THE WORLD'S CLASSICS

NINA BALATKA

LINDA TRESSEL

ANTHONY TROLLOPE (1815–82), the son of a failing London barrister, was brought up an awkward and unhappy youth amidst debt and privation. His mother maintained the family by writing, but Anthony's own first novel did not appear until 1847, when he had at length established a successful Civil Service career in the Post Office, from which he retired in 1867. After a slow start, he achieved fame, with 47 novels and some 16 other books, and sales sometimes topping 100,000. He was acclaimed an unsurpassed portraitist of the lives of the professional and landed classes, especially in his perennially popular *Chronicles of Barsetshire* (1855–67), and his six brilliant Palliser novels (1864–80). His fascinating *Autobiography* (1883) recounts his successes with an enthusiasm which stems from memories of a miserable youth. Throughout the 1870s he developed new styles of fiction, but was losing critical favour by the time of his death.

ROBERT TRACY is Professor of English and of Celtic Studies at the University of California, Berkeley. He is the author of *Trollope's Later Novels* (1978). His *Stone* (1981) is a translation of *Kamen'* (1913, 1916), poems by the Russian poet Osip Mandelstam. He has edited *The Aran Islands and Other Writings* by John Millington Synge (1962), Trollope's *The Way We Live Now* (1974), and *The Macdermots of Ballycloran* (1989).

THE WORLD'S CLASSICS

ANTHONY TROLLOPE
Nina Balatka

Linda Tressel

Edited with an Introduction by
ROBERT TRACY

Oxford   New York
OXFORD UNIVERSITY PRESS
1991

Oxford University Press, Walton Street, Oxford OX2 6DP

Oxford New York Toronto
Delhi Bombay Calcutta Madras Karachi
Petaling Jaya Singapore Hong Kong Tokyo
Nairobi Dar es Salaam Cape Town
Melbourne Auckland

and associated companies in
Berlin Ibadan

Oxford is a trade mark of Oxford University Press

First published together in one volume by Oxford University Press 1946
First issued as a World's Classics paperback 1991

British Library Cataloguing in Publication Data

Trollope, Anthony 1815–1882
Nina Balatka; Linda Tressel
I. Title   II. Tracy, Robert
823.8

ISBN 0–19–282723–5

Library of Congress Cataloging in Publication Data
Trollope, Anthony, 1815–1882.
Nina Balatka; Linda Tressel / Anthony Trollope ; edited with an
introduction by Robert Tracy.
p.   cm.—(The World's classics)
Includes bibliographical references.
I. Tracy, Robert, 1928–   . II. Trollope, Anthony, 1815–1882.
Linda Tressel. 1991. III. Title: Nina Balatka. IV. Title: Linda
Tressel. V. Series.
PR5684.N5 1991   823'.8—dc20   90–49897

ISBN 0–19–282723–5

Printed in Great Britain by
BPCC Hazell Books Ltd.
Aylesbury, Bucks

CONTENTS

INTRODUCTION

When Trollope began *Nina Balatka* on 3 November 1865, he had been a novelist for twenty years, and was at the peak both of his powers and of his reputation. He had already published fifteen novels, two substantial travel books, and two collections of short stories. Contemporary critics ranked him with Dickens, Thackeray, and George Eliot. Five Barsetshire novels had already stretched English topography to include the 'dear county' of his imagination, and Trollope had recently begun his Palliser or Parliamentary cycle of novels with *Can You Forgive Her?* (1864–5).

In his posthumously published *Autobiography*, written in 1875–6, Trollope depicts himself as blunt, hard-headed, and unimaginative, and insists that novel-writing is a trade like any other, comparable to shoemaking rather than any form of creative art. He also claims to have become uneasy about his own success, and his right to that success. 'It seemed to me that a name once earned carried with it too much favour,' he tells us;

... I had so far progressed that that which I wrote was received with too much favour ... I felt that aspirants coming up below me might do work as good as mine, and probably much better work, and yet fail to have it appreciated. In order to test this, I determined to be such an aspirant myself, and to begin a course of novels anonymously, in order that I might see whether I could succeed in obtaining a second identity,—whether as I had made one mark by such literary ability as I possessed, I might succeed in doing so again. In 1865 I began a short tale called *Nina Balatka*, which in 1866 was published anonymously in *Blackwood's Magazine*. In 1867 this was followed by another of the same length, called *Linda Tressel* ... both were written immediately after visits to the towns in which the scenes are laid, -Prague, namely, and Nuremberg. Of course I had endeavoured to change not only my manner of language, but my manner of story-telling also ... English life in them there was none. There was more of romance proper than had been usual with me. And I made an attempt at local colouring, at descriptions of scenes and places, which has not been usual with me. In all this I am confident that I was in a measure successful. In the loves, and fears, and hatreds, of both Nina and Linda, there is much that is pathetic. Prague is Prague, and Nuremberg is Nuremberg. I know that the stories are good, but they missed the object with which they had been written.[1]

Though John Blackwood reported that readers were interested in the mystery of authorship, *Blackwood's Magazine* did not noticeably increase its sales, and both novels sold poorly in book form, even when reissued under Trollope's name in 1879.[2] Nor did Trollope succeed in changing his 'manner of language'. Writing in the *Spectator*, Richard Holt Hutton recognized Trollope's style: 'no one who knows his style at all can read three pages of this tale without detecting him as plainly as if he were present in the flesh'.[3]

Trollope's experiment in anonymity suggests that he was trying to escape from himself as well as from his readers, from that tolerant but magisterial narrative voice which described the crises of characters and character types already familiar from his repeated portrayals: Mr Harding, Mrs Proudie, Archdeacon Grantly, his various country gentlemen, maidens, matriarchs, and professional men. That narrative voice often avoided judgement, but nevertheless established, by its own narrative authority, a code of behaviour against which characters are judged; the voice creates and sustains its own moral and social authority. The world of Barchester and Barset had perhaps become too predictable, too unambiguous. It is significant that, three weeks after he had completed *Nina Balatka*, Trollope began *The Last Chronicle of Barset* (1866–7), in

[1] Anthony Trollope, *An Autobiography* (1883; repr. 1950), 204–6.
[2] *The Letters of Anthony Trollope*, ed. N. John Hall, 2 vols. (1983), i. 375, 384–5; ii. 542, 724, 839.
[3] *Spectator*, 23 Mar. 1867, repr. in *Trollope: The Critical Heritage*, ed. Donald Smalley (1969), 268.

which, after killing off Mr Harding and Mrs Proudie, he announced he would write no more about Barset. In *An Autobiography* he tells us that Mrs Proudie died because he had overheard two readers complaining about her reappearances,[4] but she is more probably a victim of Trollope's self-criticism and eagerness to try something new. By separating himself from his usual characters and settings— English people in an English landscape—to write *Nina Balatka*, he perhaps freed himself to break away from Barset, and the danger of repeating himself to contentedly uncritical readers. He attempted the writer's hardest task, to abandon a successful formula. Perhaps he also needed to escape from his own relentless productivity—from the pages and pages he celebrates in *An Autobiography*. *Nina Balatka* and *Linda Tressel* are brief, economical with characters, settings, and events, unlike his panoramic novels of multiple plot.

When he came to describe his motives for writing anonymously, ten years after the fact, Trollope may have failed—or declined—to remember all of them. Critics had charged him with writing too much too rapidly. '"Author of *Nina Balatka*" may become a very convenient *nom de plume*, especially for such a very prolific writer as our friend,' John Blackwood remarked to a correspondent (3 April 1867).[5] The creation of a second authorial identity would evade the charge that he was writing too quickly and too much. More immediately, Trollope had visited Prague and Nuremberg in the autumn of 1865. His impressions of both places were vivid, his imagination strongly affected. Trollope's visits to new places usually became material for travel sketches, but many travellers had already described Nuremberg, and even Prague. Both could be thriftily used instead as settings for fiction.

These unfamiliar settings offered Trollope chances to depict lovers separated by divisions sharper than those

---

[4] *Autobiography*, 275–6.   [5] *Letters*, i. 375.

usually found in English life and fiction. Social status, money, or reputation sometimes impede his earlier fictional love affairs, but not racial or religious barriers. The opening sentence of *Nina Balatka* is at once a declaration of independence from the previous Trollope world and a new kind of dilemma for a Trollope heroine: 'Nina Balatka was a maiden of Prague, born of Christian parents, and herself a Christian—but she loved a Jew; and this is her story.' Later Trollope introduces issues of religious and racial prejudice into his English fictions. In *The Eustace Diamonds* (1871–3), Lizzie Eustace marries Joseph Emilius/Yusef Mealyus, a 'Bohemian Jew' from Prague, who turns out to be a bigamist and a murderer. In *The Way We Live Now* (1874–5), Georgiana Longstaffe, realizing that he is her last chance to marry money, is ready to marry Mr Breghert, to her family 'an old fat Jew', but very much her moral superior; in the same novel, several young men of title eagerly pursue the heiress Marie Melmotte, not caring if she is Jewish or not. Emily Wharton insists on marrying Ferdinand Lopez, allegedly a Portuguese Jew, in *The Prime Minister* (1875–6). These marriages are all abortive, or brief and disastrous. Trollope recognizes a prejudice against Jews in English society. He does not condone that prejudice, but recognizes its strength and persistence. A mixed marriage will probably provoke hostility and social isolation. Nevertheless, he suggests that Nina Balatka will find happiness with a Jewish husband, though they must leave Prague for a more tolerant community. Similarly, in *Phineas Redux* (1873–4) Phineas Finn, Irish and Catholic, commences a successful marriage with Mme Max Goesler, who has saved his life by undertaking a 'romantic' journey to Prague.

There may be yet another reason why Trollope tried to write a new kind of novel and conceal his authorship. 'You know that my novels are not sensational,' he told George Eliot, sending her a copy of *Rachel Ray*. 'In Rachel Ray I have attempted to confine myself to the commonest details

of commonplace life among the most ordinary people,
allowing myself no incident that would be even remarkable
in every day life. I have shorn my fiction of all romance.'[6]
Nina Balatka and *Linda Tressel* allowed Trollope to indulge
his usually suppressed romantic imagination. His two heroines are impulsive, passionate, willing to risk all, defy social
conventions, even to die. They live in exotic foreign cities,
whose atmospheres Trollope strives to evoke. In fact, he
returns to the mood of his first three novels, *The Macdermots
of Ballycloran* (1847), *The Kellys and the O'Kellys* (1848), and
La Vendée (1850), which are foreign in setting, romantic in
treatment—and which failed with contemporary readers.
With the success of *The Warden* (1855), Trollope had
accepted his role as chronicler of unsensational English life.
Nina Balatka and *Linda Tressel* allowed him a brief romantic
holiday. After writing them, he introduced sensational
elements more freely into his English novels. Mr Kennedy
tries to shoot Phineas Finn in a jealous rage; Finn is tried
for the murder of Mr Bonteen; Lopez throws himself in
front of a train. Trollope's two anonymous novels showed
him how to admit the sensational into ordinary life.

   Trollope's visit to Prague was to a city where political,
linguistic, and racial tensions were high. The Bohemians—
or Czechs, as they call themselves and are now generally
known—are Slavs. They were restive under Austrian rule,
which imposed German as the only legal language and
banned the use of Czech in the schools or the publication of
Czech newspapers. Trollope notes Prague's 'alas! ... Austrian barracks' (p. 5) housing an army of occupation, ready
to suppress any movement towards independence. Nationalist demonstrations in June 1848 had been met with
bullets, and an Austrian bombardment of Prague. Like
most Englishmen of his day, Trollope was sceptical about
the benefits of Habsburg rule. His brother Tom, who lived

[6] 18 October 1863; *Letters*, i. 238.

in Florence, was an ardent supporter of Italian nationalists in their successful effort to drive the Austrian armies out of Italy in the 1860s. Anthony Trollope was less ardent, but his short story 'The Last Austrian Who Left Venice'[7] generally endorses the Italian cause.

Partly because of reverses in Italy, the Austrian government tried to appear more conciliatory towards the Magyars, Czechs, and other suppressed nationalities. Soon after Trollope completed his novel, Austria's crushing defeat in the Austro-Prussian War (1866) led to further relaxations; in July 1866, when the first instalment of *Nina Balatka* appeared, Prague was occupied by Prussian troops, a situation that must have given the novel an appearance of topicality. The Czechs achieved political independence in 1918—and again in 1989.

Trollope's ability to respond strongly to a new place, and to sense its fictional possibilities, is often evident, for example in the opening paragraphs of *The Macdermots of Ballycloran* or *The American Senator*, and especially in the famous *Autobiography* passage which describes the genesis of the Barchester novels, 'conceived . . . whilst wandering . . . on a midsummer evening round the purlieus' of Salisbury Cathedral.[8] His brief stays in Prague and Nuremberg were long enough for him to recognize issues and tensions that could become a story. A projected marriage between a Catholic and a Jew would perhaps have been controversial anywhere in nineteenth-century Europe, but especially in Prague. Nina and her family are Czechs, and presumably speak Czech among themselves.[9] The Jews of Prague had

[7] *Good Words*, January 1867.

[8] *Autobiography*, 92.

[9] Trollope remembered Prague's linguistic division in *Phineas Redux* (1873–4). '"My next [witness] will be a Bohemian blacksmith named Praska,"' declares Mr Chaffanbrass, defending Phineas at his trial on the charge of murdering Mr Bonteen; '"Peter Praska,—who naturally can't speak a word of English, and unfortunately can't speak a word of German either. But we have got an interpreter . . .".' Then Peter Praska was handed up to the rostrum . . . and the man learned in Czech and also in English was placed close to him and sworn . . .' (*Phineas Redux*, 1973, ii. 235).

been liberated from onerous local laws by the Austrian
emperors, especially Joseph II (1780–90), whose Edict of
Toleration (1781) removed many Jewish disabilities. But
the Edict also encouraged Jews to learn German, and
insisted that German be used and taught in all Jewish
schools. By the mid-nineteenth century, Prague Jews
usually spoke German; Rebecca Loth addresses Nina as
'Fräulein' (p. 118). This habitual preference for German
was strongly resented by the Czechs among whom they
lived, as was Jewish loyalty to the House of Habsburg.
Nationalist demonstrations in Prague in 1848 quickly
turned into an attack on the Jewish quarter. Nina's determination to marry 'Anton Trendellsohn, the Jew' (p. 31)
raises political as well as racial and religious issues.

   In depicting Nina as she struggles with her family's
hostility to her plans, and her Jewish lover's suspicions of
her sincerity, Trollope always makes her motivation and
behaviour plausible. During his years in Ireland he had
become familiar, if not with Catholic doctrine, with the
attitudes and practices of folk Catholicism. Nina's sense
that her choice of a husband will make it impossible for her
to pray to St Nicholas is theologically flawed in just the
right way; her loyalty is not to dogma but to habitual
observance. Living in the Kleinseite or 'Little Side' of
Prague, her parish church was dedicated to St Nicholas,
and so he would be the object of her special devotion. He
was also popularly considered the patron of brides, especially dowerless brides, and of marriage generally. When
she is told that it is wrong and sinful to love a Jew, she
resists her aunt's bullying, but also avoids any discussion
with the local priest. Trollope understands the workings of
her mind perfectly when he has her take down the Virgin's
picture from her bedroom wall and hide it in a drawer; and
then, after Father Jerome's gentle rebuke, hang the picture
in its place again. Her later vagueness about her own
religious future—she wonders if she should become Jewish—lacks rationality or fervour, but is believable.

   Trollope is less assured with Anton Trendellsohn, and he

does not portray Trendellsohn's problems with the proposed marriage as fully as Nina's. He does recognize that
Trendellsohn's relatives are also horrified at the idea of a
mixed marriage. Anton's father threatens to disinherit him,
and assures him that he will become an outcast among the
Jews of Prague, who have until now seen in him a potential
leader. Finally married, the couple decide to leave Prague.

But Trollope cannot refrain from endowing Trendellsohn with certain stereotypical traits. He is eager for
money, somewhat mysterious in his dealings, and all too
ready to suspect Nina of concealing a legal document
which is rightfully his. Twice he insists on testing her
cruelly—making her search her father's desk, then
demanding that she allow a search among her own papers.
'Ninas [sic] warm frank outpouring of her love is a most
beautiful piece of painting,' John Blackwood commented,
'but as the story goes on one cannot sympathise with her in
her love for her cold suspicious Jew.' Nina's 'charm &
purity', he told Trollope, 'made me all the more savage at
the Jew when he tried to disgrace such a mistress by making
her purloin her fathers key'. Trollope later agreed that
Trendellsohn 'comes out too black. I think I'll make him
give her a diamond necklace in the last chapter'[10]—though
Trendellsohn only restores to her (in Chapter 12) her
mother's necklace, which Nina has pawned. When Blackwood later complained about the character of Ludovic
Valcarm in _Linda Tressel_, Trollope replied with a defence of
the mixture of attractive and unattractive qualities in
many of his less-than-perfect protagonists:

It is hardly possible for a novelist who depends more on character
than on incident for his interest always to make the chief
personages of his stories pleasant acquaintances. His object is to
shew what is the effect of such and such qualities on the happiness
of those on whom they act; and in doing this he can hardly
contrive that a nice young man should always be there to be
married to the nice young woman. It may be so now & again; but

[10] _Letters_, i. 337–8, 351.

not always ... I cannot admit that I am bound always to have a pleasant young man. Pleasant young men are not so common.[11]

Trollope recognizes that Trendellsohn is under extraordinary pressures, badgered by Nina's relatives and by his own community. But Trendellsohn's willingness to suspect Nina on rather flimsy grounds leaves a bad taste, and there are echoes of nineteenth-century portrayals of Shylock as villainous in his consistent mistrust. Nevertheless, we believe in Trendellsohn's suspicions. His awkward inability to be open or fair with Nina, despite his real love for her, is convincing if unattractive. He has lived his life in a place where Christians have traditionally despised Jews, and have reinforced their hatred with laws and legal disabilities. 'I do not know that there is a Christian in Prague who would feel it to be beneath him to rob a Jew, and I do not altogether blame them,' he tells Nina. 'They believe that we would rob them, and many of us do so. We are very sharp, each on the other, dealing against each other always in hatred, never in love—never even in friendship' (pp. 99–100). 'You may reproach the Jews for their specific anxiousness,' wrote Kafka, a son of the Prague ghetto, to Milena Jesenská, herself Christian and Czech:

The insecure position of Jews, insecure within themselves, insecure among people, would make it above all comprehensible that they consider themselves to be allowed to own only what they hold in their hands or between their teeth, that furthermore only palpable possessions give them the right to live, and that they will never again acquire what they once have lost but that instead it calmly swims away from them forever. From the most improbable sides Jews are threatened with danger, or let us, to be more exact, leave the dangers aside and say they are threatened with threats ... And then Milena still talks about anxiousness, gives me a blow on the chest or asks (what so far as sound and rhythm are concerned, comes to the same thing in the Czech language): 'Jste žid?'—'Are you Jewish?' Don't you see how in the 'Jste' the fist is withdrawn to gather muscle-strength? And then in the 'žid' the

[11] Trollope to Blackwood, 19 September 1867; *Letters*, i. 390.

cheerful, unfailing, forward-flying blow? These are the side-effects which the Czech language frequently possesses for the German ear.[12]

Trendellsohn is determined to escape from that anxiety and insecurity, to break out of the social isolation which Prague Jews still experienced despite the abolition of the ghetto as a place of enforced residence. He dreams of that assimilation which seemed possible as nineteenth-century Europe seemed to grow more tolerant. 'To be a Jew, always a Jew, in all things a Jew, had been ever a part of his great dream,' Trollope tells us;

It was … impossible to him … to forswear the religion of his people. To go forth and be great in commerce by deserting his creed would have been nothing to him. His ambition did not desire wealth so much as the possession of wealth in Jewish hands, without those restrictions upon its enjoyment to which Jews under his own eye had ever been subjected. It would have delighted him to think that, by means of his work, there should no longer be a Jews' quarter in Prague, but that all Prague should be ennobled and civilised and made beautiful by the wealth of Jews (p. 70).

When he realizes that Christian and Jewish intolerance of a mixed marriage will never allow him to live with Nina in Prague, he resolves to leave for more tolerant cities in Germany or England:

To be a Jew in London, they had told him, was almost better than to be a Christian … Nina should be his wife. It might be that she would follow the creed of her husband, and then all would be well. In those far cities to which he would go, it would hardly in such case be known that she had been born a Christian; or else he would show the world around him, both Jews and Christians, how well a Christian and a Jew might live together. To crush the prejudice which had dealt so hardly with his people—to make a Jew equal in all things to a Christian—this was his desire; and how could this better be fulfilled than by his union with a Christian?

[12] Franz Kafka, *Letters to Milena*, ed. Willi Haas, trans. Tania and James Stern (1953), 50–1. Kafka had to assure the sceptical Milena that he understood Czech (p. 24).

. . . 'Dark, ignorant, and foolish,' Anton said to himself, speaking of those among whom he lived; 'it is their pride to live in disgrace, while all the honours of the world are open to them if they chose to take them!' (pp. 70–1).

In naming his hero, Trollope may have recalled Moses Mendelssohn (1729–86), the major proponent of Jewish assimilation, who urged Jews literally to leave the ghetto, but, more importantly, urged them to abandon intellectual and psychological ghettoes and involve themselves with the new ideas of the eighteenth-century Enlightenment. Trollope had had his own experiences of being a social outcast; *An Autobiography* records his progress from schoolboy pariah to social equality and intimacy, and he endowed Trendell-sohn with his own first name and initials.

In Trendellsohn, Trollope has depicted the tentative, eager, prickly nervousness of a nineteenth-century Jew venturing out of the confining yet protective ghetto, determined to be received as an equal among Christians, to be respected by them, yet scarcely believing that this can happen. He has recognized the importance of this Jewish eagerness to participate more fully in public and social life, the central issue for nineteenth-century European Jews. And Trollope rightly saw Prague as a kind of frontier, where Jews were becoming financially important but were not yet accepted—a little before the time of the story, Sigmund Freud's father left Czech-speaking Moravia, where his business contended with anti-Jewish boycotts, for the more tolerant atmosphere of Vienna.

Trollope describes Prague, he reminds us, more elaborately than was 'usual with me'. His depiction emphasizes the social and religious divisions between Anton and Nina. Each lives in a long-established neighbourhood, Nina beneath the Hradschin, the ancient residence of Bohemia's kings and later of the Habsburg emperors, which also contains Prague's Catholic cathedral. Trendellsohn lives beside a constant reminder of his Jewish identity: the oldest of Prague's synagogues, celebrated by Trollope and by contemporary guidebooks as the oldest synagogue in Europe. Between the two, the Moldau River makes a literal division; several important episodes take place on the Charles Bridge, which connects their two worlds but also marks their separation. Trollope's 'local colouring' naturally draws on his own visit to the city, and also on Murray's *Handbook for Travellers in Southern Germany*. Nina and Anton move between the sights Murray recommends for tourists: the ghetto and synagogue, the Charles Bridge with its statues, the 'Theinkirche' and Grosser Ring, the Hradschin.

Trollope's Prague may also owe something to the hallucinatory Prague of George Eliot's *The Lifted Veil*, published anonymously in *Blackwood's* in July 1859, soon after Eliot herself had visited the city. The protagonist of *The Lifted Veil* is able to 'see' places and events before he experiences them, lifting a little the veil concealing the future. His first such experience is a vision of Prague that anticipates Trollope's references to the bridge and its statues, the Hradschin, and the deposed Emperor Ferdinand. Prague's people are

doomed to live on in the stale repetition of memories, like deposed and superannuated kings in their regal, gold-inwoven tatters. The city looked so thirsty that the broad river seemed to me a sheet of metal; and the blackened statues, as I passed under their blank gaze, along the unending bridge, with their ancient garments and their saintly crowns, seemed to me the real inhabitants and owners of this place . . .

When Eliot's seer visits Prague, he finds the bridge exactly as he had foreseen it. 'The old synagogue . . . with its shrunken lights, was of a piece with my vision.'[13] In her turn, George Eliot perhaps remembered Ziska Zamenoy's visit to the Prague synagogue during a service, his confusion and sense that he is in an alien world (pp. 84–5), when in *Daniel Deronda* (1876) she sent Deronda to a service at

---

[13] George Eliot, *The Lifted Veil* (1985), 11, 33–4.

Frankfurt's orthodox synagogue, where he feels himself an outsider, yet becomes socially involved. Deronda also returns to Gwendolen Harleth her pawned necklace, as Anton returns Nina's necklace.[14] Deronda's later eager assumption of his Jewish identity, and his decision against assimilation, reverses Anton Trendellsohn's course, and contrasts with Trollope's apparent approval of Anton's plans.

There are also resemblances between Trollope's Prague and the city as depicted by Franz Kafka. Both use Prague as a vast empty stage where intense personal dramas of isolation are acted out. The narrow streets among which Nina and Trendellsohn live might conceal those inaccessible law courts and dubious lawyers' offices where Joseph K. seeks counsel. Here they become a metaphor for the complexities of Nina's relationship with Anton. In *Nina Balatka*, Trollope uses setting more metaphorically than he does in his English novels, especially in the extraordinary scene when Nina climbs to the parapet of the Charles Bridge, ready to leap into the river yet deliberately placing herself beside the statue of St John Nepomucene, the protector of those in danger of drowning.

Linda Tressel bears a close, indeed sisterly resemblance to *Nina Balatka*. Again the setting is a picturesque foreign city. Again a young girl is tormented over her choice of husband, again on religious grounds, as Linda struggles with her narrow-minded and domineering aunt, who is herself dominated by a narrow Calvinism. Trollope inherited a disdain for religious zealotry from his mother, who was particularly hostile to Low-Church Evangelicals. He himself attacked Evangelical attitudes in portraying Mrs Proudie and especially Mr Slope, as early as *Barchester Towers* (1857). But in portraying Charlotte Staubach,

[14] George Eliot, *Daniel Deronda*, ed. Barbara Hardy (1987), 415–16 (bk. iv, ch. 32); 47–9 (bk. i, ch. 2).

Linda's aunt and guardian, and her efforts to force Linda into a loveless marriage, Trollope shows how far he has come in understanding a rigid religious attitude. Slope is a caricatured opportunist, Mrs Proudie a comic bully. There are superficial portraits of rigid clergymen in *The Kellys and the O'Kellys* (1848) and *Miss Mackenzie* (1865). But Charlotte Staubach is sincere in her beliefs, and well-intentioned. She tries to force Linda to marry the unattractive Peter Steinmarc because she genuinely believes she is working to save the girl's soul, and because she believes that woman's divinely appointed role is to obey, to abandon all pride and self-will. Trollope never mocks Madame Staubach. He recognizes how powerful and dangerous her certainties make her. She bears some resemblance to Mr Kennedy in *Phineas Finn* (1867–9), which Trollope completed two weeks before he began *Linda Tressel*; Kennedy re-appears in *Phineas Redux*. In her tightly ruled house, frequent attendance at church services, rigidity, and efforts to marry her niece to an unsuitable and unattractive husband, she is a harsh preliminary version of Aunt Stanbury, the 'Juno' of Exeter in *He Knew He Was Right* (1868–9). Trollope wrote *Linda Tressel* between 2 June and 10 July 1867; he began *He Knew He Was Right* four months later, on 13 November. In between he wrote *The Golden Lion of Granpere* (1872), set among the Vosges mountains in Lorraine, another tale of a (temporarily) unapproved marriage, also destined for anonymous publication, but refused on those terms by John Blackwood, who felt he had had enough of Trollope's experiment in anonymity.[15]

Blackwood had been disappointed in sales of *Nina Balatka*. With *Linda Tressel*, he was also uneasy about the story and its characters. 'I am very sorry to say that I fear you have made a blunder and so have I,' he told Trollope after reading the manuscript:

There is no adequate motive for Madame Staubachs conduct
& her persistence becomes irritatingly wearisome.

You have really no right to say that it was the Calvinistic old
jades *virtues* that caused poor Linda's sufferings . . .

Herr Molk is a capital sketch and Linda herself is excellent if
she had a man to give her heart to. Ludovic is too much of a myth
. . . the want of somebody like a man is the main defect . . .

Altho' Madame Staubach only wearies me it is possible that the
blessed newspaper critics may call her A Creation & so I shall
conclude by wishing her all success.

Trollope offered to take back the story, and a few days later
wrote to defend it: 'I wanted to shew how religion, if
misunderstood, may play the very Devil in a house;—and
as regards the "Devil" part I have succeeded according to
your own description'. Blackwood eventually came to, or at
least expressed, a more favourable opinion:

I still have slightly the feeling of impatience at the story which
frightened me at first but there is more variety than I thought &
there is strong individual human character very happily painted.
The views too of the fanatical old woman in favouring Linda with
so many stripes in this world to save her from eternal brimstone in
the next, come out much more clearly in type than in a hurried
perusal of the m.s.—as does also the character of Linda with the
haunting dread of brimstone which her early education had
planted in her mind.[16]

Trollope again uses a foreign setting to great effect.
Himself a tourist in Prague and Nuremberg, he remembers
the tourist's inevitable isolation as an outsider in depicting
the isolation of Nina Balatka and of Linda. Neither woman
can adequately communicate her anguish, neither can find
an understanding listener—a psychological isolation resem-
bling so many tourists' linguistic isolation. Because he
knows these cities only from the outside, Trollope avoids
any need to portray their societies. Nina and her father
have no friends, and are estranged from their only

[16] Blackwood to Trollope, 13 September, 11 December; Trollope to
Blackwood, 16 and 19 September 1867; *Letters*, i. 387–9, 390, 406.

relatives; Mme Staubach discourages any intercourse with the world outside her house, except for visits to church. Trollope's foreign settings make it necessary for him to focus on isolated individuals. He creates these dramas with very small casts, and often makes his stage an interior one, his heroine's mind, his actors her emotions.

Nina Balatka must cross a river to meet her lover. Linda, like Tennyson's Lady of Shalott, lives on a small island (in Nuremberg's Pegnitz River), and gazes at her lover across the intervening waters. This allows him a dramatic visit to her involving two small boats and a mighty leap, an achievement Trollope undercuts by telling us the narrow river is hardly deep enough to reach the lover's knees.

Trollope's habitual mistrust of romantic gestures is here tempered by his awareness of how much they can mean to Linda, especially when Peter Steinmarc, the suitor her aunt has chosen for her, is nearly three times her age, sedentary, snuffy, and motivated primarily by his desire to become owner of her house rather than by much interest in Linda herself. 'When Linda denounces Peter as a —— beast do you mean that she called him a damned beast?' Blackwood inquired. 'I am sure she was justified.'[17]

Linda is promised to one wrong man, and falls in love with another. Her mistaken infatuation with the insubstantial Ludovic Valcarm is a natural result of her isolation, and of the repressive regime under which she lives. Perhaps the quaint old buildings of Nuremberg made Trollope half remember his childhood encounters with the Grimm brothers' Rapunzel. Despite Blackwood's criticism, Ludovic's lack of substance is essential to Linda's self-delusion and disappointment. He is all charm and dash, and her lack of experience makes her all too ready to admire him.

Trollope's indulgence in 'more of romance proper than had been usual with me' does not extend to his treatment of Linda's elopement. It is pouring rain, and on the train to Augsburg, Linda is very cold:

[17] Blackwood to Trollope, 13 September 1867; *Letters*, i. 389.

Her feet became like ice, and then the chill crept up her body. . . .
It was still dark night, and the violent rain was pattering against
the glass, and the damp came in through the crevices, and the
wind blew bitterly upon her; and then as she turned a little to ask
her lover to find some comfort for her, some mitigation of her
pain, she perceived that he was asleep. Then the tears began to
run down her cheeks, and she told herself that it would be well if
she could die. . . . For a moment or two she had hoped that her
movement would waken Ludovic, so that she might have had the
comfort of a word; but he had only tumbled with his head hither
and thither, and had finally settled himself in a position in which
he leaned heavily upon her. . . . Gradually the day dawned, and
the two could look at each other in the grey light of the morning.
(pp. 327–9).

Hardy may have remembered this episode when he sent
Elfride Swancourt and Stephen Smith on an equally
dismal railway elopement in *A Pair of Blue Eyes* (1872–3).

Though Linda Tressel is a victim of her own romantic
yearnings as well as of her aunt's repression, she is not
without spirit, as when she exaggerates her appointed
suitor's age with shrewd vindictiveness, or threatens him. 'I
will lead you such a life!' she tells Steinmarc. 'I will make
you rue the day you first saw me. You shall wish that you
were at the quarries . . . I will disgrace you, and make your
name infamous. I will waste everything that you have.
There is nothing so bad I will not do to punish you'
(pp. 348–9). Trollope matches his observation of Nina
Balatka taking down the Virgin's picture by showing us
Linda's 'little kick' as she listens to Herr Molk praising
Steinmarc: 'according to Herr Molk . . . Peter was little
short of a municipal demigod. Prudent he was, and confidential. A man deep in the city's trust, and with money laid
out at interest. Strong and healthy he was,—indeed lusty
for his age, if Herr Molk spoke the truth. Poor Linda gave a
little kick beneath the clothes when this was said, but she
spoke no word of reply' (p. 306).

If both novels have foreign settings, they also deal with a

social class not usually central in Trollope's novels: a lower-middle class of small tradesmen, municipal employees, and failed business men. As in his novels of county or London life, where most of the characters are precisely located within a hierarchical gentry, these novels too have elaborate gradations of wealth and rank. Nina's estranged relatives are rich and socially pretentious, and Trollope lodges them in a fashionable Prague street. Linda is reminded that Steinmarc holds the office of Town Clerk, once held by her own father. Her inheritance, the 'Red House', makes her as attractive a wife in her little world as do the great dowries of Lady Glencora and Marie Melmotte in London's West End.

Trollope often condemns the outsider—Slope, Melmotte, Lopez—and endorses social cohesion and social consensus: if society generally is prejudiced against a newcomer, society may well be right. Even if society is wrong, he accepts its power to withhold social acceptance, as in *An Autobiography* he accepts his schoolfellows' cruel right to exclude him. When Lord Silverbridge proposes to marry the American Isabel Boncassen in *The Duke's Children* (1879–80), her father insists that Silverbridge guarantee that she will be accepted by his family and by society, welcomed into 'the community of Countesses and Duchesses'.[18] In *Nina Balatka* and *Linda Tressel*, however, Trollope is romantic enough to defy social conformity. Nina and Anton are allowed their love and presumably their happiness, even though all Prague, Christian and Jewish, opposes their marriage—but they must find their future elsewhere. Linda Tressel cannot accept Herr Molk's advice to marry Steinmarc because of his civic virtues and assured place in Nuremberg. She breaks under pressure, especially when she finds that Molk is right in his disdain of Ludovic Valcarm. The strain of her defiance is too much for her, and she dies. Public opinion is powerful, cannot be challenged with impunity, but can also be cruel and wrong.

[18] *The Duke's Children* (1973), 556.

While Trollope failed to establish a second literary
identity with these two novels, he did change and develop
as a novelist by writing them. After *Nina Balatka* and *Linda
Tressel*, Trollope's characters are more introspective, their
psychologies more complex. Both heroines' flights from
their native cities hint at an autobiographical element:
Trollope too was fleeing, from Barchester and Barset, with
their predictabilities and complacencies. In the periods
between and immediately following his experiments in
anonymity, Trollope admitted death into Barchester, and
produced some of his best work: *The Last Chronicle of Barset*,
Phineas Finn, *He Knew He Was Right*. As a way of freeing his
imagination for new themes and situations the experiment
was a success—and also produced these two sensitive
studies of young women, each on the edge of breakdown,
driven nearly to madness by the contrary forces that both
drive and impede them, struggling to define themselves.

Robert Tracy

Berkeley, California
17 January 1990

A NOTE ON THE TEXT

Nina Balatka, subtitled *The Story of a Maiden of Prague*, first appeared in *Blackwood's Magazine* (volumes 100–1) in seven instalments:

Part 1 (Chapters 1–2), July 1866
Part 2 (Chapters 3–5), August 1866
Part 3 (Chapters 6–7), September 1866
Part 4 (Chapters 8–9), October 1866
Part 5 (Chapters 10–12), November 1866
Part 6 (Chapters 13–14), December 1866
Conclusion (Chapters 15–16), January 1867.

The novel was published in two volumes by William Blackwood and Sons, Edinburgh, in February 1867. Unsold sheets of this edition were bound in one volume in 1879, and reissued under Trollope's name by Blackwood.

Linda Tressel was published in *Blackwood's* (volumes 102–3) in eight instalments:

Part 1 (Chapters 1–2), October 1867
Part 2 (Chapters 3–4), November 1867
Part 3 (Chapter 5), December 1867
Part 4 (Chapters 6–8), January 1868
Part 5 (Chapter 9), February 1868
Part 6 (Chapters 10–12), March 1868
Part 7 (Chapters 13–14), April 1868
Part 8 (Chapters 15–17), May 1868.

Blackwood then issued the novel in two volumes (May 1868). As with *Nina Balatka*, unsold sheets were bound in a single volume under Trollope's name and republished in 1879 or 1880.

Nina Balatka and *Linda Tressel* first appeared in the 'World's Classics' series in 1946; they were published together in a single volume. The present edition reprints that text, which has been collated with the original *Blackwood's* text.

SELECT BIBLIOGRAPHY

There is no complete edition of Trollope's works. Thirty-six titles (in sixty-two volumes), reproducing first editions, appear in *Selected Works of Anthony Trollope* (Arno Press, New York, 1981), under the general editorship of N. John Hall. James Gindin edited *Nina Balatka* and *Linda Tressel* for this series, with a valuable introduction to each. Most of Trollope's novels are available in the Oxford 'World's Classics' series. The standard bibliography is by Michael Sadleir: *Trollope: A Bibliography* (1928; repr. 1977).

Trollope's *An Autobiography* (1883) is an important work of literature in its own right, apart from the information it supplies. It is best supplemented by *The Letters of Anthony Trollope* (Stanford, Calif., 1983), ed. N. John Hall. Hall is also at work on a biography, which will supersede those by T. H. S. Escott (1913; repr. 1967), Michael Sadleir (1927), and James Pope Hennessy (1971). There is a recent (1988) biography by R. H. Super, *The Chronicler of Barsetshire*, and R. C. Terry has prepared *A Trollope Chronology* (1989); Terry's *Trollope: Interviews and Recollections* (1987) offers many glimpses of Trollope in action.

There are two bibliographies of Trollope criticism: Rafael Holling, *A Century of Trollope Criticism* (1956), and *The Reputation of Trollope: An Annotated Bibliography 1925–1975* (1978), ed. John Charles Olmsted and Jeffrey Welch. These are supplemented by Donald D. Stone's 'Trollope Studies, 1976–1981', in *Dickens Studies Annual*, 11 (1983). *Trollope: The Critical Heritage* (1969), ed. Donald Smalley, reprints reviews and criticism by Trollope's contemporaries. There are three useful collections of more recent criticism: *Anthony Trollope* (1980), ed. T. E. Bareham; *The Trollope Critics* (1980), ed. N. John Hall; *Trollope Centenary Essays* (1982), ed. John Halperin.

There are many general critical studies: Ruth ap Roberts, *Trollope: Artist and Moralist* (1971; published in the United States as *The Moral Trollope*); Bradford A. Booth, *Anthony Trollope: Aspects of His Life and Work* (1958); A. O. J. Cockshut, *Anthony Trollope: A Critical Study* (1955); John Halperin, *Trollope and Politics* (1977); Geoffrey Harvey, *The Art of Anthony Trollope* (1980); James R. Kincaid, *The Novels of Anthony Trollope* (1977); Bill Overton,

The Unofficial Trollope (1982); Robert M. Polhemus, The Changing
World of Anthony Trollope (1968); Arthur Pollard, Anthony Trollope
(1978); R. C. Terry, Anthony Trollope: The Artist in Hiding (1977);
Robert Tracy, Trollope's Later Novels (1978); and Andrew Wright,
Anthony Trollope: Dream and Art (1983). The studies by Harvey,
Kincaid, Overton, Polhemus, and Pollard comment briefly and
perceptively on Nina Balatka and/or Linda Tressel.

These two novels have rarely been the subject of periodical
articles, apart from Judith Knelman's 'Trollope's Experiment
with Anonymity' (Victorian Periodical Review, 1981) and William A.
West's 'The Anonymous Trollope' (Ariel, 1974). The portrayal of
Trendellsohn in Nina Balatka is discussed in Edgar Rosenberg's
From Shylock to Svengali (1960). Information about conditions of
Jewish life in nineteenth-century Prague appears in the three-
volume survey The Jews of Czechoslovakia (1968–84), published by
the Jewish Publication Society of America, and in The Making of
Czech Jewry (1988) by Hillel J. Kieval.

A CHRONOLOGY OF
ANTHONY TROLLOPE

Virtually all Trollope's fiction after *Framley Parsonage* (1860–1) appeared first in serial form, with book publication usually coming just prior to the final instalment of the serial.

1815   (24 Apr.) Born at 16 Keppel Street, Bloomsbury, the fourth son of Thomas and Frances Trollope.
(Summer ?) Family moves to Harrow-on-the-Hill.

1823   To Harrow School as a day-boy.

1825   To a private school at Sunbury.

1827   To school at Winchester College.

1830   Removed from Winchester and returned to Harrow.

1834   (Apr.) The family flees to Bruges to escape creditors.
(Nov.) Accepts a junior clerkship in the General Post Office, London.

1841   (Sept.) Made Postal Surveyor's Clerk at Banagher, King's County, Ireland.

1843   (mid-Sept.) Begins work on his first novel, *The Macdermots of Ballycloran*.

1844   (11 June) Marries Rose Heseltine.
(Aug.) Transferred to Clonmel, County Tipperary.

1846   (13 Mar.) Son, Henry Merivale Trollope, born.

1847   *The Macdermots of Ballycloran*, published in 3 vols. (Newby).
(27 Sept.) Son, Frederic James Anthony Trollope, born.

1848   *The Kellys and the O'Kellys; or Landlords and Tenants* 3 vols. (Colburn).
(Autumn) Moves to Mallow, County Cork.

1850   *La Vendée; An Historical Romance* 3 vols. (Colburn).
Writes *The Noble Jilt* (A play, published 1923).

1851   (1 Aug.) Sent to south-west of England on special postal mission.

1853   (29 July) Begins *The Warden* (the first of the Barsetshire novels).
(29 Aug.) Moves to Belfast as Acting Surveyor.

1854   (9 Oct.) Appointed Surveyor of Northern District of Ireland.

1855   *The Warden* 1 vol. (Longman).
Writes *The New Zealander*.
(June) Moves to Donnybrook, Dublin.

1857   *Barchester Towers* 3 vols. (Longman).

1858   *The Three Clerks* 3 vols. (Bentley).
Doctor Thorne 3 vols. (Chapman & Hall).
(Jan.) Departs for Egypt on Post Office business.
(Mar.) Visits Holy Land.
(Apr.–May) Returns via Malta, Gibraltar and Spain.
(May–Sept.) Visits Scotland and north of England on postal business.
(16 Nov.) Leaves for the West Indies on postal mission.

1859   *The Bertrams* 3 vols. (Chapman & Hall).
The West Indies and the Spanish Main 1 vol. (Chapman & Hall).
(3 July) Arrives home.
(Nov.) Leaves Ireland; settles at Waltham Cross, Hertfordshire, after being appointed Surveyor of the Euston District of England.

1860   *Castle Richmond* 3 vols. (Chapman & Hall).
First serialized fiction, *Framley Parsonage*, published in the *Cornhill Magazine*.
(Oct.) Visits, with his wife, his mother and brother in Florence; makes the acquaintance of Kate Field, a 22-year-old American for whom he forms a romantic attachment.

1861   *Framley Parsonage* 3 vols. (Smith, Elder).
Tales of All Countries 1 vol. (Chapman & Hall).
(24 Aug.) Leaves for America to write a travel book.

1862   *Orley Farm* 2 vols. (Chapman & Hall).
North America 2 vols. (Chapman & Hall).
The Struggles of Brown, Jones and Robinson: By One of the Firm 1 vol. (New York, Harper—an American piracy; first English edition 1870, Smith, Elder).
(25 Mar.) Arrives home from America.
(5 Apr.) Elected to the Garrick Club.

1863   *Tales of All Countries*, Second Series, 1 vol. (Chapman & Hall).
       Rachel Ray 2 vols. (Chapman & Hall).
       (6 Oct.) Death of his mother, Mrs Frances Trollope.

1864   *The Small House at Allington* 2 vols. (Smith, Elder).
       (12 Apr.) Elected a member of the Athenaeum Club.

1865   *Can You Forgive Her?* 2 vols. (Chapman & Hall).
       Miss Mackenzie 1 vol. (Chapman & Hall).
       Hunting Sketches 1 vol. (Chapman & Hall).

1866   *The Belton Estate* 3 vols. (Chapman & Hall).
       Travelling Sketches 1 vol. (Chapman & Hall).
       Clergymen of the Church of England 1 vol. (Chapman & Hall).

1867   *Nina Balatka* 2 vols. (Blackwood).
       The Claverings 2 vols. (Smith, Elder).
       The Last Chronicle of Barset 2 vols. (Smith, Elder).
       Lotta Schmidt and Other Stories 1 vol. (Strahan).
       (1 Sept.) Resigns from the Post Office.
       Assumes editorship of *Saint Pauls Magazine*.

1868   *Linda Tressel* 2 vols. (Blackwood).
       (11 Apr.) Leaves London for the United States on postal mission.
       (26 July) Returns from America.
       (Nov.) Stands unsuccessfully as Liberal candidate for Beverley, Yorkshire.

1869   *Phineas Finn; the Irish Member* 2 vols. (Virtue & Co).
       He Knew He Was Right 2 vols. (Strahan).
       Did He Steal It? A Comedy in Three Acts (a version of *The Last Chronicle of Barset*, privately printed by Virtue & Co).

1870   *The Vicar of Bullhampton* 1 vol. (Bradbury, Evans).
       An Editor's Tales 1 vol. (Strahan).
       The Commentaries of Caesar 1 vol. (Blackwood).
       (Jan.–July) Eased out of *Saint Pauls Magazine*.

1871   *Sir Harry Hotspur of Humblethwaite* 1 vol. (Hurst & Blackett).
       Ralph the Heir 3 vols. (Hurst & Blackett).
       (Apr.) Gives up house at Waltham Cross.
       (24 May) Sails to Australia to visit his son.
       (27 July) Arrives at Melbourne.

1872   *The Golden Lion of Granpere* 1 vol. (Tinsley).
(Jan.–Oct.) Travelling in Australia and New Zealand.
(Dec.) Returns via the United States.

1873   *The Eustace Diamonds* 3 vols. (Chapman & Hall).
Australia and New Zealand 2 vols. (Chapman & Hall).
(Apr.) Settles in Montagu Square, London.

1874   *Phineas Redux* 2 vols. (Chapman & Hall).
Lady Anna 2 vols. (Chapman & Hall).
Harry Heathcote of Gangoil. A Tale of Australian Bush Life
1 vol. (Sampson Low).

1875   *The Way We Live Now* 2 vols. (Chapman & Hall).
(1 Mar.) Leaves for Australia via Brindisi, the Suez Canal,
and Ceylon.
(4 May) Arrives in Australia.
(Aug.–Oct.) Sailing homewards.
(Oct.) Begins *An Autobiography*.

1876   *The Prime Minister* 4 vols. (Chapman & Hall).

1877   *The American Senator* 3 vols. (Chapman & Hall).
(29 June) Leaves for South Africa.
(11 Dec.) Sails for home.

1878   *South Africa* 2 vols. (Chapman & Hall).
Is He Popenjoy? 3 vols. (Chapman & Hall).
(June–July) Travels to Iceland in the yacht 'Mastiff'.
How the 'Mastiffs' Went to Iceland 1 vol. (privately printed,
Virtue & Co).

1879   *An Eye for an Eye* 2 vols. (Chapman & Hall).
Thackeray 1 vol. (Macmillan).
John Candigate 3 vols. (Chapman & Hall).
Cousin Henry 2 vols. (Chapman & Hall).

1880   *The Duke's Children* 3 vols. (Chapman & Hall).
The Life of Cicero 2 vols. (Chapman & Hall).
(July) Settles at South Harting, Sussex, near Petersfield.

1881   *Dr Wortle's School* 2 vols. (Chapman & Hall).
Ayala's Angel 3 vols. (Chapman & Hall).

1882   *Why Frau Frohmann Raised Her Prices; and Other Stories* 1 vol.
(Isbister).
The Fixed Period 2 vols. (Blackwood).
Marion Fay 3 vols. (Chapman & Hall).

Lord Palmerston 1 vol. (Isbister).
Kept in the Dark 2 vols. (Chatto & Windus).
(May) Visits Ireland to collect material for a new Irish novel.
(Aug.) Returns to Ireland a second time.
(2 Oct.) Takes rooms for the winter at Garlant's Hotel, Suffolk St., London.
(3 Nov.) Suffers paralytic stroke.
(6 Dec.) Dies in nursing home, 34 Welbeck St., London.

1883   *Mr. Scarborough's Family* 3 vols. (Chatto & Windus).
The Landleaguers (unfinished) 3 vols. (Chatto & Windus).
An Autobiography 2 vols. (Blackwood).

1884   *An Old Man's Love* 2 vols. (Blackwood).

1923   *The Noble Jilt* 1 vol. (Constable).

1927   *London Tradesmen* 1 vol. (Elkin Mathews and Marrat).

1972   *The New Zealander* 1 vol. (Oxford University Press).

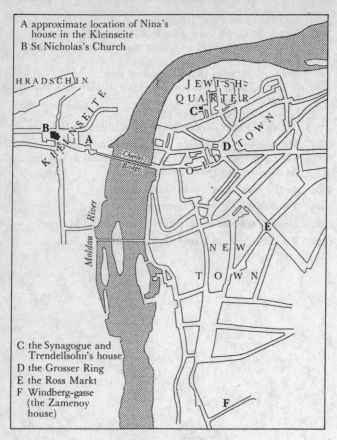

A approximate location of Nina's house in the Kleinseite
B St Nicholas's Church

C the Synagogue and Trendellsohn's house
D the Grosser Ring
E the Ross Markt
F Windberg-gasse (the Zamenoy house)

Nina Balatka's Prague

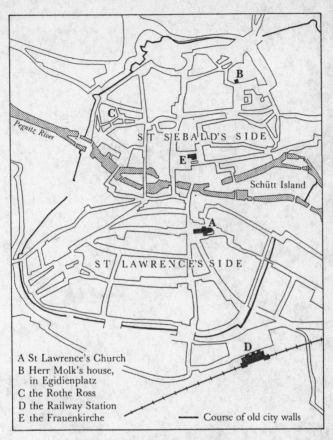

A St Lawrence's Church
B Herr Molk's house,
  in Egidienplatz
C the Rothe Ross
D the Railway Station
E the Frauenkirche

—— Course of old city walls

Linda Tressel's Nuremberg

NINA BALATKA

THE PERSONS OF THE STORY*

STEPHEN TRENDELLSOHN	.	*A Jew in Prague.*
ANTON TRENDELLSOHN		*His Son.*
KARIL ZAMENOY	. .	*A Christian Merchant of Prague.*
MADAME ZAMENOY	. .	*His Wife.*
ZISKA ZAMENOY		*Their Son.*
JOSEF BALATKA	. .	*A Broken Merchant of Prague, also a Christian.*
NINA BALATKA	. .	*His Daughter.*
RUTH JACOBI	. .	*Granddaughter of the Jew.*
REBECCA LOTH	. .	*A Jewess.*
FATHER JEROME	. .	*A Priest.*
RAPINSKI	. . .	*A Jeweller.*
LOTTA LUXA	. . .	*Servant to Madame Zamenoy.*
SOUCHEY	. . .	*Servant to Josef Balatka.*

CHAPTER I

NINA BALATKA was a maiden of Prague,* born of Christian parents, and herself a Christian—but she loved a Jew; and this is her story.

Nina Balatka was the daughter of one Josef Balatka, an old merchant of Prague, who was living at the time of this story; but Nina's mother was dead. Josef, in the course of his business, had become closely connected with a certain Jew named Trendellsohn, who lived in a mean house in the Jews' quarter in Prague—habitation in that one allotted portion of the town having been the enforced custom with the Jews then, as it still is now.* In business with Trendellsohn, the father, there was Anton, his son; and Anton Trendellsohn was the Jew whom Nina Balatka loved. Now it had so happened that Josef Balatka, Nina's father, had drifted out of a partnership with Karil Zamenoy, a wealthy Christian merchant of Prague, and had drifted into a partnership with Trendellsohn. How this had come to pass needs not to be told here, as it had all occurred in years when Nina was an infant. But in these shiftings Balatka became a ruined man, and at the time of which I write he and his daughter were almost penniless. The reader must know that Karil Zamenoy and Josef Balatka had married sisters. Josef's wife, Nina's mother, had long been dead, having died—so said Sophie Zamenoy, her sister—of a broken heart; of a heart that had broken itself in grief, because her husband had joined his fortunes with those of a Jew. Whether the disgrace of the alliance or its disastrous result may have broken the lady's heart, or whether she may have died of a pleurisy, as the doctors said, we need not inquire here. Her soul had been long at rest, and her spirit, we may hope, had ceased to fret itself in horror at contact with a Jew. But Sophie Zamenoy was alive and strong, and could still hate a Jew as intensely as Jews ever were hated in those earlier days in which hatred could satisfy itself with persecution. In her time but little power was left to Madame Zamenoy to persecute the Trendellsohns

other than that which nature had given to her in the
bitterness of her tongue. She could revile them behind
their back, or, if opportunity offered, to their faces; and
both she had done often, telling the world of Prague that
the Trendellsohns had killed her sister, and robbed her
foolish brother-in-law. But hitherto the full vial of her
wrath* had not been emptied, as it came to be emptied
afterwards; for she had not yet learned the mad iniquity
of her niece. But at the moment of which I now speak,
Nina herself knew her own iniquity, hardly knowing,
however, whether her love did or did not disgrace her.
But she did know that any thought as to that was too late.
She loved the man, and had told him so; and were he
gipsy as well as Jew, it would be required of her that she
should go out with him into the wilderness.* And Nina
Balatka was prepared to go out into the wilderness.
Karil Zamenoy and his wife were prosperous people, and
lived in a comfortable modern house in the New Town.
It stood in a straight street, and at the back of the house
there ran another straight street. This part of the city is
very little like that old Prague, which may not be so
comfortable, but which, of all cities on the earth, is
surely the most picturesque. Here lived Sophie Zamenoy; and so far up in the world had she mounted, that
she had a coach of her own in which to be drawn about
the thoroughfares of Prague and its suburbs, and a stout
little pair of Bohemian horses—ponies they were called
by those who wished to detract somewhat from Madame
Zamenoy's position. Madame Zamenoy had been at
Paris, and took much delight in telling her friends that
the carriage also was Parisian; but, in truth, it had come
no further than from Dresden. Josef Balatka and his
daughter were very, very poor; but, poor as they were,
they lived in a large house, which, at least nominally,
belonged to old Balatka himself, and which had been
his residence in the days of his better fortunes. It was in
the Kleinseite,* that narrow portion of the town which lies
on the other side of the river Moldau—the further side,
that is, from the so-called Old and New Town, on the
western side of the river, immediately under the great

hill of the Hradschin. The Old Town and the New Town are thus on one side of the river, and the Kleinseite and the Hradschin on the other. To those who know Prague, it need not here be explained that the streets of the Kleinseite are wonderful in their picturesque architecture, wonderful in their lights and shades, wonderful in their strange mixture of shops and palaces—and now, alas! also of Austrian barracks*—and wonderful in their intricacy and great steepness of ascent. Balatka's house stood in a small courtyard near to the river, but altogether hidden from it, somewhat to the right of the main street of the Kleinseite* as you pass over the bridge. A lane, for it is little more, turning from the main street between the side walls of what were once two palaces, comes suddenly into a small square, and from a corner of this square there is an open stone archway leading into a court. In this court is the door, or doors, as I may say, of the house in which Balatka lived with his daughter Nina. Opposite to these two doors was the blind wall of another residence. Balatka's house occupied two sides of the court, and no other window, therefore, besides his own looked either upon it or upon him. The aspect of the place is such as to strike with wonder a stranger to Prague,—that in the heart of so large a city there should be an abode so sequestered, so isolated, so desolate, and yet so close to the thickest throng of life. But there are others such, perhaps many others such, in Prague; and Nina Balatka, who had been born there, thought nothing of the quaintness of her abode. Immediately over the little square stood the palace of the Hradschin, the wide-spreading residence of the old kings of Bohemia, now the habitation of an ex-emperor of the House of Hapsburg,* who must surely find the thousand chambers of the royal mansion all too wide a retreat for the use of his old age. So immediately did the imperial hill tower over the spot on which Balatka lived, that it would seem at night, when the moon was shining as it shines only at Prague, that the colonnades of the palace were the upper storeys of some enormous edifice, of which the broken merchant's small courtyard formed a lower portion. The long rows of

windows would glimmer in the sheen of the night, and
Nina would stand in the gloom of the archway counting
them till they would seem to be uncountable, and wondering what might be the thoughts of those who abode there.
But those who abode there were few in number, and
their thoughts were hardly worthy of Nina's speculation.
The windows of kings' palaces look out from many
chambers. The windows of the Hradschin look out, as
we are told, from a thousand. But the rooms within have
seldom many tenants, nor the tenants, perhaps, many
thoughts. Chamber after chamber, you shall pass
through them by the score, and know by signs unconsciously recognised that there is not, and never has been,
true habitation within them. Windows almost innumer-
able are there, that they may be seen from the outside—
and such is the use of palaces. But Nina, as she would
look, would people the rooms with throngs of bright
inhabitants, and would think of the joys of happy girls
who were loved by Christian youths, and who could dare
to tell their friends of their love. But Nina Balatka was
no coward, and she had already determined that she
would at once tell her love to those who had a right to know
in what way she intended to dispose of herself. As to her
father, if only he could have been alone in the matter, she
would have had some hope of a compromise which
would have made it not absolutely necessary that she
should separate herself from him for ever in giving herself
to Anton Trendellsohn. Josef Balatka would doubtless
express horror, and would feel shame that his daughter
should love a Jew—though he had not scrupled to allow
Nina to go frequently among these people, and to use her
services with them for staving off the ill consequences of
his own idleness and ill-fortune; but he was a meek,
broken man, and was so accustomed to yield to Nina that
at last he might have yielded to her even in this. There
was, however, that Madame Zamenoy, her aunt—her
aunt with the bitter tongue; and there was Ziska Zamenoy, her cousin—her rich and handsome cousin, who
would so soon declare himself willing to become more
than cousin, if Nina would but give him one nod of

encouragement, or half a smile of welcome. But Nina hated her Christian lover, cousin though he was, as warmly as she loved the Jew. Nina, indeed, loved none of the Zamenoys—neither her cousin Ziska, nor her very Christian aunt Sophie with the bitter tongue, nor her prosperous, money-loving, acutely mercantile uncle Karil; but, nevertheless, she was in some degree so subject to them, that she knew that she was bound to tell them what path in life she meant to tread. Madame Zamenoy had offered to take her niece to the prosperous house in the Windberg-gasse* when the old house in the Kleinseite had become poor and desolate; and though this generous offer had been most fatuously* declined—most wickedly declined, as aunt Sophie used to declare—nevertheless other favours had been vouchsafed; and other favours had been accepted, with sore injury to Nina's pride. As she thought of this, standing in the gloom of the evening under the archway, she remembered that the very frock she wore had been sent to her by her aunt. But in spite of the bitter tongue, and in spite of Ziska's derision, she would tell her tale, and would tell it soon. She knew her own courage, and trusted it; and, dreadful as the hour would be, she would not put it off by one moment. As soon as Anton should desire her to declare her purpose, she would declare it; and as he who stands on a precipice, contemplating the expediency of throwing himself from the rock, will feel himself gradually seized by a mad desire to do the deed out of hand at once, so did Nina feel anxious to walk off to the Windberg-gasse, and dare and endure all that the Zamenoys could say or do. She knew, or thought she knew, that persecution could not go now beyond the work of the tongue. No priest could immure her. No law could touch her because she was minded to marry a Jew. Even the people in these days were mild and forbearing in their usages with the Jews, and she thought that the girls of the Kleinseite would not tear her clothes from her back even when they knew of her love. One thing, however, was certain. Though every rag should be torn from her—though some priest might have special power given him to persecute her—

though the Zamenoys in their wrath should be able to crush her—even though her own father should refuse to see her, she would be true to the Jew. Love to her should be so sacred that no other sacredness should be able to touch its sanctity. She had thought much of love, but had never loved before. Now she loved, and, heart and soul, she belonged to him to whom she had devoted herself. Whatever suffering might be before her, though it were suffering unto death, she would endure it if her lover demanded such endurance. Hitherto, there was but one person who suspected her. In her father's house there still remained an old dependant, who, though he was a man, was cook and housemaid, and washerwoman and servant-of-all-work; or perhaps it would be more true to say that he and Nina between them did all that the requirements of the house demanded. Souchey—for that was his name—was very faithful, but with his fidelity had come a want of reverence towards his master and mistress, and an absence of all respectful demeanour. The enjoyment of this apparent independence by Souchey himself went far, perhaps, in lieu of wages.

'Nina,' he said to her one morning, 'you are seeing too much of Anton Trendellsohn.'

'What do you mean by that, Souchey?' said the girl, sharply.

'You are seeing too much of Anton Trendellsohn,' repeated the old man.

'I have to see him on father's account. You know that. You know that, Souchey, and you shouldn't say such things.'

'You are seeing too much of Anton Trendellsohn,' said Souchey for the third time. 'Anton Trendellsohn is a Jew.' Then Nina knew that Souchey had read her secret, and was sure that it would spread from him through Lotta Luxa, her aunt's confidential maid, up to her aunt's ears. Not that Souchey would be untrue to her on behalf of Madame Zamenoy, whom he hated; but that he would think himself bound by his religious duty—he who never went near priest or mass himself—to save his mistress from the perils of the Jew. The story of her love must be told, and Nina preferred to tell it herself to having it told for her by her servant Souchey. She must see Anton. When the evening therefore had come, and there was sufficient dusk upon the bridge to allow of her passing over without observation, she put her old cloak upon her shoulders, with the hood drawn over her head, and, crossing the river, turned to the left and made her way through the narrow crooked streets which led to the Jews' quarter. She knew the path well, and could have found it with blindfold eyes. In the middle of that close and densely populated region of Prague stands the old Jewish synagogue*—the oldest place of worship belonging to the Jews in Europe, as they delight to tell you; and in a pinched-up, high-gabled house immediately behind the synagogue, at the corner of two streets, each so narrow as hardly to admit a vehicle, dwelt the Trendellsohns. On the basement floor there had once been a shop. There was no shop now, for the Trendellsohns were rich, and no longer dealt in retail matters; but there had been no care, or perhaps no ambition, at work, to alter the appearance of their residence, and the old shutters were upon the window, making the house look as though it were deserted. There was a high-pitched sharp roof over the gable, which, as the building stood alone fronting upon the synagogue, made it so remarkable, that all who knew Prague well, knew the house in which the Trendellsohns lived. Nina had often wished, as in latter days she had entered it, that it was less remarkable, so that she might have gone in and out with smaller risk of observation. It was now the beginning of September, and the clocks of the town had just struck eight as Nina put her hand on the lock of the Jew's door. As usual it was not bolted, and she was able to enter without waiting in the street for a servant to come to her. She went at once along the narrow passage and up the gloomy wooden stairs, at the foot of which there hung a small lamp, giving just light enough to expel the actual blackness of night. On the first landing Nina knocked at a door, and was desired to enter by a soft female voice. The only occupant of the room when she entered was a dark-haired

child, some twelve years old perhaps, but small in stature
and delicate, and, as appeared to the eye, almost wan.
'Well, Ruth dear,' said Nina, 'is Anton at home this
evening?'

'He is up-stairs with grandfather, Nina. Shall I tell
him?'

'If you will, dear,' said Nina, stooping down and
kissing her.

'Nice Nina, dear Nina, good Nina,' said the girl,
rubbing her glossy curls against her friend's cheeks. 'Ah,
dear, how I wish you lived here!'

'But I have a father, as you have a grandfather, Ruth.'

'And he is a Christian.'

'And so am I, Ruth.'

'But you like us, and are good, and nice, and dear—
and oh, Nina, you are so beautiful! I wish you were one
of us, and lived here. There is Miriam Harter—her hair
is as light as yours, and her eyes are as grey.'

'What has that to do with it?'

'Only I am so dark, and most of us are dark here in
Prague. Anton says that away in Palestine* our girls are
as fair as the girls in Saxony.'

'And does not Anton like girls to be dark?'

'Anton likes fair hair—such as yours—and bright grey
eyes such as you have got. I said they were green, and he
pulled my ears. But now I look, Nina, I think they are
green. And so bright! I can see my own in them, though
it is so dark. That is what they call looking babies.'*

'Go to your uncle, Ruth, and tell him that I want him
—on business.'

'I will, and he'll come to you. He won't let me come
down again, so kiss me, Nina; good-bye.'

Nina kissed the child again, and then was left alone in
the room. It was a comfortable chamber, having in it
sofas and arm-chairs—much more comfortable, Nina
used to think, than her aunt's grand drawing-room in
the Windberg-gasse, which was covered all over with a
carpet, after the fashion of drawing-rooms in Paris; but
the Jew's sitting-room was dark, with walls painted a
gloomy green colour, and there was but one small lamp

of oil upon the table. But yet Nina loved the room, and
as she sat there waiting for her lover, she wished that it
had been her lot to have been born a Jewess. Only, had
that been so, her hair might perhaps have been black,
and her eyes dark, and Anton would not have liked her.
She put her hand up for a moment to her rich brown
tresses, and felt them as she took joy in thinking that
Anton Trendellsohn loved to look upon fair beauty.

After a short while Anton Trendellsohn came down.
To those who know the outward types of his race there
could be no doubt that Anton Trendellsohn was a very
Jew among Jews. He was certainly a handsome man, not
now very young, having reached some year certainly in
advance of thirty, and his face was full of intellect. He
was slightly made, below the middle height, but was well
made in every limb, with small feet and hands, and small
ears, and a well-turned neck. He was very dark—dark
as a man can be and yet show no sign of colour in his
blood. No white man could be more dark and swarthy
than Anton Trendellsohn. His eyes, however, which
were quite black, were very bright. His jet-black hair,
as it clustered round his ears, had in it something of a curl.
Had it been allowed to grow, it would almost have hung
in ringlets; but it was worn very short, as though its
owner were jealous even of the curl. Anton Trendellsohn
was decidedly a handsome man; but his eyes were somewhat too close together in his face, and the bridge of his
aquiline nose was not sharply cut, as is mostly the case
with such a nose on a Christian face. The olive oval face
was without doubt the face of a Jew, and the mouth was
greedy, and the teeth were perfect and bright, and the
movement of the man's body was the movement of a Jew.
But not the less on that account had he behaved with
Christian forbearance to his Christian debtor, Josef
Balatka, and with Christian chivalry to Balatka's
daughter, till that chivalry had turned itself into love.

'Nina,' he said, putting out his hand, and holding hers
as he spoke; 'I hardly expected you this evening; but I am
glad to see you—very glad.'

'I hope I am not troubling you, Anton?'

'How can you trouble me? The sun does not trouble us when we want light and heat.'

'Can I give you light and heat?'

'The light and heat I love best, Nina.'

'If I thought that—if I could really think that—I would be happy still, and would mind nothing.'

'And what is it you do mind?'

'There are things to trouble us, of course. When aunt Sophie says that all of us have our troubles—even she—I suppose that even she speaks the truth.'

'Your aunt Sophie is a fool.'

'I should not mind if she were only a fool. But a fool can sometimes be right.'

'And she has been scolding you because—you—prefer a Jew to a Christian.'

'No—not yet, Anton. She does not know it yet; but she must know it.'

'Sit down, Nina.' He was still holding her by the hand; and now, as he spoke, he led her to a sofa which stood between the two windows. There he seated her, and sat by her side, still holding her hand in his. 'Yes,' he said, 'she must know it of course—when the time comes; and if she guesses it before, you must put up with her guesses. A few sharp words from a foolish woman will not frighten you, I hope.'

'No words will frighten me out of my love, if you mean that;—neither words nor anything else.'

'I believe you. You are brave, Nina. I know that. Though you will cry if one but frowns at you, yet you are brave.'

'Do not you frown at me, Anton.'

'I am one of those that do frown at times, I suppose; but I will be true to you, Nina, if you will be true to me.'

'I will be true to you—true as the sun.'

As she made her promise she turned her sweet face up to his, and he leaned over her, and kissed her.

'And what is it that has disturbed you now, Nina? What has Madame Zamenoy said to you?'

'She has said nothing—as yet. She suspects nothing—as yet.'

'Then let her remain as she is.'

'But, Anton, Souchey knows, and he will talk.'

'Souchey! And do you care for that?'

'I care for nothing—for nothing; for nothing, that is, in the way of preventing me. Do what they will, they cannot tear my love from my heart.'

'Nor can they take you away, or lock you up.'

'I fear nothing of that sort, Anton. All that I really fear is secrecy. Would it not be best that I should tell father?'

'What!—now, at once?'

'If you will let me. I suppose he must know it soon.'

'You can if you please.'

'Souchey will tell him.'

'Will Souchey dare to speak of you like that?' asked the Jew.

'Oh, yes; Souchey dares to say anything to father now. Besides, it is true. Why should not Souchey say it?'

'But you have not spoken to Souchey; you have not told him?'

'I! No indeed. I have spoken never a word to any one about that—only to you. How should I speak to another without your bidding? But when they speak to me I must answer them. If father asks me whether there be aught between you and me, shall I not tell him then?'

'It would be better to be silent for a while.'

'But shall I lie to him? I should not mind Souchey nor aunt Sophie much; but I never yet told a lie to father.'

'I do not tell you to lie.'

'Let me tell it all, Anton, and then, whatever they may say, whatever they may do, I shall not mind. I wish that they knew it, and then I could stand up against them. Then I could tell Ziska that which would make him hold his tongue for ever.'

'Ziska! Who cares for Ziska?'

'You need not, at any rate.'

'The truth is, Nina, that I cannot be married till I have settled all this about the houses in the Kleinseite. The very fact that you would be your father's heir prevents my doing so.'

'Do you think that I wish to hurry you? I would rather stay as I am, knowing that you love me.'

'Dear Nina! But when your aunt shall once know your secret, she will give you no peace till you are out of her power. She will leave no stone unturned to make you give up your Jew lover.'

'She may as well leave the turning of such stones alone.'

'But if she heard nothing of it till she heard that we were married——'

'Ah! but that is impossible. I could not do that without telling father, and father would surely tell my aunt.'

'You may do as you will, Nina; but it may be, when they shall know it, that therefore there may be new difficulty made about the houses. Karil Zamenoy has the papers, which are in truth mine—or my father's—which should be here in my iron box.' And Trendellsohn, as he spoke, put his hand forcibly on the seat beside him, as though the iron box to which he alluded were within his reach.

'I know they are yours,' said Nina.

'Yes; and without them, should your father die, I could not claim my property. The Zamenoys might say they held it on your behalf,—and you my wife at the time! Do you see, Nina? I could not stand that—I would not stand that.'

'I understand it well, Anton.'

'The houses are mine—or ours, rather. Your father has long since had the money, and more than the money. He knew that the houses were to be ours.'

'He knows it well. You do not think that he is holding back the papers?'

'He should get them for me. He should not drive me to press him for them. I know they are at Karil Zamenoy's counting-house; but your uncle told me, when I spoke to him, that he had no business with me; if I had a claim on him, there was the law. I have no claim on him. But I let your father have the money when he wanted it, on his promise that the deeds should be forthcoming. A Christian would not have been such a fool.'

'Oh, Anton, do not speak to me like that.'

'But was I not a fool? See how it is now. Were you and I to become man and wife, they would never give them up, though they are my own—my own. No; we must wait; and you—you must demand them from your uncle.'

'I will demand them. And as for waiting, I care nothing for that if you love me.'

'I do love you.'

'Then all shall be well with me; and I will ask for the papers. Father, I know, wishes that you should have all that is your own. He would leave the house to-morrow if you desired it.'

'He is welcome to remain there.'

'And now, Anton, good-night.'

'Good-night, Nina.'

'When shall I see you again?'

'When you please, and as often. Have I not said that you are light and heat to me? Can the sun rise too often for those who love it?' Then she held her hand up to be kissed, and kissed his in return, and went silently down the stairs into the street. He had said once in the course of the conversation—nay, twice, as she came to remember in thinking over it—that she might do as she would about telling her friends; and she had been almost craftily careful to say nothing herself, and to draw nothing from him, which could be held as militating against this authority, or as subsequently negativing the permission so given. She would undoubtedly tell her father—and her aunt; and would as certainly demand from her uncle those documents of which Anton Trendellsohn had spoken to her.

CHAPTER II

NINA, as she returned home from the Jews' quarter to her father's house in the Kleinseite, paused for a while on the bridge* to make some resolution—some resolution that should be fixed—as to her immediate conduct. Should she first tell her story to her father, or first to her aunt Sophie? There were reasons for and against either plan. And if to her father first, then should

she tell it to-night? She was nervously anxious to rush at
once at her difficulties, and to be known to all who
belonged to her as the girl who had given herself to the
Jew. It was now late in the evening, and the moon was
shining brightly on the palace over against her. The
colonnades seemed to be so close to her that there could
hardly be room for any portion of the city to cluster itself
between them and the river. She stood looking up at the
great building, and fell again into her trick of counting
the windows, thereby saving herself a while from the
difficult task of following out the train of her thoughts.
But what were the windows of the palace to her? So she
walked on again till she reached a spot on the bridge at
which she almost always paused a moment to perform a
little act of devotion. There, having a place in the long
row of huge statues which adorn the bridge, is the figure
of the martyr St. John Nepomucene,* who at this spot was
thrown into the river because he would not betray the
secrets of a queen's confession, and was drowned, and
who has ever been, from that period downwards, the
favourite saint of Prague—and of bridges. On the balustrade, near the figure, there is a small plate inserted in
the stone-work, and good Catholics, as they pass over the
river, put their hands upon the plate, and then kiss their
fingers. So shall they be saved from drowning and from
all perils of the water—as far, at least, as that special
transit of the river may be perilous. Nina, as a child, had
always touched the stone, and then touched her lips, and
did the act without much thought as to the saving power
of St. John Nepomucene. But now, as she carried her
hand up to her face, she did think of the deed. Had she,
who was about to marry a Jew, any right to ask for the
assistance of a Christian saint? And would such a deed
as that she now proposed to herself put her beyond the
pale of Christian aid? Would the Madonna herself
desert her should she marry a Jew? If she were to become
truer than ever to her faith—more diligent, more thoughtful, more constant in all acts of devotion—would the
blessed Mary help to save her, even though she should
commit this great sin? Would the mild-eyed, sweet

Saviour, who had forgiven so many women, who had saved from a cruel death the woman taken in adultery, who had been so gracious to the Samaritan woman at the well*—would He turn from her the graciousness of His dear eyes, and bid her go out for ever from among the faithful? Madame Zamenoy would tell her so, and so would Sister Teresa, an old nun, who was on most friendly terms with Madame Zamenoy, and whom Nina altogether hated; and so would the priest, to whom, alas! she would be bound to give faith. And if this were so, whither should she turn for comfort? She could not become a Jewess! She might call herself one; but how could she be a Jewess with her strong faith in St. Nicholas, who was the saint of her own Church,* and in St. John of the River, and in the Madonna? No; she must be an outcast from all religions, a Pariah, one devoted absolutely to the everlasting torments which lie beyond Purgatory*— unless, indeed, unless that mild-eyed Saviour would be content to take her faith and her acts of hidden worship, despite her aunt, despite that odious nun, and despite the very priest himself! She did not know how this might be with her, but she did know that all the teaching of her life was against any such hope.

But what was—what could be the good of such thoughts to her? Had not things gone too far with her for such thoughts to be useful? She loved the Jew, and had told him so; and not all the penalties with which the priests might threaten her could lessen her love, or make her think of her safety here or hereafter, as a thing to be compared with her love. Religion was much to her; the fear of the everlasting wrath of Heaven was much to her; but love was paramount! What if it were her soul? Would she not give even her soul for her love, if, for her love's sake, her soul should be required from her? When she reached the archway, she had made up her mind that she would tell her aunt first, and that she would do so early on the following day. Were she to tell her father first, her father might probably forbid her to speak on the subject to Madame Zamenoy, thinking that his own eloquence and that of the priest might prevail to put an end to so

terrible an iniquity, and that so Madame Zamenoy
might never learn the tidings. Nina, thinking of all this,
and being quite determined that the Zamenoys should
know what she intended to tell them, resolved that she
would say nothing on that night at home.

'You are very late, Nina,' said her father to her, crossly,
as soon as she entered the room in which they lived. It
was a wide apartment, having in it now but little furniture—two rickety tables, a few chairs, an old bureau in
which Balatka kept, under lock and key, all that still
belonged to him personally, and a little desk, which was
Nina's own repository.

'Yes, father, I am late; but not very late. I have been
with Anton Trendellsohn.'

'And what have you been there for now?'

'Anton Trendellsohn has been talking to me about the
papers which uncle Karil has. He wants to have them
himself. He says they are his.'

'I suppose he means that we are to be turned out of the
old house.'

'No, father; he does not mean that. He is not a cruel
man. But he says that—that he cannot settle anything
about the property without having the papers. I suppose
that is true.'

'He has the rent of the other houses,' said Balatka.

'Yes; but if the papers are his, he ought to have them.'

'Did he send for them?'

'No, father; he did not send.'

'And what made you go?'

'I am so often going there. He had spoken to me
before about this. He thinks you do not like him to come
here, and you never go there yourself.'

After this there was a pause for a few minutes, and
Nina was settling herself to her work. Then the old man
spoke again.

'Nina, I fear you see too much of Anton Trendellsohn.'
The words were the very words of Souchey; and Nina
was sure that her father and the servant had been discussing her conduct. It was no more than she had
expected, but her father's words had come very quickly

upon Souchey's speech to herself. What did it signify? Everybody would know it all before twenty-four hours had passed by. Nina, however, was determined to defend herself at the present moment, thinking that there was something of injustice in her father's remarks. 'As for seeing him often, father, I have done it because your business has required it. When you were ill in April I had to be there almost daily.'

'But you need not have gone to-night. He did not send for you.'

'But it is needful that something should be done to get for him that which is his own.' As she said this there came to her a sting of conscience, a thought that reminded her that, though she was not lying to her father in words, she was in fact deceiving him; and remembering her assertion to her lover that she had never spoken falsely to her father, she blushed with shame as she sat in the darkness of her seat.

'To-morrow, father,' she said, 'I will talk to you more about this, and you shall not at any rate say that I keep anything from you.'

'I have never said so, Nina.'

'It is late now, father. Will you not go to bed?'

Old Balatka yielded to this suggestion, and went to his bed; and Nina, after some hour or two, went to hers. But before doing so she opened the little desk that stood in the corner of their sitting-room, of which the key was always in her pocket, and took out everything that it contained. There were many letters there, of which most were on matters of business—letters which in few houses would come into the hands of such a one as Nina Balatka, but which, through the weakness of her father's health, had come into hers. Many of these she now read; some few she tore and burned in the stove, and others she tied in bundles and put back carefully into their place. There was not a paper in the desk which did not pass under her eye, and as to which she did not come to some conclusion, either to keep it or to burn it. There were no love-letters there. Nina Balatka had never yet received such a letter as that. She saw her lover too frequently to feel much

the need of written expressions of love; and such scraps
of his writing as there were in the bundles, referred
altogether to small matters of business. When she had
thus arranged her papers, she too went to bed. On the
next morning, when she gave her father his breakfast, she
was very silent. She made for him a little chocolate, and
cut for him a few slips of white bread to dip into it. For
herself, she cut a slice from a black loaf made of rye flour,
and mixed with water a small quantity of the thin sour
wine of the country. Her meal may have been worth
perhaps a couple of kreutzers,* or something less than a
penny, whereas that of her father may have cost twice as
much. Nina was a close and sparing housekeeper, but
with all her economy she could not feed three people
upon nothing. Latterly, from month to month, she had
sold one thing out of the house after another, knowing as
each article went that provision from such store as that
must soon fail her. But anything was better than taking
money from her aunt whom she hated,—except taking
money from the Jew whom she loved. From him she had
taken none, though it had been often offered. 'You have
lost more than enough by father,' she had said to him when
the offer had been made. 'What I give to the wife of my
bosom shall never be reckoned as lost,' he had answered.
She had loved him for the words, and had pressed his
hand in hers—but she had not taken his money. From
her aunt some small meagre supply had been accepted
from time to time—a florin*or two now, and a florin or
two again—given with repeated intimations on aunt
Sophie's part, that her husband Karil could not be
expected to maintain the house in the Kleinseite. Nina
had not felt herself justified in refusing such gifts from her
aunt to her father, but as each occasion came she told
herself that some speedy end must be put to this state of
things. Her aunt's generosity would not sustain her
father, and her aunt's generosity nearly killed herself.
On this very morning she would do that which would
certainly put an end to a state of things so disagreeable.
After breakfast, therefore, she started at once for the
house in the Windberg-gasse, leaving her father still in

his bed. She walked very quick, looking neither to the
right nor the left, across the bridge, along the river-side,
and then up into the straight ugly streets of the New
Town. The distance from her father's house was nearly
two miles, and yet the journey was made in half an hour.
She had never walked so quickly through the streets of
Prague before; and when she reached the end of the
Windberg-gasse, she had to pause a moment to collect
her thoughts and her breath. But it was only for a
moment, and then the bell was rung.

Yes; her aunt was at home. At ten in the morning that
was a matter of course. She was shown, not into the
grand drawing-room, which was only used on grand
occasions, but into a little back parlour which, in spite of
the wealth and magnificence of the Zamenoys, was not
so clean as the room in the Kleinseite, and certainly not
so comfortable as the Jew's apartment. There was no
carpet; but that was not much, as carpets in Prague
were not in common use. There were two tables crowded
with things needed for household purposes, half-a-dozen
chairs of different patterns, a box of sawdust close under
the wall, placed there that papa Zamenoy might spit
into it when it pleased him. There was a crowd of clothes
and linen hanging round the stove, which projected far
into the room; and spread upon the table, close to which
was placed mamma Zamenoy's chair, was an article of
papa Zamenoy's dress, on which mamma Zamenoy was
about to employ her talents in the art of tailoring. All
this, however, was nothing to Nina, nor was the dirt on
the floor much to her, though she had often thought
that if she were to go and live with aunt Sophie, she
would contrive to make some improvement as to the
cleanliness of the house.

'Your aunt will be down soon,' said Lotta Luxa as they
passed through the passage. 'She is very angry, Nina, at
not seeing you all the last week.'

'I don't know why she should be angry, Lotta. I did
not say I would come.'

Lotta Luxa was a sharp little woman, over forty years
of age, with quick green eyes and thin red-tipped nose,

looking as though Paris might have been the town of her birth rather than Prague. She wore short petticoats, clean stockings, an old pair of slippers; and in the back of her hair she still carried that Diana's dart* which maidens wear in those parts when they are not only maidens unmarried, but maidens also disengaged. No one had yet succeeded in drawing Lotta Luxa's arrow from her head, though Souchey, from the other side of the river, had made repeated attempts to do so. For Lotta Luxa had a little money of her own, and poor Souchey had none. Lotta muttered something about the thoughtless thanklessness of young people, and then took herself downstairs. Nina opened the door of the back parlour, and found her cousin Ziska sitting alone with his feet propped upon the stove.

'What, Ziska,' she said, 'you not at work by ten o'clock!'

'I was not well last night, and took physic this morning,' said Ziska. 'Something had disagreed with me.'

'I'm sorry for that, Ziska. You eat too much fruit, I suppose.'

'Lotta says it was the sausage, but I don't think it was. I'm very fond of sausage, and everybody must be ill sometimes. She'll be down here again directly;' and Ziska with his head nodded at the chair in which his mother was wont to sit.

Nina, whose mind was quite full of her business, was determined to go to work at once. 'I'm glad to have you alone for a moment, Ziska,' she said.

'And so am I very glad; only I wish I had not taken physic, it makes one so uncomfortable.'

At this moment Nina had in her heart no charity towards her cousin, and did not care for his discomfort. 'Ziska,' she said, 'Anton Trendellsohn wants to have the papers about the houses in the Kleinseite. He says that they are his, and you have them.'

Ziska hated Anton Trendellsohn, hardly knowing why he hated him. 'If Trendellsohn wants anything of us,' said he, 'why does he not come to the office? He knows where to find us.'

'Yes, Ziska, he knows where to find you; but, as he says, he has no business with you—no business as to which he can make a demand. He thinks, therefore, you would merely bid him begone.'

'Very likely. One doesn't want to see more of a Jew than one can help.'

'That Jew, Ziska, owns the house in which father lives. That Jew, Ziska, is the best friend that—that—that father has.'

'I'm sorry you think so, Nina.'

'How can I help thinking it? You can't deny, nor can uncle, that the houses belong to him. The papers got into uncle's hands when he and father were together, and I think they ought to be given up now. Father thinks that the Trendellsohns should have them. Even though they are Jews, they have a right to their own.'

'You know nothing about it, Nina. How should you know about such things as that?'

'I am driven to know. Father is ill, and cannot come himself.'

'Oh, laws! I am so uncomfortable. I never will take stuff from Lotta Luxa again. She thinks a man is the same as a horse.'

This little episode put a stop to the conversation about the title-deeds, and then Madame Zamenoy entered the room. Madame Zamenoy was a woman of a portly demeanour, well fitted to do honour by her personal presence to that carriage and horses with which Providence and an indulgent husband had blessed her. And when she was dressed in her full panoply of French millinery—the materials of which had come from England, and the manufacture of which had taken place in Prague—she looked the carriage and horses well enough. But of a morning she was accustomed to go about the house in a pale-tinted wrapper, which, pale-tinted as it was, should have been in the washing-tub much oftener than was the case with it—if not for cleanliness, then for mere decency of appearance. And the mode in which she carried her matutinal curls, done up with black pins, very visible to the eye, was not in itself

becoming. The handkerchief which she wore in lieu of
cap, might have been excused on the score of its ugliness,
as Madame Zamenoy was no longer young, had it not
been open to such manifest condemnation for other sins.
And in this guise she would go about the house from
morning to night on days not made sacred by the use of
the carriage. Now Lotta Luxa was clean in the midst of
her work; and one would have thought that the cleanliness of the maid would have shamed the slatternly ways
of the mistress. But Madame Zamenoy and Lotta Luxa
had lived together long, and probably knew each other
well.

'Well, Nina,' she said, 'so you've come at last?'

'Yes; I've come, aunt. And as I want to say something
very particular to you yourself, perhaps Ziska won't mind
going out of the room for a minute.' Nina had not sat
down since she had been in the room, and was now
standing before her aunt with almost militant firmness.
She was resolved to rush at once at the terrible subject
which she had in hand, but she could not do so in the
presence of her cousin Ziska.

Ziska groaned audibly. 'Ziska isn't well this morning,'
said Madame Zamenoy, 'and I do not wish to have him
disturbed.'

'Then perhaps you'll come into the front parlour, aunt.'

'What can there be that you cannot say before Ziska?'

'There is something, aunt,' said Nina.

If there were a secret, Madame Zamenoy decidedly
wished to hear it, and therefore, after pausing to consider
the matter for a moment or two, she led the way into the
front parlour.

'And now, Nina, what is it? I hope you have not
disturbed me in this way for anything that is a trifle.'

'It is no trifle to me, aunt. I am going to be married
to—Anton Trendellsohn.' She said the words slowly,
standing bolt-upright, at her greatest height, as she spoke
them, and looking her aunt full in the face with something of defiance both in her eyes and in the tone of her
voice. She had almost said Anton Trendellsohn, the
Jew; and when her speech was finished, and admitted of

no addition, she reproached herself with pusillanimity in that she had omitted the word which had always been so odious, and would now be doubly odious—odious to her aunt in a tenfold degree.

Madame Zamenoy stood for a while speechless—struck with horror. The tidings which she heard were so unexpected, so strange, and so abominable, that they seemed at first to crush her. Nina was her niece—her sister's child; and though she might be repudiated, reviled, persecuted, and perhaps punished, still she must retain her relationship to her injured relatives. And it seemed to Madame Zamenoy as though the marriage of which Nina spoke was a thing to be done at once, out of hand—as though the disgusting nuptials were to take place on that day or on the next, and could not now be avoided. It occurred to her that old Balatka himself was a consenting party, and that utter degradation was to fall upon the family instantly. There was that in Nina's air and manner, as she spoke of her own iniquity, which made the elder woman feel for the moment that she was helpless to prevent the evil with which she was threatened.

'Anton Trendellsohn—a Jew,' she said, at last.

'Yes, aunt; Anton Trendellsohn, the Jew. I am engaged to him as his wife.'

There was a something of doubtful futurity in the word engaged, which gave a slight feeling of relief to Madame Zamenoy, and taught her to entertain a hope that there might be yet room for escape. 'Marry a Jew, Nina,' she said; 'it cannot be possible.'

'It is possible, aunt. Other Jews in Prague have married Christians.'

'Yes, I know it. There have been outcasts among us low enough so to degrade themselves—low women who were called Christians. There has been no girl connected with decent people who has ever so degraded herself. Does your father know of this?'

'Not yet.'

'Your father knows nothing of it, and you come and tell me that you are engaged—to a Jew!' Madame Zamenoy had so far recovered herself that she was now able to let her anger mount above her misery. 'You wicked girl! Why have you come to me with such a story as this?'

'Because it is well that you should know it. I did not like to deceive you, even by secrecy. You will not be hurt. You need not notice me any longer. I shall be lost to you, and that will be all.'

'If you were to do such a thing you would disgrace us. But you will not be allowed to do it.'

'But I shall do it.'

'Nina!'

'Yes, aunt. I shall do it. Do you think I will be false to my troth?'

'Your troth to a Jew is nothing. Father Jerome will tell you so.'

'I shall not ask Father Jerome. Father Jerome, of course, will condemn me; but I shall not ask him whether or not I am to keep my promise—my solemn promise.'

'And why not?'

Then Nina paused a moment before she answered. But she did answer, and answered with that bold defiant air which at first had disconcerted her aunt.

'I will ask no one, aunt Sophie, because I love Anton Trendellsohn, and have told him that I love him.'

'Pshaw!'

'I have nothing more to say, aunt. I thought it right to tell you, and now I will go.'

She had turned to the door, and had her hand upon the lock when her aunt stopped her. 'Wait a moment, Nina. You have had your say; now you must hear me.'

'I will hear you if you say nothing against him.'

'I shall say what I please.'

'Then I will not hear you.' Nina again made for the door, but her aunt intercepted her retreat. 'Of course you can stop me, aunt, in that way if you choose.'

'You bold, bad girl!'

'You may say what you please about myself.'

'You are a bold, bad girl!'

'Perhaps I am. Father Jerome says we are all bad. And as for boldness, I have to be bold.'

'You are bold and brazen. Marry a Jew! It is the worst thing a Christian girl could do.'

'No, it is not. There are things ten times worse than that.'

'How you could dare to come and tell me!'

'I did dare, you see. If I had not told you, you would have called me sly.'

'You are sly.'

'I am not sly. You tell me I am bad and bold and brazen.'

'So you are.'

'Very likely. I do not say I am not. But I am not sly. Now, will you let me go, aunt Sophie?'

'Yes, you may go—you may go; but you may not come here again till this thing has been put an end to. Of course I shall see your father and Father Jerome, and your uncle will see the police. You will be locked up, and Anton Trendellsohn will be sent out of Bohemia. That is how it will end. Now you may go.' And Nina went her way.

Her aunt's threat of seeing her father and the priest was nothing to Nina. It was the natural course for her aunt to take, and a course in opposition to which Nina was prepared to stand her ground firmly. But the allusion to the police did frighten her. She had thought of the power which the law might have over her very often, and had spoken of it in awe to her lover. He had reassured her, explaining to her that, as the law now stood in Austria,* no one but her father could prevent her marriage with a Jew, and that he could only do so till she was of age. Now Nina would be twenty-one on the first of the coming month, and therefore would be free, as Anton told her, to do with herself as she pleased. But still there came over her a cold feeling of fear when her aunt spoke to her of the police. The law might give the police no power over her; but was there not a power in the hands of those armed men whom she saw around her on every side, and who were seldom countrymen of her own,* over and above the law? Were there not still dark dungeons and steel locks and hard hearts? Though the law might justify her, how would that serve her, if men—if men and women, were determined to persecute her? As she walked home, however, she resolved that dark dungeons and steel locks and hard hearts might do their worst against her. She had set her will upon one thing in this world, and from that one thing no persecution should drive her. They might kill her, perhaps. Yes, they might kill her; and then there would be an end of it. But to that end she would force them to come before she would yield. So much she swore to herself as she walked home on that morning to the Kleinseite.

Madame Zamenoy, when Nina left her, sat in solitary consideration for some twenty minutes, and then called for her chief confidant, Lotta Luxa. With many expressions of awe, and with much denunciation of her niece's iniquity, she told to Lotta what she had heard, speaking of Nina as one who was utterly lost and abandoned. Lotta, however, did not express so much indignant surprise as her mistress expected, though she was willing enough to join in abuse against Nina Balatka.

'That comes of letting girls go about just as they please among the men,' said Lotta.

'But a Jew!' said Madame Zamenoy. 'If it had been any kind of a Christian, I could understand it.'

'Trendellsohn has such a hold upon her, and upon her father,' said Lotta.

'But a Jew! She has been to confession, has she not?'

'Regularly,' said Lotta Luxa.

'Dear, dear! what a false hypocrite! And at mass?'

'Four mornings a week always.'

'And to tell me, after it all, that she means to marry a Jew. Of course, Lotta, we must prevent it.'

'But how? Her father will do whatever she bids him.'

'Father Jerome would do anything for me.'

'Father Jerome can do little or nothing if she has the bit between her teeth,' said Lotta. 'She is as obstinate as a mule when she pleases. She is not like other girls. You cannot frighten her out of anything.'

'I'll try, at least,' said Madame Zamenoy.

'Yes, we can try,' said Lotta.

'Would not the mayor help us—that is, if we were driven to go to that?'

'I doubt if he could do anything. He would be afraid to use a high hand. He is Bohemian. The head of the police* might do something, if we could get at him.'

'She might be taken away.'

'Where could they take her?' asked Lotta. 'No; they could not take her anywhere.'

'Not into a convent—out of the way somewhere in Italy?'

'Oh, heaven, no! They are afraid of that sort of thing now. All Prague would know of it, and would talk; and the Jews would be stronger than the priests; and the English people would hear of it, and there would be the very mischief.'*

'The times have come to be very bad, Lotta.'

'That's as may be,' said Lotta, as though she had her doubts upon the subject. 'That's as may be. But it isn't easy to put a young woman away now without her will. Things have changed—partly for the worse, perhaps, and partly for the better. Things are changing every day. My wonder is that he should wish to marry her.'

'The men think her very pretty. Ziska is mad about her,' said Madame Zamenoy.

'But Ziska is a calf to Anton Trendellsohn. Anton Trendellsohn has cut his wise teeth. Like them all, he loves his money; and she has not got a kreutzer.'

'But he has promised to marry her. You may be sure of that.'

'Very likely. A man always promises that when he wants a girl to be kind to him. But why should he stick to it? What can he get by marrying Nina,—a penniless girl, with a pauper for a father? The Trendellsohns have squeezed that sponge dry already.'

This was a new light to Madame Zamenoy, and one that was not altogether unpleasant to her eyes. That her niece should have promised herself to a Jew was dreadful, and that her niece should be afterwards jilted by the Jew was a poor remedy. But still it was a remedy, and therefore she listened.

'If nothing else can be done, we could perhaps put him against it,' said Lotta Luxa.

Madame Zamenoy on that occasion said but little more, but she agreed with her servant that it would be better to resort to any means than to submit to the degradation of an alliance with the Jew.

CHAPTER III

ON the third day after Nina's visit to her aunt, Ziska Zamenoy came across to the Kleinseite on a visit to old Balatka. In the mean time Nina had told the story of her love to her father, and the effect on Balatka had simply been, that he had not got out of his bed since. For himself he would have cared, perhaps, but little as to the Jewish marriage, had he not known that those belonging to him would have cared so much. He had no strong religious prejudice of his own, nor indeed had he strong feeling of any kind. He loved his daughter, and wished her well; but even for her he had been unable to exert himself in his younger days, and now simply expected from her hands all the comfort which remained to him in this world. The priest he knew would attack him, and to the priest he would be able to make no answer. But to Trendellsohn, Jew as he was, he would trust in worldly matters, rather than to the Zamenoys; and were it not that he feared the Zamenoys, and could not escape from his close connection with them, he would have been half inclined to let the girl marry the Jew. Souchey, indeed, had frightened him on the subject when it had first been mentioned to him; and Nina coming with her own assurance so quickly after Souchey's suspicion, had upset him; but his feeling in regard to Nina had none of that bitter anger, no touch of that abhorrence which animated the breast of his sister-in-law. When Ziska came to him he was alone in his bedroom. Ziska had heard the news, as had all the household in the Windberg-gasse, and had come over to his uncle's house to see what he could do, by his own diplomacy, to put an end to an engagement which was to him doubly calamitous. 'Uncle Josef,' he

said, sitting by the old man's bed, 'have you heard what
Nina is doing?'

'What she is doing?' said the uncle. 'What is she
doing?' Balatka feared all the Zamenoys, down to Lotta
Luxa; but he feared Ziska less than he feared any other
of the household.

'Have you heard of Anton Trendellsohn?'

'What of Anton Trendellsohn? I have been hearing
of Anton Trendellsohn for the last thirty years. I have
known him since he was born.'

'Do you wish to have him for a son-in-law?'

'For a son-in-law?'

'Yes, for a son-in-law—Anton Trendellsohn, the Jew.
Would he be a good husband for our Nina? You say
nothing, uncle Josef.'

'What am I to say?'

'You have heard of it, then? Why can you not answer
me, uncle Josef? Have you heard that Trendellsohn has
dared to ask Nina to be his wife?'

'There is not so much of daring in it, Ziska. Among
you all the poor girl is a beggar. If some one does not
take pity on her, she will starve soon.'

'Take pity on her! Do not we all take pity on her?'

'No,' said Josef Balatka, turning angrily against his
nephew; 'not a scrap of pity,—not a morsel of love. You
cannot rid yourself of her quite—of her or me—and that
is your pity.'

'You are wrong there.'

'Very well; then let me be wrong. I can understand
what is before my eyes. Look round the house and see
what we are coming to. Nina at the present moment has
not got a florin in her purse. We are starving, or next to
it, and yet you wonder that she should be willing to
marry an honest man who has plenty of money.'

'But he is a Jew!'

'Yes; he is a Jew. I know that.'

'And Nina knows it.'

'Of course she does. Do you go home and eat nothing
for a week, and then see whether a Jew's bread will
poison you.'

'But to marry him, uncle Josef!'

'It is very bad. I know it is bad, but what can I do? If she says she will do it, how can I help it? She has been a good child to me—a very good child; and am I to lie here and see her starve? You would not give to your dog the morsel of bread which she ate this morning before she went out.'

All this was a new light to Ziska. He knew that his uncle and cousin were very poor, and had halted in his love because he was ashamed of their poverty; but he had never thought of them as people hungry from want of food, or cold from want of clothes. It may be said of him, to his credit, that his love had been too strong for his shame, and that he had made up his mind to marry his cousin Nina, in spite of her poverty. When Lotta Luxa had called him a calf she had not inappropriately defined one side of his character. He was a good-looking well-grown young man, not very wise, quickly susceptible to female influences, and gifted with eyes capable of convincing him that Nina Balatka was by far the prettiest woman whom he ever saw. But, in connection with such calf-like propensities, Ziska was endowed with something of his mother's bitterness and of his father's persistency; and the old Zamenoys did not fear but that the fortunes of the family would prosper in the hands of their son. And when it was known to Madame Zamenoy and to her husband Karil that Ziska had set his heart upon having his cousin, they had expressed no displeasure at the prospect, poor as the Balatkas were. 'There is no knowing how it may go about the houses in the Kleinseite,' Karil Zamenoy had said. 'Old Trendellsohn gets the rent and the interest, but he has little or nothing to show for them—merely a written surrender from Josef, which is worth nothing.' No hindrance, therefore, was placed in the way of Ziska's suit, and Nina might have been already accepted in the Windberg-gasse had Nina chosen to smile upon Ziska. Now Ziska was told that the girl he loved was to marry a Jew because she was starving, and the tidings threw a new light upon him. Why had he not offered assistance to Nina? It was not surprising that

Nina should be so hard to him—to him who had as yet
offered her nothing in her poverty but a few cold
compliments.

'She shall have bread enough, if that is what she
wants,' said Ziska.

'Bread and kindness,' said the old man.

'She shall have kindness too, uncle Josef. I love Nina
better than any Jew in Prague can love her.'

'Why should not a Jew love? I believe the man loves
her well. Why else should he wish to make her his wife?'

'And I love her well;—and I would make her my wife.'

'You want to marry Nina!'

'Yes, uncle Josef. I wish to marry Nina. I will marry
her to-morrow—or, for that matter, to-day—if she will
have me.'

'You!—Ziska Zamenoy.'

'I,—Ziska Zamenoy.'

'And what would your mother say?'

'Both father and mother will consent. There need be
no hindrance if Nina will agree. I did not know that you
were so badly off. I did not indeed, or I would have come
to you myself and seen to it.'

Old Balatka did not answer for a while, having turned
himself in his bed to think of the proposition which had
been made to him. 'Would you not like to have me for
a son-in-law better than a Jew, uncle Josef?' said Ziska,
pleading for himself as best he knew how to plead.

'Have you ever spoken to Nina?' said the old man.

'Well, no; not exactly to say what I have said to you.
When one loves a girl as I love her, somehow—I don't
know how—But I am ready to do so at once.'

'Ah, Ziska, if you had done it sooner!'

'But is it too late? You say she has taken up with this
man because you are both so poor. She cannot like a
Jew best.'

'But she is true—so true!'

'If you mean about her promise to Trendellsohn,
Father Jerome would tell her in a minute that she should
not keep such a promise to a Jew.'

'She would not mind Father Jerome.'

'And what does she mind? Will she not mind you?'
'Me; yes,—she will mind me, to give me my food.'
'Will she not obey you?'
'How am I to bid her obey me? But I will try, Ziska.'
'You would not wish her to marry a Jew?'
'No, Ziska; certainly I should not wish it.'
'And you will give me your consent?'
'Yes,—if it be any good to you.'

'It will be good if you will be round with her, telling her that she must not do such a thing as this. Love a Jew! It is impossible. As you have been so very poor, she may be forgiven for having thought of it. Tell her that, uncle Josef; and whatever you do, be firm with her.'

'There she is in the next room,' said the father, who had heard his daughter's entrance. Ziska's face had assumed something of a defiant look while he was recommending firmness to the old man; but now that the girl of whom he had spoken was so near at hand, there returned to his brow the young calf-like expression with which Lotta Luxa was so well acquainted. 'There she is, and you will speak to her yourself now,' said Balatka.

Ziska got up to go, but as he did so he fumbled in his pocket and brought forth a little bundle of bank-notes. A bundle of bank-notes in Prague may be not little, and yet represent very little money. When bank-notes are passed for twopence and become thick with use, a man may have a great mass of paper currency in his pocket without being rich. On this occasion, however, Ziska tendered to his uncle no twopenny notes.* There was a note for five florins, and two or three for two florins, and perhaps half-a-dozen for a florin each, so that the total amount offered was sufficient to be of real importance to one so poor as Josef Balatka.

'This will help you awhile,' said Ziska, 'and if Nina will come round and be a good girl, neither you nor she shall want anything; and she need not be afraid of mother, if she will only do as I say.' Balatka had put out his hand and had taken the money, when the bedroom door was opened, and Nina came in.

'What, Ziska,' said she, 'are you here?'

'Why not? why should I not see my uncle?'

'It is very good of you, certainly; only, as you never came before—'

'I mean it for kindness, now I have come, at any rate,' said Ziska.

'Then I will take it for kindness,' said Nina.

'Why should there be quarrelling among relatives?' said the old man from among the bed-clothes.

'Why, indeed?' said Ziska.

'Why, indeed,' said Nina,—'if it could be helped?'

She knew that the outward serenity of the words spoken was too good to be a fair representation of thoughts below in the mind of any of them. It could not be that Ziska had come there to express even his own consent to her marriage with Anton Trendellsohn; and without such consent there must of necessity be a continuation of quarrelling. 'Have you been speaking to father, Ziska, about those papers?' Nina was determined that there should be no glozing* of matters, no soft words used effectually to stop her in her projected course. So she rushed at once at the subject which she thought most important in Ziska's presence.

'What papers?' said Ziska.

'The papers which belong to Anton Trendellsohn about this house and the others. They are his, and you would not wish to keep things which belong to another, even though he should be a—Jew.'

Then it occurred to Ziska that Trendellsohn might be willing to give up Nina if he got the papers, and that Nina might be willing to be free from the Jew by the same arrangement. It could not be that such a girl as Nina Balatka should prefer the love of a Jew to the love of a Christian. So at least Ziska argued in his own mind. 'I do not want to keep anything that belongs to anybody,' said Ziska. 'If the papers are with us, I am willing that they should be given up,—that is, if it be right that they should be given up.'

'It is right,' said Nina.

'I believe the Trendellsohns should have them— either father or son,' said old Balatka.

'Of course they should have them,' said Nina; 'either father or son—it makes no matter which.'

'I will try and see to it,' said Ziska.

'Pray do,' said Nina; 'it will be only just; and one would not wish to rob even a Jew, I suppose.' Ziska understood nothing of what was intended by the tone of her voice, and began to think that there might really be ground for hope.

'Nina,' he said, 'your father is not quite well. I want you to speak to me in the next room.'

'Certainly, Ziska, if you wish it. Father, I will come again to you soon. Souchey is making your soup, and I will bring it to you when it is ready.' Then she led the way into the sitting-room, and as Ziska came through, she carefully shut the door. The walls dividing the rooms were very thick, and the door stood in a deep recess, so that no sound could be heard from one room to another. Nina did not wish that her father should hear what might now pass between herself and her cousin, and therefore she was careful to shut the door close.

'Ziska,' said she, as soon as they were together, 'I am very glad that you have come here. My aunt is so angry with me that I cannot speak with her, and uncle Karil only snubs me if I say a word to him about business. He would snub me, no doubt, worse than ever now; and yet who is there here to speak of such matters if I may not do so? You see how it is with father.'

'He is not able to do much, I suppose.'

'He is able to do nothing, and there is nothing for him to do—nothing that can be of any use. But of course he should see that those who have been good to him are not —are not injured because of their kindness.'

'You mean those Jews—the Trendellsohns.'

'Yes, those Jews the Trendellsohns! You would not rob a man because he is a Jew,' said she, repeating the old words.

'They know how to take care of themselves, Nina.'

'Very likely.'

'They have managed to get all your father's property between them.'

'I don't know how that is. Father says that the business which uncle and you have was once his, and that he made it. In these matters the weakest always goes to the wall. Father has no son to help him, as uncle Karil[1] has,—and old Trendellsohn.'

'You may help him better than any son.'

'I will help him if I can. Will you and uncle give up those papers which you have kept since father left them with uncle Karil, just that they might be safe?'

This question Ziska would not answer at once. The matter was one on which he wished to negotiate, and he was driven to the necessity of considering what might be the best line for his diplomacy. 'I am sure, Ziska,' continued Nina, 'you will understand why I ask this. Father is too weak to make the demand, and uncle would listen to nothing that Anton Trendellsohn would say to him.'

'They say that you have betrothed yourself to this Jew, Nina.'

'It is true. But that has nothing to do with it.'

'He is very anxious to have the deeds?'

'Of course he is anxious. Father is old and poorly; and what would he do if father were to die?'

'Nina, he shall have them,—if he will give you up.'

Nina turned away from her cousin, and looked out from the window into the little court. Ziska could not see her face; but had he done so he would not have been able to read the smile of triumph with which for a moment or two it became brilliant. No; Anton would make no such bargain as that! Anton loved her better than any title-deeds. Had he not told her that she was his sun,—the sun that gave to him light and heat? 'If they are his own, why should he be asked to make any such bargain?' said Nina.

'Nina,' said Ziska, throwing all his passion into his voice, as he best knew how, 'it cannot be that you should love this man.'

'Why not love him?'

'A Jew!'

'Yes;—a Jew! I do love him.'

[1] ['Josef' in the lifetime editions.]

'Nina!'

'What have you to say, Ziska? Whatever you say, do not abuse him. It is my affair, not yours. You may think what you like of me for taking such a husband, but remember that he is to be my husband.'

'Nina, let me be your husband.'

'No, Ziska; that cannot be.'

'I love you. I love you fifty times better than he can do. Is not a Christian's love better than a Jew's?'

'Not to me, Ziska.'

'You cannot mean that. You cannot wish to be hated by all those who have loved you—to be reviled, and persecuted, and detested by your friends.'

'Who has loved me? Who are my friends?'

'I have loved you, Nina.'

'Ah, yes; and how have you shown it? But it is too late to speak of that now. I tell you that it is done.'

'No; it is not done yet.'

'It is done, Ziska. When I told him that I loved him, all was done that I could do.'

'Listen to me, Nina. This is absolute madness. That you should have been driven to such an engagement by your troubles, I can understand—and I can forgive it too. But now—now that you know what is before you, that you can provide every comfort for your father, and live yourself as respectably as any lady in Prague—that you can have everything, a carriage like mother's, and a house of your own, you must be mad if you still think of an engagement with a Jew.' Nina stood before him in silence, looking full into his face. He had bade her to listen, and she was determined that she would listen to the end. 'And, Nina,' he continued, 'Trendellsohn shall have what he wants. He proposes to marry you that he may make sure of the property. The very day that you say you will be my wife he shall have the deeds.'

'You think, then, that Anton Trendellsohn wants nothing more than that?'

'Nothing more.'

'I will try him. I will tell him what you say, and if that suffices him, I will not trouble him further.'

'And then you will be mine?'

'Never, Ziska,—never; not though Anton Trendellsohn were to cast me out, and I could find no shelter for my head but what that you could offer me.'

'But why not, Nina?'

'Because I do not love you. Can there be any other reason in such a matter? I do not love you. I do not care if I never see you. But him I love with all my heart. To see him is the only delight of my life. To sit beside him, with his hand in mine, and my head on his shoulder, is heaven to me. To obey him is my duty; to serve him is my pleasure. To be loved by him is the only good thing which God has given me on earth. Now, Ziska, you will know why I cannot be your wife.' Still she stood before him, and still she looked up into his face, keeping her gaze upon him even after her words were finished.

'Accursed Jew!' said Ziska.

'That is right, Ziska; curse him; it is so easy.'

'And you too will be cursed,—here and hereafter. If you marry a Jew you will be accursed to all eternity.'

'That, too, is very easy to say.'

'It is not I who say it. The priest will tell you the same.'

'Let him tell me so; it is his business, but it is not yours. You say it because you cannot have what you want yourself; that is all. When shall I call in the Ross Markt* for the papers?' In the Ross Markt was the house of business of Karil Zamenoy, and there, as Nina well knew, were kept the documents which she was so anxious to obtain. But the demand at this moment was made simply with the object of vexing Ziska, and urging him on to further anger.

'Unless you will give up Anton Trendellsohn, you had better not come to the Ross Markt.'

'I will never give him up.'

'We will see. Perhaps he will give you up after a while. It will be a fine thing to be jilted by a Jew.'

'The Jew, at any rate, shall not be jilted by the Christian. And now, if you please, I will ask you to go. I do not choose to be insulted in father's house. It is his house still.'

'Nina, I will give you one more chance.'

'You can give me no chance that will do you or me any good. If you will go, that is all I want of you now.'

For a moment or two Ziska stood in doubt as to what he would next do or say. Then he took up his hat and went away without another word. On that same evening some one rang the bell at the door of the house in the Windberg-gasse in a most humble manner—with that weak, hesitating hand which, by the tone which it produces, seems to insinuate that no one need hurry to answer such an appeal, and that the answer, when made, may be made by the lowest personage in the house. In this instance, however, Lotta Luxa did answer the bell, and not the stout Bohemian girl who acted in the household of Madame Zamenoy as assistant and fag to Lotta. And Lotta found Nina at the door, enveloped in her cloak. 'Lotta,' she said, 'will you kindly give this to my cousin Ziska?' Then, not waiting for a word, she started away so quickly that Lotta had not a chance of speaking to her, no power of uttering an audible word of abuse. When Ziska opened the parcel thus brought to him, he found it to contain all the notes which he had given to Josef Balatka.

CHAPTER IV

WHEN Nina returned to her father after Ziska's departure, a very few words made everything clear between them. 'I would not have him if there was not another man in the world,' Nina had said. 'He thinks that it is only Anton Trendellsohn that prevents it, but he knows nothing about what a girl feels. He thinks that because we are poor I am to be bought, this way or that way, by a little money. Is that a man, father, that any girl can love?' Then the father had confessed his receipt of the bank-notes from Ziska, and we already know to what result that confession had led.

Till she had delivered her packet into the hands of Lotta Luxa, she maintained her spirits by the excitement of the thing she was doing. Though she should die in the streets of hunger, she would take no money from Ziska Zamenoy. But the question now was not only of her wants, but of her father's. That she, for herself, would be justified in returning Ziska's money there could be no doubt; but was she equally justified in giving back money that had been given to her father? As she walked to the Windberg-gasse, still holding the parcel of notes in her hand, she had no such qualms of conscience; but as she returned, when it was altogether too late for repentance, she made pictures to herself of terrible scenes in which her father suffered all the pangs of want, because she had compelled him to part with this money. If she were to say one word to Anton Trendellsohn, all her trouble on that head would be over. Anton Trendellsohn would at once give her enough to satisfy their immediate wants. In a month or two, when she would be Anton's wife, she would not be ashamed to take everything from his hand; and why should she be ashamed now to take something from him to whom she was prepared to give everything? But she was ashamed to do so. She felt that she could not go to him and ask him for bread. One other resource she had. There remained to her of her mother's property a necklace, which was all that was left to her from her mother. And when this had been given to her at her mother's death, she had been especially enjoined not to part with it. Her father then had been too deeply plunged in grief to say any words on such a subject, and the gift had been put into her hands by her aunt Sophie. Even aunt Sophie had been softened at that moment, and had shown some tenderness to the orphan child. 'You are to keep it always for her sake,' aunt Sophie had said; and Nina had hitherto kept the trinket, when all other things were gone, in remembrance of her mother. She had hitherto reconciled herself to keeping her little treasure, when all other things were going, by the sacredness of the deposit; and had told herself that even for her father's sake she must not part with the gift which had come to her from her mother. But now she comforted herself by the reflection that the necklace would produce for her enough to repay her father that present from

Ziska which she had taken from him. Her father had pleaded sorely to be allowed to keep the notes. In her emotion at the moment she had been imperative with him, and her resolution had prevailed. But she thought of his entreaties as she returned home, and of his poverty and wants, and she determined that the necklace should go. It would produce for her at any rate as much as Ziska had given. She wished that she had brought it with her, as she passed the open door of a certain pawn-broker, which she had entered often during the last six months, and whither she intended to take her treasure, so that she might comfort her father on her return with the sight of the money. But she had it not, and she went home empty-handed. 'And now, Nina, I suppose we may starve,' said her father, whom she found sitting close to the stove in the kitchen, while Souchey was kneeling before it, putting in at the little open door morsels of fuel which were lamentably insufficient for the poor man's purpose of raising a fire. The weather, indeed, was as yet warm—so warm that in the middle of the day the heat was matter of complaint to Josef Balatka; but in the evening he would become chill; and as there existed some small necessity for cooking, he would beg that he might thus enjoy the warmth of the kitchen.

'Yes, we shall starve now,' said Souchey, complacently. 'There is not much doubt about our starving.'

'Souchey, I wonder you should speak like that before father,' said Nina.

'And why shouldn't he speak?' said Balatka. 'I think he has as much right as any one.'

'He has no right to make things worse than they are.'

'I don't know how I could do that, Nina,' said the servant. 'What made you take that money back to your aunt?'

'I didn't take it back to my aunt.'

'Well, to any of the family then? I suppose it came from your aunt?'

'It came from my cousin Ziska, and I thought it better to give it back. Souchey, do not you come in between

father and me. There are troubles enough; do not you
make them worse.'

'If I had been here you should never have taken it back
again,' said Souchey, obstinately.

'Father,' said Nina, appealing to the old man, 'how
could I have kept it? You knew why it was given.'

'Who is to help us if we may not take it from them?'

'To-morrow,' said Nina, 'I can get as much as he
brought. And I will, and you shall see it.'

'Who will give it you, Nina?'

'Never mind, father, I will have it.'

'She will beg it from her Jew lover,' said Souchey.

'Souchey,' said she, with her eyes flashing fire at him,
'if you cannot treat your master's daughter better than
that, you may as well go.'

'Is it not true?' demanded Souchey.

'No, it is not true; it is false. I have never taken money
from Anton; nor shall I do so till we are married.'

'And that will be never,' said Souchey. 'It is as well
to speak out at once. The priest will not let it be done.'

'All the priests in Prague cannot hinder it,' said Nina.

'That is true,' said Balatka.

'We shall see,' said Souchey. 'And in the mean time
what is the good of fighting with the Zamenoys? They
are your only friends, Nina, and therefore you take
delight in quarrelling with them. When people have
money, they should be allowed to have a little pride.'
Nina said nothing further on the occasion, though
Souchey and her father went on grumbling for an hour.
She discovered, however, from various words that her
father allowed to fall from him, that his opposition to her
marriage had nearly faded away. It seemed to be his
opinion that if she were to marry the Jew, the sooner she
did it the better. Now, Nina was determined that she
would marry the Jew, though heaven and earth should
meet in consequence. She would marry him if he would
marry her. They had told her that the Jew would jilt
her. She did not put much faith in the threat; but even
that was more probable than that she should jilt him.

On the following morning Souchey, in return, as it

were, for his cruelty to his young mistress on the preceding day, produced some small store of coin which he
declared to be the result of a further sale of the last relics
of his master's property; and Nina's journey with the
necklace to the pawnbroker was again postponed. That
day and the next were passed in the old house without
anything to make them memorable except their wearisome misery, and then Nina again went out to visit the
Jews' quarter. She told herself that she was taken there
by the duties of her position; but in truth she could
hardly bear her life without the comfort of seeing the
only person who would speak kindly to her. She was
engaged to marry this man, but she did not know when
she was to be married. She would ask no question of her
lover on that matter; but she could tell him—and she
felt herself bound to tell him—what was really her own
position, and also all that she knew of his affairs. He had
given her to understand that he could not marry her till
he had obtained possession of certain documents which
he believed to be in the possession of her uncle. And
for these documents she, with his permission, had made
application. She had at any rate discovered that they
certainly were at the office in the Ross Markt. So much
she had learned from Ziska; and so much, at any rate,
she was bound to make known to her lover. And, moreover, since she had seen him she had told all her relatives
of her engagement. They all knew now that she loved
the Jew, and that she had resolved to marry him; and of
this also it was her duty to give him tidings. The result
of her communication to her father and her relatives in
the Windberg-gasse had been by no means so terrible as
she had anticipated. The heavens and the earth had not
as yet shown any symptoms of coming together. Her
aunt, indeed, had been very angry; and Lotta Luxa and
Souchey had told her that such a marriage would not be
allowed. Ziska, too, had said some sharp words; and her
father, for the first day or two, had expostulated. But the
threats had been weak threats, and she did not find herself to be annihilated—indeed, hardly to be oppressed—
by the scolding of any of them. What the priest might

say she had not yet experienced; but opposition from other quarters had not as yet come upon her in any form that was not endurable. Her aunt had intended to consume her with wrath, but Nina had not found herself to be consumed. All this it was necessary that she should tell to Anton Trendellsohn. It was grievous to her that it should be always her lot to go to her lover, and that he should never—almost never, be able to seek her. It would in truth be never now, unless she could induce her father to receive Anton openly as his acknowledged future son-in-law; and she could hardly hope that her father would yield so far as that. Other girls, she knew, stayed till their lovers came to them, or met them abroad in public places—at the gardens and music-halls, or perhaps at church; but no such joys as these were within reach of Nina. The public gardens, indeed, were open to her and to Anton Trendellsohn as they were to others; but she knew that she would not dare to be seen in public with her Jew lover till the thing was done and she and the Jew had become man and wife. On this occasion, before she left her home, she was careful to tell her father where she was going. 'Have you any message to the Trendellsohns?' she asked. 'So you are going there again?' her father said. 'Yes, I must see them. I told you that I had a commission from them to the Zamenoys, which I have performed, and I must let them know what I did. Besides, father, if this man is to be my husband, is it not well that I should see him?' Old Balatka groaned, but said nothing further, and Nina went forth to the Jews' quarter.

On this occasion she found Trendellsohn the elder standing at the door of his own house.

'You want to see Anton,' said the Jew. 'Anton is out. He is away somewhere in the city—on business.'

'I shall be glad to see you, father, if you can spare me a minute.'

'Certainly, my child,—an hour if it will serve you. Hours are not scarce with me now, as they used to be when I was Anton's age, and as they are with him now. Hours, and minutes too, are very scarce with Anton in these days.' Then he led the way up the dark stairs to the sitting-room, and Nina followed him. Nina and the elder Trendellsohn had always hitherto been friends. Before her engagement with his son they had been affectionate friends, and since that had been made known to him there had been no quarrel between them. But the old man had hardly approved of his son's purpose, thinking that a Jew should look for the wife of his bosom among his own people, and thinking also, perhaps, that one who had so much of worldly wealth to offer as his son should receive something also of the same in his marriage. Old Trendellsohn had never uttered a word of complaint to Nina—had said nothing to make her suppose that she was not welcome to the house; but he had never spoken to her with happy, joy-giving words, as the future bride of his son. He still called her his daughter, as he had done before; but he did it only in his old fashion, using the affectionate familiarity of an old friend to a young maiden. He was a small, aged man, very thin and meagre in aspect—so meagre as to conceal in part, by the general tenuity of his aspect, the shortness of his stature. He was not even so tall as Nina, as Nina had discovered, much to her surprise. His hair was grizzled, rather than grey, and the beard on his thin, wiry, wizened face was always close shorn. He was scrupulously clean in his person, and seemed, even at his age, to take a pride in the purity and fineness of his linen. He was much older than Nina's father—more than ten years older, as he would sometimes boast; but he was still strong and active, while Nina's father was worn out with age. Old Trendellsohn was eighty, and yet he would be seen trudging about through the streets of Prague, intent upon his business of money-making; and it was said that his son Anton was not even as yet actually in partnership with him, or fully trusted by him in all his plans.

'Father,' Nina said, 'I am glad that Anton is out, as now I can speak a word to you.'

'My dear, you shall speak fifty words.'

'That is very good of you. Of course I know that the house we live in does in truth belong to you and Anton.'

'Yes, it belongs to me,' said the Jew.

'And we can pay no rent for it.'

'Is it of that you have come to speak, Nina? If so, do not trouble yourself. For certain reasons, which Anton can explain, I am willing that your father should live there without rent.'

Nina blushed as she found herself compelled to thank the Jew for his charity. 'I know how kind you have been to father,' she said.

'Nay, my daughter, there has been no great kindness in it. Your father has been unfortunate, and, Jew as I am, I would not turn him into the street. Do not trouble yourself to think of it.'

'But it was not altogether about that, father. Anton spoke to me the other day about some deeds which should belong to you.'

'They do belong to me,' said Trendellsohn.

'But you have them not in your own keeping.'

'No, we have not. It is, I believe, the creed of a Christian that he may deal dishonestly with a Jew, though the Jew who shall deal dishonestly with a Christian is to be hanged. It is strange what latitude men will give themselves under the cloak of their religion! But why has Anton spoken to you of this? I did not bid him.'

'He sent me with a message to my aunt Sophie.'

'He was wrong; he was very foolish; he should have gone himself.'

'But, father, I have found out that the papers you want are certainly in my uncle's keeping in the Ross Markt.'

'Of course they are, my dear. Anton might have known that without employing you.'

So far Nina had performed but a small part of the task which she had before her. She found it easier to talk to the old man about the title-deeds of the house in the Kleinseite than she did to tell him of her own affairs. But the thing was to be done, though the doing of it was difficult; and, after a pause, she persevered. 'And I told aunt Sophie,' she said, with her eyes turned upon the ground, 'of my engagement with Anton.'

'You did?'

'Yes; and I told father.'

'And what did your father say?'

'Father did not say much. He is poorly and weak.'

'Yes, yes; not strong enough to fight against the abomination of a Jew son-in-law. And what did your aunt say? She is strong enough to fight anybody.'

'She was very angry.'

'I suppose so, I suppose so. Well, she is right. As the world goes in Prague, my child, you will degrade yourself by marrying a Jew.'

'I want nothing prouder than to be Anton's wife,' said Nina.

'And to speak sooth,' said the old man, 'the Jew will degrade himself fully as much by marrying you.'

'Father, I would not have that. If I thought that my love would injure him, I would leave him.'

'He must judge for himself,' said Trendellsohn, relenting somewhat.

'He must judge for himself and for me too,' said Nina.

'He will be able, at any rate, to keep a house over your head.'

'It is not for that,' said Nina, thinking of her cousin Ziska's offer. She need not want for a house and money if she were willing to sell herself for such things as them.

'Anton will be rich, Nina, and you are very poor.'

'Can I help that, father? Such as I am, I am his. If all Prague were mine I would give it to him.'

The old man shook his head. 'A Christian thinks that it is too much honour for a Jew to marry a Christian, though he be rich, and she have not a ducat for her dower.'

'Father, your words are cruel. Do you believe I would give Anton my hand if I did not love him? I do not know much of his wealth; but, father, I might be the promised wife of a Christian to-morrow, who is, perhaps, as rich as he—if that were anything.'

'And who is that other lover, Nina?'

'It matters not. He can be nothing to me—nothing in that way. I love Anton Trendellsohn, and I could not be the wife of any other but him.'

'I wish it were otherwise. I tell you so plainly to your face. I wish it were otherwise. Jews and Christians have married in Prague, I know, but good has never come of it. Anton should find a wife among his own people; and you—it would be better for you to take that other offer of which you spoke.'

'It is too late, father.'

'No, Nina, it is not too late. If Anton would be wise, it is not too late.'

'Anton can do as he pleases. It is too late for me. If Anton thinks it well to change his mind, I shall not reproach him. You can tell him so, father,—from me.'

'He knows my mind already, Nina. I will tell him, however, what you say of your own friends. They have heard of your engagement, and are angry with you, of course.'

'Aunt Sophie and her people are angry.'

'Of course they will oppose it. They will set their priests at you, and frighten you almost to death. They will drive the life out of your young heart with their curses. You do not know what sorrows are before you.'

'I can bear all that. There is only one sorrow that I fear. If Anton is true to me, I will not mind all the rest.'

The old man's heart was softened towards her. He could not bring himself to say a word to her of direct encouragement, but he kissed her before she went, telling her that she was a good girl, and bidding her have no care as to the house in the Kleinseite. As long as he lived, and her father, her father should not be disturbed. And as for deeds, he declared, with something of a grim smile on his old visage, that though a Jew had always a hard fight to get his own from a Christian, the hard fighting did generally prevail at last. 'We shall get them, Nina, when they have put us to such trouble and expense as their laws may be able to devise. Anton knows that as well as I do.'

At the door of the house Nina found the old man's grand-daughter waiting for her. Ruth Jacobi was the girl's name, and she was the orphaned child of a daughter of old Trendellsohn. Father and mother were both dead;

and of her father, who had been dead long, Ruth had no memory. But she still wore some remains of the black garments which had been given to her at her mother's funeral; and she still grieved bitterly for her mother, having no woman with her in that gloomy house, and no other child to comfort her. Her grandfather and her uncle were kind to her—kind after their own gloomy fashion; but it was a sad house for a young girl, and Ruth, though she knew nothing of any better abode, found the days to be very long, and the months to be very wearisome.

'What has he been saying to you, Nina?' the girl asked, taking hold of her friend's dress, to prevent her escape into the street. 'You need not be in a hurry for a minute. He will not come down.'

'I am not afraid of him, Ruth.'

'I am, then. But perhaps he is not cross to you.'

'Why should he be cross to me?'

'I know why, Nina, but I will not say. Uncle Anton has been out all the day, and was not home to dinner. It is much worse when he is away.'

'Is Anton ever cross to you, Ruth?'

'Indeed he is,—sometimes. He scolds much more than grandfather. But he is younger, you know.'

'Yes; he is younger, certainly.'

'Not but what he is very old, too; much too old for you, Nina. When I have a lover I will never have an old man.'

'But Anton is not old.'

'Not like grandfather, of course. But I should like a lover who would laugh and be gay. Uncle Anton is never gay. My lover shall be only two years older than myself. Uncle Anton must be twenty years older than you, Nina.'

'Not more than ten—or twelve at the most.'

'He is too old to laugh and dance.'

'Not at all, dear; but he thinks of other things.'

'I should like a lover to think of the things that I think about. It is all very well being steady when you have got babies of your own; but that should be after ever so long.

I should like to keep my lover as a lover for two years. And all that time he should like to dance with me, and to hear music, and to go about just where I would like to go.'

'And what then, Ruth?'

'Then? Why, then I suppose I should marry him, and become stupid like the rest. But I should have the two years to look back at and to remember. Do you think, Nina, that you will ever come and live here when you are married?'

'I do not know that I shall ever be married, Ruth.'

'But you mean to marry uncle Anton?'

'I cannot say. It may be so.'

'But you love him, Nina?'

'Yes, I love him. I love him with all my heart. I love him better than all the world besides. Ruth, you cannot tell how I love him. I would lie down and die if he were to bid me.'

'He will never bid you do that.'

'You think that he is old, and dull, and silent, and cross. But when he will sit still and not say a word to me for an hour together, I think that I almost love him the best. I only want to be near him, Ruth.'

'But you do not like him to be cross.'

'Yes, I do. That is, I like him to scold me if he is angry. If he were angry, and did not scold a little, I should think that he was really vexed with me.'

'Then you must be very much in love, Nina?'

'I am in love—very much.'

'And does it make you happy?'

'Happy! Happiness depends on so many things. But it makes me feel that there can only be one real unhappiness; and unless that should come to me, I shall care for nothing. Good-bye, love. Tell your uncle that I was here, and say—say to him when no one else can hear, that I went away with a sad heart because I had not seen him.'

It was late in the evening when Anton Trendellsohn came home, but Ruth remembered the message that had been intrusted to her, and managed to find a moment in

which to deliver it. But her uncle took it amiss, and
scolded her. 'You two have been talking nonsense
together here half the day, I suppose.'

'I spoke to her for five minutes, uncle; that was all.'

'Did you do your lessons with Madame Pulsky?'

'Yes, I did, uncle—of course. You know that.'

'I know that it is a pity you should not be better
looked after.'

'Bring Nina home here and she will look after me.'

'Go to bed, miss—at once, do you hear?'

Then Ruth went off to her bed, wondering at Nina's
choice, and declaring to herself, that if ever she took in
hand a lover at all, he should be a lover very different
from her uncle, Anton Trendellsohn.

CHAPTER V

THE more Madame Zamenoy thought of the terrible
tidings which had reached her, the more determined
did she become to prevent the degradation of the connection with which she was threatened. She declared to
her husband and son that all Prague were already talking
of the horror, forgetting, perhaps, that any knowledge
which Prague had on the subject must have come from
herself. She had, indeed, consulted various persons on
the subject in the strictest confidence. We have already
seen that she had told Lotta Luxa and her son, and she
had, of course, complained frequently on the matter to
her husband. She had unbosomed herself to one or two
trusty female friends who lived near her, and she had
applied for advice and assistance to two priests. To
Father Jerome she had gone as Nina's confessor, and she
had also applied to the reverend pastor who had the
charge of her own little peccadilloes. The small amount
of assistance which her clerical allies offered to her had
surprised her very much. She had, indeed, gone so far
as to declare to Lotta that she was shocked by their
indifference. Her own confessor had simply told her that
the matter was in the hands of Father Jerome, as far as

it could be said to belong to the Church at all; and had
satisfied his conscience by advising his dear friend to use
all the resources which female persecution put at her
command. 'You will frighten her out of it, Madame
Zamenoy, if you go the right way about it,' said the priest.
Madame Zamenoy was well inclined to go the right way
about it, if she only knew how. She would make Nina's
life a burden to her if she could only get hold of the girl,
and would scruple at no threats as to this world or the
next. But she thought that her priest ought to have done
more for her in such a crisis than simply giving her such
ordinary counsel. Things were not as they used to be,
she knew; but there was even yet something of the pre-
stige of power left to the Church, and there were convents
with locks and bars, and excommunication might still be
made terrible, and public opinion, in the shape of outside
persecution, might, as Madame Zamenoy thought, have
been brought to bear. Nor did she get much more
comfort from Father Jerome. His reliance was placed
chiefly on operations to be carried on with the Jew; and,
failing them, on the opposition which the Jew would
experience among his own people. 'They think more of
it than we do,' said Father Jerome.

'How can that be, Father Jerome?'

'Well, they do. He would lose caste among all his
friends by such a marriage, and would, I think, destroy
all his influence among them. When he perceives this
more fully he will be shy enough about it himself.
Besides, what is he to get?'

'He will get nothing.'

'He will think better of it. And you might manage
something with those deeds. Of course he should have
them sooner or later, but they might be surrendered as
the price of his giving her up. I should say it might be
managed.'

All this was not comfortable for Madame Zamenoy;
and she fretted and fumed till her husband had no peace
in his house, and Ziska almost wished that he might hear
no more of the Jew and his betrothal. She could not even
commence her system of persecution, as Nina did not go

near her, and had already told Lotta Luxa that she must decline to discuss the question of her marriage any further. So, at last, Madame Zamenoy found herself obliged to go over in person to the house in the Kleinseite. Such visits had for many years been very rare with her. Since her sister's death and the days in which the Balatkas had been prosperous, she had preferred that all intercourse between the two families should take place at her own house; and thus, as Josef Balatka himself rarely left his own door, she had not seen him for more than two years. Frequent intercourse, however, had been maintained, and aunt Sophie knew very well how things were going on in the Kleinseite. Lotta had no compunctions as to visiting the house, and Lotta's eyes were very sharp. And Nina had been frequently in the Windberg-gasse, having hitherto believed it to be her duty to attend to her aunt's behests. But Nina was no longer obedient, and Madame Zamenoy was compelled to go herself to her brother-in-law, unless she was disposed to leave the Balatkas absolutely to their fate. Let her do what she would, Nina must be her niece, and therefore she would yet make a struggle.

On this occasion Madame Zamenoy walked on foot, thinking that her carriage and horses might be too con-spicuous at the arched gate in the little square. The carriage did not often make its way over the bridge into the Kleinseite, being used chiefly among the suburbs of the New Town, where it was now well known and quickly recognised; and she did not think that this was a good opportunity for breaking into new ground with her equipage. She summoned Lotta to attend her, and after her one o'clock dinner took her umbrella in her hand and went forth. She was a stout woman, probably not more than forty-five years of age, but a little heavy, perhaps from too much indulgence with her carriage. She walked slowly, therefore; and Lotta, who was nimble of foot and quick in all her ways, thanked her stars that it did not suit her mistress to walk often through the city.

'How very long the bridge is, Lotta!' said Madame Zamenoy.

'Not longer, ma'am, than it always has been,' said Lotta, pertly.

'Of course it is not longer than it always has been; I know that: but still I say it is very long. Bridges are not so long in other places.'

'Not where the rivers are narrower,' said Lotta. Madame Zamenoy trudged on, finding that she could get no comfort from her servant, and at last reached Balatka's door. Lotta, who was familiar with the place, entered the house first, and her mistress followed her. Hanging about the broad passage which communicated with all the rooms on the ground-floor, they found Souchey, who told them that his master was in bed, and that Nina was at work by his bedside. He was sent in to announce the grand arrival, and when Madame Zamenoy entered the sitting-room Nina was there to meet her.

'Child,' she said, 'I have come to see your father.'

'Father is in bed, but you can come in,' said Nina.

'Of course I can go in,' said Madame Zamenoy; 'but before I go in let me know this. Has he heard of the disgrace which you purpose to bring upon him?'

Nina drew herself up and made no answer; whereupon Lotta spoke. 'The old gentleman knows all about it, ma'am, as well as you do.'

'Lotta, let the child speak for herself. Nina, have you had the audacity to tell your father—that which you told me?'

'I have told him everything,' said Nina; 'will you come into his room?' Then Madame Zamenoy lifted up the hem of her garment and stepped proudly into the old man's chamber.

By this time Balatka knew what was about to befall him, and was making himself ready for the visit. He was well aware that he should be sorely perplexed as to what he should say in the coming interview. He could not speak lightly of such an evil as this marriage with a Jew; nor when his sister-in-law should abuse the Jews could he dare to defend them. But neither could he bring himself to say evil words of Nina, or to hear evil words spoken of her without making some attempt to screen her. It might be best, perhaps, to lie under the bed-clothes and say nothing, if only his sister-in-law would allow him to lie there. 'Am I to come in with you, aunt Sophie?' said Nina. 'Yes, child,' said the aunt; 'come and hear what I have to say to your father.' So Nina followed her aunt, and Lotta and Souchey were left in the sitting-room.

'And how are you, Souchey?' said Lotta, with unusual kindness of tone. 'I suppose you are not so busy but you can stay with me a few minutes while she is in there?'

'There is not so much to do that I cannot spare the time,' said Souchey.

'Nothing to do, I suppose, and less to get?' said Lotta.

'That's about it, Lotta; but you wouldn't have had me leave them?'

'A man has to look after himself in the world; but you were always easy-minded, Souchey.'

'I don't know about being so easy-minded. I know what would make me easy-minded enough.'

'You'll have to be servant to a Jew now.'

'No; I'll never be that.'

'I suppose he gives you something at odd times?'

'Who? Trendellsohn? I never saw the colour of his money yet, and do not wish to see it.'

'But he comes here—sometimes?'

'Never, Lotta. I haven't seen Anton Trendellsohn within the doors these six months.'

'But she goes to him?'

'Yes; she goes to him.'

'That's worse—a deal worse.'

'I told her how it was when I saw her trotting off so often to the Jews' quarter. "You see too much of Anton Trendellsohn," I said to her; but it didn't do any good.'

'You should have come to us, and have told us.'

'What, Madame there? I could never have brought myself to that; she is so upsetting, Lotta.'

'She is upsetting, no doubt; but she don't upset me. Why didn't you tell me, Souchey?'

'Well, I thought that if I said a word to her, perhaps that would be enough. Who could believe that she would throw herself at once into a Jew's arms—such a fellow as Anton Trendellsohn, too, old enough to be her father, and she the bonniest girl in all Prague?'

'Handsome is that handsome does, Souchey.'

'I say she's the sweetest girl in all Prague; and more's the pity she should have taken such a fancy as this.'

'She mustn't marry him, of course, Souchey.'

'Not if it can be helped, Lotta.'

'It must be helped. You and I must help it, if no one else can do so.'

'That's easy said, Lotta.'

'We can do it, if we are minded—that is, if you are minded. Only think what a thing it would be for her to be the wife of a Jew! Think of her soul, Souchey!'

Souchey shuddered. He did not like being told of people's souls, feeling probably that the misfortunes of this world were quite heavy enough for a poor wight like himself, without any addition in anticipation of futurity. 'Think of her soul, Souchey,' repeated Lotta, who was at all points a good churchwoman.

'It's bad enough any way,' said Souchey.

'And there's our Ziska would take her to-morrow in spite of the Jew.'

'Would he now?'

'That he would, without anything but what she stands up in. And he'd behave very handsome to any one that would help him.'

'He'd be the first of his name that ever did, then. I have known the time when old Balatka there, poor as he is now, would give a florin when Karil Zamenoy begrudged six kreutzers.'

'And what has come of such giving? Josef Balatka is poor, and Karil Zamenoy bids fair to be as rich as any merchant in Prague. But no matter about that. Will you give a helping hand? There is nothing I wouldn't do for you, Souchey, if we could manage this between us.'

'Would you now?' And Souchey drew near, as though some closer bargain might be practicable between them.

'I would indeed; but, Souchey, talking won't do it.'

'What will do it?'

Lotta paused a moment, looking round the room carefully, till suddenly her eyes fell on a certain article which lay on Nina's work-table. 'What am I to do?' said Souchey, anxious to be at work with the prospect of so great a reward.

'Never mind,' said Lotta, whose tone of voice was suddenly changed. 'Never mind it now at least. And, Souchey, I think you'd better go to your work. We've been gossiping here ever so long.'

'Perhaps five minutes; and what does it signify?'

'She'd think it so odd to find us here together in the parlour.'

'Not odd at all.'

'Just as though we'd been listening to what they'd been saying. Go now, Souchey—there's a good fellow; and I'll come again the day after to-morrow and tell you. Go, I say. There are things that I must think of by myself.' And in this way she got Souchey to leave the room.

'Josef,' said Madame Zamenoy, as she took her place standing by Balatka's bedside—'Josef, this is very terrible;' Nina also was standing close by her father's head, with her hand upon her father's pillow. Balatka groaned, but made no immediate answer.

'It is terrible, horrible, abominable, and damnable,' said Madame Zamenoy, bringing out one epithet after the other with renewed energy. Balatka groaned again. What could he say in reply to such an address?

'Aunt Sophie,' said Nina, 'do not speak to father like that. He is ill.'

'Child,' said Madame Zamenoy. 'I shall speak as I please. I shall speak as my duty bids me speak. Josef, this that I hear is very terrible. It is hardly to be believed that any Christian girl should think of marrying—a Jew.'

'What can I do?' said the father. 'How can I prevent her?'

'How can you prevent her, Josef? Is she not your daughter? Does she mean to say, standing there, that she will not obey her father? Tell me, Nina, will you or will you not obey your father?'

'That is his affair, aunt Sophie; not yours.'

'His affair! It is his affair, and my affair, and all our affairs. Impudent girl!—brazen-faced, impudent, bad girl! Do you not know that you would bring disgrace upon us all?'

'You are thinking about yourself, aunt Sophie; and I must think for myself.'

'You do not regard your father, then?'

'Yes, I do regard my father. He knows that I regard him. Father, is it true that I do not regard you?'

'She is a good daughter,' said the father.

'A good daughter, and talk of marrying a Jew!' said Madame Zamenoy. 'Has she your permission for such a marriage? Tell me that at once, Josef, that I may know. Has she your sanction for—for—for this accursed abomination?' Then there was silence in the room for a few moments. 'You can at any rate answer a plain question, Josef,' continued Madame Zamenoy. 'Has Nina your leave to betroth herself to the Jew, Trendell-sohn?'

'No, I have not got his leave,' said Nina.

'I am speaking to your father, miss,' said the enraged aunt.

'Yes; you are speaking very roughly to father, and he is ill. Therefore I answer for him.'

'And has he not forbidden you to think of marrying this Jew?'

'No, he has not,' said Nina.

'Josef, answer for yourself like a man,' said Madame Zamenoy. 'Have you not forbidden this marriage? Do you not forbid it now? Let me at any rate hear you say that you have forbidden it.' But Balatka found silence to be his easiest course, and answered not at all. 'What am I to think of this?' continued Madame Zamenoy. 'It cannot be that you wish your child to be the wife of a Jew!'

'You are to think, aunt Sophie, that father is ill, and that he cannot stand against your violence.'

'Violence, you wicked girl! It is you that are violent.'

'Will you come out into the parlour, aunt?'

'No, I will not come out into the parlour. I will not stir from this spot till I have told your father all that I think about it. Ill, indeed! What matters illness when it is a question of eternal damnation!' Madame Zamenoy put so much stress upon the latter word that her brother-in-law almost jumped from under the bed-clothes. Nina raised herself, as she was standing, to her full height, and a smile of derision came upon her face. 'Oh, yes!—I daresay you do not mind it,' said Madame Zamenoy. 'I daresay you can laugh now at all the pains of hell. Castaways such as you are always blind to their own danger; but your father, I hope, has not fallen so far as to care nothing for his religion, though he seems to have forgotten what is due to his family.'

'I have forgotten nothing,' said old Balatka.

'Why then do you not forbid her to do this thing?' demanded Madame Zamenoy. But the old man had recognised too well the comparative security of silence to be drawn into argument, and therefore merely hid himself more completely among the clothes. 'Am I to get no answer from you, Josef?' said Madame Zamenoy. No answer came, and therefore she was driven to turn again upon Nina.

'Why are you doing this thing, you poor deluded creature? Is it the man's money that tempts you?'

'It is not the man's money. If money could tempt me, I could have it elsewhere, as you know.'

'It cannot be love for such a man as that. Do you not know that he and his father between them have robbed your father of everything?'

'I know nothing of the kind.'

'They have; and he is now making a fool of you in order that he may get whatever remains.'

'Nothing remains. He will get nothing.'

'Nor will you. I do not believe that after all he will ever marry you. He will not be such a fool.'

'Perhaps not, aunt; and in that case you will have your wish.'

'But no one can ever speak to you again after such a condition. Do you think that I or your uncle could have you at our house when all the world shall know that you have been jilted by a Jew?'

'I will not trouble you by going to your house.'

'And is that all the satisfaction I am to have?'

'What do you want me to say?'

'I want you to say that you will give this man up, and return to your duty as a Christian.'

'I will never give him up—never. I would sooner die.'

'Very well. Then I shall know how to act. You will not be a bit nearer marrying him; I can promise you that. You are mistaken if you think that in such a matter as this a girl like you can do just as she pleases.' Then she turned again upon the poor man in bed. 'Josef Balatka, I am ashamed of you. I am indeed—I am ashamed of you.'

'Aunt Sophie,' said Nina, 'now that you are here, you can say what you please to me; but you might as well spare father.'

'I will not spare him. I am ashamed of him—thoroughly ashamed of him. What can I think of him when he will lie there and not say a word to save his daughter from the machinations of a filthy Jew?'

'Anton Trendellsohn is not a filthy Jew.'

'He is a robber. He has cheated your father out of everything.'

'He is no robber. He has cheated no one. I know who has cheated father, if you come to that.'

'Whom do you mean, hussey?'

'I shall not answer you; but you need not tell me any more about the Jews cheating us. Christians can cheat as well as Jews, and can rob from their own flesh and blood too. I do not care for your threats, aunt Sophie, nor for your frowns. I did care for them, but you have said that which makes it impossible that I should regard them any further.'

'And this is what I get for all my trouble—for all your uncle's generosity!' Again Nina smiled. 'But I suppose the Jew gives more than we have given, and therefore is preferred. You poor creature—poor wretched creature!'

During all this time Balatka remained silent; and at last,

after very much more scolding, in which Madame Zamenoy urged again and again the terrible threat of eternal
punishment, she prepared herself for going. 'Lotta Luxa,'
she said—'where is Lotta Luxa?' She opened the door,
and found Lotta Luxa seated demurely by the window.
'Lotta,' she said, 'I shall go now, and shall never come
back to this unfortunate house. You hear what I say;
I shall never return here. As she makes her bed, so must
she lie on it. It is her own doing, and no one can save
her. For my part, I think that the Jew has bewitched her.'

'Like enough,' said Lotta.

'When once we stray from the Holy Church, there is
no knowing what terrible evils may come upon us,' said
Madame Zamenoy.

'No indeed, ma'am,' said Lotta Luxa.

'But I have done all in my power.'

'That you have, ma'am.'

'I feel quite sure, Lotta, that the Jew will never marry
her. Why should a man like that, who loves money
better than his soul, marry a girl who has not a kreutzer
to bless herself?'

'Why indeed, ma'am! It's my mind that he don't
think of marrying her.'

'And, Jew as he is, he cares for his religion. He will
not bring trouble upon everybody belonging to him by
taking a Christian for his wife.'

'That he will not, ma'am, you may be sure,' said Lotta.

'And where will she be then? Only fancy, Lotta—
to have been jilted by a Jew!' Then Madame Zamenoy,
without addressing herself directly to Nina, walked out of
the room; but as she did so she paused in the doorway,
and again spoke to Lotta. 'To be jilted by a Jew, Lotta!
Think of that.'

'I should drown myself,' said Lotta Luxa. And then
they both were gone.

The idea that the Jew might jilt her disturbed Nina
more than all her aunt's anger, or than any threats as to
the penalties she might have to encounter in the next
world. She felt a certain delight, an inward satisfaction,
in giving up everything for her Jew lover—a satisfaction

which was the more intense, the more absolute was the
rejection and the more crushing the scorn which she
encountered on his behalf from her own people. But to
encounter this rejection and scorn, and then to be thrown
over by the Jew, was more than she could endure. And
would it, could it, be so? She sat down to think of it; and
as she thought of it terrible fears came upon her. Old
Trendellsohn had told her that such a marriage on his
son's part would bring him into great trouble; and old
Trendellsohn was not harsh with her as her aunt was
harsh. The old man, in his own communications with
her, had always been kind and forbearing. And then
Anton himself was severe to her. Though he would now
and again say some dear, well-to-be-remembered happy
word, as when he told her that she was his sun, and that
he looked to her for warmth and light, such soft speakings
were few with him and far between. And then he never
mentioned any time as the probable date of their marriage. If only a time could be fixed, let it be ever so
distant, Nina thought that she could still endure all the
cutting taunts of her enemies. But what would she do if
Anton were to announce to her some day that he found
himself, as a Jew, unable to marry with her as a Christian? In such a case she thought that she must drown
herself, as Lotta had suggested to her.

As she sat thinking of this, her eyes suddenly fell upon
the one key which she herself possessed, and which, with
a woman's acuteness of memory, she perceived to have
been moved from the spot on which she had left it. It
was the key of the little desk which stood in the corner
of the parlour, and in which, on the top of all the papers,
was deposited the necklace with which she intended to
relieve the immediate necessities of their household. She
at once remembered that Lotta had been left for a long
time in the room, and with anxious, quick suspicion she
went to the desk. But her suspicions had wronged Lotta.
There, lying on a bundle of letters, was the necklace, in
the exact position in which she had left it. She kissed the
trinket, which had come to her from her mother, replaced
it carefully, and put the key into her pocket.

What should she do next? How should she conduct herself in her present circumstances? Her heart prompted her to go off at once to Anton Trendellsohn and tell him everything; but she greatly feared that Anton would not be glad to see her. She knew that it was not well that a girl should run after her lover; but yet how was she to live without seeing him? What other comfort had she? and from whom else could she look for guidance? She declared to herself at last that she, in her position, would not be stayed by ordinary feelings of maiden reserve. She would tell him everything, even to the threat on which her aunt had so much depended, and would then ask him for his counsel. She would describe to him, if words from her could describe them, all her difficulties, and would promise to be guided by him absolutely in everything. 'Everything,' she would say to him, 'I have given up for you. I am yours entirely, body and soul. Do with me as you will.' If he should then tell her that he would not have her, that he did not want the sacrifice, she would go away from him—and drown herself. But she would not go to him to-day—no, not to-day; not perhaps to-morrow. It was but a day or two as yet since she had been over at the Trendellsohns' house, and though on that occasion she had not seen Anton, Anton of course would know that she had been there. She did not wish him to think that she was hunting him. She would wait yet two or three days—till the next Sunday morning perhaps—and then she would go again to the Jews' quarter. On the Christian Sabbath Anton was always at home, as on that day business is suspended in Prague both for Christian and Jew.

Then she went back to her father. He was still lying with his face turned to the wall, and Nina, thinking that he slept, took up her work and sat by his side. But he was awake, and watching. 'Is she gone?' he said, before her needle had been plied a dozen times.

'Aunt Sophie? Yes, father, she has gone.'

'I hope she will not come again.'

'She says that she will never come again.'

'What is the use of her coming here? We are lost and

are perishing. We are utterly gone. She will not help
us, and why should she disturb us with her curses?'

'Father, there may be better days for us yet.'

'How can there be better days when you are bringing
down the Jew upon us? Better days for yourself, perhaps,
if mere eating and drinking will serve you.'

'Oh, father!'

'Have you not ruined everything with your Jew lover?
Did you not hear how I was treated? What could I say
to your aunt when she stood there and reviled us?'

'Father, I was so grateful to you for saying nothing!'

'But I knew that she was right. A Christian should not
marry a Jew. She said it was abominable; and so it is.'

'Father, father, do not speak like that! I thought that
you had forgiven me. You said to aunt Sophie that I was
a good daughter. Will you not say the same to me—to
me myself?'

'It is not good to love a Jew.'

'I do love him, father. How can I help it now? I
cannot change my heart.'

'I suppose I shall be dead soon,' said old Balatka,
'and then it will not matter. You will become one of
them, and I shall be forgotten.'

'Father, have I ever forgotten you?' said Nina, throwing herself upon him on his bed. 'Have I not always
loved you? Have I not been good to you? Oh, father,
we have been true to each other through it all. Do not
speak to me like that at last.'

CHAPTER VI

ANTON TRENDELLSOHN had learned from his father that
Nina had spoken to her aunt about the title-deeds of
the houses in the Kleinseite, and that thus, in a roundabout way, a demand had been made for them. 'Of course,
they will not give them up,' he had said to his father.
'Why should they, unless the law makes them? They
have no idea of honour or honesty to one of us.' The elder
Jew had then expressed his opinion that Josef Balatka

should be required to make the demand as a matter of business, to enforce a legal right; but to this Anton had replied that the old man in the Kleinseite was not in a condition to act efficiently in the matter himself. It was to him that the money had been advanced, but to the Zamenoys that it had in truth been paid; and Anton declared his purpose of going to Karil Zamenoy, and himself making his demand. And then there had been a discussion, almost amounting to a quarrel, between the two Trendellsohns as to Nina Balatka. Poor Nina need not have added another to her many causes of suffering by doubting her lover's truth. Anton Trendellsohn, though not given to speak of his love with that demonstrative vehemence to which Nina had trusted in her attempts to make her friends understand that she could not be talked out of her engagement, was nevertheless sufficiently firm in his purpose. He was a man very constant in all his purposes, whom none who knew him would have supposed likely to jeopardise his worldly interests for the love of a Christian girl, but who was very little apt to abandon aught to which he had set his hand because the voices of those around him might be against him. He had thought much of his position as a Jew before he had spoken of love to the penniless Christian maiden who frequented his father's house, pleading for her father in his poverty; but the words when spoken meant much, and Nina need not have feared that he would forget them. He was a man not much given to dalliance, not requiring from day to day the soft sweetness of a woman's presence to keep his love warm; but his love could maintain its own heat, without any softness or dalliance. Had it not been so, such a girl as Nina would hardly have surrendered to him her whole heart as she had done.

'You will fall into trouble about the maiden,' the elder Trendellsohn had said.

'True, father; there will be trouble enough. In what that we do is there not trouble?'

'A man in the business of his life must encounter labour and grief and disappointment. He should take to him a wife to give him ease in these things, not one who will be an increase to his sorrows.'

'That which is done is done.'

'My son, this thing is not done.'

'She has my plighted word, father. Is not that enough?'

'Nina is a good girl. I will say for her that she is very good. I have wished that you might have brought to my house as your wife the child of my old friend Baltazar Loth; but if that may not be, I would have taken Nina willingly by the hand—had she been one of us.'

'It may be that God will open her eyes.'

'Anton, I would not have her eyes opened by anything so weak as her love for a man. But I have said that she was good. She will hear reason; and when she shall know that her marriage among us would bring trouble on us, she will restrain her wishes. Speak to her, Anton, and see if it be not so.'

'Not for all the wealth which all our people own in Bohemia! Father, to do so would be to demand, not to ask. If she love me, could she refuse such a request were I to ask it?'

'I will speak a word to Nina, my son, and the request shall come from her.'

'And if it does, I will never yield to it. For her sake I would not yield, for I know she loves me. Neither for my own would I yield; for as truly as I worship God, I love her better than all the world beside. She is to me my cup of water when I am hot and athirst, my morsel of bread when I am faint with hunger. Her voice is the only music which I love. The touch of her hand is so fresh that it cools me when I am in fever. The kiss of her lips is so sweet and balmy that it cures when I shake with an ague fit. To think of her when I am out among men fighting for my own, is such a joy, that now, methinks now, that I have had it belonging to me, I could no longer fight were I to lose it. No, father; she shall not be taken from me. I love her, and I will keep her.'

Oh that Nina could have heard him! How would all her sorrows have fled from her, and left her happy in her poverty! But Anton Trendellsohn, though he could speak after this manner to his father, could hardly bring himself to talk of his feelings to the woman who would have given her eyes, could she for his sake have spared them, to hear him. Now and again, indeed, he would say a word, and then would frown and become gloomy, as though angry with himself for such outward womanly expression of what he felt. As it was, the words fell upon ears which they delighted not. 'Then, my son, you will live to rue the day in which you first saw her,' said the elder Jew. 'She will be a bone of contention in your way that will separate you from all your friends. You will become neither Jew nor Christian, and will be odious alike to both. And she will be the same.'

'Then, father, we will bear our sorrows together.'

'Yes; and what happens when sorrows come from such causes? The man learns to hate the woman who has caused them, and ill-uses her, and feels himself to be a Cain upon the earth, condemned by all, but by none so much as by himself. Do you think that you have strength to bear the contempt of all those around you?'

Anton waited a moment or two before he answered, and then spoke very slowly. 'If it be necessary to bear so much, I will at least make the effort. It may be that I shall find the strength.'

'Nothing then that your father says to you avails aught?'

'Nothing, father, on that matter. You should have spoken sooner.'

'Then you must go your own way. As for me, I must look for another son to bear the burden of my years.' And so they parted.

Anton Trendellsohn understood well the meaning of the old man's threat. He was quite alive to the fact that his father had expressed his intention to give his wealth and his standing in trade and the business of his house to some younger Jew, who would be more true than his own son to the traditional customs of their tribes. There was Ruth Jacobi, his granddaughter—the only child of the house—who had already reached an age at which she might be betrothed; and there was Samuel Loth, the son of Baltazar Loth, old Trendellsohn's oldest friend. Anton Trendellsohn did not doubt who might be the adopted child to be taken to fill his place. It has been already explained that there was no partnership actually existing between the two Trendellsohns. By degrees the son had slipt into the father's place, and the business by which the house had grown rich had for the last five or six years been managed chiefly by him. But the actual results of the son's industry and the son's thrift were still in the possession of the father. The old man might no doubt go far towards ruining his son if he were so minded.

Dreams of a high ambition had, from very early years, flitted across the mind of the younger Trendellsohn till they had nearly formed themselves into a settled purpose. He had heard of Jews in Vienna, in Paris, and in London, who were as true to their religion as any Jew of Prague, but who did not live immured in a Jews' quarter, like lepers separate and alone in some loathed corner of a city otherwise clean. These men went abroad into the world as men, using the wealth with which their industry had been blessed, openly as the Christians used it. And they lived among Christians as one man should live with his fellow-men—on equal terms, giving and taking, honouring and honoured. As yet it was not so with the Jews of Prague, who were still bound to their old narrow streets, to their dark houses, to their mean modes of living, and who, worst of all, were still subject to the isolated ignominy of Judaism. In Prague a Jew was still a Pariah. Anton's father was rich—very rich. Anton hardly knew what was the extent of his father's wealth, but he did know that it was great. In his father's time, however, no change could be made. He did not scruple to speak to the old man of these things; but he spoke of them rather as dreams, or as distant hopes, than as being the basis of any purpose of his own. His father would merely say that the old house, looking out upon the ancient synagogue, must last him his time, and that the changes of which Anton spoke must be postponed—not till he died—but till such time as he should feel it right to give up the things of this world. Anton Trendellsohn, who knew his father well, had resolved that he would wait patiently for everything till his father should have gone to his last home, knowing that nothing but death would close the old man's interest in the work of his life. But he had been content to wait —to wait, to think, to dream, and only in part to hope. He still communed with himself daily as to that House of Trendellsohn which might, perhaps, be heard of in cities greater than Prague, and which might rival in the grandeur of its wealth those mighty commercial names* which had drowned the old shame of the Jew in the new glory of their great doings. To be a Jew in London, they had told him, was almost better than to be a Christian, provided that he was rich, and knew the ways of trade, —was better for such purposes as were his purposes. Anton Trendellsohn believed that he would be rich, and was sure that he knew the ways of trade; and therefore he nursed his ambition, and meditated what his action should be when the days of his freedom should come to him.

Then Nina Balatka had come across his path. To be a Jew, always a Jew, in all things a Jew, had been ever a part of his great dream. It was as impossible to him as it would be to his father to forswear the religion of his people. To go forth and be great in commerce by deserting his creed would have been nothing to him. His ambition did not desire wealth so much as the possession of wealth in Jewish hands, without those restrictions upon its enjoyment to which Jews under his own eye had ever been subjected. It would have delighted him to think that, by means of his work, there should no longer be a Jews' quarter in Prague, but that all Prague should be ennobled and civilised and made beautiful by the wealth of Jews. Wealth must be his means, and therefore he was greedy; but wealth was not his last or only aim, and therefore his greed did not utterly destroy his heart. Then Nina Balatka had come across his path, and he was compelled to shape his dreams anew. How could a Jew among Jews hold up his head as such who had taken to his bosom a Christian wife?

But again he shaped his dreams aright—so far aright that he could still build the castles of his imagination to his own liking. Nina should be his wife. It might be that she would follow the creed of her husband, and then all would be well. In those far cities to which he would go, it would hardly in such case be known that she had been born a Christian; or else he would show the world around him, both Jews and Christians, how well a Christian and a Jew might live together. To crush the prejudice which had dealt so hardly with his people—to make a Jew equal in all things to a Christian—this was his desire; and how could this better be fulfilled than by his union with a Christian? One thing at least was fixed with him—one thing was fixed, even though it should mar his dreams. He had taken the Christian girl to be part of himself, and nothing should separate them. His father had spoken often to him of the danger which he would incur by marrying a Christian, but had never before uttered any word approaching to a personal threat. Anton had felt himself to be so completely the mainspring of the business in which they were both engaged—was so perfectly aware that he was so regarded by all the commercial men of Prague—that he had hardly regarded the absence of any positive possession in his father's wealth as detrimental to him. He had been willing that it should be his father's while his father lived, knowing that any division would be detrimental to them both. He had never even asked his father for a partnership, taking everything for granted. Even now he could not quite believe that his father was in earnest. It could hardly be possible that the work of his own hands should be taken from him because he had chosen a bride for himself! But this he felt, that should his father persevere in the intention which he had expressed, he would be upheld in it by every Jew of Prague. 'Dark, ignorant, and foolish,' Anton said to himself, speaking of those among whom he lived; 'it is their pride to live in disgrace, while all the honours of the world are open to them if they chose to take them!'

He did not for a moment think of altering his course of

action in consequence of what his father had said to him. Indeed, as regarded the business of the house, it would stand still altogether were he to alter it. No successor could take up the work when he should leave it. No other hand could continue the webs which were of his weaving. So he went forth, as the errands of the day called him, soon after his father's last words were spoken, and went through his work as though his own interest in it were in no danger.

On that evening nothing was said on the subject between him and his father, and on the next morning he started immediately after breakfast for the Ross Markt, in order that he might see Karil Zamenoy, as he had said that he would do. The papers, should he get them, would belong to his father, and would at once be put into his father's hands. But the feeling that it might not be for his own personal advantage to place them there did not deter him. His father was an old man, and old men were given to threaten. He at least would go on with his duty.

It was about eleven o'clock in the day when he entered the open door of the office in the Ross Markt, and found Ziska and a young clerk sitting opposite to each other at their desks. Anton took off his hat and bowed to Ziska, whom he knew slightly, and asked the young man if his father were within.

'My father is here,' said Ziska, 'but I do not know whether he can see you.'

'You will ask him, perhaps,' said Trendellsohn.

'Well, he is engaged. There is a lady with him.'

'Perhaps he will make an appointment with me, and I will call again. If he will name an hour, I will come at his own time.'

'Cannot you say to me, Herr Trendellsohn, that which you wish to say to him?'

'Not very well.'

'You know that I am in partnership with my father.'

'He and you are happy to be so placed together. But if your father can spare me five minutes, I will take it from him as a favour.'

Then, with apparent reluctance, Ziska came down from his seat and went into the inner room. There he remained some time, while Trendellsohn was standing, hat in hand, in the outer office. If the changes which he hoped to effect among his brethren could be made, a Jew in Prague should, before long, be asked to sit down as readily as a Christian. But he had not been asked to sit, and he therefore stood holding his hat in his hand during the ten minutes that Ziska was away. At last young Zamenoy returned, and, opening the door, signified to the Jew that his father would see him at once if he would enter. Nothing more had been said about the lady, and there, when Trendellsohn went into the room, he found the lady, who was no other than Madame Zamenoy herself. A little family council had been held, and it had been settled among them that the Jew should be seen and heard.

'So, sir, you are Anton Trendellsohn,' began Madame Zamenoy, as soon as Ziska was gone—for Ziska had been told to go—and the door was shut.

'Yes, madame; I am Anton Trendellsohn. I had not expected the honour of seeing you, but I wish to say a few words on business to your husband.'

'There he is; you can speak to him.'

'Anything that I can do, I shall be very happy,' said Karil Zamenoy, who had risen from his chair to prevent the necessity of having to ask the Jew to sit down.

'Herr Zamenoy,' began the Jew, 'you are, I think, aware that my father has purchased from your friend and brother-in-law, Josef Balatka, certain houses in the Kleinseite, in one of which the old man still lives.'

'Upon my word, I know nothing about it,' said Zamenoy—'nothing, that is to say, in the way of business;' and the man of business laughed. 'Mind I do not at all deny that you did so—you or your father, or the two together. Your people are getting into their hands lots of houses all over the town; but how they do it nobody knows. They are not bought in fair open market.'

'This purchase was made by contract, and the price was paid in full before the houses were put into our hands.'

'They are not in your hands now, as far as I know.'

'Not the one, certainly, in which Balatka lives. Motives of friendship——'

'Friendship!' said Madame Zamenoy, with a sneer.

'And now motives of love,' continued Anton, 'have induced us to leave the use of that house with Josef Balatka.'

'Love!' said Madame Zamenoy, springing from her chair; 'love indeed! Do not talk to me of love for a Jew.'

'My dear, my dear!' said her husband, expostulating.

'How dares he come here to talk of his love? It is filthy—it is worse than filthy—it is profane.'

'I came here, madame,' continued Anton, 'not to talk of my love, but of certain documents or title-deeds respecting those houses, which should be at present in my father's custody. I am told that your husband has them in his safe custody.'

'My husband has them not,' said Madame Zamenoy.

'Stop, my dear—stop,' said the husband.

'Not that he would be bound to give them up to you if he had got them, or that he would do so; but he has them not.'

'In whose hands are they then?'

'That is for you to find out, not for us to tell you.'

'Why should not all the world be told, so that the proper owner may have his own?'

'It is not always so easy to find out who is the proper owner,' said Zamenoy the elder.

'You have seen this contract before, I think,' said Trendellsohn, bringing forth a written paper.

'I will not look at it now at any rate. I have nothing to do with it, and I will have nothing to do with it. You have heard Madame Zamenoy declare that the deed which you seek is not here. I cannot say whether it is here or no. I do not say—as you will be pleased to remember. If it were here it would be in safe keeping for my brother-in-law, and only to him could it be given.'

'But will you not say whether it is in your hands? You know well that Josef Balatka is ill, and cannot attend to such matters.'

'And who has made him ill, and what has made him ill?' said Madame Zamenoy. 'Ill! of course he is ill. Is it not enough to make any man ill to be told that his daughter is to marry a Jew?'

'I have not come hither to speak of that,' said Trendellsohn.

'But I speak of it; and I tell you this, Anton Trendellsohn—you shall never marry that girl.'

'Be it so; but let me at any rate have that which is my own.'

'Will you give her up if it is given to you?'

'It is here then?'

'No; it is not here. But will you abandon this mad thought if I tell you where it is?'

'No; certainly not.'

'What a fool the man is!' said Madame Zamenoy. 'He comes to us for what he calls his property because he wants to marry the girl, and she is deceiving him all the while. Go to Nina Balatka, Trendellsohn, and she will tell you who has the document. She will tell you where it is, if it suits her to do so.'

'She has told me, and she knows that it is here.'

'She knows nothing of the kind, and she has lied. She has lied in order that she may rob you. Jew as you are, she will be too many for you. She will rob you, with all her seeming simplicity.'

'I trust her as I do my own soul,' said Trendellsohn.

'Very well; I tell you that she, and she only, knows where these papers are. For aught I know, she has them herself. I believe that she has them. Ziska,' said Madame Zamenoy, calling aloud—'Ziska, come hither;' and Ziska entered the room. 'Ziska, who has the title-deeds of your uncle's houses in the Kleinseite?' Ziska hesitated a moment without answering. 'You know, if anybody does,' said his mother; 'tell this man, since he is so anxious, who has got them.'

'I do not know why I should tell him my cousin's secrets.'

'Tell him, I say. It is well that he should know.'

'Nina has them, as I believe,' said Ziska, still hesitating.

'Nina has them!' said Trendellsohn.

'Yes; Nina Balatka,' said Madame Zamenoy. 'We tell you, to the best of our knowledge at least. At any rate, they are not here.'

'It is impossible that Nina should have them,' said Trendellsohn. 'How should she have got them?'

'That is nothing to us,' said Madame Zamenoy. 'The whole thing is nothing to us. You have heard all that we can tell you, and you had better go.'

'You have heard more than I would have told you myself,' said Ziska, 'had I been left to my opinion.'

Trendellsohn stood pausing for a moment, and then he turned to the elder Zamenoy. 'What do you say, sir? Is it true that these papers are at the house in the Kleinseite?'

'I say nothing,' said Karil Zamenoy. 'It seems to me that too much has been said already.'

'A great deal too much,' said the lady. 'I do not know why I should have allowed myself to be surprised into giving you any information at all. You wish to do us the heaviest injury that one man can do another, and I do not know why we should speak to you at all. Now you had better go.'

'Yes; you had better go,' said Ziska, holding the door open, and looking as though he were inclined to threaten. Trendellsohn paused for a moment on the threshold, fixing his eyes full upon those of his rival; but Ziska neither spoke nor made any further gesture, and then the Jew left the house.

'I would have told him nothing,' said the elder Zamenoy when they were left alone.

'My dear, you don't understand; indeed you do not,' said his wife. 'No stone should be left unturned to prevent such a horrid marriage as this. There is nothing I would not say—nothing I would not do.'

'But I do not see that you are doing anything.'

'Leave this little thing to me, my dear—to me and Ziska. It is impossible that you should do everything yourself. In such a matter as this, believe me that a woman is best.'

'But I hate anything that is really dishonest.'

'There shall be no dishonesty,—none in the world. You don't suppose that I want to get the dirty old tumble-down houses. God forbid! But you would not give up everything to a Jew! Oh, I hate them! I do hate them! Anything is fair against a Jew.' If such was Madame Zamenoy's ordinary doctrine, it may well be understood that she would scruple at using no weapon against a Jew who was meditating so great an injury against her as this marriage with her niece. After this little discussion old Zamenoy said no more, and Madame Zamenoy went home to the Windberg-gasse.

Trendellsohn, as he walked homewards, was lost in amazement. He wholly disbelieved the statement that the document he desired was in Nina's hands, but he thought it possible that it might be in the house in the Kleinseite. It was, after all, on the cards that old Balatka was deceiving him. The Jew was by nature suspicious, though he was also generous. He could be noble in his confidence, and at the same time could become at a moment distrustful. He could give without grudging, and yet grudge the benefits which came of his giving. Neither he nor his father had ever positively known in whose custody were the title-deeds which he was so anxious to get into his own hands. Balatka had said that they must be with the Zamenoys, but even Balatka had never spoken as of absolute knowledge. Nina, indeed, had declared positively that they were in the Ross Markt, saying that Ziska had so stated in direct terms; but there might be a mistake in this. At any rate he would interrogate Nina, and if there were need, would not spare the old man any questions that could lead to the truth. Trendellsohn, as he thought of the possibility of such treachery on Balatka's part, felt that, without, compunction, he could be very cruel, even to an old man, under such circumstances as those.

CHAPTER VII

MADAME ZAMENOY and her son no doubt understood each other's purposes, and there was another person in the house who understood them—Lotta Luxa, namely; but Karil Zamenoy had been kept somewhat in the dark. Touching that piece of parchment as to which so much anxiety had been expressed, he only knew that he had, at his wife's instigation, given it into her hand in order that she might use it in some way for putting an end to the foul betrothal between Nina and the Jew. The elder Zamenoy no doubt understood that Anton Trendellsohn was to be bought off by the document; and he was not unwilling to buy him off so cheaply, knowing as he did that the houses were in truth the Jew's property: but Madame Zamenoy's scheme was deeper than this. She did not believe that the Jew was to be bought off at so cheap a price; but she did believe that it might be possible to create such a feeling in his mind as would make him abandon Nina out of the workings of his own heart. Ziska and his mother were equally anxious to save Nina from the Jew, but not exactly with the same motives. He had received a promise, both from his father and mother, before anything was known of the Jew's love, that Nina should be received as a daughter-in-law, if she would accept his suit; and this promise was still in force. That the girl whom he loved should love a Jew, distressed and disgusted Ziska; but it did not deter him from his old purpose. It was shocking, very shocking, that Nina should so disgrace herself; but she was not on that account less pretty or less charming in her cousin's eyes. Madame Zamenoy, could she have had her own will, would have rescued Nina from the Jew—firstly, because Nina was known all over Prague to be her niece—and, secondly, for the good of Christianity generally; but the girl herself, when rescued, she would willingly have left to starve in the poverty of the old house in the Kleinseite, as a punishment for her sin in having listened to a Jew.

'I would have nothing more to say to her,' said the mother to her son.

'Nor I either,' said Lotta, who was present. 'She has demeaned herself far too much to be a fit wife for Ziska.'

'Hold your tongue, Lotta; what business have you to speak about such a matter?' said the young man.

'All the same, Ziska, if I were you, I would give her up,' said the mother.

'If you were me, mother, you would not give her up. If every man is to give up the girl he likes because somebody else interferes with him, how is anybody to get married at all? It's the way with them all.'

'But a Jew, Ziska!'

'So much the more reason for taking her away from him.' Then Ziska went forth on a certain errand, the expediency of which he had discussed with his mother.

'I never thought he'd be so firm about it, ma'am,' said Lotta to her mistress.

'If we could get Trendellsohn to turn her off, he would not think much of her afterwards,' said the mother. 'He wouldn't care to take the Jew's leavings.'

'But he seems to be so obstinate,' said Lotta. 'Indeed I did not think there was so much obstinacy in him.'

'Of course he is obstinate while he thinks the other man is to have her,' said the mistress; 'but all that will be changed when the girl is alone in the world.'

It was a Saturday morning, and Ziska had gone out with a certain fixed object. Much had been said between him and his mother since Anton Trendellsohn's visit to the office, and it had been decided that he should now go and see the Jew in his own home. He should see him and speak him fair, and make him understand if possible that the whole question of the property should be settled as he wished it—if he would only give up his insane purpose of marrying a Christian girl. Ziska would endeavour also to fill the Jew's mind with suspicion against Nina. The former scheme was Ziska's own; the second was that in which Ziska's mother put her chief trust. 'If once he can be made to think that the girl is deceiving him, he will quarrel with her utterly,' Madame Zamenoy had said.

On Saturday there is but little business done in Prague, because Saturday is the Sabbath of the Jews. The shops

are of course open in the main streets of the town, but
banks and counting-houses are closed, because the Jews
will not do business on that day—so great is the prepon-
derance of the wealth of Prague in the hands of that
people! It suited Ziska, therefore, to make his visit on a
Saturday, both because he had but little himself to do
on that day, and because he would be almost sure to find
Trendellsohn at home. As he made his way across the
bottom of the Kalowrat-strasse and through the centre of
the city to the narrow ways of the Jews' quarter, his
heart somewhat misgave him as to the result of his visit.
He knew very well that a Christian was safe among the
Jews from any personal ill-usage; but he knew also that
such a one as he would be known personally to many of
them as a Christian rival, and probably as a Christian
enemy in the same city, and he thought that they would
look at him askance. Living in Prague all his life, he had
hardly been above once or twice in the narrow streets
which he was now threading. Strangers who come to
Prague visit the Jews' quarter as a matter of course, and
to such strangers the Jews of Prague are invariably
courteous. But the Christians of the city seldom walk
through the heart of the Jews' locality, or hang about
the Jews' synagogue, or are seen among their houses
unless they have special business. The Jews' quarter,
though it is a banishment to the Jews from the fairer
portions of the city, is also a separate and somewhat
sacred castle in which they may live after their old fashion
undisturbed. As Ziska went on, he became aware that
the throng of people was unusually great, and that the
day was in some sort more peculiar than the ordinary
Jewish Sabbath. That the young men and girls should
be dressed in their best clothes was, as a matter of course,
incidental to the day; but he could perceive that there
was an outward appearance of gala festivity about them
which could not take place every week. The tall bright-
eyed black-haired girls stood talking in the streets, with
something of boldness in their gait and bearing, dressed
many of them in white muslin, with bright ribbons and
full petticoats, and that small bewitching Hungarian hat

which they delight to wear. They stood talking somewhat loudly to each other, or sat at the open windows;
while the young men in black frock-coats and black hats,
with crimson cravats, clustered by themselves, wishing,
but not daring so early in the day, to devote themselves
to the girls, who appeared, or attempted to appear, unaware of their presence. Who can say why it is that those
encounters, which are so ardently desired by both sides,
are so rarely able to get themselves commenced till the
enemies have been long in sight of each other? But so it
is among Jews and Christians, among rich and poor,
out under the open sky, and even in the atmosphere of
the ball-room, consecrated though it be to such purposes.
Go into any public dancing-room of Vienna, where the
girls from the shops and the young men from their desks
congregate to waltz and make love, and you shall observe
that from ten to twelve they will dance as vigorously as at
a later hour, but that they will hardly talk to each other
till the mellowness of the small morning hours has come
upon them.

Among these groups in the Jewish quarter Ziska made
his way, conscious that the girls eyed him and whispered
to each other something as to his presence, and conscious
also that the young men eyed him also, though they did
so without speaking of him as he passed. He knew that
Trendellsohn lived close to the synagogue, and to the
synagogue he made his way. And as he approached the
narrow door of the Jews' church, he saw that a crowd of
men stood round it, some in high caps and some in black
hats, but all habited in short muslin shirts, which they
wore over their coats. Such dresses he had seen before,
and he knew that these men were taking part from time
to time in some service within the synagogue. He did
not dare to ask of one of them which was Trendellsohn's
house, but went on till he met an old man alone just at
the back of the building, dressed also in a high cap and
shirt, which shirt, however, was longer than those he had
seen before. Plucking up his courage, he asked of the old
man which was the house of Anton Trendellsohn.

'Anton Trendellsohn has no house,' said the old man;

'but that is his father's house, and there Anton Trendell-sohn lives. I am Stephen Trendellsohn, and Anton is my son.'

Ziska thanked him, and, crossing the street to the house, found that the door was open, and that two girls were standing just within the passage. The old man had gone, and Ziska, turning, had perceived that he was out of sight before he reached the house.

'I cannot come till my uncle returns,' said the younger girl.

'But, Ruth, he will be in the synagogue all day,' said the elder, who was that Rebecca Loth of whom the old Jew had spoken to his son.

'Then all day I must remain,' said Ruth; 'but it may be he will be in by one.' Then Ziska addressed them, and asked if Anton Trendellsohn did not live there.

'Yes; he lives there,' said Ruth, almost trembling, as she answered the handsome stranger.

'And is he at home?'

'He is in the synagogue,' said Ruth. 'You will find him there if you will go in.'

'But they are at worship there,' said Ziska, doubtingly.

'They will be at worship all day, because it is our festival,' said Rebecca, with her eyes fixed upon the ground; 'but if you are a Christian they will not object to your going in. They like that Christians should see them. They are not ashamed.'

Ziska, looking into the girl's face, saw that she was very beautiful; and he saw also at once that she was exactly the opposite of Nina, though they were both of a height. Nina was fair, with grey eyes, and smooth brown hair which seemed to demand no special admiration, though it did in truth add greatly to the sweet delicacy of her face; and she was soft in her gait, and appeared to be yielding and flexible in all the motions of her body. You would think that if you were permitted to embrace her, the outlines of her body would form themselves to yours, as though she would in all things fit herself to him who might be blessed by her love. But Rebecca Loth was dark, with large dark-blue eyes and jet black tresses,

which spoke out loud to the beholder to their own love-
liness. You could not fail to think of her hair and of her
eyes, as though they were things almost separate from
herself. And she stood like a queen, who knew herself to
be all a queen, strong on her limbs, wanting no support,
somewhat hard withal, with a repellant beauty that
seemed to disdain while it courted admiration, and
utterly rejected the idea of that caressing assistance which
men always love to give, and which women often love to
receive. At the present moment she was dressed in a
frock of white muslin, looped round the skirt, and bright
with ruby ribbons. She had on her feet coloured boots,
which fitted them to a marvel, and on her glossy hair a
small new hat, ornamented with the plumage of some
strange bird. On her shoulders she wore a coloured
jacket, open down the front, sparkling with jewelled
buttons, over which there hung a chain with a locket.
In her ears she carried long heavy earrings of gold. Were
it not that Ziska had seen others as gay in their apparel
on his way, he would have fancied that she was tricked
out for the playing of some special part, and that she
should hardly have shown herself in the streets with her
gala finery. Such was Rebecca Loth the Jewess, and
Ziska almost admitted to himself that she was more
beautiful than Nina Balatka.

'And are you also of the family?' Ziska asked.

'No; she is not of the family,' said Ruth. 'She is my
particular friend, Rebecca Loth. She does not live here.
She lives with her brother and her mother.'

'Ruth, how foolish you are! What does it signify to the
gentleman?'

'But he asked, and so I supposed he wanted to know.'

'I have to apologise for intruding on you with any
questions, young ladies,' said Ziska; 'especially on a day
which seems to be solemn.'

'That does not matter at all,' said Rebecca. 'Here is
my brother, and he will take you into the synagogue if
you wish to see Anton Trendellsohn.' Samuel Loth, her
brother, then came up and readily offered to take Ziska
into the midst of the worshippers. Ziska would have

escaped now from the project could he have done so
without remark; but he was ashamed to seem afraid to
enter the building, as the girls seemed to make so light
of his doing so. He therefore followed Rebecca's brother,
and in a minute or two was inside the narrow door.

The door was very low and narrow, and seemed to be
choked up by men with short white surplices,* but nevertheless he found himself inside, jammed among a crowd
of Jews; and a sound of many voices, going together in a
sing-song wail or dirge, met his ears. His first impulse
was to take off his hat, but that was immediately replaced
upon his head, he knew not by whom; and then he
observed that all within the building were covered. His
guide did not follow him, but whispered to someone what
it was that the stranger required. He could see that those
inside the building were all clothed in muslin shirts of
different lengths, and that it was filled with men, all of
whom had before them some sort of desk, from which
they were reading, or rather wailing out their litany.
Though this was the chief synagogue in Prague, and, as
being the so-called oldest in Europe, is a building of some
consequence in the Jewish world, it was very small.
There was no ceiling, and the high-pitched roof, which
had once probably been coloured, and the walls, which
had once certainly been white, were black with the dirt
of ages.* In the centre there was a cage, as it were, or
iron grille,* within which five or six old Jews were placed,
who seemed to wail louder than the others. Round the
walls there was a row of men inside stationary desks, and
outside them another row, before each of whom there
was a small movable standing desk, on which there was
a portion of the law of Moses. There seemed to be no
possible way by which Ziska could advance, and he
would have been glad to retreat had retreat been possible.
But first one Jew and then another moved their desks for
him, so that he was forced to advance, and some among
them pointed to the spot where Anton Trendellsohn was
standing. But as they pointed, and as they moved their
desks to make a pathway, they still sang and wailed con-
tinuously, never ceasing for an instant in their long, loud,

melancholy song of prayer. At the further end there seemed to be some altar, in front of which the High Priest* wailed louder than all, louder even than the old men within the cage; and even he, the High Priest, was forced to move his desk to make way for Ziska. But, apparently without displeasure, he moved it with his left hand, while he swayed his right hand backwards and forwards as though regulating the melody of the wail. Beyond the High Priest Ziska saw Anton Trendellsohn, and close to the son he saw the old man whom he had met in the street, and whom he recognised as Anton's father. Old Trendellsohn seemed to take no notice of him, but Anton had watched him from his entrance, and was prepared to speak to him, though he did not discontinue his part in the dirge till the last moment.

'I had a few words to say to you, if it would suit you,' said Ziska, in a low voice.

'Are they of import?' Trendellsohn asked. 'If so, I will come to you.'

Ziska then turned to make his way back, but he saw that this was not to be his road for retreat. Behind him the movable phalanx had again formed itself into close rank, but before him the wailing wearers of the white shirts were preparing for the commotion of his passage by grasping the upright stick of their movable desks in their hands. So he passed on, making the entire round of the synagogue; and when he got outside the crowded door, he found that the younger Trendellsohn had followed him. 'We had better go into the house,' said Anton; 'it will not be well for us to talk here on any matter of business. Will you follow me?'

Then he led the way into the old house, and there at the front door still stood the two girls talking to each other.

'You have come back, uncle,' said Ruth.

'Yes; for a few moments, to speak to this gentleman.'

'And will you return to the synagogue?'

'Of course I shall return to the synagogue.'

'Because Rebecca wishes me to go out with her,' said the younger girl, in a plaintive voice.

'You cannot go out now. Your grandfather will want you when he returns.'

'But, uncle Anton, he will not come till sunset.'

'My mother wished to have Ruth with her this afternoon if it were possible,' said Rebecca, hardly looking at Anton as she spoke to him; 'but of course if you will not give her leave I must return without her.'

'Do you not know, Rebecca,' said Anton, 'that she is needful to her grandfather?'

'She could be back before sunset.'

'I will trust to you, then, that she is brought back.' Ruth, as soon as she heard the words, scampered up-stairs to array herself in such finery as she possessed, while Rebecca still stood at the door.

'Will you not come in, Rebecca, while you wait for her?' said Anton.

'Thank you, I will stand here. I am very well here.'

'But the child will be ever so long making herself ready. Surely you will come in.'

But Rebecca was obstinate, and kept her place at the door. 'He has that Christian girl there with him day after day,' she said to Ruth as they went away together. 'I will never enter the house while she is allowed to come there.'

'But Nina is very good,' said Ruth.

'I do not care for her goodness.'

'Do you not know that she is to be uncle Anton's wife?'

'They have told me so, but she shall be no friend of mine, Ruth. Is it not shameful that he should wish to marry a Christian?'

When the two men had reached the sitting-room in the Jew's house, and Ziska had seated himself, Anton Trendellsohn closed the door, and asked, not quite in anger, but with something of sternness in his voice, why he had been disturbed while engaged in an act of worship.

'They told me that you would not mind my going in to you,' said Ziska, deprecating his wrath.

'That depends on your business. What is it that you have to say to me?'

'It is this. When you came to us the other day in the

Ross Markt, we were hardly prepared for you. We did not expect you.'

'Your mother could hardly have received me better had she expected me for a twelvemonth.'

'You cannot be surprised that my mother should be vexed. Besides, you would not be angry with a lady for what she might say.'

'I care but little what she says. But words, my friend, are things, and are often things of great moment. All that, however, matters very little. Why have you done us the honour of coming to our house?'

Even Ziska could perceive, though his powers of perception in such matters were perhaps not very great, that the Jew in the Jews' quarter, and the Jew in the Ross Markt, were very different persons. Ziska was now sitting while Anton Trendellsohn was standing over him. Ziska, when he remembered that Anton had not been seated in his father's office—had not been asked to sit down—would have risen himself, and have stood during the interview, but he did not know how to leave his seat. And when the Jew called him his friend, he felt that the Jew was getting the better of him—was already obtaining the ascendant. 'Of course we wish to prevent this marriage,' said Ziska, dashing at once at his subject.

'You cannot prevent it. The law allows it. If that is what you have come to do, you may as well return.'

'But listen to me, my friend,' said Ziska, taking a leaf out of the Jew's book. 'Only listen to me, and then I shall go.'

'Speak, then, and I will listen; but be quick.'

'You want, of course, to be made right about those houses?'

'My father, to whom they belong, wishes to be made right, as you call it.'

'It is all the same thing. Now, look here. The truth is this. Everything shall be settled for you, and the whole thing given up regularly into your hands, if you will only give over about Nina Balatka.'

'But I will not give over about Nina Balatka. Am I to be bribed out of my love by an offer of that which is already mine own? But that you are in my father's house, I would be wrathful with you for making me such an offer.'

'Why should you seek a Christian wife, with such maidens among you as her whom I saw at the door?'

'Do not mind the maiden whom you saw at the door. She is nothing to you.'

'No; she is nothing to me. Of course, the lady is nothing to me. If I were to come here looking for her, you would be angry, and would bid me seek for beauty among my own people. Would you not do so? Answer me now.'

'Like enough. Rebecca Loth has many friends who would take her part.'

'And why should we not take Nina's part—we who are her friends?'

'Have you taken her part? Have you comforted her when she was in sorrow? Have you wiped her tears when she wept? Have you taken from her the stings of poverty, and striven to make the world to her a pleasant garden. She has no mother of her own. Has yours been a mother to her? Why is it that Nina Balatka has cared to receive the sympathy and the love of a Jew? Ask that girl whom you saw at the door for some corner in her heart, and she will scorn you. She, a Jewess, will scorn you, a Christian. She would so look at you that you would not dare to repeat your prayer. Why is it that Nina has not so scorned me? We are lodged poorly here, while Nina's aunt has a fine house in the New Town. She has a carriage and horses, and the world around her is gay and bright. Why did Nina come to the Jews' quarter for sympathy, seeing that she, too, has friends of her own persuasion? Take Nina's part, indeed! It is too late now for you to take her part. She has chosen for herself, and her resting-place is to be here.' Trendellsohn, as he spoke, put his hand upon his breast, within the fold of his waistcoat; but Ziska hardly understood that his doing so had any special meaning. Ziska supposed that the 'here' of which the Jew spoke was the old house in which they were at the moment talking to each other.

'I am sure we have meant to be kind to her,' said Ziska.

'You see the effect of your kindness. I tell you this only in answer to what you said as to the young woman whom you saw at the door. Have you aught else to say to me? I utterly decline that small matter of traffic which you have proposed to me.'

'It was not traffic exactly.'

'Very well. What else is there that I can do for you?'

'I hardly know how to go on, as you are so—so hard in all that you say.'

'You will not be able to soften me, I fear.'

'About the houses—though you say that I am trafficking, I really wish to be honest with you.'

'Say what you have to say, then, and be honest.'

'I have never seen but one document which conveys the ownership of those houses.'

'Let my father, then, have that one document.'

'It is in Balatka's house.'

'That can hardly be possible,' said Trendellsohn.

'As I am a Christian gentleman,' said Ziska, 'I believe it to be in that house.'

'As I am a Jew, sir, fearing God,' said the other, 'I do not believe it. Who in that house has the charge of it?'

Ziska hesitated before he replied. 'Nina, as I think,' he said at last. 'I suppose Nina has it herself.'

'Then she would be a traitor to me.'

'What am I to say as to that?' said Ziska, smiling. Trendellsohn came to him and sat down close at his side, looking closely into his face. Ziska would have moved away from the Jew, but the elbow of the sofa did not admit of his receding; and then, while he was thinking that he would escape by rising from his seat, Anton spoke again in a low voice—so low that it was almost a whisper, but the words seemed to fall direct into Ziska's ears, and to hurt him. 'What are you to say? You called yourself just now a Christian gentleman. Neither the one name nor the other goes for aught with me. I am neither the one nor the other. But I am a man;—and I ask you, as another man, whether it be true that Nina Balatka has that paper in her possession—in her own possession, mind you, I say.' Ziska had hesitated before, but his hesitation now was much more palpable. 'Why do you not answer me?' continued the Jew. 'You have made this accusation against her. Is the accusation true?'

'I think she has it,' said Ziska. 'Indeed I feel sure of it.'

'In her own hands?'

'Oh yes;—in her own hands. Of course it must be in her own hands.'

'Christian gentleman,' said Anton, rising again from his seat, and now standing opposite to Ziska, 'I disbelieve you. I think that you are lying to me. Despite your Christianity, and despite your gentility—you are a liar. Now, sir, unless you have anything further to say to me, you may go.'

Ziska, when thus addressed, rose of course from his seat. By nature he was not a coward, but he was unready, and knew not what to do or to say on the spur of the moment. 'I did not come here to be insulted,' he said.

'No; you came to insult me, with two falsehoods in your mouth, either of which proves the other to be a lie. You offer to give me up the deeds on certain conditions, and then tell me that they are with the girl! If she has them, how can you surrender them? I do not know whether so silly a story might prevail between two Christians, but we Jews have been taught among you to be somewhat observant. Sir, it is my belief that the document belonging to my father is in your father's desk in the Ross Markt.'

'By heaven, it is in the house in the Kleinseite.'

'How could you then have surrendered it?'

'It could have been managed.'

It was now the Jew's turn to pause and hesitate. In the general conclusion to which his mind had come, he was not far wrong. He thought that Ziska was endeavouring to deceive him in the spirit of what he said, but that as regarded the letter, the young man was endeavouring to adhere to some fact for the salvation of his conscience as a Christian. If Anton Trendellsohn could but find out in what lay the quibble, the discovery might be very serviceable to him. 'It could have been managed

—could it?' he said, speaking very slowly. 'Between you and her, perhaps.'

'Well, yes; between me and Nina;—or between some of us,' said Ziska.

'And cannot it be managed now?'

'Nina is not one of us now. How can we deal with her?'

'Then I will deal with her myself. I will manage it if it is to be managed. And, sir, if I find that in this matter you have told me the simple truth—not the truth, mind you, as from a gentleman, or the truth as from a Christian, for I suspect both—but the simple truth as from man to man, then I will express my sorrow for the harsh words I have used to you.' As he finished speaking, Trendellsohn held the door of the room open in his hand, and Ziska, not being ready with any answer, passed through it and descended the stairs. The Jew followed him and also held open the house door, but did not speak again as Ziska went out. Nor did Ziska say a word, the proper words not being ready to his tongue. The Jew returned at once into the synagogue, having during the interview with Ziska worn the short white surplice in which he had been found; and Ziska returned at once to his own house in the Windberg-gasse.

CHAPTER VIII

EARLY on the following morning—the morning of the Christian Sunday—Nina Balatka received a note, a very short note, from her lover the Jew. 'Dearest, meet me on the bridge this evening at eight. I will be at your end of the right-hand pathway exactly at eight. Thine, ever and always, A. T.' Nina, directly she had read the words, rushed out to the door in order that she might give assurance to the messenger that she would do as she was bidden; but the messenger was gone, and Nina was obliged to reconcile herself to the prospect of silent obedience. The note, however, had made her very happy, and the prospect pleased her well. It was on this very day that she had intended to go to her lover; but it was in all respects much pleasanter to her that her lover should come to her. And then, to walk with him was of all things the most delightful, especially in the gloom of the evening, when no eyes could see her,—no eyes but his own. She could hang upon his arm, and in this way she could talk more freely with him than in any other. And then the note had in it more of the sweetness of a love-letter than any written words which she had hitherto received from him. It was very short, no doubt, but he had called her 'Dearest,' instead of 'Dear Nina,' as had been his custom, and then he had declared that he was hers ever and always. No words could have been sweeter. She was glad that the note was so short, because there was nothing in it to mar her pleasure. Yes, she would be there at eight. She was quite determined that she would not keep him waiting.

At half-past seven she was on the bridge. There could be no reason, she thought, why she should not walk across it to the other side and then retrace her steps, though in doing so she was forced, by the rule of the road upon the bridge, to pass to the Old Town by the right-hand pathway in going, while he must come to her by the opposite side. But she would walk very quickly and watch very closely. If she did not see him as she crossed and recrossed, she would at any rate be on the spot indicated at the time named. The autumn evenings had become somewhat chilly, and she wrapped her thin cloak close round her, as she felt the night air as she came upon the open bridge. But she was not cold. She told herself that she could not and would not be cold. How could she be cold when she was going to meet her lover? The night was dark, for the moon was now gone and the wind was blowing; but there were a few stars bright in the heaven, and when she looked down through the parapets of the bridge, there was just light enough for her to see the black water flowing fast beneath her. She crossed quickly to the figure of St. John, that she might look closely on those passing on the other side, and after a few moments recrossed the road. It was the figure of the saint, St. John Nepomucene, who was thrown from this very bridge and drowned, and who has ever since been the protector of good Christians from the fate which he himself had suffered. Then Nina bethought herself whether she was a good Christian, and whether St. John of the Bridge would be justified in interposing on her behalf, should she be in want of him. She had strong doubts as to the validity of her own Christianity, now that she loved a Jew; and feared that it was more than probable that St. John would do nothing for her, were she in such a strait as that in which he was supposed to interfere. But why now should she think of any such danger? Lotta Luxa had told her to drown herself when she should find herself to have been jilted by her Jew lover; but her Jew lover was true to her; she had his dear words at that moment in her bosom, and in a few moments her hand would be resting on his arm. So she passed on from the statue of St. John, with her mind made up that she did not want St. John's aid. Some other saint she would want, no doubt, and she prayed a little silent prayer to St. Nicholas, that he would allow her to marry the Jew without taking offence at her. Her circumstances had been very hard, as the saint must know, and she had meant to do her best. Might it not be possible, if the saint would help her, that she might convert her husband? But as she thought of this, she shook her head. Anton Trendellsohn was not a man to be changed in his religion by any words which she could use. It would be much more probable, she knew, that the conversion would be the other way. And she thought she would not mind that, if only it could be a real conversion. But if she were induced to say that she was a Jewess, while she still believed in St. Nicholas and St. John, and in the beautiful face of the dear Virgin,—if to please her husband she were to call herself a Jewess while she was at heart a Christian,—then her state would be very wretched. She prayed again to St. Nicholas to keep her from that state. If she were to become a Jewess, she hoped that St. Nicholas would let her go altogether, heart and soul, into Judaism.

When she reached the end of the long bridge she looked anxiously up the street by which she knew that he must come, endeavouring to discover his figure by the glimmering light of an oil-lamp that hung at an angle in the street, or by the brighter glare which came from the gas in a shop-window by which he must pass. She stood thus looking and looking till she thought he would never come. Then she heard the clock in the old watch-tower of the bridge over her head strike three-quarters, and she became aware that, instead of her lover being after his time, she had yet to wait a quarter of an hour for the exact moment which he had appointed. She did not in the least mind waiting. She had been a little uneasy when she thought that he had neglected or forgotten his own appointment. So she turned again and walked back towards the Kleinseite, fixing her eyes, as she had so often done, on the rows of windows which glittered along the great dark mass of the Hradschin Palace. What were they all doing up there, those slow and faded courtiers to an ex-Emperor, that they should want to burn so many candles? Thinking of this she passed the tablet on the bridge, and, according to her custom, put the end of her fingers on it. But as she was raising her hand to her mouth to kiss it she remembered that the saint might not like such service from one who was already half a Jew at heart, and she refrained. She refrained, and then considered whether the bridge might not topple down with her into the stream because of her iniquity. But it did not topple down, and now she was standing beyond any danger from the water at the exact spot which Trendellsohn had named. She stood still lest she might possibly miss him by moving, till she was again cold. But she did not regard that, though she pressed her cloak closely round her limbs. She did not move till she heard the first sound of the bell as it struck eight, and then she gave a little jump as she found that her lover was close upon her.

'So you are here, Nina,' he said, putting his hand upon her arm.

'Of course I am here, Anton. I have been looking, and looking, and looking, thinking you never would come; and how did you get here?'

'I am as punctual as the clock, my love.'

'Oh yes, you are punctual, I know; but where did you come from?'

'I came down the hill from the Hradschin. I have had business there. It did not occur to your simplicity that I could reach you otherwise than by the direct road from my own home.'

'I never thought of your coming from the side of the Hradschin,' said Nina, wondering whether any of those lights she had seen could have been there for the use of Anton Trendellsohn. 'I am so glad you have come to me. It is so good of you.'

'It is good of you to come and meet me, my own one. But you are cold. Let us walk, and you will be warmer.'

Nina, who had already put her hand upon her lover's arm, thrust it in a little farther, encouraged by such sweet words; and then he took her little hand in his, and drew her still nearer to him, till she was clinging to him very closely. 'Nina, my own one,' he said again. He had never before been in so sweet a mood with her. Walk with him? Yes; she would walk with him all night if he would let her. Instead of turning again over the bridge as she had expected, he took her back into the Kleinseite, not bearing round to the right in the direction of her own house, but going up the hill into a large square, round which the pathway is covered by the overhanging houses, as is common for avoidance of heat in Southern cities. Here, under the low colonnade, it was very dark, and the passengers going to and fro were not many. At each angle of the square where the neighbouring streets entered it, in the open space, there hung a dull, dim oil-lamp; but other light there was none. Nina, however, did not mind the darkness while Anton Trendellsohn was with her. Even when walking close under the but-tresses of St. Nicholas*—of St. Nicholas, who could not but have been offended—close under the very niche in which stood the statue of the saint—she had no uncomfortable qualms. When Anton was with her she did not much regard the saints. It was when she was alone that those thoughts on her religion came to disturb her mind.

'I do so like walking with you,' she said. 'It is the nicest way of talking in the world.'

'I want to ask you a question, Nina,' said Anton; 'or perhaps two questions.' The tight grasping clasp made on his arm by the tips of her fingers relaxed itself a little as she heard his words, and remarked their altered tone. It was not, then, to be all love; and she could perceive that he was going to be serious with her, and, as she feared, perhaps angry. Whenever he spoke to her on any matter of business, his manner was so very serious as to assume in her eyes, when judged by her feelings, an appearance of anger. The Jew immediately felt the little movement of her fingers, and hastened to reassure her. 'I am quite sure that your answers will satisfy me.'

'I hope so,' said Nina. But the pressure of her hand upon his arm was not at once repeated.

'I have seen your cousin Ziska, Nina; indeed, I have seen him twice lately; and I have seen your uncle and your aunt.'

'I suppose they did not say anything very pleasant about me.'

'They did not say anything very pleasant about anybody or about anything. They were not very anxious to be pleasant; but that I did not mind.'

'I hope they did not insult you, Anton?'

'We Jews are used as yet to insolence from Christians, and do not mind it.'

'They shall never more be anything to me, if they have insulted you.'

'It is nothing, Nina. We bear those things, and think that such of you Christians as use that liberty of a vulgar tongue, which is still possible towards a Jew in Prague, are simply poor in heart and ignorant.'

'They are poor in heart and ignorant.'

'I first went to your uncle's office in the Ross Markt, where I saw him and your aunt and Ziska. And afterwards Ziska came to me, at our own house. He was tame enough then.'

'To your own house?'

'Yes; to the Jews' quarter. Was it not a condescension?

He came into our synagogue and ferreted me out. You may be sure that he had something very special to say when he did that. But he looked as though he thought that his life were in danger among us.'

'But, Anton, what had he to say?'

'I will tell you. He wanted to buy me off.'

'Buy you off!'

'Yes; to bribe me to give you up. Aunt Sophie does not relish the idea of having a Jew for her nephew.'

'Aunt Sophie!—but I will never call her Aunt Sophie again. Do you mean that they offered you money?'

'They offered me property, my dear, which is the same. But they did it economically, for they only offered me my own. They were kind enough to suggest that if I would merely break my word to you, they would tell me how I could get the title-deeds of the houses, and thus have the power of turning your father out into the street.'

'You have the power. He would go at once if you bade him.'

'I do not wish him to go. As I have told you often, he is welcome to the use of the house. He shall have it for his life, as far as I am concerned. But I should like to have what is my own.'

'And what did you say?' Nina, as she asked the question, was very careful not to tighten her hold upon his arm by the weight of a single ounce.

'What did I say? I said that I had many things that I valued greatly, but that I had one thing that I valued more than gold or houses—more even than my right.'

'And what is that?' said Nina, stopping suddenly, so that she might hear clearly every syllable of the words which were to come. 'What is that?' She did not even yet add an ounce to the pressure; but her fingers were ready.

'A poor thing,' said Anton; 'just the heart of a Christian girl.'

Then the hand was tightened, or rather the two hands, for they were closed together upon his arm; and his other arm was wound round her waist; and then, in the gloom of the dark colonnade, he pressed her to his bosom, and

kissed her lips and her forehead, and then her lips again.
'No,' he said, 'they have not bribed high enough yet to
get from me my treasure—my treasure.'

'Dearest, am I your treasure?'

'Are you not? What else have I that I make equal to
you?' Nina was supremely happy—triumphant in her
happiness. She cared nothing for her aunt, nothing for
Lotta Luxa and her threats; and very little at the present
moment even for St. Nicholas or St. John of the Bridge.
To be told by her lover that she was his own treasure,
was sufficient to banish for the time all her miseries and
all her fears.

'You are my treasure. I want you to remember that,
and to believe it,' said the Jew.

'I will believe it,' said Nina, trembling with anxious
eagerness. Could it be possible that she would ever
forget it?

'And now I will ask my questions. Where are those
title-deeds?'

'Where are they?' said she, repeating his question.

'Yes; where are they?'

'Why do you ask me? And why do you look like that?'

'I want you to tell me where they are, to the best of
your knowledge.'

'Uncle Karil has them,—or else Ziska.'

'You are sure of that?'

'How can I be sure? I am not sure at all. But Ziska
said something which made me feel sure of it, as I told
you before. And I have supposed always that they must
be in the Ross Markt. Where else can they be?'

'Your aunt says that you have got them.'

'That I have got them?'

'Yes, you. That is what she intends me to understand.'
The Jew had stopped at one of the corners, close under
the little lamp, and looked intently into Nina's face as he
spoke to her.

'And you believe her?' said Nina.

But he went on without noticing her question. 'She
intends me to believe that you have got them, and are
keeping them from me fraudulently! cheating me, in

point of fact;—that you are cheating me, so that you may have some hold over the property for your own purposes. That is what your aunt wishes me to believe. She is a wise woman, is she not? and very clever. In one breath she tries to bribe me to give you up, and in the next she wants to convince me that you are not worth keeping.'

'But, Anton——'

'Nay, Nina, I will not put you to the trouble of protestation. Look at that star. I should as soon suspect the light which God has placed in the heaven of misleading me, as I should suspect you.'

'Oh, Anton, dear Anton, I do so love you for saying that! Would it be possible that I should keep anything from you?'

'I think you would keep nothing from me. Were you to do so, you could not be my own love any longer. A man's wife must be true to him in everything, or she is not his wife. I could endure not only no fraud from you, but neither could I endure falsehood.'

'I have never been false to you. With God's help I never will be false to you.'

'He has given you His help. He has made you truehearted, and I do not doubt you. Now answer me another question. Is it possible that your father should have the paper?'

Nina paused a moment, and then she replied with eagerness, 'Quite impossible. I am sure that he knows nothing of it more than you know.' When she had so spoken they walked in silence for a few yards, but Anton did not at once reply to her. 'You do not think that father is keeping anything from you, do you?' said Nina.

'I do not know,' said the Jew. 'I am not sure.'

'You may be sure. You may be quite sure. Father is at least honest.'

'I have always thought so.'

'And do you not think so still?'

'Look here, Nina. I do not know that there is a Christian in Prague who would feel it to be beneath him to rob a Jew, and I do not altogether blame them. They believe that we would rob them, and many of us do so.

We are very sharp, each on the other, dealing against each other always in hatred, never in love—never even in friendship.'

'But, for all that, my father has never wronged you.'

'He should not do so, for I am endeavouring to be kind to him. For your sake, Nina, I would treat him as though he were a Jew himself.'

'He has never wronged you;—I am sure that he has never wronged you.'

'Nina, you are more to me than you are to him.'

'Yes, I am—I am your own; but yet I will declare that he has never wronged you.'

'And I should be more to you than he is.'

'You are more—you are everything to me; but, still, I know that he has never wronged you.'

Then the Jew paused again, still walking onwards through the dark colonnade with her hand upon his arm. They walked in silence the whole side of the large square, Nina waiting patiently to hear what would come next, and Trendellsohn considering what words he would use. He did suspect her father, and it was needful to his purpose that he should tell her so; and it was needful also, as he thought, that she should be made to understand that in her loyalty and truth to him she must give up her father, or even suspect her father, if his purpose required that she should do so. Though she were still a Christian herself, she must teach herself to look at other Christians, even at those belonging to herself, with Jewish eyes. Unless she could do so she would not be true and loyal to him with that truth and loyalty which he required. Poor Nina! It was the dearest wish of her heart to be true and loyal to him in all things; but it might be possible to put too hard a strain even upon such love as hers. 'Nina,' the Jew said, 'I fear your father. I think that he is deceiving us.'

'No, Anton, no! he is not deceiving you. My aunt and uncle and Ziska are deceiving you.'

'They are trying to deceive me, no doubt; but as far as I can judge from their own words and looks, they do believe that at this moment the document which I want is in your father's house. As far as I can judge their thoughts from their words, they think that it is there.'

'It is not there,' said Nina, positively.

'That is what we must find out. Your uncle was silent. He said nothing, or next to nothing.'

'He is the best of the three, by far,' said Nina.

'Your aunt is a clever woman in spite of her blunder about you; and had I dealt with her only I should have thought that she might have expressed herself as she did, and still have had the paper in her own keeping. I could not read her mind as I could read his. Women will lie better than men.'

'But men can lie too,' said Nina.

'Your cousin Ziska is a fool.'

'He is a fox,' said Nina.

'He is a fool in comparison with his mother. And I had him in my own house, under my thumb, as it were. Of course he lied. Of course he tried to deceive me. But, Nina, he believes that the document is here,—in your house. Whether it be there or not, Ziska thinks that it is there.'

'Ziska is more fox than fool,' said Nina.

'Let that be as it may, I tell you the truth of him. He thinks it is here. Now, Nina, you must search for it.'

'It is not there, Anton. I tell you of my own knowledge, it is not in the house. Come and search yourself. Come to-morrow. Come to-night, if you will.'

'It would be of no use. I could not search as you can do. Tell me, Nina; has your father no place locked up which is not open to you?'

'Yes; he has his old desk; you know it, where it stands in the parlour.'

'You never open that?'

'No, never; but there is nothing there—nothing of that nature.'

'How can you tell? Or he can keep it about his person?'

'He keeps it nowhere. He has not got it. Dear Anton, put it out of your head. You do not know my cousin Ziska. That he has it in his own hands I am now sure.'

'And I, Nina, am sure that it is here in the Kleinseite —or at least am sure that he thinks it to be so. The question now is this: Will you obey me in what directions I may give you concerning it?' Nina could not bring herself to give an unqualified reply to this demand on the spur of the moment. Perhaps it occurred to her that the time for such implicit obedience on her part had hardly yet come—that as yet at least she must not be less true to her father than to her lover. She hesitated, therefore, in answering him. 'Do you not understand me, Nina?' he said, roughly. 'I asked you whether you will do as I would have you do, and you make no reply. We two, Nina, must be one in all things, or else we must be apart—in all things.'

'I do not know what it is you wish of me,' she said, trembling.

'I wish you to obey me.'

'But suppose——'

'I know that you must trust me first before you can obey me.'

'I do trust you. You know that I trust you.'

'Then you should obey me.'

'But not to suspect my own father!'

'I do not ask you to suspect him.'

'But you suspect him?'

'Yes; I do. I am older than you, and know more of men and their ways than you can do. I do suspect him. You must promise me that you will search for this deed.'

Again she paused, but after a moment or two a thought struck her, and she replied eagerly, 'Anton, I will tell you what I will do. I will ask him openly. He and I have always been open to each other.'

'If he is concealing it, do you think he will tell you?'

'Yes, he would tell me. But he is not concealing it.'

'Will you look?'

'I cannot take his keys from him and open his box.'

'You mean that you will not do as I bid you?'

'I cannot do it. Consider of it, Anton. Could you treat your own father in such a way?'

'I would cling to you sooner than to him. I have told

him so, and he has threatened to turn me penniless from
his house. Still I shall cling to you,—because you are my
love. I shall do so if you are equally true to me. That is
my idea of love. There can be no divided allegiance.'

And this also was Nina's idea of love—an idea up to
which she had striven to act and live when those around
her had threatened her with all that earth and heaven
could do to her if she would not abandon the Jew. But
she had anticipated no such trial as that which had now
come upon her. 'Dear Anton,' she said, appealing to
him weakly in her weakness, 'if you did but know how
I love you!'

'You must prove your love.'

'Am I not ready to prove it? Would I not give up
anything, everything, for you?'

'Then you must assist me in this thing, as I am desiring
you.' As he said this they had reached the corner from
whence the street ran in the direction of the bridge, and
into this he turned instead of continuing their walk round
the square. She said nothing as he did so; but accompanied him, still leaning upon his arm. He walked on
quickly and in silence till they came to the turn which
led towards Balatka's house, and then he stopped. 'It is
late,' said he, 'and you had better go home.'

'May I not cross the bridge with you?'

'You had better go home.' His voice was very stern,
and as she dropped her hand from his arm she felt it to
be impossible to leave him in that way. Were she to do
so, she would never be allowed to speak to him or to see
him again. 'Good-night,' he said, preparing to turn
from her.

'Anton, Anton, do not leave me like that.'

'How then shall I leave you? Shall I say that it does
not matter whether you obey me or no? It does matter.
Between you and me such obedience matters everything.
If we are to be together, I must abandon everything for
you, and you must comply in everything with me.' Then
Nina, leaning close upon him, whispered into his ear that
she would obey him.

CHAPTER IX

NINA's misery as she went home was almost complete. She had not, indeed, quarrelled with her lover, who had again caressed her as she left him, and assured her of his absolute confidence, but she had undertaken a task against which her very soul revolted. It gave her no comfort to say to herself that she had undertaken to look for that which she knew she would not find, and that therefore her search could do no harm. She had, in truth, consented to become a spy upon her father, and was so to do in furtherance of the views of one who suspected her father of fraud, and who had not scrupled to tell her that her father was dishonest. Now again she thought of St. Nicholas, as she heard the dull chime of the clock from the saint's tower, and found herself forced to acknowledge that she was doing very wickedly in loving a Jew. Of course troubles would come upon her. What else could she expect? Had she not endeavoured to throw behind her and to trample under foot all that she had learned from her infancy under the guidance of St. Nicholas? Of course the saint would desert her. The very sound of the chime told her that he was angry with her. How could she hope again that St. John would be good to her? Was it not to be expected that the black-flowing river over which she understood him to preside would become her enemy and would swallow her up,— as Lotta Luxa had predicted? Before she returned home, when she was quite sure that Anton Trendellsohn had already passed over, she went down upon the bridge, and far enough along the causeway to find herself over the river, and there, crouching down, she looked at the rapid-running silent black stream beneath her. The waters were very silent and very black, but she could still see or feel that they were running rapidly. And they were cold, too. She herself at the present moment was very cold. She shuddered as she looked down, pressing her face against the stone-work, with her two hands resting on two of the pillars of the parapet. It would be very terrible.

She did not think that she much cared for death. The world had been so hard to her, and was growing so much harder, that it would be a good thing to get away from it. If she could become ill and die, with a good kind nun standing by her bedside, and with the cross pressed to her bosom, and with her eyes fixed on the sweet face of the Virgin Mother as it was painted in the little picture in her room,—in that way she thought that death might even be grateful. But to be carried away she knew not whither in the cold, silent, black-flowing Moldau! And yet she half believed the prophecy of Lotta. Such a quiet death as that she had pictured to herself could not be given to her! What nun would come to her bedside,— to the bed of a girl who had declared to all Prague that she intended to marry a Jew? For weeks past she had feared even to look at the picture of the Virgin.

'I'm afraid you'll think I am very late, father,' she said, as soon as she reached home.

Her father muttered something, but not angrily, and she soon busied herself about him, doing some little thing for his comfort, as was her wont. But as she did so she could not but remember that she had undertaken to be a spy upon him, to secrete his key, and to search surreptitiously for that which he was supposed to be keeping fraudulently. As she sat by him empty-handed —for it was Sunday night, and as a Christian she never worked with a needle upon the Sunday*—she told herself that she could not do it. Could there be any harm done were she to ask him now, openly, what papers he kept in that desk? But she desired to obey her lover where obedience was possible, and he had expressly forbidden her to ask any such question. She sat, therefore, and said no word that could tend to ease her suffering; and then, when the time came, she went suffering to her bed.

On the next day there seemed to come to her no opportunity for doing that which she had to do. Souchey was in and out of the house all the morning, explaining to her that they had almost come to the end of the flour and of the potatoes which he had bought, that he himself had swallowed on the previous evening the last tip of the

great sausage—for, as he had alleged, it was no use a
fellow dying of starvation outright—and that there was
hardly enough of chocolate left to make three cups.
Nina had brought out her necklace and had asked
Souchey to take it to the shop and do the best with it he
could; but Souchey had declined the commission, alleging that he would be accused of having stolen it; and
Nina had then prepared to go herself, but her father had
called her, and he had come out into the sitting-room
and had remained there during the afternoon, so that
both the sale of the trinket and the search in the desk had
been postponed. The latter she might have done at
night, but when the night came the deed seemed to be
more horrid than it would be even in the day.

She observed also, more accurately than she had ever
done before, that he always carried the key of his desk
with him. He did not, indeed, put it under his pillow,
or conceal it in bed, but he placed it with an old spectacle-
case which he always carried, and a little worn pocket-
book which Nina knew to be empty, on a low table
which stood at his bed-head; and now during the whole
of the afternoon he had the key on the table beside him.
Nina did not doubt but that she could take the key while
he was asleep; for when he was even half asleep—which
was perhaps his most customary state—he would not stir
when she entered the room. But if she took it at all, she
would do so in the day. She could not bring herself to
creep into the room in the night, and to steal the key in
the dark. As she lay in bed she still thought of it. She
had promised her lover that she would do this thing.
Should she resolve not to do it, in spite of that promise,
she must at any rate tell Anton of her resolution. She
must tell him, and then there would be an end of everything. Would it be possible for her to live without her
love?

On the following morning it occurred to her that she
might perhaps be able to induce her father to speak of
the houses, and of those horrid documents of which she
had heard so much, without disobeying any of Trendellsohn's behests. There could, she thought, be no harm in

her asking her father some question as to the ownership
of the houses, and as to the Jew's right to the property.
Her father had very often declared in her presence that
old Trendellsohn could turn him into the street at any
moment. There had been no secrets between her and
her father as to their poverty, and there could be no
reason why her tongue should now be silenced, so long
as she refrained from any positive disobedience to her
lover's commands. That he must be obeyed she still
recognised as the strongest rule of all—obeyed, that is,
till she should go to him and lay down her love at his
feet, and give back to him the troth which he had given her.

'Father,' she said to the old man about noon that day,
'I suppose this house does belong to the Trendellsohns?'

'Of course it does,' said he, crossly.

'Belongs to them altogether, I mean?' she said.

'I don't know what you call altogether. It does belong
to them, and there's an end of it. What's the good of
talking about it?'

'Only if so, they ought to have those deeds they are so
anxious about. Everybody ought to have what is his own.
Don't you think so, father?'

'I am keeping nothing from them,' said he; 'you don't
suppose that I want to rob them?'

'Of course you do not.' Then Nina paused again.
She was drawing perilously near to forbidden ground, if
she were not standing on it already; and yet she was very
anxious that the subject should not be dropped between
her and her father.

'I'm sure you do not want to rob any one, father.
But——'

'But what? I suppose young Trendellsohn has been
talking to you again about it. I suppose he suspects me;
if so, no doubt, you will suspect me too.'

'Oh, father! how can you be so cruel?'

'If he thinks the papers are here, it is his own house;
let him come and search for them.'

'He will not do that, I am sure.'

'What is it he wants, then? I can't go out to your
uncle and make him give them up.'

'They are, then, with uncle?'

'I suppose so; but how am I to know? You see how they treat me. I cannot go to them, and they never come to me;—except when that woman comes to scold.'

'But they can't belong to uncle.'

'Of course they don't.'

'Then why should he keep them? What good can they do him? When I spoke to Ziska, Ziska said they should be kept, because Trendellsohn is a Jew; but surely a Jew has a right to his own. We at any rate ought to do what we can for him, Jew as he is, since he lets us live in his house.'

The slight touch of irony which Nina had thrown into her voice when she spoke of what was due to her lover even though he was a Jew was not lost upon her father. 'Of course you would take his part against a Christian,' he said.

'I take no one's part against any one,' said she, 'except so far as right is concerned. If we take a Jew's money, I think we should give him the thing which he purchases.'

'Who is keeping him from it?' said Balatka, angrily.

'Well;—I suppose it is my uncle,' replied Nina.

'Why cannot you let me be at peace then?'

Having so said he turned himself round to the wall, and Nina felt herself to be in a worse position than ever. There was nothing now for her but to take the key, or else to tell her lover that she would not obey him. There could be no further hope in diplomacy. She had just resolved that she could not take the key—that in spite of her promise she could not bring herself to treat her father after such fashion as that—when the old man turned suddenly round upon her again, and went back to the subject.

'I have got a letter somewhere from Karil Zamenoy,' said he, 'telling me that the deed is in his own chest.'

'Have you, father?' said she, anxiously, but struggling to repress her anxiety.

'I had it, I know. It was written ever so long ago— before I had settled with the Trendellsohns; but I have seen it often since. Take the key and unlock the desk, and bring me the bundle of papers that are tied with an old tape; or—stop—bring me all the papers.' With trembling hand Nina took the key. She was now desired by her father to do exactly that which her lover wished her to have done; or, better still, her father was about to do the thing himself. She would at any rate have positive proof that the paper was not in her father's desk. He had desired her to bring all the papers, so that there would be no doubt left. She took the key very gently,—as softly as was possible to her, and went slowly into the other room. When there she unlocked the desk and took out the bundle of letters tied with an old tape which lay at the top ready to her hand. Then she collected together the other papers, which were not many, and without looking at them carried them to her father. She studiously avoided any scrutiny of what there might be, even by so much as a glance of her eye. 'This seems to be all there is, father, except one or two old account-books.'

He took the bundle, and with feeble hands untied the tape and moved the documents, one by one. Nina felt that she was fully warranted in looking at them now, as her father was in fact showing them to her. In this way she would be able to give evidence in his favour without having had recourse to any ignoble practice. The old man moved every paper in the bundle, and she could see that they were all letters. She had understood that the deed for which Trendellsohn had desired her to search was written on a larger paper than any she now saw, and that she might thus know it at once. There was, certainly, no such deed among the papers which her father slowly turned over, and which he slowly proceeded to tie up again with the old tape. 'I am sure I saw it the other day,' he said, fingering among the loose papers while Nina looked on with anxious eyes. Then at last he found the letter from Karil Zamenoy, and having read it himself, gave it her to read. It was dated seven or eight years back, at a time when Balatka was only on his way to ruin—not absolutely ruined, as was the case with him now—and contained an offer on Zamenoy's part to give

safe custody to certain documents which were named,
and among which the deed now sought for stood first.

'And has he got all those other papers?' Nina asked.

'No! he has none of them, unless he has this. There
is nothing left but this one that the Jew wants.'

'And uncle Karil has never given that back?'

'Never.'

'And it should belong to Stephen Trendellsohn?'

'Yes, I suppose it should.'

'Who can wonder, then, that they should be anxious
and inquire after it, and make a noise about it? Will not
the law make uncle Karil give it up?'

'How can the law prove that he has got it? I know
nothing about the law. Put them all back again.' Then
Nina replaced the papers and locked the desk. She had,
at any rate, been absolutely and entirely successful in her
diplomacy, and would be able to assure Anton Trendellsohn, of her own knowledge, that that which he sought
was not in her father's keeping.

On the same day she went out to sell her necklace.
She waited till it was nearly dark—till the first dusk of
evening had come upon the street—and then she crossed
the bridge and hurried to a jeweller's shop in the Grosser
Ring which she had often observed, and at which she
knew such trinkets as hers were customarily purchased.
The Grosser Ring is an open space—such as we call a
square—in the oldest part of the town, and in it stand
the Town Hall and the Theinkirche—which may be
regarded as the most special church in Prague, as there
for many years were taught the doctrines of Huss,* the
great Reformer of Bohemia. Here, in the Grosser Ring,
there was generally a crowd of an evening, as Nina knew,
and she thought that she could go in and out of the
jeweller's shop without observation. She believed that
she might be able to borrow money on her treasure,
leaving it as a deposit; and this, if possible, she would do.
There were regular pawnbrokers in the town, by whom
no questions would be made, who, of course, would lend
her money in the ordinary way of their trade; but she
believed that such people would advance to her but a

very small portion of the value of her necklace; and then,
if, as would be too probable, she could not redeem it, the
necklace would be gone, and gone without a price!

'Yes, it is my own, altogether my own—my very own.'
She had to explain all the circumstances to the jeweller,
and at last, with a view of quelling any suspicion, she
told the jeweller what was her name, and explained how
poor were the circumstances of her house. 'But you must
be the niece of Madame Zamenoy, in the Windberg-
gasse,' said the jeweller. And then, when Nina with
hesitation acknowledged that such was the case, the man
asked her why she did not go to her rich aunt, instead of
selling a trinket which must be so valuable.

'No!' said Nina, 'I cannot do that. If you will lend
me something of its value, I shall be so much obliged
to you.'

'But Madame Zamenoy would surely help you?'

'We would not take it from her. But we will not speak
of that, sir. Can I have the money?' Then the jeweller
gave her a receipt for the necklace and took her receipt
for the sum he lent her. It was more than Nina had
expected, and she rejoiced that she had so well completed
her business. Nevertheless she wished that the jeweller
had known nothing of her aunt. She was hardly out of
the shop before she met her cousin Ziska, and she so met
him that she could not escape him. She heard his voice,
indeed, almost as soon as she recognised him, and had
stopped at his summons before she had calculated whether
it might not be better to run away. 'What, Nina! is that
you?' said Ziska, taking her hand before she knew how
to refuse it to him.

'Yes; it is I,' said Nina.

'What are you doing here?'

'Why should I not be in the Grosser Ring as well as
another? It is open to rich and poor.'

'So is Rapinsky's shop; but poor people do not generally have much to do there.' Rapinsky was the name of
the jeweller who had advanced the money to Nina.

'No, not much,' said Nina. 'What little they have to
sell is soon sold.'

'And have you been selling anything?'

'Nothing of yours, Ziska.'   •

'But have you been selling anything?'

'Why do you ask me? What business is it of yours?'

'They say that Anton Trendellsohn, the Jew, gives you all that you want,' said Ziska.

'Then they say lies,' said Nina, her eyes flashing fire upon her Christian lover through the gloom of the evening. 'Who says so? You say so. No one else would be mean enough to be so false.'

'All Prague says so.'

'All Prague! I know what that means. And did all Prague go to the Jews' quarter last Saturday, to tell Anton Trendellsohn that the paper which he wants, and which is his own, was in father's keeping? Was it all Prague told that falsehood also?' There was a scorn in her face as she spoke which distressed Ziska greatly, but which he did not know how to meet or how to answer. He wanted to be brave before her; and he wanted also to show his affection for her, if only he knew how to do so, without making himself humble in her presence.

'Shall I tell you, Nina, why I went to the Jews' quarter on Saturday?'

'No; tell me nothing. I wish to hear nothing from you. I know enough without your telling me.'

'I wish to save you if it be possible, because—because I love you.'

'And I—I never wish to see you again, because I hate you. I hate you, because you have been cruel. But let me tell you this; poor as we are, I have never taken a farthing of Anton's money. When I am his wife, as I hope to be—as I hope to be—I will take what he gives me as though it came from heaven. From you!—I would sooner die in the street than take a crust of bread from you.' Then she darted from him, and succeeded in escaping without hearing the words with which he replied to her angry taunts. She was woman enough to understand that her keenest weapon for wounding him would be an expression of unbounded love and confidence as to the man who was his rival; and therefore, though she was compelled to deny that she had lived on the charity of her lover, she had coupled her denial with an assurance of her faith and affection, which was, no doubt, bitter enough in Ziska's ears. 'I do believe that she is witched,' he said, as he turned away towards his own house. And then he reflected wisely on the backward tendency of the world in general, and regretted much that there was no longer given to priests in Bohemia the power of treating with salutary ecclesiastical severity patients suffering in the way in which his cousin Nina was afflicted.

Nina had hardly got out of the Grosser Ring into the narrow street which leads from thence towards the bridge, when she encountered her other lover. He was walking slowly down the centre of the street when she passed him, or would have passed him, had not she recognised his figure through the gloom. 'Anton,' she said, coming up to him and touching his arm as lightly as was possible, 'I am so glad to meet you here.'

'Nina?'

'Yes; Nina.'

'And what have you been doing?'

'I don't know that I want to tell you; only that I like to tell you everything.'

'If so, you can tell me this.' Nina, however, hesitated. 'If you have secrets, I do not want to inquire into them,' said the Jew.

'I would rather have no secrets from you, only——'

'Only what?'

'Well; I will tell you. I had a necklace; and we are not very rich, you know, at home; and I wanted to get something for father, and——'

'You have sold it?'

'No; I have not sold it. The man was very civil, indeed quite kind, and he lent me some money.'

'But the kind man kept the necklace, I suppose.'

'Of course he kept the necklace. You would not have me borrow money from a stranger, and leave him nothing?'

'No; I would not have you do that. But why not borrow from one who is no stranger?'

'I do not want to borrow at all,' said Nina, in her lowest tone.

'Are you ashamed to come to me in your trouble?'

'Yes,' said Nina. 'I should be ashamed to come to you for money. I would not take it from you.'

He did not answer her at once, but walked on slowly while she kept close to his side.

'Give me the jeweller's docket,' he said at last. Nina hesitated for a moment, and then he repeated his demand in a sterner voice. 'Nina, give me the jeweller's docket.' Then she put her hand in her pocket and gave it him. She was very averse to doing so, but she was more averse to refusing him aught that he asked of her.

'I have got something to tell you, Anton,' she said, as soon as he had put the jeweller's paper into his purse.

'Well—what is it?'

'I have seen every paper and every morsel of everything that is in father's desk, and there is no sign of the deed you want.'

'And how did you see them?'

'He showed them to me.'

'You told him, then, what I had said to you?'

'No; I told him nothing about it. He gave me the key, and desired me to fetch him all the papers. He wanted to find a letter which uncle Karil wrote him ever so long ago. In that letter uncle Karil acknowledges that he has the deed.'

'I do not doubt that in the least.'

'And what is it you do doubt, Anton?'

'I do not say I doubt anything.'

'Do you doubt me, Anton?'

There was a little pause before he answered her—the slightest moment of hesitation. But had it been but half as much, Nina's ear and Nina's heart would have detected it. 'No,' said Anton, 'I am not saying that I doubt any one.'

'If you doubt me, you will kill me. I am at any rate true to you. What is it you want? What is it you think?'

'They tell me that the document is in the house in the Kleinseite.'

'Who are they? Who is it that tells you?'

'More than one. Your uncle and aunt said so;—and Ziska Zamenoy came to me on purpose to repeat the same.'

'And would you believe what Ziska says? I have hardly thought it worth my while to tell you that Ziska——'

'To tell me what of Ziska?'

'That Ziska pretends to—to want that I should be his wife. I would not look at him if there were not another man in Prague. I hate him. He is a liar. Would you believe Ziska?'

'And another has told me.'

'Another?' said Nina, considering.

'Yes, another.'

'Lotta Luxa, I suppose.'

'Never mind. They say indeed that it is you who have the deed.'

'And you believe them?'

'No, I do not believe them. But why do they say so?'

'Must I explain that? How can I tell? Anton, do you not believe that the woman who loves you will be true to you?'

Then he paused again—'Nina, sometimes I think that I have been mad to love a Christian.'

'What have I been then? But I do love you, Anton— I love you better than all the world. I care nothing for Jew or Christian. When I think of you, I care nothing for heaven or earth. You are everything to me, because I love you. How could I deceive you?'

'Nina, Nina, my own one!' he said.

'And as I love you, so do you love me? Say that you love me also.'

'I do,' said he—'I love you as I love my own soul.'

Then they parted; and Nina, as she went home, tried to make herself happy with the assurance which had been given to her by the last words her lover had spoken; but still there remained with her that suspicion of a doubt which, if it really existed, would be so cruel an injury to her love.

CHAPTER X

SOME days passed on after the visit to the jeweller's shop,
—perhaps ten or twelve,—before Nina heard from or
saw her lover again; and during that time she had no
tidings from her relatives in the Windberg-gasse. Life
went on very quietly in the old house, and not the less
quietly because the proceeds of the necklace saved Nina
from any further immediate necessity of searching for
money. The cold weather had come, or rather weather
that was cold in the morning and cold in the evening,
and old Balatka kept his bed altogether. His state was
such that no one could say why he should not get up and
dress himself, and he himself continued to speak of some
future time when he would do so; but there he was, lying
in his bed, and Nina told herself that in all probability
she would never see him about the house again. For herself, she was becoming painfully anxious that some day
should be fixed for her marriage. She knew that she was,
herself, ignorant in such matters; and she knew also that
there was no woman near her from whom she could seek
counsel. Were she to go to some matron of the neighbourhood, her neighbour would only rebuke her, because
she loved a Jew. She had boldly told her relatives of her
love, and by doing so had shut herself out from all assistance from them. From even her father she could get no
sympathy; though with him her engagement had become
so far a thing sanctioned, that he had ceased to speak of
it in words of reproach. But when was it to be? She had
more than once made up her mind that she would ask
her lover, but her courage had never as yet mounted
high enough in his presence to allow her to do so. When
he was with her, their conversation always took such a
turn that before she left him she was happy enough if she
could only draw from him an assurance that he was not
forgetting to love her. Of any final time for her marriage
he never said a word. In the mean time she and her
father might starve! They could not live on the price of
a necklace for ever. She had not made up her mind—

she never could make up her mind—as to what might be
best for her father when she should be married; but she
had made up her mind that when that happy time should
come, she would simply obey her husband. He would
tell her what would be best for her father. But in the
mean time there was no word of her marriage; and now
she had been ten days in the Kleinseite without once
having had so much as a message from her lover. How
was it possible that she should continue to live in such a
condition as this?

She was sitting one morning very forlorn in the big
parlour, looking out upon the birds who were pecking
among the dust in the courtyard below, when her eye
just caught the drapery of the dress of some woman who
had entered the arched gateway. Nina, from her place
by the window, could see out through the arch, and no
one therefore could come through their gate while she
was at her seat without passing under her eye; but on
this occasion the birds had distracted her attention, and
she had not caught a sight of the woman's face or figure.
Could it be her aunt come to torture her again—her and
her father? She knew that Souchey was down-stairs,
hanging somewhere in idleness about the door, and
therefore she did not leave her place. If it were indeed
her aunt, her aunt might come up there to seek her. Or
it might possibly be Lotta Luxa, who, next to her aunt,
was of all women the most disagreeable to Nina. Lotta,
indeed, was not so hard to bear as aunt Sophie, because
Lotta could be answered sharply, and could be told to go,
if matters proceeded to extremities. In such a case Lotta
no doubt would not go; but still the power of desiring
her to do so was much. Then Nina remembered that
Lotta never wore her petticoats so full as was the morsel
of drapery which she had seen. And as she thought of
this there came a low knock at the door. Nina, without
rising, desired the stranger to come in. Then the door
was gently opened, and Rebecca Loth the Jewess stood
before her. Nina had seen Rebecca, but had never spoken
to her. Each girl had heard much of the other from their
younger friend Ruth Jacobi. Ruth was very intimate

with them both, and Nina had been willing enough to be
told of Rebecca, as had Rebecca also to be told of Nina.
'Grandfather wants Anton to marry Rebecca,' Ruth had
said more than once; and thus Nina knew well that
Rebecca was her rival. 'I think he loves her better than
his own eyes,' Ruth had said to Rebecca, speaking of her
uncle and Nina. But Rebecca had heard from a thousand
sources of information that he who was to have been her
lover had forgotten his own people and his own religion,
and had given himself to a Christian girl. Each, therefore, now knew that she looked upon an enemy and a
rival; but each was anxious to be very courteous to her
enemy.

Nina rose from her chair directly she saw her visitor,
and came forward to meet her. 'I suppose you hardly
know who I am, Fräulein?' said Rebecca.

'Oh, yes,' said Nina, with her pleasantest smile; 'you
are Rebecca Loth.'

'Yes, I am Rebecca Loth, the Jewess.'

'I like the Jews,' said Nina.

Rebecca was not dressed now as she had been dressed
on that gala occasion when we saw her in the Jews'
quarter. Then she had been as smart as white muslin
and bright ribbons and velvet could make her. Now she
was clad almost entirely in black, and over her shoulders
she wore a dark shawl, drawn closely round her neck.
But she had on her head, now as then, that peculiar
Hungarian hat which looks almost like a coronet in
front, and gives an aspect to the girl who wears it half
defiant and half attractive; and there were there, of
course, the long, glossy, black curls, and the dark-blue
eyes, and the turn of the face, which was so completely
Jewish in its hard, bold, almost repellent beauty. Nina
had said that she liked the Jews, but when the words
were spoken she remembered that they might be open
to misconstruction, and she blushed. The same idea
occurred to Rebecca, but she scorned to take advantage
of even a successful rival on such a point as that. She
would not twit Nina by any hint that this assumed liking
for the Jews was simply a special predilection for one Jew

in particular. 'We are not ungrateful to you for coming among us and knowing us,' said Rebecca. Then there was a slight pause, for Nina hardly knew what to say to her visitor. But Rebecca continued to speak. 'We hear that in other countries the prejudice against us is dying away, and that Christians stay with Jews in their houses, and Jews with Christians, eating with them and drinking with them. I fear it will never be so in Prague.'

'And why not in Prague? I hope it may. Why should we not do in Prague as they do elsewhere?'

'Ah, the feeling is too firmly settled here. We have our own quarter, and live altogether apart. A Christian here will hardly walk with a Jew, unless it be from counter to counter, or from bank to bank. As for their living together—or even eating in the same room—do you ever see it?'

Nina of course understood the meaning of this. That which the girl said to her was intended to prove to her how impossible it was that she should marry a Jew, and live in Prague with a Jew as his wife; but she, who had stood her ground before aunt Sophie, who had never flinched for a moment before all the threats which could be showered upon her from the Christian side, was not going to quail before the opposition of a Jewess, and that Jewess a rival!

'I do not know why we should not live to see it,' said Nina.

'It must take long first—very long,' said Rebecca. 'Even now, Fräulein, I fear you will think that I am very intrusive in coming to you. I know that a Jewess has no right to push her acquaintance upon a Christian girl.' The Jewess spoke very humbly of herself and of her people; but in every word she uttered there was a slight touch of irony which was not lost upon Nina. Nina could not but bethink herself that she was poor—so poor that everything around her, on her, and about her, told of poverty; while Rebecca was very rich, and showed her wealth even in the sombre garments which she had chosen for her morning visit. No idea of Nina's poverty had crossed Rebecca's mind, but Nina herself could not but remember it when she felt the sarcasm implied in her visitor's self-humiliation.

'I am glad that you have come to me—very glad indeed, if you have come in friendship.' Then she blushed as she continued, 'To me, situated as I am, the friendship of a Jewish maiden would be a treasure indeed.'

'You intend to speak of——'

'I speak of my engagement with Anton Trendellsohn. I do so with you because I know that you have heard of it. You tell me that Jews and Christians cannot come together in Prague, but I mean to marry a Jew. A Jew is my lover. If you will say that you will be my friend, I will love you indeed. Ruth Jacobi is my friend; but then Ruth is so young.'

'Yes, Ruth is very young. She is a child. She knows nothing.'

'A child's friendship is better than none.'

'Ruth is very young. She cannot understand. I too love Ruth Jacobi. I have known her since she was born. I knew and loved her mother. You do not remember Ruth Trendellsohn. No; your acquaintance with them is only of the other day.'

'Ruth's mother has been dead seven years,' said Nina.

'And what are seven years? I have known them for four-and-twenty.'

'Nay; that cannot be.'

'But I have. That is my age, and I was born, so to say, in their arms. Ruth Trendellsohn was ten years older than I—only ten.'

'And Anton?'

'Anton was a year older than his sister; but you know Anton's age. Has he never told you his age?'

'I never asked him; but I know it. There are things one knows as a matter of course. I remember his birth-day always.'

'It has been a short always.'

'No, not so short. Two years is not a short time to know a friend.'

'But he has not been betrothed to you for two years?'

'No; not betrothed to me.'

'Nor has he loved you so long; nor you him?'

'For him, I can only speak of the time when he first told me so.'

'And that was but the other day—but the other day, as I count the time.' To this Nina made no answer. She could not claim to have known her lover from so early a date as Rebecca Loth had done, who had been, as she said, born in the arms of his family. But what of that? Men do not always love best those women whom they have known the longest. Anton Trendellsohn had known her long enough to find that he loved her best. Why then should this Jewish girl come to her and throw in her teeth the shortness of her intimacy with the man who was to be her husband? If she, Nina, had also been a Jewess, Rebecca Loth would not then have spoken in such a way. As she thought of this she turned her face away from the stranger, and looked out among the sparrows who were still pecking among the dust in the court. She had told Rebecca at the beginning of their interview that she would be delighted to find a friend in a Jewess, but now she felt sorry that the girl had come to her. For Anton's sake she would bear with much from one whom he had known so long. But for that thought she would have answered her visitor with short courtesy. As it was, she sat silent and looked out upon the birds.

'I have come to you now,' said Rebecca Loth, 'to say a few words to you about Anton Trendellsohn. I hope you will not refuse to listen.'

'That will depend on what you say.'

'Do you think it will be for his good to marry a Christian?'

'I shall leave him to judge of that,' replied Nina, sharply.

'It cannot be that you do not think of it. I am sure you would not willingly do an injury to the man you love.'

'I would die for him, if that would serve him.'

'You can serve him without dying. If he takes you for his wife, all his people will turn against him. His own father will become his enemy.'

'How can that be? His father knows of it, and yet he is not my enemy.'

'It is as I tell you. His father will disinherit him. Every Jew in Prague will turn his back upon him. He knows it now. Anton knows it himself, but he cannot be the first to say the word that shall put an end to your engagement.'

'Jews have married Christians in Prague before now,' said Nina, pleading her own cause with all the strength she had.

'But not such a one as Anton Trendellsohn. An unconsidered man may do that which is not permitted to those who are more in note.'

'There is no law against it now.'

'That is true. There is no law. But there are habits stronger than law. In your own case, do you not know that all the friends you have in the world will turn their backs upon you? And so it would be with him. You two would be alone—neither as Jews nor as Christians—with none to aid you, with no friend to love you.'

'For myself I care nothing,' said Nina. 'They may say, if they like, that I am no Christian.'

'But how will it be with him? Can you ever be happy if you have been the cause of ruin to your husband?'

Nina was again silent for a while, sitting with her face turned altogether away from the Jewess. Then she rose suddenly from her chair, and, facing round almost fiercely upon the other girl, asked a question, which came from the fulness of her heart, 'And you—you yourself, what is it that you intend to do? Do you wish to marry him?'

'I do,' said Rebecca, bearing Nina's gaze without dropping her own eyes for a moment. 'I do. I do wish to be the wife of Anton Trendellsohn.'

'Then you shall never have your wish—never. He loves me, and me only. Ask him, and he will tell you so.'

'I have asked him, and he has told me so.' There was something so serious, so sad, and so determined in the manner of the young Jewess, that it almost cowed Nina—almost drove her to yield before her visitor. 'If he has

told you so,' she said—; then she stopped, not wishing
to triumph over her rival.

'He has told me so; but I knew it without his telling.
We all know it. I have not come here to deceive you, or
to create false suspicions. He does love you. He cares
nothing for me, and he does love you. But is he therefore
to be ruined? Which had he better lose? All that he has
in the world, or the girl that has taken his fancy?'

'I would sooner lose the world twice over than lose
him.'

'Yes; but you are only a woman. Think of his position.
There is not a Jew in all Prague respected among us as
he is respected. He knows more, can do more, has more
of wit and cleverness, than any of us. We look to him to
win for the Jews in Prague something of the freedom
which Jews have elsewhere,—in Paris and in London.
If he takes a Christian for his wife, all this will be
destroyed.'

'But all will be well if he were to marry you!'

Now it was Rebecca's turn to pause; but it was not for
long. 'I love him dearly,' she said; 'with a love as warm
as yours.'

'And therefore I am to be untrue to him,' said Nina,
again seating herself.

'And were I to become his wife,' continued Rebecca,
not regarding the interruption, 'it would be well with
him in a worldly point of view. All our people would be
glad, because there has been friendship between the
families from of old. His father would be pleased, and he
would become rich; and I also am not without some
wealth of my own.'

'While I am poor,' said Nina; 'so poor that,—look here,
I can only mend my rags. There, look at my shoes. I
have not another pair to my feet. But if he likes me, poor
and ragged, better than he likes you, rich—' She got so
far, raising her voice as she spoke; but she could get no
farther, for her sobs stopped her voice.

But while she was struggling to speak, the other girl
rose and knelt at Nina's feet, putting her long tapering
fingers upon Nina's threadbare arms, so that her forehead

was almost close to Nina's lips. 'He does,' said Rebecca.
'It is true—quite true. He loves you, poor as you are,
ten times—a hundred times—better than he loves me,
who am not poor. You have won it altogether by yourself, with nothing of outside art to back you. You have
your triumph. Will not that be enough for a life's contentment?'

'No;—no, no,' said Nina. 'No, it will not be enough.'
But her voice now was not altogether sorrowful. There
was in it something of a wild joy which had come to her
heart from the generous admission which the Jewess
made. She did triumph as she remembered that she had
conquered with no other weapons than those which
nature had given her.

'It is more of contentment than I shall ever have,' said
Rebecca. 'Listen to me. If you will say to me that you
will release him from his promise, I will swear to you by
the God whom we both worship, that I will never become
his wife—that he shall never touch me or speak to me in
love.' She had risen before she made this proposal, and
now stood before Nina with one hand raised, with her
blue eyes fixed upon Nina's face, and a solemnity in her
manner which for a while startled Nina into silence.
'You will believe my word, I am sure,' said Rebecca.

'Yes, I would believe you,' said Nina.

'Shall it be a bargain between us? Say so, and whatever is mine shall be mine and yours too. Though a Jew
may not make a Christian his wife, a Jewish girl may love
a Christian maiden;—and then, Nina, we shall both
know that we have done our very best for him whom we
both love better than all the world beside.'

Nina was again silent, considering the proposition that
had been made to her. There was one thing that she did
not see; one point of view in which the matter had not
been presented to her. The cause for her sacrifice had
been made plain to her, but why was the sacrifice of the
other also to become necessary? By not yielding she
might be able to keep her lover to herself; but if she were
to be induced to abandon him—for his sake, so that he
might not be ruined by his love for her—why, in that

case, should he not take the other girl for his wife? In such a case Nina told herself that there would be no world left for her. There would be nothing left for her beyond the accomplishment of Lotta Luxa's prophecy. But yet, though she thought of this, though in her misery she half resolved that she would give up Anton, and not exact from Rebecca the oath which the Jewess had tendered, still, in spite of that feeling, the dread of a rival's success helped to make her feel that she could never bring herself to yield.

'Shall it be as I say?' said Rebecca; 'and shall we, dear, be friends while we live?'

'No,' said Nina, suddenly.

'You cannot bring yourself to do so much for the man you love?'

'No, I cannot. Could you throw yourself from the bridge into the Moldau, and drown yourself?'

'Yes,' said Rebecca, 'I could. If it would serve him, I think that I could do so.'

'What! in the dark, when it is so cold? The people would see you in the daytime.'

'But I would live, that I might hear of his doings, and see his success.'

'Ah! I could not live without feeling that he loved me.'

'But what will you think of his love when it has ruined him? Will it be pleasant then? Were I to do that, then —then I should bethink myself of the cold river and the dark night, and the eyes of the passers-by whom I should be afraid to meet in the daytime. I ask you to be as I am. Who is there that pities me? Think again, Nina. I know you would wish that he should be prosperous.'

Nina did think again, and thought long. And she wept, and the Jewess comforted her, and many words were said between them beyond those which have been here set down; but, in the end, Nina could not bring herself to say that she would give him up. For his sake had she not given up her uncle and her aunt, and St. John and St. Nicholas—and the very Virgin herself, whose picture she had now removed from the wall beside her bed to a dark drawer? How could she give up that which was everything she had in the world—the very life of her bosom? 'I will ask him—him himself,' she said at last, hoarsely. 'I will ask him, and do as he bids me. I cannot do anything unless it is as he bids me.'

'In this matter you must act on your own judgment, Nina.'

'No, I will not. I have no judgment. He must judge for me in everything. If he says it is better that we should part, then—then—then I will let him go.'

After this Rebecca left the room and the house. Before she went, she kissed the Christian girl; but Nina did not remember that she had been kissed. Her mind was so full, not of thought, but of the suggestion that had been made to her, that it could now take no impression from anything else. She had been recommended to do a thing as her duty—as a paramount duty towards him who was everything to her—the doing of which it would be impossible that she should survive. So she told herself when she was once more alone, and had again seated herself in the chair by the window. She did not for a moment accuse Rebecca of dealing unfairly with her. It never occurred to her as possible that the Jewess had come to her with false views of her own fabrication. Had she so believed, her suspicions would have done great injustice to her rival; but no such idea presented itself to Nina's mind. All that Rebecca had said to her had come to her as though it were gospel. She did believe that Trendellsohn, as a Jew, would injure himself greatly by marrying a Christian. She did believe that the Jews of Prague would treat him somewhat as the Christians would treat herself. For herself such treatment would be nothing, if she were but once married; but she could understand that to him it would be ruinous. And Nina believed also that Rebecca had been entirely disinterested in her mission—that she came thither, not to gain a lover for herself, but to save from injury the man she loved, without reference to her own passion. Nina knew that Rebecca was strong and good, and acknowledged also that she herself was weak and selfish. She thought that she ought to have been persuaded to make the sacrifice, and once or twice she almost resolved that she would follow Rebecca to the Jews' quarter and tell her that it should be made. But she could not do it. Were she to do so, what would be left to her? With him she could bear anything, everything. To starve would hardly be bitter to her, so that his arm could be round her waist, and that her head could be on his shoulder. And, moreover, was she not his to do with as he pleased? After all her promises to him, how could she take upon herself to dispose of herself otherwise than as he might direct?

But then some thought of the missing document came back upon her, and she remembered in her grief that he suspected her—that even now he had some frightful doubt as to her truth to him—her faith, which was, alas, alas! more firm and bright towards him than towards that heavenly Friend whose aid would certainly suffice to bring her through all her troubles, if only she could bring herself to trust as she asked it. But she could trust only in him, and he doubted her! Would it not be better to do as Rebecca said, and make the most of such contentment as might come to her from her triumph over herself? That would be better—ten times better than to be abandoned by him—to be deserted by her Jew lover, because the Jew would not trust her, a Christian! On either side there could be nothing for her but death; but there is a choice even of deaths. If she did the thing herself, she thought that there might be something sweet even in the sadness of her last hour—something of the flavour of sacrifice. But should it be done by him, in that way there lay nothing but the madness of desolation! It was her last resolve, as she still sat at the window counting the sparrows in the yard, that she would tell him everything, and leave it to him to decide. If he would say that it was better for them to part, then he might go; and Rebecca Loth might become his wife, if he so wished it.

CHAPTER XI

ON one of these days old Trendellsohn went to the
office of Karil Zamenoy, in the Ross Markt, with
the full determination of learning in truth what there
might be to be learned as to that deed which would be so
necessary to him, or to those who would come after him,
when Josef Balatka might die. He accused himself of
having been foolishly soft-hearted in his transactions
with this Christian, and reminded himself from time to
time that no Jew in Prague would have been so treated
by any Christian. And what was the return made to
him? Among them they had now secreted that of which
he should have enforced the rendering before he had
parted with his own money; and this they did because
they knew that he would be unwilling to take harsh legal
proceedings against a bed-ridden old man! In this frame
of mind he went to the Ross Markt, and there he was
assured over and over again by Ziska Zamenoy—for
Karil Zamenoy was not to be seen—that Nina Balatka
had the deed in her own keeping. The name of Nina
Balatka was becoming very grievous to the old man.
Even he, when the matter had first been broached to
him, had not recognised all the evils which would come
from a marriage between his son and a Christian maiden;
but of late his neighbours had been around him, and he
had looked into the thing, and his eyes had been opened,
and he had declared to himself that he would not take a
Christian girl into his house as his daughter-in-law. He
could not prevent the marriage. The law would be on
his son's side. The law of the Christian kingdom in which
he lived allowed such marriages, and Anton, if he
executed the contract which would make the marriage
valid, would in truth be the girl's husband. But—and
Trendellsohn, as he remembered the power which was still
in his hands, almost regretted that he held it—if this
thing were done, his son must go out from his house, and
be his son no longer.

The old man was very proud of his son. Rebecca had

said truly that no Jew in Prague was so respected among Jews as Anton Trendellsohn. She might have added, also, that none was more highly esteemed among Christians. To lose such a son would be a loss indeed. 'I will share everything with him, and he shall go away out of Bohemia,' Trendellsohn had said to himself. 'He has earned it, and he shall have it. He has worked for me—for us both—without asking me, his father, to bind myself with any bond. He shall have the wealth which is his own, but he shall not have it here. Ah! if he would but take that other one as his bride, he should have everything, and his father's blessing—and then he would be the first instead of the last among his people.' Such was the purpose of Stephen Trendellsohn towards his son; but this, his real purpose, did not hinder him from threatening worse things. To prevent the marriage was his great object; and if threats would prevent it, why should he not use them?

But now he had conceived the idea that Nina was deceiving his son—that Nina was in truth holding back the deed with some view which he could hardly fathom. Ziska Zamenoy had declared, with all the emphasis in his power, that the document was, to the best of his belief, in Nina's hands; and though Ziska's emphasis would not have gone far in convincing the Jew, had the Jew's mind been turned in the other direction, now it had its effect. 'And who gave it her?' Trendellsohn had asked. 'Ah, there you must excuse me,' Ziska had answered; 'though, indeed, I could not tell you if I would. But we have nothing to do with the matter. We have no claim upon the houses. It is between you and the Balatkas.' Then the Jew had left the Zamenoys' office, and had gone home, fully believing that the deed was in Nina's hands.

'Yes, it is so—she is deceiving you,' he said to his son that evening.

'No, father. I think not.'

'Very well. You will find, when it is too late, that my words are true. Have you ever known a Christian who thought it wrong to rob a Jew?'

'I do not believe that Nina would rob me.'

'Ah! that is the confidence of what you call love. She is honest, you think, because she has a pretty face.'

'She is honest, I think, because she loves me.'

'Bah! Does love make men honest, or women either? Do we not see every day how these Christians rob each other in their money dealings when they are marrying? What was the girl's name?—old Thibolski's daughter—how they robbed her when they married her, and how her people tried their best to rob the lad she married. Did we not see it all?'

'It was not the girl who did it—not the girl herself.'

'Why should a woman be honester than a man? I tell you, Anton, that this girl has the deed.'

'Ziska Zamenoy has told you so?'

'Yes, he has told me. But I am not a man to be deceived because such a one as Ziska wishes to deceive me. You, at least, know me better than that. That which I tell you, Ziska himself believes.'

'But Ziska may believe wrongly.'

'Why should he do so? Whose interest can it be to make this thing seem so, if it be not so? If the girl have the deed, you can get it more readily from her than from the Zamenoys. Believe me, Anton, the deed is with the girl.'

'If it be so, I shall never believe again in the truth of a human being,' said the son.

'Believe in the truth of your own people,' said the father. 'Why should you seek to be wiser than them all?'

The father did not convince the son, but the words which he had spoken helped to create a doubt which already had almost an existence of its own. Anton Trendellsohn was prone to suspicions, and now was beginning to suspect Nina, although he strove hard to keep his mind free from such taint. His better nature told him that it was impossible that she should deceive him. He had read the very inside of her heart, and knew that her only delight was in his love. He understood perfectly the weakness and faith and beauty of her feminine nature, and her trusting, leaning softness was to his harder spirit as water to a thirsting man in the desert. When she clung to him, promising to obey him in everything, the touch of her hands, and the sound of her voice, and the beseeching glance of her loving eyes, were food and drink to him. He knew that her presence refreshed him and cooled him—made him young as he was growing old, and filled his mind with sweet thoughts which hardly came to him but when she was with him. He had told himself over and over again that it must be good for him to have such a one for his wife, whether she were Jew or Christian. He knew himself to be a better man when she was with him than at other moments of his life. And then he loved her. He was thinking of her hourly, though his impatience to see her was not as hers to be with him. He loved her. But yet—yet—what if she should be deceiving him? To be able to deceive others, but never to be deceived himself, was to him, unconsciously, the glory which he desired. To be deceived was to be disgraced. What was all his wit and acknowledged cunning if a girl—a Christian girl—could outwit him? For himself, he could see clearly enough into things to be aware that, as a rule, he could do better by truth than he could by falsehood. He was not prone to deceive others. But in such matters he desired ever to have the power with him—to keep, as it were, the upper hand. He would fain read the hearts of others entirely, and know their wishes, and understand their schemes, whereas his own heart and his own desires and his own schemes should only be legible in part. What if, after all, he were unable to read the simple tablets of this girl's mind—tablets which he had regarded as being altogether in his own keeping?

He went forth for a while, walking slowly through the streets, as he thought of this, wandering without an object, but turning over in his mind his father's words. He knew that his father was anxious to prevent his marriage. He knew that every Jew around him—for now the Jews around him had all heard of it—was keenly anxious to prevent so great a disgrace. He knew all that his father had threatened, and he was well aware how complete was his father's power. But he could stand against all that, if only Nina were true to him. He would go away from Prague. What did it matter? Prague was not all the world. There were cities better, nobler, richer than Prague, in which his brethren, the Jews, would not turn their backs upon him because he had married a Christian. It might be that he would have to begin the world again; but for that, too, he would be prepared. Nina had shown that she could bear poverty. Nina's torn boots and threadbare dress, and the utter absence of any request ever made with regard to her own comfort, had not been lost upon him. He knew how noble she was in bearing— how doubly noble she was in never asking. If only there was nothing of deceit at the back to mar it all!

He passed over the bridge, hardly knowing whither he was going, and turned directly down towards Balatka's house. As he did so he observed that certain repairs were needed in an adjoining building which belonged to his father, and determined that a mason should be sent there on the next day. Then he turned in under the archway, not passing through it into the court, and there he stood looking up at the window, in which Nina's small solitary lamp was twinkling. He knew that she was sitting by the light, and that she was working. He knew that she would be raised almost to a seventh heaven of delight if he would only call her to the door and speak to her a dozen words before he returned to his home. But he had no thought of doing it. Was it possible that she should have this document in her keeping?—that was the thought that filled his mind. He had bribed Lotta Luxa, and Lotta had sworn by her Christian gods that the deed was in Nina's hands. If the thing was false, why should they all conspire to tell the same falsehood? And yet he knew that they were false in their natures. Their manner, the words of each of them, betrayed something of falsehood to his well-tuned ear, to his acute eye, to his sharp senses. But with Nina—from Nina herself—every-thing that came from her spoke of truth. A sweet savour of honesty hung about her breath, and was a blessing to him when he was near enough to her to feel it. And yet he told himself that he was bound to doubt. He stood for some half-hour in the archway, leaning against the stonework at the side, and looking up at the window where Nina was sitting. What was he to do? How should he carry himself in this special period of his life? Great ideas about the destiny of his people were mingled in his mind with suspicions as to Nina, of which he should have been, and probably was, ashamed. He would certainly take her away from Prague. He had already perceived that his marriage with a Christian would be regarded in that stronghold of prejudice in which he lived with so much animosity as to impede, and perhaps destroy, the utility of his career. He would go away, taking Nina with him. And he would be careful that she should never know, by a word or a look, that he had in any way suffered for her sake. And he swore to himself that he would be soft to her, and gentle, loving her with a love more demonstrative than he had hitherto exhibited. He knew that he had been stern, exacting, and sometimes harsh. All that should be mended. He had learned her character, and perceived how absolutely she fed upon his love; and he would take care that the food should always be there, palpably there, for her sustenance. But —but he must try her yet once more before all this could be done for her. She must pass yet once again through the fire; and if then she should come forth as gold she should be to him the one pure ingot which the earth contained. With how great a love would he not repay her in future days for all that she would have suffered for his sake!

But she must be made to go through the fire again.* He would tax her with the possession of the missing deed, and call upon her to cleanse herself from the accusation which was made against her. Once again he would be harsh with her—harsh in appearance only—in order that his subsequent tenderness might be so much more tender! She had already borne much, and she must be made to endure once again. Did not he mean to endure much for her sake? Was he not prepared to recommence the troubles and toil of his life all from the beginning, in order that she might be that life's companion? Surely he had the right to put her through the fire, and prove her as never gold was proved before.

At last the little light was quenched, and Anton Trendellsohn felt that he was alone. The unseen companion of his thoughts was no longer with him, and it was useless for him to remain there standing in the archway. He blew her a kiss from his lips, and blessed her in his heart, and protested to himself that he knew she would come out of the fire pure altogether and proved to be without dross. And then he went his way. In the mean time Nina, chill and wretched, crept to her cold bed, all unconscious of the happiness that had been so near her. 'If he thinks I can be false to him, it will be better to die,' she said to herself, as she drew the scanty clothing over her shivering shoulders.

As she did so her lover walked home, and having come to a resolution which was intended to be definite as to his love, he allowed his thoughts to run away with him to other subjects. After all, it would be no evil to him to leave Prague. At Prague how little was there of progress either in thought or in things material! At Prague a Jew could earn money, and become rich—might own half the city; and yet at Prague he could only live as an outcast. As regarded the laws of the land, he, as a Jew, might fix his residence anywhere in Prague or around Prague; he might have gardens, and lands, and all the results of money; he might put his wife into a carriage twice as splendid as that which constituted the great social triumph of Madame Zamenoy;—but so strong against such a mode of life were the traditional prejudices of both Jews and Christians, that any such fashion of living would be absolutely impossible to him. It would not be good for him that he should remain at Prague. Knowing his father as he did, he could not believe that the old man would be so unjust as to let him go altogether empty-handed. He had toiled, and had been successful; and something of the corn which he had garnered would surely be rendered to him. With this—or, if need be, without it—he and his Christian wife would go forth and see if the world was not wide enough to find them a spot on which they might live without the contempt of those around them.

Though Nina had quenched her lamp and had gone to bed, it was not late when Trendellsohn reached his home, and he knew that he should find his father waiting for him. But his father was not alone. Rebecca Loth was sitting with the old man, and they had just supped together when Anton entered the room. Ruth Jacobi was also there, waiting till her friend should go, before she also went to her bed.

'How are you, Anton?' said Rebecca, giving her hand to the man she loved. 'It is strange to see you in these days.'

'The strangeness, Rebecca, comes from no fault of my own. Few men, I fancy, are more constant to their homes than I am.'

'You sleep here and eat here, I daresay.'

'My business lies mostly out, about the town.'

'Have you been about business now, uncle Anton?' said Ruth.

'Do not ask forward questions, Ruth,' said the uncle. 'Rebecca, I fear, teaches you to forget that you are still a child.'

'Do not scold her,' said the old man. 'She is a good girl.'

'It is Anton that forgets that nature is making Ruth a young woman,' said Rebecca.

'I do not want to be a young woman a bit before uncle Anton likes it,' said Ruth. 'I don't mind waiting ever so long for him. When he is married he will not care what I am.'

'If that be so, you may be a woman very soon,' said Rebecca.

'That is more than you know,' said Anton, turning very sharply on her. 'What do you know of my marriage, or when it will be?'

'Are you scolding her too?' said the elder Trendellsohn.

'Nay, father; let him do so,' said Rebecca. 'He has known me long enough to scold me if he thinks that I deserve it. You are gentle to me and spoil me, and it is only well that one among my old friends should be sincere enough to be ungentle.'

'I beg your pardon, Rebecca, if I have been un-courteous.'

'There can be no pardon where there is no offence.'

'If you are ashamed to hear of your marriage,' said the father, 'you should be ashamed to think of it.'

Then there was silence for a few seconds before any one spoke. The girls did not dare to speak after words so serious from the father to the son. It was known to both of them that Anton could hardly bring himself to bear a rebuke even from his father, and they felt that such a rebuke as this, given in their presence, would be altogether unendurable. Every one in the room understood the exact position in which each stood to the other. That Rebecca would willingly have become Anton's wife, that she had refused various offers of marriage in order that ultimately it might be so, was known to Stephen Tren-dellsohn, and to Anton himself, and to Ruth Jacobi. There had not been the pretence of any secret among them in the matter. But the subject was one which could hardly be discussed by them openly. 'Father,' said Anton, after a while, during which the black thunder-cloud which had for an instant settled on his brow had managed to dispel itself without bursting into a visible storm—'father, I am neither ashamed to think of my intended marriage nor to speak of it. There is no question of shame. But it is unpleasant to make such a subject matter of general conversation when it is a source of trouble instead of joy among us. I wish I could have made you happy by my marriage.'

'You will make me very wretched.'

'Then let us not talk about it. It cannot be altered. You would not have me false to my plighted word?'

Again there was silence for some minutes, and then Rebecca spoke,—the words coming from her in the lowest possible accents.

'It can be altered without breach of your plighted word. Ask the young woman what she herself thinks. You will find that she knows that you are both wrong.'

'Of course she knows it,' said the father.

'I will ask her nothing of the kind,' said the son.

'It would be of no use,' said Ruth.

After this Rebecca rose to take her leave, saying something of the falseness of her brother Samuel, who had promised to come for her and to take her home. 'But he is with Miriam Harter,' said Rebecca, 'and, of course, he will forget me.'

'I will go home with you,' said Anton.

'Indeed you shall not. Do you think I cannot walk alone through our own streets in the dark without being afraid?'

'I am well aware that you are afraid of nothing; but nevertheless, if you will allow me, I will accompany you.' There was no sufficient cause for her to refuse his company, and the two left the house together.

As they descended the stairs, Rebecca determined that she would have the first word in what might now be said between them. She had suggested that this marriage with the Christian girl might be abandoned without the disgrace upon Anton of having broken his troth, and she had thereby laid herself open to a suspicion of having worked for her own ends,—of having done so with unmaidenly eagerness to gratify her own love. Something on the subject must be said—would be said by him if not by her—and therefore she would explain herself at once. She spoke as soon as she found herself by his side in the street. 'I regretted what I said upstairs, Anton, as soon as the words were out of my mouth.'

'I do not know that you said anything to regret.'

'I told you that if in truth you thought this marriage to be wrong—'

'Which I do not.'

'Pardon me, my friend, for a moment. If you had so thought, I said that there was a mode of escape without falsehood or disgrace. In saying so I must have seemed to urge you to break away from Nina Balatka.'

'You are all urging me to do that.'

'Coming from the others, such advice cannot even seem to have an improper motive.' Here she paused, feeling the difficulty of her task,—aware that she could not conclude it without an admission which no woman willingly makes. But she shook away the impediment bracing herself to the work, and went on steadily with her speech. 'Coming from me, such motive may be imputed—nay, it must be imputed.'

'No motive is imputed that is not believed by me to be good and healthy and friendly.'

'Our friends,' continued Rebecca, 'have wished that you and I should be husband and wife. That is now impossible.'

'It is impossible,—because Nina will be my wife.'

'It is impossible, whether Nina should become your wife or should not become your wife. I do not say this from any girlish pride. Before I knew that you loved a Christian woman, I would willingly have been—as our friends wished. You see I can trust you enough for candour. When I was young they told me to love you, and I obeyed them. They told me that I was to be your wife, and I taught myself to be happy in believing them. I now know that they were wrong, and I will endeavour to teach myself another happiness.'

'Rebecca, if I have been in fault—'

'You have never been in fault. You are by nature too stern to fall into such faults. It has been my misfortune— perhaps rather I should say my difficulty—that till of late you have given me no sign by which I could foresee my lot. I was still young, and I still believed what they told me,—even though you did not come to me as lovers come. Now I know it all; and as any such thoughts—or wishes, if you will—as those I used to have can never return to me, I may perhaps be felt by you to be free to use what liberty of counsel old friendship may give me. I know you will not misunderstand me—and that is all. Do not come further with me.'

He called to her, but she was gone, escaping from him with quick running feet through the dark night; and he returned to his father's house, thinking of the girl that had left him.

CHAPTER XII

AGAIN some days passed by without any meeting between Nina and her lover, and things were going
very badly with the Balatkas in the old house. The
money that had come from the jeweller was not indeed
all expended, but Nina looked upon it as her last resource,
till marriage should come to relieve her; and the time
of her marriage seemed to be as far from her as ever. So the
kreutzers were husbanded as only a woman can husband
them, and new attempts were made to reduce the little
expenses of the little household.

'Souchey, you had better go. You had indeed,' said
Nina. 'We cannot feed you.' Now Souchey had himself
spoken of leaving them some days since, urged to do so
by his Christian indignation at the abominable betrothal
of his mistress. 'You said the other day that you would
do so, and it will be better.'

'But I shall not.'

'Then you will be starved.'

'I am starved already, and it cannot be worse. I dined
yesterday on what they threw out to the dogs in the meat-
market.'

'And where will you dine to-day?'

'Ah, I shall dine better to-day. I shall get a meal in
the Windberg-gasse.'

'What! at my aunt's house?'

'Yes; at your aunt's house. They live well there, even
in the kitchen. Lotta will have for me some hot soup, a
mess of cabbage, and a sausage. I wish I could bring it
away from your aunt's house to the old man and yourself.'

'I would sooner fall in the gutter than eat my aunt's
meat.'

'That is all very fine for you, but I am not going to
marry a Jewess. Why should I quarrel with your aunt,
or with Lotta Luxa? If you would give up the Jew, Nina,
your aunt's house would be open to you; yes,—and
Ziska's house.'

'I will not give up the Jew,' said Nina, with flashing
eyes.

'I suppose not. But what will you do when he gives you up? What if Ziska then should not be so forward?'

'Of all those who are my enemies, and whom I hate because they are so cruel, I hate Ziska the worst. Go and tell him so, since you are becoming one of them. In doing so much you cannot at any rate do me harm.'

Then she took herself off, forgetting in her angry spirit the prudential motives which had induced her to begin the conversation with Souchey. But Souchey, though he was going to Madame Zamenoy's house to get his dinner, and was looking forward with much eagerness to the mess of hot cabbage and the cold sausage, had by no means become 'one of them' in the Windberg-gasse. He had had more than one interview of late with Lotta Luxa, and had perceived that something was going on, of which he much desired to be at the bottom. Lotta had some scheme, which she was half willing and half unwilling to reveal to him, by which she hoped to prevent the threatened marriage between Nina and the Jew. Now Souchey was well enough inclined to take a part in such a scheme,—provided it did not in any way make him a party with the Zamenoys in things general against the Balatkas. It was his duty as a Christian—though he himself was rather slack in the performance of his own religious duties—to put a stop to this horrible marriage if he could do so; but it behoved him to be true to his master and mistress, and especially true to them in opposition to the Zamenoys. He had in some sort been carrying on a losing battle against the Zamenoys all his life, and had some of the feelings of a martyr,—telling himself that he had lost a rich wife by doing so. He would go on this occasion and eat his dinner and be very confidential with Lotta; but he would be very discreet, would learn more than he told, and, above all, would not betray his master or mistress.

Soon after he was gone, Anton Trendellsohn came over to the Kleinseite, and, ringing at the bell of the house, received admission from Nina herself. 'What! you, Anton?' she said, almost jumping into his arms, and then restraining herself. 'Will you come up? It is so long since I have seen you.'

'Yes—it is long. I hope the time is soon coming when there shall be no more of such separation.'

'Is it? Is it indeed?'

'I trust it is.'

'I suppose as a maiden I ought to be coy, and say that I would prefer to wait; but, dearest love, sorrow and trouble have banished all that. You will not love me less because I tell you that I count the minutes till I may be your wife.'

'No; I do not love you less on that account. I would have you be true and faithful in all things.'

Though the words themselves were assuring, there was something in the tone of his voice which repressed her. 'To you I am true and faithful in all things; as faithful as though you were already my husband. What were you saying of a time that is soon coming?'

He did not answer her question, but turned the subject away into another channel. 'I have brought something for you,' he said—'something which I hope you will be glad to have.'

'Is it a present?' she asked. As yet he had never given her anything that she could call a gift, and it was to her almost a matter of pride that she had taken nothing from her Jew lover, and that she would take nothing till it should be her right to take everything.

'Hardly a present; but you shall look at it as you will. You remember Rapinsky, do you not?' Now Rapinsky was the jeweller in the Grosser Ring, and Nina, though she well remembered the man and the shop, did not at the moment remember the name. 'You will not have forgotten this at any rate,' said Trendellsohn, bringing the necklace from out of his pocket.

'How did you get it?' said Nina, not putting out her hand to take it, but looking at it as it lay upon the table.

'I thought you would be glad to have it back again.'

'I should be glad if—'

'If what? Will it be less welcome because it comes through my hands?'

'The man lent me money upon it, and you must have paid the money.'

'What if I have? I like your pride, Nina; but be not too proud. Of course I have paid the money. I know Rapinsky, who deals with us often. I went to him after you spoke to me, and got it back again. There is your mother's necklace.'

'I am sorry for this, Anton.'

'Why sorry?'

'We are so poor that I shall be driven to take it elsewhere again. I cannot keep such a thing in the house while father wants. But better he should want than—'

'Than what, Nina?'

'There would be something like cheating in borrowing money on the same thing twice.'

'Then put it by, and I will be your lender.'

'No; I will not borrow from you. You are the only one in the world that I could never repay. I cannot borrow from you. Keep this thing, and if I am ever your wife, then you shall give it me.'

'If you are ever my wife?'

'Is there no room for such an if? I hope there is not, Anton. I wish it were as certain as the sun's rising. But people around us are so cruel! It seems, sometimes, as though the world were against us. And then you, yourself——'

'What of me myself, Nina?'

'I do not think you trust me altogether; and unless you trust me, I know you will not make me your wife.'

'That is certain; and yet I do not doubt that you will be my wife.'

'But do you trust me? Do you believe in your heart of hearts that I know nothing of that paper for which you are searching?' She paused for a reply, but he did not at once make any. 'Tell me,' she went on saying, with energy, 'are you sure that I am true to you in that matter, as in all others? Though I were starving—and it is nearly so with me already—and though I loved you beyond even all heaven, as I do, I do—I would not become your wife if you doubted me in any tittle. Say that you doubt me, and then it shall be all over.' Still he did not speak. 'Rebecca Loth will be a fitter wife for you than I can be,' said Nina.

'If you are not my wife, I shall never have a wife,' said Trendellsohn.

In her ecstasy of delight, as she heard these words, she took up his hand and kissed it; but she dropped it again, as she remembered that she had not yet received the assurance that she needed. 'But you do believe me about this horrid paper?'

It was necessary that she should be made to go again through the fire. In deliberate reflection he had made himself aware that such necessity still existed. It might be that she had some inner reserve as to duty towards her father. There was, possibly, some reason which he could not fathom why she should still keep something back from him in this matter. He did not, in truth, think that it was so, but there was the chance. There was the chance, and he could not bear to be deceived. He felt assured that Ziska Zamenoy and Lotta Luxa believed that this deed was in Nina's keeping. Indeed, he was assured that all the household of the Zamenoys so believed. 'If there be a God above us, it is there,' Lotta had said, crossing herself. He did not think it was there; he thought that Lotta was wrong, and that all the Zamenoys were wrong, by some mistake which he could not fathom; but still there was the chance, and Nina must be made to bear this additional calamity.

'Do you think it impossible,' said he, 'that you should have it among your own things?'

'What! without knowing that I have it?' she asked.

'It may have come to you with other papers,' he said, 'and you may not quite have understood its nature.'

'There, in that desk, is every paper that I have in the world. You can look if you suspect me. But I shall not easily forgive you for looking.' Then she threw down the key of her desk upon the table. He took it up and fingered it, but did not move towards the desk. 'The greatest treasure there,' she said, 'are scraps of your own, which I have been a fool to value, as they have come from a man who does not trust me.'

He knew that it would be useless for him to open the desk. If she were secreting anything from him, she was not hiding it there. 'Might it not possibly be among your clothes?' he asked.

'I have no clothes,' she answered, and then strode off across the wide room, towards the door of her father's apartment. But after she had grasped the handle of the door, she turned again upon her lover. 'It may, however, be well that you should search my chamber and my bed. If you will come with me, I will show you the door. You will find it to be a sorry place for one who was your affianced bride.'

'Who *is* my affianced bride,' said Trendellsohn.

'No, sir!—who *was*, but is so no longer. You will have to ask my pardon,—at my feet, before I will let you speak to me again as my lover. Go and search. Look for your deed,—and then you shall see that I will tear out my own heart rather than submit to the ill-usage of distrust from one who owes me so much faith as you do.'

'Nina,' he said.

'Well, sir.'

'I do trust you.'

'Yes—with a half trust;—with one eye closed, while the other is watching me. You think you have so conquered me that I will be good to you, and yet cannot keep yourself from listening to those who whisper that I am bad to you. Sir, I fear they have been right when they told me that a Jew's nature would surely shock me at last.'

The dark frowning cloud, which she had so often observed with fear, came upon his brow; but she did not fear him now. 'And do you too taunt me with my religion?' he said.

'No, not so—not with your religion, Anton; but with your nature.'

'And how can I help my nature?'

'I suppose you cannot help it, and I am wrong to taunt you. I should not have taunted you. I should only have said that I will not endure the suspicion either of a Christian or of a Jew.'

He came up to her now, and put out his arm as though he were about to embrace her. 'No,' she said; 'not again, till you have asked my pardon for distrusting me, and have given me your solemn word that you distrust me no longer.'

He paused a moment in doubt; then put his hat on his head and prepared to leave her. She had behaved very well, but still he would not be weak enough to yield to her in everything at once. As to opening her desk, or going up-stairs into her room, that he felt to be quite impossible. Even his nature did not admit of that. But neither did his nature allow him to ask her pardon and to own that he had been wrong. She had said that he must implore her forgiveness at her feet. One word, however, one look, would have sufficed. But that word and that look were, at the present moment, out of his power. 'Good-bye Nina,' he said. 'It is best that I should leave you now.'

'By far the best; and you will take the necklace with you, if you please.'

'No; I will leave that. I cannot keep a trinket that was your mother's.'

'Take it, then, to the jeweller's, and get back your money. It shall not be left here. I will have nothing from your hands.' He was so far cowed by her manner that he took up the necklace and left the house, and Nina was once more alone.

What they had told her of her lover was after all true. That was the first idea that occurred to her as she sat in her chair, stunned by the sorrow that had come upon her. They had dinned into her ears their accusations, not against the man himself, but against the tribe to which he belonged, telling her that a Jew was, of his very nature, suspicious, greedy, and false. She had perceived early in her acquaintance with Anton Trendellsohn that he was clever, ambitious, gifted with the power of thinking as none others whom she knew could think; and that he had words at his command, and was brave, and was endowed with a certain nobility of disposition which prompted him to wish for great results rather than for small advantages. All this had conquered her, and had made her resolve to think that a Jew could be as good as a Christian. But now, when the trial of the man had in truth come, she found that those around her had been right in what they had said. How base must be the nature which could prompt a man to suspect a girl who had been true to him as Nina had been true to her lover!

She would never see him again—never! He had left the room without even answering the question which she had asked him. He would not even say that he trusted her. It was manifest that he did not trust her, and that he believed at this moment that she was endeavouring to rob him in this matter of the deed. He had asked her if she had it in her desk or among her clothes, and her very soul revolted from the suspicion so implied. She would never speak to him again. It was all over. No; she would never willingly speak to him again.

But what would she do? For a few minutes she fell back, as is so natural with mortals in trouble, upon that religion which she had been so willing to outrage by marrying the Jew. She went to a little drawer and took out a string of beads which had lain there unused since she had been made to believe that the Virgin and the saints would not permit her marriage with Anton Trendellsohn. She took out the beads,—but she did not use them. She passed no berries through her fingers to check the number of prayers said, for she found herself unable to say any prayer at all. If he would come back to her, and ask her pardon—ask it in truth at her feet—she would still forgive him, regardless of the Virgin and the saints. And if he did not come back, what was the fate that Lotta Luxa had predicted for her, and to which she had acknowledged to herself that she would be driven to submit? In either case how could she again come to terms with St. John and St. Nicholas? And how was she to live? Should she lose her lover, as she now told herself would certainly be her fate, what possibility of life was left to her? From day to day and from week to week she had put off to a future hour any definite consideration of what she and her father should do in their poverty, believing that it might be postponed till her marriage would make all things easy. Her future mode of living had often been discussed between her and her lover, and she had been candid enough in explaining to him that she could not leave her father desolate. He had always replied that his wife's father should want for nothing, and she had been delighted to think that she could with joy accept that from her husband which nothing would induce her to accept from her lover. This thought had sufficed to comfort her, as the evil of absolute destitution was close upon her. Surely the day of her marriage would come soon.

But now it seemed to her to be certain that the day of her marriage would never come. All those expectations must be banished, and she must look elsewhere,—if elsewhere there might be any relief. She knew well that if she would separate herself from the Jew, the pocket of her aunt would be opened to relieve the distress of her father—would be opened so far as to save the old man from perishing of want. Aunt Sophie, if duly invoked, would not see her sister's husband die of starvation. Nay, aunt Sophie would doubtless so far stretch her Christian charity as to see that her niece was in some way fed, if that niece would be duly obedient. Further still, aunt Sophie would accept her niece as the very daughter of her house, as the rising mistress of her own establishment, if that niece would only consent to love her son. Ziska was there as a husband in Anton's place, if Ziska might only gain acceptance.

But Nina, as she rose from her chair and walked backwards and forwards through her chamber, telling herself all these things, clenched her fist, and stamped her foot, as she swore to herself that she would dare all that the saints could do to her, that she would face all the terrors of the black dark river, before she would succumb to her cousin Ziska. As she worked herself into wrath, thinking now of the man she loved, and then of the man she did not love, she thought that she could willingly perish,—

if it were not that her father lay there so old and so helpless. Gradually, as she magnified to herself the terrible
distresses of her heart, the agony of her yearning love for
a man who, though he loved her, was so unworthy of her
perfect faith, she began to think that it would be well to
be carried down by the quick, eternal, almighty stream
beyond the reach of the sorrow which encompassed her.
When her father should leave her she would be all alone
—alone in the world, without a friend to regard her, or
one living human being on whom she, a girl, might rely
for protection, shelter, or even for a morsel of bread.
Would St. Nicholas cover her from the contumely of the
world, or would St. John of the Bridges feed her? Did
she in her heart of hearts believe that even the Virgin
would assist her in such a strait? No; she had no such
belief. It might be that such real belief had never been
hers. She hardly knew. But she did know that now, in
the hour of her deep trouble, she could not say her
prayers and tell her beads, and trust valiantly that the
goodness of heaven would suffice to her in her need.

In the mean time Souchey had gone off to the Windberg-gasse, and had gladdened himself with the soup,
with the hot mess of cabbage and the sausage, supplied by
Madame Zamenoy's hospitality. The joys of such a
moment are unknown to any but those who, like Souchey,
have been driven by circumstances to sit at tables very
ill supplied. On the previous day he had fed upon offal
thrown away from a butcher's stall, and habit had made
such feeding not unfamiliar to him. As he walked from
the Kleinseite through the Old Town to Madame Zamenoy's bright-looking house in the New Town, he had
comforted himself greatly with thoughts of the coming
feast. The representation which his imagination made to
him of the banquet sufficed to produce happiness, and he
went along hardly envying any man. His propensities at
the moment were the propensities of a beast. And yet he
was submitting himself to the terrible poverty which made
so small a matter now a matter of joy to him, because
there was a something of nobility within him which made
him true to the master who had been true to him, when

they had both been young together. Even now he resolved, as he sharpened his teeth, that through all the
soup and all the sausage he would be true to the Balatkas.
He would be true even to Nina Balatka,—though he
recognised it as a paramount duty to do all in his power
to save her from the Jew.

He was seated at the table in the kitchen almost as
soon as he had entered the house in the Windberg-gasse,
and found his plate full before him. Lotta had felt that
there was no need of the delicacy of compliment in feeding a man who was so undoubtedly hungry, and she had
therefore bade him at once fall to. 'A hearty meal is a
thing you are not used to,' she had said, 'and it will do
your old bones a deal of good.' The address was not
complimentary, especially as coming from a lady in
regard to whom he entertained tender feelings; but
Souchey forgave the something of coarse familiarity
which the words displayed, and, seating himself on the
stool before the victuals, gave play to the feelings of
the moment. 'There's no one to measure what's left of the
sausage,' said Lotta, instigating him to new feats.

'Ain't there now?' said Souchey, responding to the
sound of the trumpet. 'I always thought she had the devil's
own eye in looking after what was used in the kitchen.'

'The devil himself winks sometimes,' said Lotta, cutting
another half-inch off from the unconsumed fragment,
and picking the skin from the meat with her own fair
fingers. Hitherto Souchey had been regardless of any
such niceness in his eating, the skin having gone with the
rest; but now he thought that the absence of the outside
covering and the touch of Lotta's fingers were grateful to
his appetite.

'Souchey,' said Lotta, when he had altogether done,
and had turned his stool round to the kitchen fire, 'where
do you think Nina would go if she were to marry—a Jew?'
There was an abrupt solemnity in the manner of the
question which at first baffled the man, whose breath was
heavy with the comfortable repletion which had been
bestowed upon him.

'Where would she go to?' he said, repeating Lotta's words.

'Yes, Souchey, where would she go to? Where would be her eternal home? What would become of her soul? Do you know that not a priest in Prague would give her absolution though she were on her dying bed? Oh, holy Mary, it's a terrible thing to think of! It's bad enough for the old man and her to be there day after day without a morsel to eat; and I suppose if it were not for Anton Trendellsohn it would be bad enough with them——'

'Not a gulden, then, has Nina ever taken from the Jew —nor the value of a gulden,* as far as I can judge between them.'

'What matters that, Souchey? Is she not engaged to him as his wife? Can anything in the world be so dreadful? Don't you know she'll be—damned for ever and ever?' Lotta, as she uttered the terrible words, brought her face close to Souchey's, looking into his eyes with a fierce glare. Souchey shook his head sorrowfully, owning thereby that his knowledge in the matter of religion did not go to the point indicated by Lotta Luxa. 'And wouldn't anything, then, be a good deed that would prevent that?'

'It's the priests that should do it among them.'

'But the priests are not the men they used to be, Souchey. And it is not exactly their fault neither. There are so many folks about in these days who care nothing who goes to glory and who does not, and they are too many for the priests.'

'If the priests can't fight their own battle, I can't fight it for them,' said Souchey.

'But for the old family, Souchey, that you have known so long! Look here; you and I between us can prevent it.'

'And how is it to be done?'

'Ah! that's the question. If I felt that I was talking to a real Christian that had a care for the poor girl's soul, I would tell you in a moment.'

'So I am; only her soul isn't my business.'

'Then I cannot tell you this. I can't do it unless you acknowledge that her welfare as a Christian is the business of us all. Fancy, Souchey, your mistress married to a filthy Jew!'

'For the matter of that, he isn't so filthy neither.'

'An abominable Jew! But, Souchey, she will never fall out with him. We must contrive that he shall quarrel with her. If she had a thing about her that he did not want her to have, couldn't you contrive that he should know it?'

'What sort of thing? Do you mean another lover, like?'

'No, you gander. If there was anything of that sort I could manage it myself. But if she had a thing locked up —away from him, couldn't you manage to show it to him? He's very generous in rewarding, you know.'

'I don't want to have anything to do with it,' said Souchey, getting up from his stool and preparing to take his departure. Though he had been so keen after the sausage, he was above taking a bribe in such a matter as this.

'Stop, Souchey, stop. I didn't think that I should ever have to ask anything of you in vain.'

Then she put her face very close to his, so that her lips touched his ear, and she laid her hand heavily upon his arm, and she was very confidential. Souchey listened to the whisper till his face grew longer and longer. ''Tis for her soul,' said Lotta—'for her poor soul's sake. When you can save her by raising your hand, would you let her be damned for ever?'

But she could exact no promise from Souchey except that he would keep faith with her, and that he would consider deeply the proposal made to him. Then there was a tender farewell between them, and Souchey returned to the Kleinseite.

CHAPTER XIII

FOR two days after this Nina heard nothing from the Jews' quarter, and in her terrible distress her heart almost became softened towards the man who had so deeply offended her. She began to tell herself, in the weariness of her sorrow, that men were different from women, and, of their nature, more suspicious; that no woman had a right to expect every virtue in her lover, and that no woman had less of such right than she herself, who had so little to give in return for all that Anton proposed to bestow upon her. She began to think that she could forgive him, even for his suspicion, if he would only come to be forgiven. But he came not, and it was only too plain to her that she could not be the first to go to him after what had passed between them.

And then there fell another crushing sorrow upon her. Her father was ill—so ill that he was like to die. The doctor came to him,—some son of Galen*who had known the merchant in his prosperity,—and, with kind assurances, told Nina that her father, though he could pay nothing, should have whatever assistance medical attention could give him; but he said, at the same time, that medical attention could give no aid that would be of permanent service. The light had burned down in the socket, and must go out. The doctor took Nina by the hand, and put his own hand upon her soft tresses, and spoke kind words to console her. And then he said that the sick man ought to take a few glasses of wine every day; and as he was going away, turned back again, and promised to send the wine from his own house. Nina thanked him, and plucked up something of her old spirit during his presence, and spoke to him as though she had no other care than that of her father's health; but as soon as the doctor was gone she thought again of her Jew lover. That her father should die was a great grief. But when she should be alone in the old house, with the corpse lying on the bed, would Anton Trendellsohn come to her then?

He did not come to her now, though he knew of her father's illness. She sent Souchey to the Jews' quarter to tell the sad news,—not to him, but to old Trendellsohn. 'For the sake of the property it is right that he should know,' Nina said to herself, excusing to herself on this plea her weakness in sending any message to the house of Anton Trendellsohn till he should have come and asked her pardon. But even after this he came not. She listened to every footstep that entered the courtyard. She could not keep herself from going to the window, and from looking into the square. Surely now, in her deep sorrow, in her solitude, he would come to her. He would come and say one word,—that he did trust her, that he would trust her! But no; he came not at all; and the hours of the day and the night followed slowly and surely upon each other, as she sat by her father's bed watching the last quiver of the light in the socket.

But though Trendellsohn did not come himself, there came to her a messenger from the Jew's house—a messenger from the Jew's house, but not a messenger from Anton Trendellsohn. 'Here is a girl from the—Jew,' said Souchey, whispering into her ear as she sat at her father's bedside;—'one of themselves. Shall I tell her to go away, because he is so ill?' And Souchey pointed to his master's head on the pillow. 'She has got a basket, but she can leave that.'

Nina, however, was by no means inclined to send the Jewess away, rightly guessing that the stranger was her friend Ruth. 'Stop here, Souchey, and I will go to her,' Nina said. 'Do not leave him till I return. I will not be long.' She would not have let a dog go without a word that had come from Anton's house or from Anton's presence. Perhaps he had written to her. If there were but a line to say, 'Pardon me; I was wrong,' everything might yet be right. But Ruth Jacobi was the bearer of no note from Anton, nor indeed had she come on her present message with her uncle's knowledge. She had put a heavy basket on the table, and now, running forward, took Nina by the hands, and kissed her.

'We have been so sorry, all of us, to hear of your father's illness,' said Ruth.

'Father is very ill,' said Nina. 'He is dying.'

'Nay, Nina; it may be that he is not dying. Life and death both are in the hands of God.'

'Yes; it is in God's hands of course; but the doctor says that he will die.'

'The doctors have no right to speak in that way,' said Ruth, 'for how can they know God's pleasure? It may be that he will recover.'

'Yes; it may be,' said Nina. 'It is good of you to come

to me, Ruth. I am so glad you have come. Have you any —any—message?' If he would only ask to be forgiven through Ruth, or even if he had sent a word that might be taken to show that he wished to be forgiven, it should suffice.

'I have—brought—a few things in a basket,' said Ruth, almost apologetically.

Then Nina lifted the basket. 'You did not surely carry this through the streets?'

'I had Shadrach, our boy, with me. He carried it. It is not from me, exactly; though I have been so glad to come with it.'

'And who sent it?' said Nina, quickly, with her fingers trembling on its lid. If Anton had thought to send anything to her, that anything should suffice.

'It was Rebecca Loth who thought of it, and who asked me to come,' said Ruth.

Then Nina drew back her fingers as though they were burned, and walked away from the table with quick angry steps. 'Why should Rebecca Loth send anything to me?' she said. 'What is there in the basket?'

'She has written a little line. It is at the top. But she has asked me to say—'

'What has she asked you to say? Why should she say anything to me?'

'Nay, Nina; she is very good, and she loves you.'

'I do not want her love.'

'I am to say to you that she has heard of your distress, and she hopes that a girl like you will let a girl like her do what she can to comfort you.'

'She cannot comfort me.'

'She bade me say that if she were ill, or in sorrow, there is no hand from which she would so gladly take comfort as from yours;—for the sake, she said, of a mutual friend.'

'I have no—friend,' said Nina.

'Oh, Nina, am not I your friend? Do not I love you?'

'I do not know. If you do love me now, you must cease to love me. You are a Jewess, and I am a Christian, and we must live apart. You, at least, must live. I wish you would tell the boy that he may take back the basket.'

'There are things in it for your father, Nina; and, Nina, surely you will read Rebecca's note?'

Then Ruth went to the basket, and from the top she took out Rebecca's letter, and gave it to Nina, and Nina read it. It was as follows:—

'I shall always regard you as very dear to me, because our hearts have been turned in the same way. It may not be perhaps that we shall know each other much at first; but I hope the days may come when we shall be much older than we are now, and that then we may meet and be able to talk of what has passed without pain. I do not know why a Jewess and a Christian woman should not be friends.

'I have sent a few things which may perhaps be of comfort to your father. In pity to me do not refuse them. They are such as one woman should send to another. And I have added a little trifle for your own use. At the present moment you are poor as to money, though so rich in the gifts which make men love. On my knees before you I ask you to accept from my hand what I send, and to think of me as one who would serve you in more things if it were possible. Yours, if you will let me, affectionately,

REBECCA.

'I see when I look at them that the shoes will be too big.'

She stood for a while apart from Ruth, with the open note in her hand, thinking whether or no she would accept the gifts which had been sent. The words which Rebecca had written had softened her heart, especially those in which the Jewess had spoken openly to her of her poverty. 'At the present moment you are poor as to money,' the girl had said, and had said it as though such poverty were, after all, but a small thing in their relative positions one to another. That Nina should be loved, and Rebecca not loved, was a much greater thing. For her father's sake she would take the things sent,—and for Rebecca's sake. She would take even the shoes, which she wanted so sorely. She remembered well, as she read the last word, how, when Rebecca had been with her, she herself had pointed to the poor broken slippers which she wore, not meaning to excite such compassion as had now been shown. Yes, she would accept it all—as one woman should take such things from another.

'You will not make Shadrach carry them back?' said Ruth, imploring her.

'But he;—has he sent nothing?—not a word?' She would have thought herself to be utterly incapable, before Ruth had come, of showing so much weakness; but her reserve gave way as she admitted in her own heart the kindness of Rebecca, and she became conquered and humbled. She was so terribly in want of his love at this moment! 'And has he sent no word of a message to me?'

'I did not tell him that I was coming.'

'But he knows;—he knows that father is so ill.'

'Yes; I suppose he has heard that, because Souchey came to the house. But he has been out of temper with us all, and unhappy, for some days past. I know that he is unhappy when he is so harsh with us.'

'And what has made him unhappy?'

'Nay, I cannot tell you that. I thought perhaps it was because you did not come to him. You used to come and see us at our house.'

Dear Ruth! Dearest Ruth, for saying such dear words! She had done more than Rebecca by the sweetness of the suggestion. If it were really the case that he were un-happy because they had parted from each other in anger, no further forgiveness would be necessary.

'But how can I come, Ruth?' she said. 'It is he that should come to me.'

'You used to come.'

'Ah, yes. I came first with messages from father, and then because I loved to hear him talk to me. I do not mind telling you, Ruth, now. And then I came because, —because he said I was to be his wife. I thought that if I was to be his wife it could not be wrong that I should go to his father's house. But now that so many people know it,—that they talk about it so much,—I cannot go to him now.'

'But you are not ashamed of being engaged to him—because he is a Jew!'

'No,' said Nina, raising herself to her full height; 'I am not ashamed of him. I am proud of him. To my thinking there is no man like him. Compare him and Ziska, and Ziska becomes hardly a man at all. I am very proud to think that he has chosen me.'

'That is well spoken, and I shall tell him.'

'No, you must not tell him, Ruth. Remember that I talk to you as a friend, and not as a child.'

'But I will tell him, because then his brow will become smooth, and he will be happy. He likes to think that people know him to be clever; and he will be glad to be told that you understand him.'

'I think him greater and better than all men; but, Ruth, you must not tell him what I say—not now, at least—for a reason.'

'What reason, Nina?'

'Well; I will tell you, though I would not tell any one else in the world. When we parted last I was angry with him—very angry with him.'

'He had been scolding you, perhaps?'

'I should not mind that—not in the least. He has a right to scold me.'

'He has a right to scold me, I suppose; but I mind it very much.'

'But he has no right to distrust me, Ruth. I wish he could see my heart and all my mind, and know every thought in my breast, and then he would feel that he could trust me. I would not deceive him by a word or a look for all the world. He does not know how true I am to him, and that kills me.'

'I will tell him everything.'

'No, Ruth; tell him nothing. If he cannot find it out without being told, telling will do no good. If you thought a person was a thief, would you change your mind because the person told you he was honest? He must find it out for himself if he is ever to know it.'

When Ruth was gone, Nina knew that she had been comforted. To have spoken about her lover was in itself much; and to have spoken about him as she had done seemed almost to have brought him once more near to her. Ruth had declared that Anton was sad, and had suggested to Nina that the cause of his sadness was the same as her own. There could not but be comfort in this. If he really wished to see her, would he not come over to the Kleinseite? There could be no reason why he should not visit the girl he intended to marry, and whom he was longing to see. Of course he had business which must occupy his time. He could not give up every moment to thoughts of love, as she could do. She told herself all this, and once more endeavoured to be comforted.

And then she unpacked the basket. There were fresh eggs, and a quantity of jelly, and some soup in a jug ready to be made hot, and such delicacies as invalids will eat when their appetites will serve for nothing else. And Nina, as she took these things out, thought only of her father. She took them as coming for him altogether, without any reference to her own use. But at the bottom of the basket there were stockings, and a handkerchief or two, and a petticoat, and a pair of shoes. Should she throw them out among the ashes behind the kitchen, or should she press them to her bosom as treasures to be loved as long as a single thread of them might hang together? She had taken such alms before—from her aunt Sophie—taking them in bitterness of spirit, and wearing them as though they were made of sackcloth, very sore to the skin. The acceptance of such things, even from her aunt, had been gall to her; but, in the old days, no idea of refusing them had come to her. Of course she must submit herself to her aunt's charity, because of her father's poverty. And garments had come to her which were old and worn, bearing unmistakable signs of Lotta's coarse but reparative energies,—raiment against which her feminine niceness would have rebelled, had it been possible for her, in her misfortunes, to indulge her feminine niceness.

But there was a sweet scent of last summer's roses on the things which now lay in her lap, and each article was of the best; and, though each had been worn, they were all such as one girl would lend to another who was her dearest friend,—who was to be made welcome to the wardrobe as though it were her own. There was something of the tenderness of love in the very folding, and respect as well as friendship in the care of the packing. Her aunt's left-off clothes had come to her in a big roll, fastened with a corking-pin. But Rebecca, with delicate fingers, had made each article of her tribute to look pretty, as though for the dress of such a one as Nina prettiness and care must always be needed. It was not possible for her to refuse a present sent to her with so many signs of tenderness.

And then she tried on the shoes. Of all the things she needed these were the most necessary. At her first glance she thought that they were new; but she perceived that they had been worn, and she liked them the better on that account. She put her feet into them and found that they were in truth a little too large for her. And this, even this, tended in some sort to gratify her feelings and soothe the asperity of her grief. 'It is only a quarter of a size,' she said to herself, as she held up her dress that she might look at her feet. And thus she resolved that she would accept her rival's kindness.

On the following morning the priest came—that Father Jerome whom she had known as a child, and from whom she had been unable to obtain ghostly comfort* since she had come in contact with the Jew. Her aunt and her father, Souchey and Lotta Luxa, had all threatened her with Father Jerome; and when it had become manifest to her that it would be necessary that the priest should visit her father in his extremity, she had at first thought that it would be well for her to hide herself. But the cowardice of this had appeared to her to be mean, and she had resolved that she would meet her old friend at her father's bedside. After all, what would his bitterest words be to her after such words as she had endured from her lover?

Father Jerome came, and she received him in the parlour. She received him with downcast eyes and a demeanour of humility, though she was resolved to flare

up against him if he should attack her too cruelly. But
the man was as mild to her and as kind as ever he had
been in her childhood, when he would kiss her, and call
her his little nun, and tell her that if she would be a good
girl she should always have a white dress and roses at the
festival of St. Nicholas. He put his hand on her head and
blessed her, and did not seem to have any abhorrence of
her because she was going to marry a Jew. And yet he
knew it.

He asked a few words as to her father, who was indeed
better on this morning than he had been for the last few
days, and then he passed on into the sick man's room.
And there, after a few faintest words of confession from
the sick man, Nina knelt by her father's bedside, while
the priest prayed for them both, and forgave the sinner
his sins, and prepared him for his further journey with
such preparation as the extreme unction* of his Church
would afford.

When the prayer and the ceremony were over, and the
viaticum*had been duly administered, the priest returned
into the parlour, and Nina followed him. 'He is stronger
than I had expected to find him,' said Father Jerome.

'He has rallied a little, Father, because you were
coming. You may be sure that he is very ill.'

'I know that he is very ill, but I think that he may still
last some days. Should it be so, I will come again.'
After that Nina thought that the priest would have gone;
but he paused for a few moments as though hesitating,
and then spoke again, putting down his hat, which he had
taken up. 'But what is all this that I hear about you, Nina?'

'All what?' said Nina, blushing.

'They tell me that you have engaged yourself to marry
Anton Trendellsohn, the Jew.' She stood before him
confessing her guilt by her silence. 'Is it true, Nina?'
he asked.

'It is true.'

'I am very sorry for that,—very sorry. Could you not
bring yourself to love some Christian youth, rather than
a Jew? Would it not be better, do you think, to do so—
for your soul's sake?'

'It is too late now, Father.'

'Too late! No; it can never be too late to repent of evil.'

'But why should it be evil, Father Jerome? It is permitted; is it not?'

'The law permits it, certainly.'

'And when I am a Jew's wife, may I not go to mass?'

'Yes;—you may go to mass. Who can hinder you?'

'And if I pray devoutly, will not the saints hear me?'

'It is not for me to limit their mercy. I think that they will hear all prayers that are addressed to them with faith and humility.'

'And you, Father, will you not give me absolution if I am a Jew's wife?'

'I would ten times sooner give it you as the wife of a Christian, Nina. My absolution would be nothing to you, Nina, if the while you had a deep sin upon your conscience.' Then the priest went, being unwilling to endure further questioning, and Nina seated herself in a glow of triumph. And this was the worst that she would have to endure from the Church after all her aunt's threatenings,—after Lotta's bitter words, and the reproaches of all around her! Father Jerome—even Father Jerome himself, who was known to be the strictest priest on that side of the river in opposing the iniquities of his flock—did not take upon himself to say that her case as a Christian would be hopeless, were she to marry the Jew! After that she went to the drawer in her bedroom, and restored the picture of the Virgin to its place.

CHAPTER XIV

FATHER JEROME had been very mild with Nina, but his mildness did not produce any corresponding feelings of gentleness in the breasts of Nina's relatives in the Windberg-gasse. Indeed, it had the contrary effect of instigating Madame Zamenoy and Lotta Luxa to new exertions. Nina, in her triumph, could not restrain herself from telling Souchey that Father Jerome did not by any means think so badly of her as did the others; and Souchey,

partly in defence of Nina, and partly in quest of further
sound information on the knotty religious difficulty
involved, repeated it all to Lotta. Among them they
succeeded in cutting Souchey's ground from under him
as far as any defence of Nina was concerned, and they
succeeded also in solving his religious doubts. Poor
Souchey was at last convinced that the best service he
could render to his mistress was to save her from marrying the Jew, let the means by which this was to be done
be, almost, what they might.

As the result of this teaching, Souchey went late one
afternoon to the Jews' quarter. He did not go thither
direct from the house in the Kleinseite, but from Madame
Zamenoy's abode, where he had again dined previously
in Lotta's presence. Madame Zamenoy herself had con-
descended to enlighten his mind on the subject of Nina's
peril, and had gone so far as to invite him to hear a few
words on the subject from a priest on that side of the
water.* Souchey had only heard Nina's report of what
Father Jerome had said, but he was listening with his
own ears while the other priest declared his opinion that
things would go very badly with any Christian girl who
might marry a Jew. This sufficed for him; and then—
having been so far enlightened by Madame Zamenoy
herself—he accepted a little commission, which took him
to the Jew's house. Lotta had had much difficulty in
arranging this; for Souchey was not open to a bribe in
the matter, and on that account was able to press his
legitimate suit very closely. Before he would start on his
errand to the Jew, Lotta was almost obliged to promise
that she would yield.

It was late in the afternoon when he got to Trendellsohn's house. He had never been there before,[1] though he
well knew the exact spot on which it stood, and had often
looked up at the windows, regarding the place with
unpleasant suspicions; for he knew that Trendellsohn
was now the owner of the property that had once been

---

[1] [This is an error on Trollope's part. On p. 152 Nina 'sent
Souchey to the Jews' quarters to tell the sad news' and on
p. 156 Rebecca says: 'Souchey came to the house'.]

his master's, and, of course, as a good Christian, he believed that the Jew had obtained Balatka's money by robbery and fraud. He hesitated a moment before he presented himself at the door, having some fear at his heart. He knew that he was doing right, but these Jews in their own quarter were uncanny, and might be dangerous! To Anton Trendellsohn, over in the Klein-seite, Souchey could be independent, and perhaps on occasions a little insolent; but of Anton Trendellsohn in his own domains he almost acknowledged to himself that he was afraid. Lotta had told him that, if Anton were not at home, his commission could be done as well with the old man; and as he at last made his way round the synagogue to the house door, he determined that he would ask for the elder Jew. That which he had to say, he thought, might be said easier to the father than to the son.

The door of the house stood open, and Souchey, who, in his confusion, missed the bell, entered the passage. The little oil-lamp still hung there, giving a mysterious glimmer of light, which he did not at all enjoy. He walked on very slowly, trying to get courage to call, when, of a sudden, he perceived that there was a figure of a man standing close to him in the gloom. He gave a little start, barely suppressing a scream, and then perceived that the man was Anton Trendellsohn himself. Anton, hearing steps in the passage, had come out from the room on the ground-floor, and had seen Souchey before Souchey had seen him.

'You have come from Josef Balatka's,' said the Jew. 'How is the old man?'

Souchey took off his cap and bowed, and muttered something as to his having come upon an errand. 'And my master is something better to-day,' he said, 'thanks be to God for all His mercies!'

'Amen,' said the Jew.

'But it will only last a day or two; no more than that,' said Souchey. 'He has had the doctor and the priest, and they both say that it is all over with him for this world.'

'And Nina—you have brought some message probably from her?'

'No—no indeed; that is, not exactly; not to-day, Herr Trendellsohn. The truth is, I had wished to speak a word or two to you about the maiden; but perhaps you are engaged—perhaps another time would be better.'

'I am not engaged, and no other time could be better.'

They were still out in the passage, and Souchey hesitated. That which he had to say it would behove him to whisper into the closest privacy of the Jew's ear—into the ear of the old Jew or of the young. 'It is something very particular,' said Souchey.

'Very particular—is it?' said the Jew.

'Very particular indeed,' said Souchey. Then Anton Trendellsohn led the way back into the dark room on the ground-floor from whence he had come, and invited Souchey to follow him. The shutters were up, and the place was seldom used. There was a counter running through it, and a cross-counter, such as are very common when seen by the light of day in shops; but the place seemed to be mysterious to Souchey; and always afterwards, when he thought of this interview, he remembered that his tale had been told in the gloom of a chamber that had never been arranged for honest Christian purposes.

'And now, what is it you have to tell me?' said the Jew.

After some fashion Souchey told his tale, and the Jew listened to him without a word of interruption. More than once Souchey had paused, hoping that the Jew would say something; but not a sound had fallen from Trendellsohn till Souchey's tale was done.

'And it is so—is it?' said the Jew when Souchey ceased to speak. There was nothing in his voice which seemed to indicate either sorrow or joy, or even surprise.

'Yes, it is so,' said Souchey.

'And how much am I to pay you for the information?' the Jew asked.

'You are to pay me nothing,' said Souchey.

'What! you betray your mistress gratis?'

'I do not betray her,' said Souchey. 'I love her and the

old man too. I have been with them through fair
weather and through foul. I have not betrayed her.'

'Then why have you come to me with this story?'

The whole truth was almost on Souchey's tongue. He
had almost said that his sole object was to save his mistress
from the disgrace of marrying a Jew. But he checked
himself, then paused a moment, and then left the room
and the house abruptly. He had done his commission,
and the fewer words which he might have with the Jew
after that the better.

On the following morning Nina was seated by her
father's bedside, when her quick ear caught through the
open door the sound of a footstep in the hall below. She
looked for a moment at the old man, and saw that if not
sleeping he appeared to sleep. She leaned over him for a
moment, gave one gentle touch with her hand to the bed-
clothes, then crept out into the parlour, and closed behind
her the door of the bedroom. When in the middle of the
outer chamber she listened again, and there was clearly
a step on the stairs. She listened again, and she knew
that the step was the step of her lover. He had come to
her at last, then. Now, at this moment, she lost all remembrance of her need of forgiving him. Forgiving him!
What could there be to be forgiven to one who could
make her so happy as she felt herself to be at this moment?
She opened the door of the room just as he had raised his
hand to knock, and threw herself into his arms. 'Anton,
dearest, you have come at last. But I am not going to
scold. I am so glad that you have come, my own one!'

While she was yet speaking, he brought her back into
the room, supporting her with his arm round her waist;
and when the door was closed he stood over her still
holding her up, and looking down into her face, which
was turned up to his. 'Why do you not speak to me,
Anton?' she said. But she smiled as she spoke, and there
was nothing of fear in the tone of her voice, for his look
was kind, and there was love in his eyes.

He stooped down over her, and fastened his lips upon
her forehead. She pressed herself closer against his
shoulder, and shutting her eyes, as she gave herself up to

the rapture of his embrace, told herself that now all should be well with them.

'Dear Nina,' he said.

'Dearest, dearest Anton,' she replied.

And then he asked after her father; and the two sat together for a while, with their knees almost touching, talking in whispers as to the condition of the old man. And they were still so sitting, and still so talking, when Nina rose from her chair, and put up her forefinger with a slight motion for silence, and a pretty look of mutual interest—as though Anton were already one of the same family; and, touching his hair lightly with her hand as she passed him, that he might feel how delighted she was to be able so to touch him, she went back to the door of the bedroom on tiptoe, and, lifting the latch without a sound, put in her head and listened. But the sick man had not stirred. His face was still turned from her, as though he slept, and then, again closing the door, she came back to her lover.

'He is quite quiet,' she said, whispering.

'Does he suffer?'

'I think not; he never complains. When he is awake he will sit with my hand within his own, and now and again there is a little pressure.'

'And he says nothing?'

'Very little; hardly a word now and then. When he does speak, it is of his food.'

'He can eat, then?'

'A morsel of jelly, or a little soup. But, Anton, I must tell you—I tell you everything, you know—where do you think the things that he takes have come from? But perhaps you know.'

'Indeed I do not.'

'They were sent to me by Rebecca Loth.'

'By Rebecca!'

'Yes; by your friend Rebecca. She must be a good girl.'

'She is a good girl, Nina.'

'And you shall know everything; see—she sent me these,' and Nina showed her shoes; 'and the very stockings I have on; I am not ashamed that you should know.'

'Your want, then, has been so great as that?'

'Father has been very poor. How should he not be poor when nothing is earned? And she came here, and she saw it.'

'She sent you these things?'

'Yes, Ruth came with them; there was a great basket with nourishing food for father. It was very kind of her. But, Anton, Rebecca says that I ought not to marry you, because of our religion. She says all the Jews in Prague will become your enemies.'

'We will not stay in Prague; we will go elsewhere. There are other cities besides Prague.'

'Where nobody will know us?'

'Where we will not be ashamed to be known.'

'I told Rebecca that I would give you back all your promises, if you wished me to do so.'

'I do not wish it. I will not give you back your promises, Nina.'

The enraptured girl again clung to him. 'My own one,' she said, 'my darling, my husband; when you speak to me like that, there is no girl in Bohemia so happy as I am. Hush! I thought it was father. But no; there is no sound. I do not mind what any one says to me, as long as you are kind.'

She was now sitting on his knee, and his arm was round her waist, and she was resting her head against his brow; he had asked for no pardon, but all the past was entirely forgiven; why should she even think of it again? Some such thought was passing through her mind, when he spoke a word, and it seemed as though a dagger had gone into her heart. 'About that paper, Nina?' Accursed document, that it should be brought again between them to dash the cup of joy from her lips at such a moment as this! She disengaged herself from his embrace, almost with a leap. 'Well! what about the paper?' she said.

'Simply this, that I would wish to know where it is.'

'And you think I have it?'

'No; I do not think so; I am perplexed about it, hardly knowing what to believe; but I do not think you have it; I think that you know nothing of it.'

'Then why do you mention it again, reminding me of the cruel words which you spoke before?'

'Because it is necessary for both our sakes. I will tell you plainly just what I have heard: your servant Souchey has been with me, and he says that you have it.'

'Souchey!'

'Yes; Souchey. It seemed strange enough to me, for I had always thought him to be your friend.'

'Souchey has told you that I have got it?'

'He says that it is in that desk,' and the Jew pointed to the old depository of all the treasures which Nina possessed.

'He is a liar.'

'I think he is so, though I cannot tell why he should have so lied; but I think he is a liar; I do not believe that it is there; but in such a matter it is well that the fact should be put beyond all dispute. You will not object to my looking into the desk?' He had come there with a fixed resolve that he would demand to search among her papers. It was very unpleasant to him, and he knew that his doing so would be painful to her; but he told himself that it would be best for them both that he should persevere.

'Will you open it, or shall I?' he said, and as he spoke, she looked into his face, and saw that all tenderness and love were banished from it, and that the hard suspicious greed of the Jew was there instead.

'I will not unlock it,' she said; 'there is the key, and you can do as you please.' Then she flung the key upon the table, and stood with her back up against the wall, at some ten paces distant from the spot where the desk stood. He took up the key, and placed it remorselessly in the lock, and opened the desk, and brought all the papers forth on to the table which stood in the middle of the room.

'Are all my letters to be read?' she asked.

'Nothing is to be read,' he said.

'Not that I should mind it; or at least I should have cared but little ten minutes since. There are words there may make you think I have been a fool, but a fool only too faithful to you.'

He made no answer to this, but moved the papers one
by one carefully till he came to a folded document larger
than the others. Why dwell upon it? Of course it was
the deed for which he was searching. Nina, when from
her station by the wall she saw that there was something
in her lover's hands of which she had no knowledge—
something which had been in her own desk without her
privity*—came forward a step or two, looking with all
her eyes. But she did not speak till he had spoken; nor did
he speak at once. He slowly unfolded the document, and
perused the heading of it; then he refolded it, and placed
it on the table, and stood there with his hand upon it.

'This,' said he, 'is the paper for which I am looking.
Souchey, at any rate, is not a liar.'

'How came it there?' said Nina, almost screaming in
her agony.

'That I know not; but Souchey is not a liar; nor were
your aunt and her servant liars in telling me that I
should find it in your hands.'

'Anton,' she said, 'as the Lord made me, I knew not of
it;' and she fell on her knees before his feet.

He looked down upon her, scanning every feature of
her face and every gesture of her body with hard inquiring
eyes. He did not stoop to raise her, nor, at the moment,
did he say a word to comfort her. 'And you think that I
stole it and put it there?' she said. She did not quail
before his eyes, but seemed, though kneeling before him,
to look up at him as though she would defy him. When
first she had sunk upon the ground, she had been weak,
and wanted pardon though she was ignorant of all offence;
but his hardness, as he stood with his eyes fixed upon her,
had hardened her, and all her intellect, though not her
heart, was in revolt against him. 'You think that I have
robbed you?'

'I do not know what to think,' he said.

Then she rose slowly to her feet, and, collecting the
papers which he had strewed upon the table, put them
back slowly into the desk, and locked it.

'You have done with this now,' she said, holding the
key in her hand.

'Yes; I do not want the key again.'

'And you have done with me also?'

He paused a moment or two to collect his thoughts, and then he answered her. 'Nina, I would wish to think about this before I speak of it more fully. What step I may next take I cannot say without considering it much. I would not wish to pain you if I could help it.'

'Tell me at once what it is that you believe of me?'

'I cannot tell you at once. Rebecca Loth is friendly to you, and I will send her to you to-morrow.'

'I will not see Rebecca Loth,' said Nina. 'Hush! there is father's voice. Anton, I have nothing more to say to you;—nothing—nothing.' Then she left him, and went into her father's room.

For some minutes she was busy by her father's bed, and went about her work with a determined alacrity, as though she would wipe out of her mind altogether, for the moment, any thought about her love and the Jew and the document that had been found in her desk; and for a while she was successful, with a consciousness, indeed, that she was under the pressure of a terrible calamity which must destroy her, but still with an outward presence of mind that supported her in her work. And her father spoke to her, saying more to her than he had done for days past, thanking her for her care, patting her hand with his, caressing her, and bidding her still be of good cheer, as God would certainly be good to one who had been so excellent a daughter. 'But I wish, Nina, he were not a Jew,' he said suddenly.

'Dear father, we will not talk of that now.'

'And he is a stern man, Nina.'

But on this subject she would speak no further, and therefore she left the bedside for a moment, and offered him a cup, from which he drank. When he had tasted it he forgot the matter that had been in his mind, and said no further word as to Nina's engagement.

As soon as she had taken the cup from her father's hand, she returned to the parlour. It might be that Anton was still there. She had left him in the room, and had shut her ears against the sound of his steps, as though she were resolved that she would care nothing ever again for his coming or going. He was gone, however, and the room was empty, and she sat down in solitude, with her back against the wall, and began to realise her position. He had told her that others accused her, but that he had not suspected her. He had not suspected her, but he had thought it necessary to search, and had found in her possession that which had made her guilty in his eyes!

She would never see him again—never willingly. It was not only that he would never forgive her, but that she could never now be brought to forgive him. He had stabbed her while her words of love were warmest in his ear. His foul suspicions had been present to his mind even while she was caressing him. He had never known what it was to give himself up really to his love for one moment. While she was seated on his knee, with her head pressed against his, his intellect had been busy with the key and the desk, as though he were a policeman looking for a thief, rather than a lover happy in the endearments of his mistress. Her vivid mind pictured all this to her, filling her full with every incident of the insult she had endured. No. There must be an end of it now. If she could see her aunt that moment, or Lotta, or even Ziska, she would tell them that it should be so. She would say nothing to Anton;—no, not a word again, though both might live for an eternity; but she would write a line to Rebecca Loth, and tell the Jewess that the Jew was now free to marry whom he would among his own people. And some of the words that she thought would be fitting for such a letter occurred to her as she sat there. 'I know now that a Jew and a Christian ought not to love each other as we loved. Their hearts are different.' That was her present purpose, but, as will be seen, she changed it afterwards.

But ever and again as she strengthened her resolution, her thoughts would run from her, carrying her back to the sweet rapture of some moment in which the man had been gracious to her; and even while she was struggling to teach herself to hate him, she would lean her head on one side, as though by doing so she might once more touch his brow with hers; and unconsciously she would put out her fingers, as though they might find their way into his hand. And then she would draw them back with a shudder, as though recoiling from the touch of an adder.

Hours had passed over her before she began to think whence had come the paper which Trendellsohn had found in her desk; and then, when the idea of some fraud presented itself to her, that part of the subject did not seem to her to be of great moment. It mattered but little who had betrayed her. It might be Rebecca, or Souchey, or Ruth, or Lotta, or all of them together. His love, his knowledge of her whom he loved, should have carried him aloft out of the reach of any such poor trick as that! What mattered it now who had stolen her key, and gone like a thief to her desk, and laid this plot for her destruction? That he should have been capable of being deceived by such a plot against her was enough for her. She did not even speak to Souchey on the subject. In the course of the afternoon he came across her as she moved about the house, looking ashamed, not daring to meet her eyes, hardly able to mutter a word to her. But she said not a syllable to him about her desk. She could not bring herself to plead the cause between her and her lover before her father's servant.

The greater part of the day she passed by her father's bedside, but whenever she could escape from the room, she seated herself in the chair against the wall, endeavouring to make up her mind as to the future. But there was much more of passion than of thought within her breast. Never, never, never would she forgive him! Never again would she sit on his knee caressing him. Never again would she even speak to him. Nothing would she take from his hand, or from the hands of his friends! Nor would she ever stoop to take aught from her aunt, or from Ziska. They had triumphed over her. She knew not how. They had triumphed over her, but the triumph should be very bitter to them—very bitter, if there was any touch of humanity left among them.

Later in the day there came to be something of motion in the house. Her father was worse in health, was going fast, and the doctor was again there. And in these moments Souchey was with her, busy in the dying man's room; and there were gentle kind words spoken between him and Nina—as would be natural between such persons at such a time. He knew that he had been a traitor, and the thought of his treachery was heavy at his heart; but he perceived that no immediate punishment was to come upon him, and it was some solace to him that he could be sedulous and gentle and tender. And Nina, though she knew that the man had given his aid in destroying her, bore with him not only without a hard word, but almost without a severe thought. What did it matter what such a one as Souchey could do?

In the middle watches of that night the old man died, and Nina was alone in the world. Souchey, indeed, was with her in the house, and took from her all painful charge of the bed at which now her care could no longer be of use. And early in the morning, while it was yet dark, Lotta came down, and spoke words to her, of which she remembered nothing. And then she knew that her aunt Sophie was there, and that some offers were made to her at which she only shook her head. 'Of course you will come up to us,' aunt Sophie said. And she made many more suggestions, in answer to all of which Nina only shook her head. Then her aunt and Nina, with Lotta's aid, fixed upon some plan,—Nina hardly knew what,—as to the morrow. She did not care to know what it was that they fixed. They were going to leave her alone for this day, and the day would be very long. She told herself that it would be long enough for her.

The day was very long. When her aunt had left her she saw no one but Souchey and an old woman who was busy in the bedroom which was now closed. She had stood at the foot of the bed with her aunt, but after that she did not return to the chamber. It was not only her father who, for her, was now lying dead. She had loved her father well, but with a love infinitely greater she had loved another; and that other one was now dead to her also. What was there left to her in the world? The charity of her aunt, and Lotta's triumph, and Ziska's love? No indeed! She would bear neither the charity, nor the triumph, nor the love. One other visitor came to the house that day. It was Rebecca Loth. But Nina refused to see Rebecca. 'Tell her,' she said to Souchey, 'that I cannot see a stranger while my father is lying dead.' How often did the idea occur to her, throughout the terrible length of that day, that 'he' might come to her? But he came not. 'So much the better,' she said to herself. 'Were he to come, I would not see him.'

Late in the evening, when the little lamp in the room had been already burning for some hour or two, she called Souchey to her. 'Take this note,' she said, 'to Anton Trendellsohn.'

'What! to-night?' said Souchey, trembling.

'Yes, to-night. It is right that he should know that the house is now his own, to do what he will with it.'

Then Souchey took the note, which was as follows:—

'My father is dead, and the house will be empty to-morrow. You may come and take your property without fear that you will be troubled by

'NINA BALATKA.'

CHAPTER XV

WHEN Souchey left the room with the note, Nina went to the door and listened. She heard him turn the lock below, and heard his step out in the courtyard, and listened till she knew that he was crossing the square. Then she ran quickly up to her own room, put on her hat and her old worn cloak—the cloak which aunt Sophie had given her—and returned once more into the parlour. She looked round the room with anxious eyes, and seeing her desk, she took the key from her pocket and put it into the lock. Then there came a thought into her mind as to the papers; but she resolved that the thought need not arrest her, and she left the key in the lock with the papers untouched. Then she went to the door of her father's room, and stood there for a moment with her hand upon the latch. She tried it ever so gently, but she found that the door was bolted. The bolt, she knew, was on her side, and she could withdraw it; but she did not do so, seeming to take the impediment as though it were a sufficient bar against her entrance. Then she ran down the stairs rapidly, opened the front door, and found herself out in the night air.

It was a cold windy night—not so late, indeed, as to have made her feel that it was night, had she not come from the gloom of the dark parlour, and the glimmer of her one small lamp. It was now something beyond the middle of October, and at present it might be eight o'clock. She knew that there would be moonlight, and she looked up at the sky; but the clouds were all dark, though she could see that they were moving along with the gusts of wind. It was very cold, and she drew her cloak closer about her as she stepped out into the archway.

Up above her, almost close to her in the gloom of the night, there was the long colonnade of the palace, with the lights glimmering in the windows as they always glimmered. She allowed herself for a moment to think who might be there in those rooms—as she had so often thought before. It was possible that Anton might be there. He had been there once before at this time in the evening, as he himself had told her. Wherever he might be, was he thinking of her? But if he thought of her, he was thinking of her as one who had deceived him, who had tried to rob him. Ah! the day would soon come in which he would learn that he had wronged her. When that day should come, would his heart be bitter within him? 'He will certainly be unhappy for a time,' she said; 'but he is hard and will recover, and she will console him. It will be better so. A Christian and a Jew should never love each other.'

As she stood the clouds were lifted for a moment from the face of the risen moon, and she could see by the pale clear light the whole façade of the palace as it ran along the steep hillside above her. She could count the arches, as she had so often counted them by the same light. They

seemed to be close over her head, and she stood there
thinking of them, till the clouds had again skurried across
the moon's face, and she could only see the accustomed
glimmer in the windows. As her eye fell upon the well-
known black buildings around her, she found that it was
very dark. It was well for her that it should be so dark.
She never wanted to see the light again.

There was a footstep on the other side of the square,
and she paused till it had passed away beyond the reach
of her ears. Then she came out from under the archway,
and hurried across the square to the street which led to
the bridge. It was a dark gloomy lane, narrow, and
composed of high buildings without entrances, the sides
of barracks and old palaces.* From the windows above
her head on the left, she heard the voices of soldiers.
A song was being sung, and she could hear the words.
How cruel it was that other people should have so much
of light-hearted joy in the world, but that for her everything should have been so terribly sad! The wind, as it
met her, seemed to penetrate to her bones. She was very
cold! But it was useless to regard that. There was no
place on the face of the earth that would ever be warm
for her.

As she passed along the causeway leading to the
bridge, a sound with which she was very familiar met her
ears. They were singing vespers* under the shadow of one
of the great statues which are placed one over each arch
of the bridge. There was a lay friar* standing by a little
table, on which there was a white cloth and a lighted
lamp and a small crucifix; and above the crucifix, supported against the stonework of the bridge, there was a
picture of the Virgin with her Child, and there was a
tawdry wreath of paper flowers, so that by the light of the
lamp you could see that a little altar had been prepared.
And on the table there was a plate containing kreutzers,
into which the faithful who passed and took a part in the
evening psalm of praise, might put an offering for the
honour of the Virgin, and for the benefit of the poor friar
and his brethren in their poor cloisters at home. Nina
knew all about it well. Scores of times had she stood on

the same spot upon the bridge, and sung the vesper hymn, ere she passed on to the Kleinseite.

And now she paused and sang it once again. Around the table upon the pavement there stood perhaps thirty or forty persons, most of them children, and the remainder girls perhaps of Nina's age. And the friar stood close by the table, leaning idly against the bridge, with his eye wandering from the little plate with the kreutzers to the passers-by who might possibly contribute. And ever and anon he with drawling voice would commence some sentence of the hymn, and then the girls and children would take it up, well knowing the accustomed words; and their voices as they sang would sound sweetly across the waters, the loud gurgling of which, as they ran beneath the arch, would be heard during the pauses.

And Nina stopped and sang. When she was a child she had sung there very often, and the friar of those days would put his hand upon her head and bless her, as she brought her small piece of tribute to his plate. Of late, since she had been at variance with the Church by reason of the Jew, she had always passed by rapidly, as though feeling that she had no longer any right to take part in such a ceremony. But now she had done with the Jew, and surely she might sing the vesper song. So she stopped and sang, remembering not the less as she sang, that that which she was about to do, if really done, would make all such singing unavailing for her.

But then, perhaps, even yet it might not be done. Lotta's first prediction, that the Jew would desert her, had certainly come true; and Lotta's second prediction, that there would be nothing left for her but to drown herself, seemed to her to be true also. She had left the house in which her father's dead body was still lying, with this purpose. Doubly deserted as she now was by lover and father, she could live no longer. It might, however, be possible that that saint who was so powerful over the waters might yet do something for her,—might yet interpose on her behalf, knowing, as he did, of course, that all idea of marriage between her, a Christian, and her Jew lover had been abandoned. At any rate she

stood and sang the hymn, and when there came the
accustomed lull at the end of the verse, she felt in her
pocket for a coin, and, taking a piece of ten kreutzers,
she stepped quickly up to the plate and put it in. A day
or two ago ten kreutzers was an important portion of the
little sum which she still had left in hand, but now ten
kreutzers could do nothing for her. It was at any rate
better that the friar should have it than that her money
should go with her down into the blackness of the river.
Nevertheless she did not give the friar all. She saw one
girl whispering to another as she stepped up to the table,
and she heard her own name. 'That is Nina Balatka.'
And then there was an answer which she did not hear,
but which she was sure referred to the Jew. The girls
looked at her with angry eyes, and she longed to stop and
explain to them that she was no longer betrothed to the
Jew. Then, perhaps, they would be gentle with her, and
she might yet hear a kind word spoken to her before she
went. But she did not speak to them. No; she would
never speak to man or woman again. What was the use
of speaking now? No sympathy that she could receive
would go deep enough to give relief to such wounds as
hers.

As she dropped her piece of money into the plate her
eyes met those of the friar, and she recognised at once a
man whom she had known years ago, at the same spot
and engaged in the same work. He was old and haggard,
and thin and grey, and very dirty; but there came a smile
over his face as he also recognised her. He could not
speak to her, for he had to take up a verse in the hymn,
and drawl out the words which were to set the crowd
singing, and Nina had retired back again before he was
silent. But she knew that he had known her, and she
almost felt that she had found a friend who would be kind
to her. On the morrow, when inquiry would be made—
and aunt Sophie would certainly be loud in her inquiries
—this friar would be able to give some testimony respecting her.

She passed on altogether across the bridge, in order
that she might reach the spot she desired without observa-

tion—and perhaps also with some halting idea that she might thus postpone the evil moment. The figure of St. John Nepomucene rested on the other balustrade of the bridge, and she was minded to stand for a while under its shadow. Now, at Prague it is the custom that they who pass over the bridge shall always take the right-hand path as they go; and she, therefore, in coming from the Kleinseite, had taken that opposite to the statue of the saint. She had thought of this, and had told herself that she would cross the roadway in the middle of the bridge; but at that moment the moon was shining brightly: and then, too, the night was long. Why need she be in a hurry?

At the further end of the bridge she stood a while in the shade of the watch-tower, and looked anxiously around her. When last she had been over in the Old Town, within a short distance of the spot where she now stood, she had chanced to meet her lover. What if she should see him now? She was sure that she would not speak to him. And yet she looked very anxiously up the dark street, through the glimmer of the dull lamps. First there came one man, and then another, and a third; and she thought, as her eyes fell upon them, that the figure of each was the figure of Anton Trendellsohn. But as they emerged from the darker shadow into the light that was near, she saw that it was not so, and she told herself that she was glad. If Anton were to come and find her there, it might be that he would disturb her purpose. But yet she looked again before she left the shadow of the tower. Now there was no one passing in the street. There was no figure there to make her think that her lover was coming either to save her or to disturb her.

Taking the pathway on the other side, she turned her face again towards the Kleinseite, and very slowly crept along under the balustrade of the bridge. This bridge over the Moldau is remarkable in many ways, but it is specially remarkable for the largeness of its proportions. It is very long, taking its spring from the shore a long way before the actual margin of the river; it is of a fine

breadth: the side-walks to it are high and massive; and
the groups of statues with which it is ornamented, though
not in themselves of much value as works of art, have a
dignity by means of their immense size which they lend
to the causeway, making the whole thing noble, grand,
and impressive. And below, the Moldau runs with a
fine, silent, dark volume of water,—a very sea of waters
when the rains have fallen and the little rivers have been
full, though in times of drought great patches of ugly dry
land are to be seen in its half-empty bed. At the present
moment there were no such patches; and the waters ran
by, silent, black, in great volumes, and with unchecked
rapid course. It was only by pausing specially to listen
to them that the passer-by could hear them as they
glided smoothly round the piers of the bridge. Nina did
pause and did hear them. They would have been almost
less terrible to her, had the sound been rougher and
louder.

On she went, very slowly. The moon, she thought,
had disappeared altogether before she reached the cross
inlaid in the stone on the bridge-side, on which she was
accustomed to lay her fingers, in order that she might
share somewhat of the saint's power over the river. At
that moment, as she came up to it, the night was very
dark. She had calculated that by this time the light of
the moon would have waned, so that she might climb to
the spot which she had marked for herself without observation. She paused, hesitating whether she would put
her hand upon the cross. It could not at least do her any
harm. It might be that the saint would be angry with
her, accusing her of hypocrisy; but what would be the
saint's anger for so small a thing amidst the multitudes
of charges that would be brought against her? For that
which she was going to do now there could be no absolution given. And perhaps the saint might perceive that
the deed on her part was not altogether hypocritical—
that there was something in it of a true prayer. He might
see this, and intervene to save her from the waters. So
she put the palm of her little hand full upon the cross,
and then kissed it heartily, and after that raised it up

again till it rested on the foot of the saint. As she stood there she heard the departing voices of the girls and children singing the last verse of the vesper hymn, as they followed the friar off the causeway of the bridge into the Kleinseite.

She was determined that she would persevere. She had endured that which made it impossible that she should recede, and had sworn to herself a thousand times that she would never endure that which would have to be endured if she remained longer in this cruel world. There would be no roof to cover her now but the roof in the Windberg-gasse, beneath which there was to her a hell upon earth. No; she would face the anger of all the saints rather than eat the bitter bread which her aunt would provide for her. And she would face the anger of all the saints rather than fall short in her revenge upon her lover. She had given herself to him altogether,—for him she had been half-starved, when, but for him, she might have lived as a favoured daughter in her aunt's house,—for him she had made it impossible to herself to regard any other man with a spark of affection,—for his sake she had hated her cousin Ziska—her cousin who was handsome, and young, and rich, and had loved her, —feeling that the very idea that she could accept love from any one but Anton had been an insult to her. She had trusted Anton as though his word had been gospel to her. She had obeyed him in everything, allowing him to scold her as though she were already subject to his rule; and, to speak the truth, she had enjoyed such treatment, obtaining from it a certain assurance that she was already his own. She had loved him entirely, had trusted him altogether, had been prepared to bear all that the world could fling upon her for his sake, wanting nothing in return but that he should know that she was true to him.

This he had not known, nor had he been able to understand such truth. It had not been possible to him to know it. The inborn suspicion of his nature had broken out in opposition to his love, forcing her to acknowledge to herself that she had been wrong in loving a Jew. He had been unable not to suspect her of some vile scheme

by which she might possibly cheat him of his property, if
at the last moment she should not become his wife. She
told herself that she understood it all now—that she
could see into his mind, dark and gloomy as were its
recesses. She had wasted all her heart upon a man who
had never even believed in her; and would she not be
revenged upon him? Yes, she would be revenged, and
she would cure the malady of her own love by the only
possible remedy within her reach.

The statue of St. John Nepomucene is a single figure,
standing in melancholy weeping posture on the balustrade
of the bridge, without any of that ponderous strength of
widespread stone which belongs to the other groups.
This St. John is always pictured to us as a thin, melancholy, half-starved saint, who has had all the life washed
out of him by his long immersion. There are saints to
whom a trusting religious heart can turn, relying on their
apparent physical capabilities. St. Mark, for instance, is
always a tower of strength, and St. Christopher is very
stout, and St. Peter carries with him an ancient man-
liness which makes one marvel at his cowardice when he
denied his Master. St. Lawrence, too, with his gridiron,
and St. Bartholomew with his flaying-knife and his own
skin* hanging over his own arm, look as though they
liked their martyrdom, and were proud of it, and could
be useful on an occasion. But this St. John of the Bridges
has no pride in his appearance, and no strength in his
look. He is a mild, meek saint, teaching one rather by his
attitude how to bear with the malice of the waters, than
offering any protection against their violence. But now,
at this moment, his aid was the only aid to which Nina
could look with any hope. She had heard of his rescuing
many persons from death amidst the current of the
Moldau. Indeed she thought that she could remember
having been told that the river had no power to drown
those who could turn their minds to him when they were
struggling in the water. Whether this applied only to those
who were in sight of his statue on the bridge of Prague,
or whether it was good in all rivers of the world, she did
not know. Then she tried to think whether she had ever

heard of any case in which the saint had saved one who had—who had done the thing which she was now about to do. She was almost sure that she had never heard of such a case as that. But, then, was there not something special in her own case? Was not her suffering so great, her condition so piteous, that the saint would be driven to compassion in spite of the greatness of her sin? Would he not know that she was punishing the Jew by the only punishment with which she could reach him? She looked up into the saint's wan face, and fancied that no eyes were ever so piteous, no brow ever so laden with the deep suffering of compassion. But would this punishment reach the heart of Anton Trendellsohn? Would he care for it? When he should hear that she had—destroyed her own life because she could not endure the cruelty of his suspicion, would the tidings make him unhappy? When last they had been together he had told her, with all that energy which he knew so well how to put into his words, that her love was necessary to his happiness. 'I will never release you from your promises,' he had said, when she offered to give him back his troth because of the ill-will of his people. And she still believed him. Yes, he did love her. There was something of consolation to her in the assurance that the strings of his heart would be wrung when he should hear of this. If his bosom were capable of agony, he would be agonised.

It was very dark at this moment, and now was the time for her to climb upon the stonework and hide herself behind the drapery of the saint's statue. More than once, as she had crossed the bridge, she had observed the spot, and had told herself that if such a deed were to be done, that would be the place for doing it. She had always been conscious, since the idea had entered her mind, that she would lack the power to step boldly up on to the parapet and go over at once, as the bathers do when they tumble headlong into the stream that has no dangers for them. She had known that she must crouch, and pause, and think of it, and look at it, and nerve herself with the memory of her wrongs. Then, at some moment in which her heart was wrung to the utmost, she would gradually slacken her hold, and the dark, black, silent river should take her. She climbed up into the niche, and found that the river was very far from her, though death was so near to her and the fall would be so easy. When she became aware that there was nothing between her and the great void space below her, nothing to guard her, nothing left to her in all the world to protect her, she retreated, and descended again to the pavement. And never in her life had she moved with more care, lest, inadvertently, a foot or a hand might slip, and she might tumble to her doom against her will.

When she was again on the pathway she remembered her note to Anton—that note which was already in his hands. What would he think of her if she were only to threaten the deed, and then not perform it? And would she allow him to go unpunished? Should he triumph, as he would do if she were now to return to the house which she had told him she had left? She clasped her hands together tightly, and pressed them first to her bosom and then to her brow, and then again she returned to the niche from which the fall into the river must be made. Yes, it was very easy. The plunge might be taken at any moment. Eternity was before her, and of life there remained to her but the few moments in which she might cling there and think of what was coming. Surely she need not begrudge herself a minute or two more of life.

She was very cold, so cold that she pressed herself against the stone in order that she might save herself from the wind that whistled round her. But the water would be colder still than the wind, and when once there she could never again be warm. The chill of the night, and the blackness of the gulf before her, and the smooth rapid gurgle of the dark moving mass of waters beneath, were together more horrid to her imagination than even death itself. Thrice she released herself from her backward pressure against the stone, in order that she might fall forward and have done with it, but as often she found herself returning involuntarily to the protection which still remained to her. It seemed as though she could not fall. Though she would have thought that another must have gone directly to destruction if placed where she was crouching—though she would have trembled with agony to see any one perched in such danger—she appeared to be firm fixed. She must jump forth boldly, or the river would not take her. Ah! what if it were so—that the saint who stood over her, and whose cross she had so lately kissed, would not let her perish from beneath his feet? In these moments her mind wandered in a maze of religious doubts and fears, and she entertained, unconsciously, enough of doctrinal scepticism to found a school of freethinkers. Could it be that God would punish her with everlasting torments because in her agony she was driven to this as her only mode of relief? Would there be no measuring of her sins against her sorrows, and no account taken of the simplicity of her life? She looked up towards heaven, not praying in words, but with a prayer in her heart. For her there could be no absolution, no final blessing. The act of her going would be an act of terrible sin. But God would know all, and would surely take some measure of her case. He could save her if He would, despite every priest in Prague. More than one passenger had walked by while she was crouching in her niche beneath the statue—had passed by and had not seen her. Indeed, the night at present was so dark, that one standing still and looking for her would hardly be able to define her figure. And yet, dark as it was, she could see something of the movement of the waters beneath her, some shimmer produced by the gliding movement of the stream. Ah! she would go now and have done with it. Every moment that she remained was but an added agony.

Then, at that moment, she heard a voice on the bridge near her, and she crouched close again, in order that the passenger might pass by without noticing her. She did not wish that any one should hear the splash of her plunge, or be called on to make ineffectual efforts to save her. So she would wait again. The voice drew nearer to her, and suddenly she became aware that it was Souchey's voice. It was Souchey, and he was not alone. It must be Anton who had come out with him to seek her, and to save her. But no. He should have no such relief as that from his coming sorrow. So she clung fast, waiting till they should pass, but still leaning a little towards the causeway, so that, if it were possible, she might see the figures as they passed. She heard the voice of Souchey quite plain, and then she perceived that Souchey's companion was a woman. Something of the gentleness of a woman's voice reached her ear, but she could distinguish no word that was spoken. The steps were now very close to her, and with terrible anxiety she peeped out to see who might be Souchey's companion. She saw the figure, and she knew at once by the hat that it was Rebecca Loth. They were walking fast, and were close to her now. They would be gone in an instant.

On a sudden, at the very moment that Souchey and Rebecca were in the act of passing beneath the feet of the saint, the clouds swept by from off the disc of the waning moon, and the three faces were looking at each other in the clear pale light of the night. Souchey started back and screamed. Rebecca leaped forward and put the grasp of her hand tight upon the skirt of Nina's dress, first one hand and then the other, and, pressing forward with her body against the parapet, she got a hold also of Nina's foot. She perceived instantly what was the girl's purpose, but, by God's blessing on her efforts, there should be no cold form found in the river that night; or, if one, then there should be two. Nina kept her hold against the figure, appalled, dumbfounded, awe-stricken, but still with some inner consciousness of salvation that comforted her. Whether her life was due to the saint or to the Jewess she knew not, but she acknowledged to herself silently that death was beyond her reach, and she was grateful.

'Nina,' said Rebecca. Nina still crouched against the stone, with her eyes fixed on the other girl's face; but she was unable to speak. The clouds had again obscured the moon, and the air was again black, but the two now could see each other in the darkness, or feel that they did so. 'Nina, Nina—why are you here?'

'I do not know,' said Nina, shivering.

'For the love of God take care of her,' said Souchey, 'or she will be over into the river.'

'She cannot fall now,' said Rebecca. 'Nina, will you not come down to me? You are very cold. Come down, and I will warm you.'

'I am very cold,' said Nina. Then gradually she slid down into Rebecca's arms, and was placed sitting on a little step immediately below the figure of St. John. Rebecca knelt by her side, and Nina's head fell upon the shoulder of the Jewess. Then she burst into the violence of hysterics, but after a moment or two a flood of tears relieved her.

'Why have you come to me?' she said. 'Why have you not left me alone?'

'Dear Nina, your sorrows have been too heavy for you to bear.'

'Yes; they have been very heavy.'

'We will comfort you, and they shall be softened.'

'I do not want comfort. I only want to—to—to go.'

While Rebecca was chafing Nina's hands and feet, and tying a handkerchief from off her own shoulders round Nina's neck, Souchey stood over them, not knowing what to propose. 'Perhaps we had better carry her back to the old house,' he said.

'I will not be carried back,' said Nina.

'No, dear; the house is desolate and cold. You shall not go there. You shall come to our house, and we will do for you the best we can there, and you shall be comfortable. There is no one there but mother, and she is kind and gracious. She will understand that your father has died, and that you are alone.'

Nina, as she heard this, pressed her head and shoulders close against Rebecca's body. As it was not to be allowed to her to escape from all her troubles, as she had thought to do, she would prefer the neighbourhood of the Jews to that of any Christians. There was no Christian now who would say a kind word to her. Rebecca spoke to her very kindly, and was soft and gentle with her. She could not go where she would be alone. Even if left to do so, all physical power would fail her. She knew that she was weak as a child is weak, and that she must submit to be governed. She thought it would be better to be governed by Rebecca Loth at the present moment than by any one else whom she knew. Rebecca had spoken of her mother, and Nina was conscious of a faint wish that there had been no such person in her friend's house; but this was a minor trouble, and one which she could afford to disregard amidst all her sorrows. How much more terrible would have been her fate had she been carried away to aunt Sophie's house! 'Does he know?' she said, whispering the question into Rebecca's ear.

'Yes, he knows. It was he who sent me.' Why did he not come himself? That question flashed across Nina's mind,—and it was present also to Rebecca. She knew that it was the question which Nina, within her heart, would silently ask. 'I was there when the note came,' said Rebecca, 'and he thought that a woman could do more than a man. I am so glad he sent me—so very glad. Shall we go, dear?'

Then Nina rose from her seat, and stood up, and began to move slowly. Her limbs were stiff with cold, and at first she could hardly walk; but she did not feel that she would be unable to make the journey. Souchey came to her side, but she rejected his arm petulantly. 'Do not let him come,' she said to Rebecca. 'I will do whatever you tell me; I will indeed.' Then the Jewess said a word or two to the old man, and he retreated from Nina's side, but stood looking at her till she was out of sight. Then he returned home to the cold desolate house in the Kleinseite, where his only companion was the lifeless body of his old master. But Souchey, as he left his young mistress, made no complaint of her treatment of him. He knew that he had betrayed her, and brought her close upon the step of death's door. He could understand it all now. Indeed he had understood it all since the first word that Anton Trendellsohn had spoken after reading Nina's note.

'She will destroy herself,' Anton had said.

'What! Nina, my mistress?' said Souchey. Then, while Anton had called Rebecca to him, Souchey had seen it all. 'Master,' he said, when the Jew returned to him, 'it was Lotta Luxa who put the paper in the desk. Nina knew nothing of its being there.' Then the Jew's heart sank coldly within him, and his conscience became hot within his bosom. He lost nothing of his presence of mind, but simply hurried Rebecca upon her errand. 'I shall see you again to-night,' he said to the girl.

'You must come then to our house,' said Rebecca. 'It may be that I shall not be able to leave it.'

Rebecca, as she led Nina back across the bridge, at first said nothing further. She pressed the other girl's arm within her own, and there was much of tenderness and regard in the pressure. She was silent, thinking, perhaps, that any speech might be painful to her companion. But Nina could not restrain herself from a question, 'What will they say of me?'

'No one, dear, shall say anything.'

'But he knows.'

'I know not what he knows, but his knowledge, whatever it be, is only food for his love. You may be sure of his love, Nina—quite sure, quite sure. You may take my word for that. If that has been your doubt, you have doubted wrongly.'

Not all the healing medicines of Mercury, not wine from the flasks of the gods,* could have given Nina life and strength as did those words from her rival's lips. All her memory of his offences against her had again gone in her thought of her own sin. Would he forgive her and still love her? Yes; she was a weak woman—very weak; but she had that one strength which is sufficient to atone for all feminine weakness,—she could really love; or rather, having loved, she could not cease to love. Anger had no effect on her love, or was as water thrown on blazing coal, which makes it burn more fiercely. Ill usage could not crush her love. Reason, either from herself or others, was unavailing against it. Religion had no power over it. Her love had become her religion to Nina. It took the place of all things both in heaven and earth. Mild as she was by nature, it made her a tigress to those who opposed it. It was all the world to her. She had tried to die, because

her love had been wounded; and now she was ready to
live again because she was told that her lover—the lover
who had used her so cruelly—still loved her. She pressed
Rebecca's arm close into her side. 'I shall be better
soon,' she said. Rebecca did not doubt that Nina would
soon be better, but of her own improvement she was by
no means so certain.

They walked on through the narrow crooked streets
into the Jews' quarter, and soon stood at the door of
Rebecca's house. The latch was loose, and they entered,
and they found a lamp ready for them on the stairs.
'Had you not better come to my bed for to-night?' said
Rebecca.

'Only that I should be in your way, I should be so
glad.'

'You shall not be in my way. Come, then. But first
you must eat and drink.' Though Nina declared that she
could not eat a morsel, and wanted no drink but water,
Rebecca tended upon her, bringing the food and wine
that were in truth so much needed. 'And now, dear, I
will help you to bed. You are yet cold, and there you
will be warm.'

'But when shall I see him?'

'Nay, how can I tell? But, Nina, I will not keep him
from you. He shall come to you here when he chooses—
if you choose it also.'

'I do choose it—I do choose it,' said Nina, sobbing in
her weakness—conscious of her weakness.

While Rebecca was yet assisting Nina—the Jewess
kneeling as the Christian sat on the bedside—there came
a low rap at the door, and Rebecca was summoned away.
'I shall be but a moment,' she said, and she ran down
to the front door.

'Is she here?' said Anton, hoarsely.

'Yes, she is here.'

'The Lord be thanked! And can I not see her?'

'You cannot see her now, Anton. She is very weary,
and all but in bed.'

'To-morrow I may come?'

'Yes, to-morrow.'

'And, tell me, how did you find her? Where did you find her?'

'To-morrow, Anton, you shall be told,—whatever there is to tell. For to-night, is it not enough for you to know that she is with me? She will share my bed, and I will be as a sister to her.'

Then Anton spoke a word of warm blessing to his friend, and went his way home.

CHAPTER XVI

EARLY in the following year, while the ground was yet bound with frost, and the great plains of Bohemia were still covered with snow, a Jew and his wife took their leave of Prague, and started for one of the great cities of the west. They carried with them but little of the outward signs of wealth, and but few of those appurtenances of comfort which generally fall to the lot of brides among the rich; the man, however, was well to do in the world, and was one who was not likely to bring his wife to want. It need hardly be said that Anton Trendellsohn was the man, and that Nina Balatka was his wife.

On the eve of their departure, Nina and her friend the Jewess had said farewell to each other. 'You will write to me from Frankfort?' said Rebecca.

'Indeed I will,' said Nina; 'and you, you will write to me often, very often?'

'As often as you will wish it.'

'I shall wish it always,' said Nina; 'and you can write; you are clever. You know how to make your words say what there is in your heart.'

'But you have been able to make your face more eloquent than any words.'

'Rebecca, dear Rebecca! Why was it that he did not love such a one as you rather than me? You are more beautiful.'

'But he at least has not thought so.'

'And you are so clever and so good; and you could have given him help which I never can give him.'

'He does not want help. He wants to have by his side
a sweet soft nature that can refresh him by its contrast to
his own. He has done right to love you, and to make you
his wife; only, I could wish that you were as we are in
religion.' To this Nina made no answer. She could not
promise that she would change her religion, but she
thought that she would endeavour to do so. She would
do so if the saints would let her. 'I am glad you are
going away, Nina,' continued Rebecca. 'It will be better
for him and better for you.'

'Yes, it will be better.'

'And it will be better for me also.' Then Nina threw
herself on Rebecca's neck and wept. She could say
nothing in words in answer to that last assertion. If
Rebecca really loved the man who was now the husband
of another, of course it would be better that they should
be apart. But Nina, who knew herself to be weak, could
not understand that Rebecca, who was so strong, should
have loved as she had loved.

'If you have daughters,' said Rebecca, 'and if he will
let you name one of them after me, I shall be glad.' Nina
swore that if God gave her such a treasure as a daughter,
that child should be named after the friend who had
been so good to her.

There were also a few words of parting between Anton
Trendellsohn and the girl who had been brought up to
believe that she was to be his wife; but though there was
friendship in them, there was not much of tenderness.
'I hope you will prosper where you are going,' said
Rebecca, as she gave the man her hand.

'I do not fear but that I shall prosper, Rebecca.'

'No; you will become rich, and perhaps great—as
great, that is, as we Jews can make ourselves.'

'I hope you will live to hear that the Jews are not
crushed elsewhere as they are here in Prague.'

'But, Anton, you will not cease to love the old city
where your fathers and friends have lived so long?'

'I will never cease to love those, at least, whom I leave
behind me. Farewell, Rebecca;' and he attempted to
draw her to him as though he would kiss her. But she

withdrew from him, very quietly, with no mark of anger, with no ostentation of refusal. 'Farewell,' she said. 'Perhaps we shall see each other after many years.'

Trendellsohn, as he sat beside his young wife in the post-carriage which took them out of the city, was silent till he had come nearly to the outskirts of the town; and then he spoke. 'Nina,' he said, 'I am leaving behind me, and for ever, much that I love well.'

'And it is for my sake,' she said. 'I feel it daily, hourly. It makes me almost wish that you had not loved me.'

'But I take with me that which I love infinitely better than all that Prague contains. I will not, therefore, allow myself a regret. Though I should never see the old city again, I will always look upon my going as a good thing done.' Nina could only answer him by caressing his hand, and by making internal oaths that her very best should be done in every moment of her life to make him contented with the lot he had chosen.

There remains very little of the tale to be told—nothing, indeed, of Nina's tale—and very little to be explained. Nina slept in peace at Rebecca's house that night on which she had been rescued from death upon the bridge —or, more probably, lay awake anxiously thinking what might yet be her fate. She had been very near to death —so near that she shuddered, even beneath the warmth of the bed-clothes, and with the protection of her friend so close to her, as she thought of those long dreadful minutes she had passed crouching over the river at the feet of the statue. She had been very near to death, and for a while could hardly realise the fact of her safety. She knew that she was glad to have been saved; but what might come next was, at that moment, all vague, uncertain, and utterly beyond her own control. She hardly ventured to hope more than that Anton Trendellsohn would not give her up to Madame Zamenoy. If he did, she must seek the river again, or some other mode of escape from that worst of fates. But Rebecca had assured her of Anton's love, and in Rebecca's words she had a certain, though a dreamy, faith. The night was long, but she wished it to be longer. To be there and to feel

that she was warm and safe was almost happiness for her
after the misery she had endured.

On the next day, and for a day or two afterwards, she
was feverish and she did not rise, but Rebecca's mother
came to her, and Ruth,— and at last Anton himself. She
never could quite remember how those few days were
passed, or what was said, or how it came to be arranged
that she was to stay for a while in Rebecca's house; that
she was to stay there for a long while,—till such time as
she should become a wife, and leave it for a house of her
own. She never afterwards had any clear conception,
though she very often thought of it all, how it came to be
a settled thing among the Jews around her, that she was
to be Anton's wife, and that Anton was to take her away
from Prague. But she knew that her lover's father had
come to her, and that he had been kind, and that there
had been no reproach cast upon her for the wickedness
she had attempted. Nor was it till she found herself
going to mass all alone on the third Sunday that she
remembered that she was still a Christian, and that her
lover was still a Jew. 'It will not seem so strange to you
when you are away in another place,' Rebecca said to her
afterwards. 'It will be good for both of you that you
should be away from Prague.'

Nor did Nina hear much of the attempts which the
Zamenoys made to rescue her from the hands of the Jews.
Anton once asked her very gravely whether she was quite
certain that she did not wish to see her aunt. 'Indeed, I
am,' said Nina, becoming pale at the idea of the suggested
meeting. 'Why should I see her? She has always been
cruel to me.' Then Anton explained to her that Madame
Zamenoy had made a formal demand to see her niece,
and had even lodged with the police a statement that
Nina was being kept in durance in the Jews' quarter; but
the accusation was too manifestly false to receive attention even when made against a Jew, and Nina had
reached an age which allowed her to choose her own
friends without interposition from the law. 'Only,' said
Anton, 'it is necessary that you should know your own
mind.'

'I do know it,' said Nina, eagerly.

And she saw Madame Zamenoy no more, nor her uncle Karil, nor her cousin Ziska. Though she lived in the same city with them for three months after the night on which she had been taken to Rebecca's house, she never again was brought into contact with her relations. Lotta she once saw, when walking in the street with Ruth; and Lotta too saw her, and endeavoured to address her: but Nina fled, to the great delight of Ruth, who ran with her; and Lotta Luxa was left behind at the street corner.

I do not know that Nina ever had a more clearly-defined idea of the trick that Lotta had played upon her, than was conveyed to her by the sight of the deed as it was taken from her desk, and the knowledge that Souchey had put her lover upon the track. She soon learned that she was acquitted altogether by Anton, and she did not care for learning more. Of course there had been a trick. Of course there had been deceit. Of course her aunt and Lotta Luxa and Ziska, who was the worst of them all, had had their hands in it! But what did it signify? They had failed, and she had been successful. Why need she inquire farther?

But Souchey, who repented himself thoroughly of his treachery, spoke his mind freely to Lotta Luxa. 'No,' said he, 'not if you had ten times as many florins, and were twice as clever, for you nearly drove me to be the murderer of my mistress.'

THE END

LINDA TRESSEL

THE PERSONS OF THE STORY*

HERR MOLK	*A Magistrate at Nuremberg.*
PETER STEINMARC	*Town-Clerk to the City Magistrates.*
MADAME STAUBACH	*A Widow living in the Red House.*
LINDA TRESSEL	*Her Niece.*
LUDOVIC VALCARM	*A Young Man of Nuremberg, cousin to Steinmarc.*
JACOB HEISSE	*An Upholsterer at Nuremberg.*
FANNY HEISSE	*His Daughter—afterwards married to Max Bogen.*
TETCHEN	*Servant to Madame Staubach.*
STOBE	*A Brewer's Hacker.*
MAX BOGEN	*A Young Lawyer of Augsburg.*

CHAPTER I

THE troubles and sorrows of Linda Tressel, who is the heroine of the little story now about to be told, arose from the too rigid virtue of her nearest and most loving friend,—as troubles will sometimes come from rigid virtue when rigid virtue is not accompanied by sound sense, and especially when it knows little or nothing of the softness of mercy.

The nearest and dearest friend of Linda Tressel was her aunt, the widow Staubach—Madame Charlotte Staubach, as she had come to be called in the little town of Nuremberg where she lived. In Nuremberg all houses are picturesque, but you shall go through the entire city and find no more picturesque abode than the small red house with the three gables close down by the river-side in the Schütt island—the little island made by the river Pegnitz in the middle of the town.* They who have seen the widow Staubach's house will have remembered it, not only because of its bright colour and its sharp gables, but also because of the garden which runs between the house and the water's edge. And yet the garden was no bigger than may often nowadays be seen in the balconies of the mansions of Paris and of London. Here Linda Tressel lived with her aunt, and here also Linda had been born.

Linda was the orphan of Herr Tressel, who had for many years been what we may call town-clerk to the magistrates of Nuremberg. Chance in middle life had taken him to Cologne—a German city indeed, as was his own, but a city so far away from Nuremberg that its people and its manners were as strange to him as though he had gone beyond the reach of his own mother-tongue. But here he had married, and from Cologne had brought home his bride to the picturesque, red, gabled house by the water's side in his own city. His wife's only sister had also married, in her own town; and that sister was the virtuous but rigid aunt Charlotte, to live with whom had been the fate in life of Linda Tressel.

It need not be more than told in the fewest words that the town-clerk and the town-clerk's wife both died when Linda was but an infant, and that the husband of her aunt Charlotte died also. In Nuremberg there is no possession so much coveted and so dearly loved as that of the house in which the family lives. Herr Tressel had owned the house with the three gables, and so had his father before him, and to the father it had come from an uncle whose name had been different,—and to him from some other relative. But it was an old family property, and, like other houses in Nuremberg, was to be kept in the hands of the family while the family might remain, unless some terrible ruin should supervene.

When Linda was but six years old, her aunt, the widow, came to Nuremberg to inhabit the house which the Tressels had left as an only legacy to their daughter; but it was understood when she did so that a right of living in the house for the remainder of her days was to belong to Madame Staubach because of the surrender she thus made of whatever of a home was then left to her in Cologne. There was probably no deed executed to this effect; nor would it have been thought that any deed was necessary. Should Linda Tressel, when years had rolled on, be taken as a wife, and should the husband live in the red house, there would still be room for Linda's aunt. And by no husband in Nuremberg, who should be told that such an arrangement had been anticipated, would such an arrangement be opposed. Mothers-in-law, aunts, maiden sisters, and dependent female relatives, in all degrees, are endured with greater patience and treated with a gentler hand in patient Bavaria* than in some lands farther west where life is faster, and in which men's shoulders are more easily galled by slight burdens. And as poor little Linda Tressel had no other possession but the house, as all other income, slight as it might be, was to be brought with her by aunt Charlotte, aunt Charlotte had at least a right to the free use of the roof over her head. It is necessary that so much should be told; but Linda's troubles did not come from the divided right which she had in her father's house. Linda's troubles, as has before

been said, sprang not from her aunt's covetousness, but
from her aunt's virtue—perhaps we might more truly say,
from her aunt's religion.

Nuremberg is one of those German cities in which a
stranger finds it difficult to understand the religious idio-
syncrasies of the people. It is in Bavaria, and Bavaria,
as he knows, is Roman Catholic. But Nuremberg is
Protestant, and the stranger, when he visits the two cathedrals—those of St. Sebald and St. Lawrence*—finds it
hard to believe that they should not be made to resound
with masses, so like are they in all respects to other
Romanist cathedrals which he has seen. But he is told
that they are Lutheran and Protestant, and he is obliged
to make himself aware that the prevailing religion of
Nuremberg is Lutheran, in spite of what to him are the
Catholic appearances of the churches. Now the widow
Staubach was among Protestants the most Protestant,
going far beyond the ordinary amenities of Lutheran
teaching, as at present taught, in her religious observances, her religious loves, and her religious antipathies.
The ordinary Lutheran of the German cities does not
wear his religion very conspicuously. It is not a trouble
to him in his daily life, causing him to live in terror as to
the life to come. That it is a comfort to him let us not
doubt. But it has not on him generally that outward,
ever palpable, unmistakable effect, making its own of his
gait, his countenance, his garb, his voice, his words, his
eyes, his thoughts, his clothes, his very sneeze, his cough,
his sighs, his groans, which is the result of Calvinistic
impressions thoroughly brought home to the mind and
lovingly entertained in the heart. Madame Staubach was
in truth a German Anabaptist, but it will be enough
for us to say that her manners and gait were the manners and gait of a Calvinist.*

While Linda Tressel was a child she hardly knew that
her aunt was peculiar in her religious ideas. That mode
of life which comes to a child comes naturally, and Linda,
though she was probably not allowed to play as freely as
did the other bairns* around her, though she was taken
more frequently to the house of worship which her aunt

frequented, and targed more strictly in the reading of
godly books, did not know till she was a child no longer,
that she was subjected to harder usage than others endured. But when Linda was eleven, the widow was persuaded by a friend that it was her duty to send her niece
to school; and when Linda at sixteen ceased to be a school
girl, she had learned to think that the religion of her
aunt's neighbours was a more comfortable religion than
that practised by her aunt; and when she was eighteen,
she had further learned to think that the life of certain
neighbour girls was a pleasanter life than her own. When
she was twenty, she had studied the subject more deeply,
and had told herself that though her spirit was prone to
rebel against her aunt, that though she would fain have
been allowed to do as did other girls of twenty, yet she
knew her aunt to be a good woman, and knew that it
behoved her to obey. Had not her aunt come all the way
from Cologne, from the distant city of Rhenish Prussia,
to live in Nuremberg for her sake, and should she be un-
faithful and rebellious? Now Madame Staubach understood and appreciated the proneness to rebellion in her
niece's heart, but did not quite understand, and perhaps
could not appreciate, the attempt to put down that rebellion which the niece was ever making from day to
day.

I have said that the widow Staubach had brought with
her to Nuremberg some income upon which to live in the
red house with the three gables. Some small means of her
own she possessed, some few hundred florins*a-year, which
were remitted to her punctually from Cologne; but this
would not have sufficed even for the moderate wants of
herself, her niece, and of the old maid Tetchen, who
lived with them, and who had lived with Linda's mother.
But there was a source of income very ready to the widow's
hand, and of which it was a matter of course that she
should in her circumstances avail herself. She and her
niece could not fill the family home, and a portion of it
was let to a lodger. This lodger was Herr Steinmarc—
Peter Steinmarc, who had been clerk to Linda's father
when Linda's father had been clerk to the city magistrates,

and who was now clerk to the city magistrates himself. Peter Steinmarc in the old days had inhabited a garret in the house, and had taken his meals at his master's table; but now the first floor of the house was his own, the big airy pleasant chamber looking out from under one gable on to the clear water, and the broad passage under the middle gable, and the square large bedroom—the room in which Linda had been born—under the third gable. The windows from these apartments all looked out on to the slow-flowing but clear stream, which ran so close below them that the town-clerk might have sat and fished from his windows had he been so minded; for there was no road there—only the narrow slip of a garden no broader than a balcony. And opposite, beyond the river, where the road ran, there was a broad place,—the Ruden Platz; and every house surrounding this was picturesque with different colours, and with many gables, and the points of the houses rose up in sharp pyramids, of which every brick and every tile was in its place, sharp, clear, well formed, and appropriate, in those very inches of space which each was called upon to fill. For in Nuremberg it is the religion of the community that no house shall fall into decay, that no form of city beauty shall be allowed to vanish, that nothing of picturesque antiquity shall be changed. From age to age, though stones and bricks are changed, the buildings are the same, and the medieval forms remain, delighting the taste of the traveller as they do the pride of the burgher. Thus it was that Herr Steinmarc, the clerk of the magistrates in Nuremberg, had for his use as pleasant an abode as the city could furnish him.

Now it came to pass that, during the many years of their residence beneath the same roof, there grew up a strong feeling of friendship between Peter Steinmarc and the widow Staubach, so strong that in most worldly matters the widow would be content to follow her friend Peter's counsels without hesitation. And this was the case although Peter by no means lived in accordance with the widow's tenets as to matters of religion. It is not to be understood that Peter was a godless man,—not so especi-

ally, or that he lived a life in any way scandalous, or open
to special animadversion from the converted; but he was
a man of the world, very fond of money, very fond of
business, doing no more in the matter of worship than
is done ordinarily by men of the world,—one who would
not scruple to earn a few gulden* on the Sunday if such
earning came in his way, who liked his beer and his pipe,
and, above all things, liked the fees and perquisites of
office on which he lived and made his little wealth. But
though thus worldly he was esteemed much by Madame
Staubach, who rarely, on his behalf, put forth that voice
of warning which was so frequently heard by her niece.

But there are women of the class to which Madame
Staubach belonged who think that the acerbities of religion are intended altogether for their own sex. That
men ought to be grateful to them who will deny? Such
women seem to think that Heaven will pardon that hardness of heart which it has created in man, and which the
affairs of the world seem almost to require; but that it
will extend no such forgiveness to the feminine creation.
It may be necessary that a man should be stiff-necked,
self-willed, eager on the world, perhaps even covetous
and given to worldly lusts. But for a woman, it behoves
her to crush herself, so that she may be at all points submissive, self-denying, and much-suffering. She should be
used to thorns in the flesh, and to thorns in the spirit too.
Whatever may be the thing she wants, that thing she
should not have. And if it be so that, in her feminine
weakness, she be not able to deny herself, there should
be those around her to do the denial for her. Let her crush
herself as it becomes a poor female to do, or let there be
some other female to crush her if she lack the strength,
the purity, and the religious fervour which such self-
crushing requires. Poor Linda Tressel had not much
taste for crushing herself, but Providence had supplied
her with one who had always been willing to do that
work for her. And yet the aunt had ever dearly loved her
niece, and dearly loved her now in these days of our story.
If your eye offend you, shall you not pluck it out?*
After a sort Madame Staubach was plucking out her own

eye when she led her niece such a life of torment as will be described in these pages.

When Linda was told one day by Tetchen the old servant that there was a marriage on foot between Herr Steinmarc and aunt Charlotte, Linda expressed her disbelief in very strong terms. When Tetchen produced many arguments to show why it should be so, and put aside as of no avail all the reasons given by Linda to show that such a marriage could hardly be intended, Linda was still incredulous. 'You do not know aunt Charlotte, Tetchen;—not as I do.' said Linda.

'I've lived in the same house with her for fourteen years,' said Tetchen, angrily.

'And yet you do not know her. I am sure she will not marry Peter Steinmarc. She will never marry anybody. She does not think of such things.'

'Pooh!' said Tetchen; 'all women think of them. Their heads are always together, and Peter talks as though he meant to be master of the house, and he tells her everything about Ludovic. I heard them talking about Ludovic for the hour together the other night.'

'You shouldn't listen, Tetchen.'

'I didn't listen, miss. But when one is in and out one cannot stop one's ears. I hope there isn't going to be anything wrong between 'em about the house.'

'My aunt will never do anything wrong, and my aunt will never marry Peter Steinmarc.' So Linda declared in her aunt's defence, and in her latter assertion she was certainly right. Madame Staubach was not minded to marry Herr Steinmarc; but she might have done so had she wished it, for Herr Steinmarc asked her to take him more than once.

At this time the widow Staubach was a woman not much over forty years of age; and though it can hardly be said she was comely, yet she was not without a certain prettiness which might have charms in the judgment of Herr Steinmarc. She was very thin, and her face was pale, and here and there was the beginning of a wrinkle telling as much of trouble as of years; but her eyes were bright and clear, and her smooth hair, of which but the

edge was allowed to be seen beneath her cap, was of as
rich a brown as when she had married Gasper Staubach,*
now more than twenty years ago; and her teeth were
white and perfect, and the oval of her face had not been
impaired by time, and her step, though slow, was light
and firm, and her voice, though sad, was low and soft.
In talking to men—to such a man as was Herr Steinmarc—her voice was always low and soft, though there
would be a sharp note in it now and again when she
would be speaking to Tetchen or her niece. Whether it
was her gentle voice, or her bright eyes, or the edge of
soft brown hair beneath her cap, or some less creditable
feeling of covetousness in regard to the gabled house in
the Schütt island, shall not here be even guessed; but it
was the fact that Herr Steinmarc had more than once
asked Madame Staubach to be his wife when Tetchen
first imparted her suspicion to Linda.

'And what were they saying about Ludovic?' asked
Linda, when Tetchen, for the third time came to Linda
with her tidings. Now Linda had scolded Tetchen for
listening to her aunt's conversation about Ludovic, and
Tetchen thought it unjust that she should be interrogated
on the subject after being so treated.

'I told you, miss, I didn't hear anything;—only just
the name.'

'Very well, Tetchen; that will do; only I hope you
won't say such things of aunt Charlotte anywhere else.'

'What harm have I said, Linda? surely to say of a
widow that she's to be married to an honest man is not
to say harm.'

'But it is not true, Tetchen; and you should not say it.'
Then Tetchen departed quite unconvinced, and Linda
began to reflect how far her life would be changed for
the better or for the worse, if Tetchen's tidings should
ever be made true. But, as has been said before, Tetchen's
tidings were never to be made true.

But Madame Staubach did not resent the offer made
to her. When Peter Steinmarc told her that she was a
lone woman, left without guidance or protection, she
allowed the fact, admitting that guidance would be good

for her. When he went on to say that Linda also was in need of protection, she admitted that also. 'She is in sore need,' Madame Staubach said, 'the poor thoughtless child.' And when Herr Steinmarc spoke of her pecuniary condition, reminding the widow that were she left without the lodger the two women could hardly keep the old family roof over their head, Madame Staubach acknowledged it all, and perhaps went very suddenly to the true point by expressing an opinion that everything would be much better arranged if the house were the property of Herr Steinmarc himself. 'It isn't good that women should own houses,' said Madame Staubach; 'it should be enough for them that they are permitted to use them.' Then Herr Steinmarc went on to explain that if the widow would consent to become his wife, he thought he could so settle things that for their lives, at any rate, the house should be in his care and management. But the widow would not consent even to speak of such an arrangement as possible. She spoke a word, with a tear in her eye, of the human lord and master who had lived with her for two happy years, and said another word with some mystical allusion to a heavenly husband; and after that Herr Steinmarc felt that he could not plead his cause further with any hope of success. 'But why should not Linda be your wife?' said Madame Staubach, as her disappointed suitor was about to retire.

The idea had never struck the man's mind before, and now, when the suggestion was made to him, he was for a while stricken dumb. Why should he not marry Linda Tressel, the niece; gay, pretty, young, sweet as youth and prettiness and gaiety could make her, a girl than whom there was none prettier, none sweeter, in all Nuremberg —and the real owner, too, of the house in which he lived, —instead of the aunt, who was neither gay, nor sweet, nor young; who, though she was virtuous, self-denying, and meek, possessed certainly but few feminine charms? Herr Steinmarc, though he was a man not by any means living outside the pale of the Church to which he belonged, was not so strongly given to religious observances as to have preferred the aunt because of her piety and

sanctity of life. He was not hypocrite enough to suggest
to Madame Staubach that any such feeling warmed his
bosom. Why should not Linda be his wife? He sat himself down again in the arm-chair from which he had risen,
and began to consider the question.

In the first place, Herr Steinmarc was at this time
nearly fifty years old, and Linda Tressel was only twenty.
He knew Linda's age well, for he had been an inhabitant
of the garret up-stairs when Linda was born. What would
the Frau Tressel have said that night had any one pro-
phesied to her that her little daughter would hereafter
be offered as a wife to her husband's penniless clerk up-
stairs? But penniless clerks often live to fill their masters'
shoes, and do sometimes marry their masters' daughters.
And then Linda was known throughout Nuremberg to
be the real owner of the house with the three gables,
and Herr Steinmarc had an idea that the Nuremberg
magistrates would rise up against him were he to offer
to marry the young heiress. And there was a third difficulty: Herr Steinmarc, though he had no knowledge on
the subject, though his suspicions were so slight that he
had never mentioned them to his old friend the widow,
though he was aware that he had barely a ground for
the idea, still had an idea, that Linda Tressel's heart
was no longer at Linda's own disposal.

But nevertheless the momentous question which had
been so suddenly asked him was one which certainly
deserved the closest consideration. It showed him, at any
rate, that Linda's nearest friend would help him were
he inclined to prosecute such a suit, and that she saw
nothing out of course, nothing anomalous, in the proposition. It would be very nice to be the husband of a
pretty, gay, sweet-tempered, joyous young girl. It would
be very nice to marry the heiress of the house, and to
become its actual owner and master, and it would be
nice also to be preferred to him of whom Peter Steinmarc
had thought as the true possessor of Linda's heart. If
Linda were once his wife, Linda, he did not doubt, would
be true to him. In such case Linda, whom he knew to
be a good girl, would overcome any little prejudice of her

girlhood. Other men of fifty had married girls of twenty, and why should not he, Peter Steinmarc, the well-to-do, comfortable, and, considering his age, good-looking town-clerk of the city of Nuremberg? He could not bring him-self to tell Madame Staubach that he would transfer his affections to her niece on that occasion on which the question was first asked. He would take a week, he said, to consider. He took the week; but made up his mind on the first day of the week, and at the end of the week declared to Madame Staubach that he thought the plan to be a good plan.

After that there was much discussion before any further step was taken, and Tetchen was quite sure that their lodger was to be married to Linda's aunt. There was much discussion, and the widow, shocked, perhaps, at her own cruelty, almost retreated from the offer she had made. But Herr Steinmarc was emboldened, and was now eager, and held her to her own plan. It was a good plan, and he was ready. He found that he could love the maiden, and he wished to take her to his bosom at once. For a few days the widow's heart relented; for a few days there came across her breast a frail, foolish, human idea of love and passion, and the earthly joy of two young beings, happy in each other's arms. For a while she thought with regret of what she was about to do, of the sacrifice to be made, of the sorrow to be en-dured, of the deathblow to be given to those dreams of love, which doubtless had arisen, though hitherto they were no more than dreams. Madame Staubach, though she was now a saint, had been once a woman, and knew as well as any woman of what nature are the dreams of love which fill the heart of a girl. It was because she knew them so well, that she allowed herself only a few hours of such weakness. What! should she hesitate be-tween heaven and hell, between God and devil, between this world and the next, between sacrifice of time and sacrifice of eternity, when the disposal of her own niece, her own child, her nearest and dearest, was concerned? Was it not fit that the world should be crushed in the bosom of a young girl? and how could it be crushed so effectually as by marrying her to an old man, one whom she respected, but who was otherwise distasteful to her—one who, as a husband, would at first be abhorrent to her? As Madame Staubach thought of heaven then, a girl who loved and was allowed to indulge her love could hardly go to heaven. 'Let it be so,' she said to Peter Steinmarc after a few days of weak vacillation,—'let it be so. I think that it will be good for her.' Then Peter Steinmarc swore that it would be good for Linda—that it should be good for Linda. His care should be so great that Linda might never doubt the good. 'Peter Steinmarc, I am thinking of her soul,' said Madame Staubach. 'I am thinking of that too,' said Peter; 'one has, you know, to think of everything in turns.'

Then there came to be a little difficulty as to the manner in which the proposition should be first made to Linda Tressel. Madame Staubach thought that it should be made by Peter himself, but Peter was of opinion that if the ice were first broken by Madame Staubach, final success might be more probably achieved. 'She owes you obedience, my friend, and she owes me none, as yet,' said Peter. There seemed to be so much of truth in this that Madame Staubach yielded, and undertook to make the first overture to Linda on behalf of her lover.

CHAPTER II

LINDA TRESSEL was a tall, light-built, active young woman, in full health, by no means a fine lady, very able and very willing to assist Tetchen in the work of the house, or rather to be assisted by Tetchen in doing it, and fit at all points to be the wife of any young burgher in Nuremberg. And she was very pretty withal, with eager, speaking eyes, and soft luxurious tresses, not black, but of so very dark a brown as to be counted black in some lights. It was her aunt's care to have these tresses confined, so that nothing of their wayward obstinacy in curling might be seen by the eyes of men; and Linda strove to obey her aunt, but the curls would sometimes be too strong for Linda, and would be seen over her shoulders and across her back, tempting the eyes of men sorely. Peter Steinmarc had so seen them many a time, and thought much of them when the offer of Linda's hand was first made to him. Her face, like that of her aunt, was oval in its form, and her complexion was dark and clear. But perhaps her greatest beauty consisted in the half-soft, half-wild expression of her face, which, while it seemed to declare to the world that she was mild, gentle, and, for the most part, silent, gave a vague, doubtful promise of something that might be beyond, if only her nature were sufficiently awakened, creating a hope and mysterious longing for something more than might be expected from a girl brought up under the severe thraldom of Madame Charlotte Staubach,—creating a hope, or perhaps it might be a fear. And Linda's face in this respect was the true reflex of her character. She lived with her aunt a quiet, industrious, sober life, striving to be obedient, striving to be religious with the religion of her aunt. She had almost brought herself to believe that it was good for her heart to be crushed. She had quite brought herself to wish to believe it. She had within her heart no desire for open rebellion against domestic authority. The world was a dangerous, bad world, in which men were dust and women something lower than dust. She would tell herself so very often, and strive to believe herself when she did so. But, for all this, there was a yearning for something beyond her present life, for something that should be of the world, worldly. When she heard profane music she would long to dance. When she heard the girls laughing in the public gardens she would long to stay and laugh with them. Pretty ribbons and bright-coloured silks were a snare to her. When she could shake out her curly locks in the retirement of her own little chamber, she liked to feel them and to know that they were pretty.

But these were the wiles with which the devil catches the souls of women, and there were times when she believed that the devil was making an especial struggle to possess himself of her. There were moments in which she almost thought that the devil would succeed, and that, perhaps, it was but of little use for her to carry on any longer the futile contest. Would it not be pleasant to give up the contest, and to laugh and talk and shout and be merry, to dance, and wear bright colours, and be gay in company with young men, as did the other girls around her? As for those other girls, their elder friends did not seem on their account to be specially in dread of Satan. There was Fanny Heisse who lived close to them, who had been Linda's friend when they went to school together. Fanny did just as she pleased, was always talking with young men, wore the brightest ribbons that the shops produced, was always dancing, seemed to be bound by no strict rules on life; and yet everybody spoke well of Fanny Heisse, and now Fanny was to be married to a young lawyer from Augsburg. Could it be the fact that the devil had made sure of Fanny Heisse? Linda had been very anxious to ask her aunt a question on that subject, but had been afraid. Whenever she attempted to discuss any point of theology with her aunt, such attempts always ended in renewed assurances of the devil's greediness, and in some harder, more crushing rule by which the devil's greed might be outwitted.

Then there came a time of terrible peril, and poor Linda was in greater doubt than ever. Fanny Heisse, who was to be married to the Augsburg lawyer, had long been accustomed to talk to young men, to one young man after another, so that young men had come to be almost nothing to her. She had selected one as her husband because it had been suggested to her that she had better settle herself in life; and this special one was well-to-do, and good-looking, and pleasant-mannered, and good-tempered. The whole thing with Fanny Heisse had seemed to go as though flirting, love, and marriage all came naturally, without danger, without care, and without disappointment. But a young man had now spoken to her, to Linda,—had spoken to her words that she did not dare to repeat to any one,—had spoken to her twice, thrice, and she had not rebuked him. She had not, at least, rebuked him with that withering scorn which the circumstances had surely required, and which would have made him know that she regarded him as one sent purposely from the Evil One to tempt her. Now again had come upon her some terrible half-formed idea that it would be well to give up the battle and let the Evil One make free with his prey. But, in truth, her heart within her had so palpitated with emotion when these words had been spoken and been repeated, that she had lacked the strength to carry on the battle properly. How send a daring young man from you with withering scorn, when there lacks power to raise the eyes, to open or to close the lips, to think even at the moment whether such scorn is deserved, or something very different from scorn?

The young man had not been seen by Linda's eyes for nearly a month, when Peter Steinmarc and Madam Staubach settled between them that the ice should be broken. On the following morning aunt Charlotte prepared herself for the communication to be made, and, when she came in from her market purchases, went at once to her task. Linda was found by her aunt in their lodger's sitting-room, busy with brooms and brushes, while Tetchen on her knees was dry-rubbing the polished board round the broad margin of the room. 'Linda,' said Madame Staubach, 'I have that which I wish to say to you; would you come with me for a while?' Then Linda followed her aunt to Madame Staubach's own chamber, and as she went there came over her a guilty fear. Could it be that her aunt had heard of the words which the young man had spoken to her?

'Linda,' said Madame Staubach, 'sit down,—there, in my chair. I have a proposition to make to you of much importance,—of very great importance. May the Lord grant that the thing that I do shall be right in His sight!'

'To make to me, aunt?' said Linda, now quite astray as to her aunt's intention. She was sure, at least, that there was no danger about the young man. Had it been her aunt's purpose to rebuke her for aught that she had done, her aunt's manner and look would have been very different,—would have been hard, severe, and full of denunciation. As it was, Madame Staubach almost hesitated in her words, and certainly had assumed much less than her accustomed austerity.

'I hope, Linda, that you know that I love you.'

'I am sure that you love me, aunt Charlotte. But why do you ask me?'

'If there be any one in this world that I do love, it is you, my child. Who else is there left to me? Were it not for you, the world with all its troubles would be nothing to me, and I could prepare myself to go in peace when He should be pleased to take me.'

'But why do you say this now, aunt Charlotte?'

'I will tell you why I say it now. Though I am hardly an old woman yet——'

'Of course you are not an old woman.'

'I wish I were older, that I might be nearer to my rest. But you are young, and it is necessary that your future life should be regarded. Whether I go hence or remain here it will be proper that some settlement should be made for you.' Then Madame Staubach paused, and Linda began to think that her aunt had on her mind some scheme about the house. When her aunt had spoken of going hence or remaining here, Linda had not been quite sure whether the goings and remainings spoken of were wholly spiritual or whether there was any reference to things worldly and temporal. Could it be that Tetchen was after all right in her surmise? Was it possible that her aunt was about to be married to Peter Steinmarc? But she said nothing; and after a while her aunt went on very slowly with her proposition. 'Yes, Linda, some settlement for your future life should be made. You know that the house in which we live is your own.'

'It is yours and mine together, aunt.'

'No, Linda; the house is your own. And the furniture in it is yours too; so that Herr Steinmarc is your lodger. It is right that you should understand all this; but I think too well of my own child to believe that she will ever on that account be disobedient or unruly.'

'That will never make a difference.'

'No, Linda; I am sure it will not. Providence has been

pleased to put me in the place of both father and mother to you. I will not say that I have done my duty by you——'

'You have, aunt, always,' said Linda, taking her aunt's hand and pressing it affectionately.

'But I have found, and I expect to find, a child's obedience. It is good that the young should obey their elders, and should understand that those in authority over them should know better than they can do themselves what is good for them.' Linda was now altogether astray in her thoughts and anticipations. Her aunt had very frequently spoken to her in this strain; nay, a week did not often pass by without such a speech. But then the speeches would come without the solemn prelude which had been made on this occasion, and would be caused generally by some act or word or look or movement on the part of Linda of which Madame Staubach had found herself obliged to express disapprobation. On the present occasion the conversation had been commenced without any such expression. Her aunt had even deigned to commend the general tenor of her life. She had dropped the hand as soon as her aunt began to talk of those in authority, and waited with patience till the gist of the lecture should be revealed to her. 'I hope you will understand this now, Linda. That which I shall propose to you is for your welfare, here and hereafter, even though it may not at first seem to you to be agreeable.'

'What is it, aunt?' said Linda, jumping up quickly from her seat.

'Sit down, my child, and I will tell you.' But Linda did not reseat herself at once. Some terrible fear had come upon her,—some fear of she knew not what,—and she found it to be almost impossible to remain quiet at her aunt's knee. 'Sit down, Linda, when I ask you.' Then Linda did sit down; but she had altogether lost that look of quiet, passive endurance which her face and figure had borne when she was first asked to listen to her aunt's words. 'The time in your life has come, my dear, when I as your guardian have to think whether it is not well that you should be—married.'

'But I do not want to be married,' said Linda, jumping up again.

'My dearest child, it would be better that you should listen to me. Marriage, you know, is an honourable state.'

'Yes, I know, of course. But, aunt Charlotte——'

'Hush, my dear.'

'A girl need not be married unless she likes.'

'If I were dead, with whom would you live? Who would there be to guard you and guide you?'

'But you are not going to die.'

'Linda, that is very wicked.'

'And why can I not guide myself?'

'Because you are young, and weak, and foolish. Because it is right that they who are frail, and timid, and spiritless, should be made subject to those who are strong and able to hold dominion and to exact obedience.' Linda did not at all like being told that she was spiritless. She thought that she might be able to show spirit enough were it not for the duty that she owed to her aunt. And as for obedience, though she were willing to obey her aunt, she felt that her aunt had no right to transfer her privilege in that respect to another. But she said nothing, and her aunt went on with her proposition.

'Our lodger, Peter Steinmarc, has spoken to me, and he is anxious to make you his wife.'

'Peter Steinmarc!'

'Yes, Linda; Peter Steinmarc.'

'Old Peter Steinmarc!'

'He is not old. What has his being old to do with it?'

'I will never marry Peter Steinmarc, aunt Charlotte.'

Madame Staubach had not expected to meet with immediate and positive obedience. She had thought it probable that there might be some opposition shown to her plan when it was first brought forward. Indeed, how could it be otherwise, when marriage was suggested abruptly to such a girl as Linda Tressel, even though the suggested husband had been an Apollo?* What young woman could have said, 'Oh, certainly; whenever you please, aunt Charlotte,' to such a proposition? Feeling

this, Madame Staubach would have gone to work by degrees,—would have opened her siege by gradual trenches,
and have approached the citadel by parallels, before she
attempted to take it by storm, had she known anything
of the ways and forms of such strategy. But though she
knew that there were such ways and forms of strategy
among the ungodly, out in the world with the worldly,
she had practised none such herself, and knew nothing
of the mode in which they should be conducted. On this
subject, if on any, her niece owed to her obedience, and
she would claim that obedience as hers of right. Though
Linda would at first be startled, she would probably be
not the less willing to obey at last, if she found her guardian stern and resolute in her demand. 'My dear,' she
said, 'you have probably not yet had time to think of the
marriage which I have proposed to you.'

'I want no time to think of it.'

'Nothing in life should be accepted or rejected without
thinking, Linda,—nothing except sin; and thinking cannot be done without time.'

'This would be sin—a great sin!'

'Linda, you are very wicked.'

'Of course, I am wicked.'

'Herr Steinmarc is a most respectable man. There is no
man in all Nuremberg more respected than Herr Steinmarc.' This was doubtless Madame Staubach's opinion
of Peter Steinmarc, but it may be that Madame Staubach
was not qualified to express the opinion of the city in
general on that subject. 'He holds the office which your
father held before him, and for many years has inhabited
the best rooms in your father's house.'

'He is welcome to the rooms if he wants them,' said
Linda. 'He is welcome to the whole house if you choose
to give it to him.'

'That is nonsense, Linda. Herr Steinmarc wants nothing
that is not his of right.'

'I am not his of right,' said Linda.

'Will you listen to me? You are much mistaken if you
think that it is because of your trumpery house that this
honest man wishes to make you his wife.' We must

suppose that Madame Staubach suffered some qualm of
conscience as she proffered this assurance, and that she
repented afterwards of the sin she committed in making
a statement which she could hardly herself have believed
to be exactly true. 'He knew your father before you were
born, and your mother; and he has known me for many
years. Has he not lived with us ever since you can
remember?'

'Yes,' said Linda; 'I remember him ever since I was a
very little girl,—as long as I can remember anything,—
and he seemed to be as old then as he is now.'

'And why should he not be old? Why should you want
a husband to be young and foolish and headstrong as
you are yourself;—perhaps some one who would drink
and gamble and go about after strange women?'

'I don't want any man for a husband,' said Linda.

'There can be nothing more proper than that Herr
Steinmarc should make you his wife. He has spoken to
me and he is willing to undertake the charge.'

'The charge!' almost screamed Linda, in terrible disgust.

'He is willing to undertake the charge, I say. We shall
then still live together, and may hope to be able to maintain a God-fearing household, in which there may be as
little opening to the temptations of the world as may be
found in any well-ordered house.'

'I do not believe that Peter Steinmarc is a God-fearing
man.'

'Linda, you are very wicked to say so.'

'But if he were, it would make no difference.'

'Linda!'

'I only know that he loves his money better than anything in the world, and that he never gives a kreutzer to
any one, and that he won't subscribe to the hospital, and
he always thinks that Tetchen takes his wine, though
Tetchen never touches a drop.'

'When he has a wife she will look after these things.'

'I will never look after them,' said Linda.

The conversation was brought to an end as soon after
this as Madame Staubach was able to close it. She had
done all that she had intended to do, and had done it

with as much of good result as she had expected. She
had probably not thought that Linda would be quite so
fierce as she had shown herself; but she had expected
tears, and more of despair, and a clearer protestation of
abject misery in the proposed marriage. Linda's mind
would now be filled with the idea, and probably she might
by degrees reconcile herself to it, and learn to think that
Peter was not so very old a man. At any rate it would
now be for Peter himself to carry on the battle.

Linda, as soon as she was alone, sat down with her
hands before her and with her eyes fixed, gazing on
vacancy, in order that she might realise to herself the
thing proposed to her. She had said very little to her
aunt of the nature of the misery which such a marriage
seemed to offer to her,—not because her imagination
made for her no clear picture on the subject, not because
she did not foresee unutterable wretchedness in such a
union. The picture of such wretchedness had been very
palpable to her. She thought that no consideration on
earth would induce her to take that mean-faced old man
to her breast as her husband, her lord—as the one being
whom she was to love beyond everybody else in this
world. The picture was clear enough, but she had argued
to herself, unconsciously, that any description of that
picture to her aunt would seem to suppose that the con-
summation of the picture was possible. She preferred therefore to declare that the thing was impossible,—an affair
the completion of which would be quite out of the question. Instead of assuring her aunt that it would have
made her miserable to have to look after Peter Steinmarc's wine, she at once protested that she never would
take upon herself that duty. 'I am not his of right,' she
had said; and as she said it, she resolved that she would
adhere to that protest. But when she was alone she
remembered her aunt's demand, her own submissiveness,
her old habits of obedience, and above all she remembered the fear that would come over her that she was
giving herself to the devil in casting from her her obedience on such a subject, and then she became very wretched.
She told herself that sooner or later her aunt would

conquer her, that sooner or later that mean-faced old man, with his snuffy fingers, and his few straggling hairs brushed over his bald pate, with his big shoes spreading here and there because of his corns, and his ugly, loose, square, snuffy coat, and his old hat which he had worn so long that she never liked to touch it, would become her husband, and that it would be her duty to look after his wine, and his old shoes, and his old hat, and to have her own little possessions doled out to her by his penuriousness. Though she continued to swear to herself that heaven and earth together should never make her become Herr Steinmarc's wife, yet at the same time she continued to bemoan the certainty of her coming fate. If they were both against her—both, with the Lord on their sides—how could she stand against them with nothing to aid her,—nothing, but the devil, and a few words spoken to her by one whom hitherto she had never dared to answer?

The house in which Linda and Madame Staubach lived, of which the three gables faced towards the river, and which came so close upon the stream that there was but a margin six feet broad between the wall and the edge of the water, was approached by a narrow street or passage, which reached as far as the end of the house, where there was a small gravelled court or open place, perhaps thirty feet square. Opposite to the door of the red house was the door of that in which lived Fanny Heisse with her father and mother. They indeed had another opening into one of the streets of the town, which was necessary, as Jacob Heisse was an upholsterer, and required an exit from his premises for chairs and tables. But to the red house with the three gables there was no other approach than by the narrow passage which ran between the river and the back of Heisse's workshop. Thus the little courtyard was very private, and Linda could stand leaning on the wicket-gate which divided the little garden from the court, without being subject to the charge of making herself public to the passers-by. Not but what she might be seen when so standing by those in the Ruden Platz on the other side of the river, as had often been pointed out to her by her aunt. But it was a habit with her to stand there, perhaps because while so standing she would often hear the gay laugh of her old friend Fanny, and would thus, at second hand, receive some impress from the gaiety of the world without. Now, in her musing, without thinking much of whither she was going, she went slowly down the stairs and out of the door, and stood leaning upon the gate looking over the river at the men who were working in the front of the warehouses. She had not been there long when Fanny ran across to her from the door of her father's house. Fanny Heisse was a bright broad-faced girl, with light hair, and laughing eyes, and a dimple on her chin, freckled somewhat, with a pug nose, and a large mouth. But for all this Fanny Heisse was known throughout Nuremberg as a pretty girl.

'Linda, what do you think?' said Fanny. 'Papa was at Augsburg yesterday, and has just come home, and it is all to come off the week after next.'

'And you are happy?'

'Of course I'm happy. Why shouldn't a girl be happy? He's a good fellow and deserves it all, and I mean to be such a wife to him! Only he is to let me dance. But you don't care for dancing?'

'I have never tried it—much.'

'No; your people think it wicked. I am so glad mine don't. But, Linda, you'll be let come to my marriage—will you not? I do so want you to come. I was making up the party just now with mother and his sister Marie. Father brought Marie home with him. And we have put you down for one. But, Linda, what ails you? Does anything ail you?' Fanny might well ask, for the tears were running down Linda's face.

'It is nothing particular.'

'Nay, but it is something particular—something very particular. Linda, you mope too much.'

'I have not been moping now. But, Fanny, I cannot talk to you about it. I cannot indeed—not now. Do not be angry with me if I go in and leave you.' Then Linda ran in, and went up to her bedroom and bolted the door.

CHAPTER III

PETER STEINMARC had a cousin in a younger generation than himself, who lived in Nuremberg, and who was named Ludovic Valcarm. The mother of this young man had been Peter's first cousin, and when she died Ludovic had in some sort fallen into the hands of his relative the town-clerk. Ludovic's father was still alive; but he was a thriftless, aimless man, who had never been of service either to his wife or children, and at this moment no one knew where he was living, or what he was doing. No one knew, unless it was his son Ludovic, who never received much encouragement in Nuremberg to talk about his father. At the present moment, Peter Steinmarc and his cousin, though they had not actually quarrelled, were not on the most friendly terms. As Peter, in his younger days, had been clerk to old Tressel, so had Ludovic been brought up to act as clerk to Peter; and for three or four years the young man had received some small modicum of salary from the city chest, as a servant in the employment of the city magistrates. But of late Ludovic had left his uncle's office, and had entered the service of certain brewers in Nuremberg, who were more liberal in their views as to wages than were the city magistrates. Peter Steinmarc had thought ill of his cousin for making this change. He had been at the trouble of pointing out to Ludovic how he himself had in former years sat upon the stool in the office in the town-hall, from whence he had been promoted to the arm-chair; and had almost taken upon himself to promise that the good fortune of Ludovic should be as great as his own, if only Ludovic for the present would be content with the stool. But young Valcarm, who by this time was four-and-twenty, told his cousin very freely that the stool in the town-hall suited him no longer, and that he liked neither the work nor the wages. Indeed, he went further than this, and told his kinsman that he liked the society of the office as little as he did either the wages or the work. It may naturally be supposed that this was not said till there had been some unpleasant words spoken

by the town-clerk to his assistant,—till the authority of
the elder had been somewhat stretched over the head of
the young man; but it may be supposed also that when
such words had once been spoken, Peter Steinmarc did
not again press Ludovic Valcarm to sit upon the official
stool.

Ludovic had never lived in the garret of the red house
as Peter himself had done. When the suggestion that he
should do so had some years since been made to Madame
Staubach, that prudent lady, foreseeing that Linda would
soon become a young woman, had been unwilling to sanction the arrangement. Ludovic, therefore, had housed
himself elsewhere, and had been free of the authority of
the town-clerk when away from his office. But he had
been often in his cousin's rooms, and there had grown
up some acquaintance between him and aunt Charlotte
and Linda. It had been very slight;—so thought aunt
Charlotte. It has been as slight as her precautions could
make it. But Ludovic, nevertheless, had spoken such
words to Linda that Linda had been unable to answer
him; and though Madame Staubach was altogether
ignorant that such iniquity had been perpetrated, Peter
Steinmarc had shrewdly guessed the truth.

Rumours of a very ill sort had reached the red house
respecting Ludovic Valcarm. When Linda had interrogated Tetchen as to the nature of the things that were
said of Ludovic in that conversation between Peter and
Madame Staubach which Tetchen had overheard, she
had not asked without some cause. She knew that evil
things were said of the young man, and that evil words
regarding him had been whispered by Peter into her
aunt's ears;—that such whisperings had been going on
almost ever since the day on which Ludovic had declined to return again to the official stool; and she knew,
she thought that she knew, that such whisperings were not
altogether undeserved. There was a set of young men
in Nuremberg of whom it was said that they had a
bad name among their elders,—that they drank spirits
instead of beer, that they were up late at nights, that
they played cards among themselves, that they were

very unfrequent at any house of prayer, that they belonged to some turbulent political society which had, to the grief of all the old burghers, been introduced into Nuremberg from Munich,* that, they talked of women as women are talked of in Paris and Vienna and other strongholds of iniquity, and that they despised altogether the old habits and modes of life of their forefathers. They were known by their dress. They wore high round hats like chimney-pots,—such as were worn in Paris,—and satin stocks, and tight-fitting costly coats of fine cloth, and long pantaloons, and they carried little canes in their hands, and gave themselves airs, and were very unlike what the young men of Nuremberg used to be. Linda knew their appearance well, and thought that it was not altogether unbecoming. But she knew also,—for she had often been so told,—that they were dangerous men, and she was grieved that Ludovic Valcarm should be among their number.

But now—now that her aunt had spoken to her of that horrid plan in reference to Peter Steinmarc, what would Ludovic Valcarm be to her? Not that he could ever have been anything. She knew that, and had known it from the first, when she had been unable to answer him with the scorn which his words had deserved. How could such a one as she be mated with a man so unsuited to her aunt's tastes, to her own modes of life, as Ludovic Valcarm? And yet she could have wished that it might be otherwise. For a moment once,—perhaps for moments more than once,—there had been ideas that no mission could be more fitting for such a one as she than that of bringing back to the right path such a young man as Ludovic Valcarm. But then,—how to begin to bring a young man back? She knew that she would not be allowed to accept his love; and now,—now that the horrid plan had been proposed to her, any such scheme was more impracticable, more impossible than ever. Ah, how she hated Peter Steinmarc as she thought of all this!

For four or five days after this, not a word was said to Linda by any one on the hated subject. She kept out of Peter Steinmarc's way as well as she could, and made herself busy through the house with an almost frantic energy. She was very good to her aunt, doing every behest that was put upon her, and going through her religious services with a zeal which almost seemed to signify that she liked them. She did not leave the house once except in her aunt's company, and restrained herself even from leaning over the wicket-gate and listening to the voice of Fanny Heisse. There were moments during these days in which she thought that her opposition to her aunt's plan had had the desired effect, and that she was not to be driven mad by the courtship of Peter Steinmarc. Surely five days would not have elapsed without a word had not the plan been deserted. If that were the case, how good would she be! If that were the case, she would resolve, on her aunt's behalf, to be very scornful to Ludovic Valcarm.

But though she had never gone outside the house without her aunt, though she had never even leaned on the front wicket, yet she had seen Ludovic. It had been no fault of hers that he had spied her from the Ruden Platz, and had kissed his hand to her, and had made a sign to her which she had only half understood,—by which she had thought that he had meant to imply that he would come to her soon. All this came from no fault of hers. She knew that the centre warehouse in the Ruden Platz opposite belonged to the brewers, Sach Brothers,* by whom Valcarm was employed. Of course it was necessary that the young man should be among the workmen, who were always moving barrels about before the warehouse, and that he should attend to his employers' business. But he need not have made the sign, or kissed his hand, when he stood hidden from all eyes but hers beneath the low dark archway; nor, for the matter of that, need her eyes have been fixed upon the gateway after she had once perceived that Ludovic was on the Ruden Platz.

What would happen to her if she were to declare boldly that she loved Ludovic Valcarm, and intended to become his wife, and not the wife of old Peter Steinmarc? In the first place, Ludovic had never asked her to be his wife;—but on that head she had almost no

doubt at all. Ludovic would ask her quickly enough, she
was very sure, if only he received sufficient encouragement. And as far as she understood the law of the
country in which she lived, no one could, she thought,
prevent her from marrying him. In such case she would
have a terrible battle with her aunt; but her aunt could
not lock her up, nor starve her into submission. It would
be very dreadful, and no doubt all good people,—all
those whom she had been accustomed to regard as good,
—would throw her over and point at her as one abandoned. And her aunt's heart would be broken, and
the world,—the world as she knew it,—would pretty
nearly collapse around her. Nevertheless she could do
it. But were she to do so, would it not simply be
that she would have allowed the Devil to get the victory,
and that she would have given herself for ever and ever,
body and soul, to the Evil One? And then she made a
compact with herself,—a compact which she hoped was
not a compact with Satan also. If they on one side
would not strive to make her marry Peter Steinmarc,
she on the other side would say nothing, not a word, to
Ludovic Valcarm.

She soon learned, however, that she had not as yet
achieved her object by the few words which she had
spoken to her aunt. Those words had been spoken on a
Monday. On the evening of the following Saturday
she sat with her aunt in their own room down-stairs,
in the chamber immediately below that occupied by
Peter Steinmarc. It was a summer evening in August,
and Linda was sitting at the window, with some household needlework in her lap, but engaged rather in watching the warehouse opposite than in sedulous attention
to her needle. Her eyes were fixed upon the little doorway, not expecting that any one would be seen there,
but full of remembrance of the figure of him who had
stood there and had kissed his hand. Her aunt, as was
her wont on every Saturday, was leaning over a little
table intent on some large book of devotional service,
with which she prepared herself for the Sabbath. Close
as was her attention now and always to the volume, she

would not on ordinary occasions have allowed Linda's eyes to stray for so long a time across the river without recalling them by some sharp word of reproof; but on this evening she sat and read and said nothing. Either she did not see her niece, so intent was she on her good work, or else, seeing her, she chose, for reasons of her own, to be as one who did not see. Linda was too intent upon her thoughts to remember that she was sinning with the sin of idleness, and would have still gazed across the river had she not heard a heavy footstep in the room above her head, and the fall of a creaking shoe on the stairs, a sound which she knew full well, and stump, bump, dump, Peter Steinmarc was descending from his own apartments to those of his neighbours below him. Then immediately Linda withdrew her eyes from the archway, and began to ply her needle with diligence. And Madame Staubach looked up from her book, and became uneasy on her chair. Linda felt sure that Peter was not going out for an evening stroll, was not in quest of beer and a friendly pipe at the Rothe Ross. He was much given to beer and a friendly pipe at the Rothe Ross;* but Linda knew that he would creep down-stairs somewhat softly when his mind was that way given; not so softly but what she would hear his steps and know whither they were wending; but now, from the nature of the sound, she was quite sure that he was not going to the inn which he frequented. She threw a hurried glance round upon her aunt, and was quite sure that her aunt was of the same opinion. When Herr Steinmarc paused for half a minute outside her aunt's door, and then slowly turned the lock, Linda was not a bit surprised; nor was Madame Staubach surprised. She closed her book with dignity, and sat awaiting the address of her neighbour.

'Good evening, ladies,' said Peter Steinmarc.

'Good evening, Peter,' said Madame Staubach. It was many years now since these people had first known each other, and the town-clerk was always called Peter by his old friend. Linda spoke not a word of answer to her lover's salutation.

'It has been a beautiful summer day,' said Peter.

'A lovely day,' said Madame Staubach, 'through the Lord's favour to us.'

'Has the fraulein* been out?' asked Peter.

'No; I have not been out,' said Linda, almost savagely.

'I will go and leave you together,' said Madame Staubach, getting up from her chair.

'No, aunt, no,' said Linda. 'Don't go away; pray, do not go away.'

'It is fitting that I should do so,' said Madame Staubach, as with one hand sh ' gently pushed back Linda, who was pressing to the door after her. 'You will stay, Linda, and hear what our friend will say; and remember, Linda, that he speaks with my authority and with my heartfelt prayer that he may prevail.'

'He will never prevail,' said Linda. But neither Madame Staubach nor Peter Steinmarc heard what she said.

Linda had already perceived, perturbed as she was in her mind, that Herr Steinmarc had prepared himself carefully for this interview. He had brought a hat with him into the room, but it was not the hat which had so long been distasteful to her. And he had got on clean bright shoes, as large indeed as the old dirty ones, because Herr Steinmarc was not a man to sacrifice his corns for love; but still shoes that were decidedly intended to be worn only on occasions. And he had changed his ordinary woollen shirt for white linen, and had taken out his new brown frock-coat*which he always wore on those high days in Nuremberg on which the magistrates appeared with their civic collars.* But, perhaps, the effect which Linda noted most keenly was the debonair fashion in which the straggling hairs had been disposed over the bald pate. For a moment or two a stranger might almost have believed that the pate was not bald.

'My dear young friend,' began the town-clerk, 'your aunt has, I think, spoken to you of my wishes.' Linda muttered something, she knew not what. But though her words were not intelligible, her looks were so, and were not of a kind to have been naturally conducive to much hope in the bosom of Herr Steinmarc. 'Of course, I can understand, Linda, how much this must have taken you by surprise at first. But that surprise will wear off, and I trust that you may gradually come to regard me as your future husband without—without—without anything like fear, you know, or feelings of that kind.' Still she did not speak. 'If you become my wife, Linda, I will do my best to make you always happy.'

'I shall never become your wife, never—never—never.'

'Do not speak so decidedly as that, Linda.'

'I must speak decidedly. I do speak decidedly. I can't speak any other way. You know very well, Herr Steinmarc, that you oughtn't to ask me. It is very wrong of you, and very wicked.'

'Why is it wrong, Linda? Why is it wicked?'

'If you want to get married, you should marry some one as old as yourself.'

'No, Linda, that is not so. It is always thought becoming that the man should be older than the wife.'

'But you are three times as old as I am, and that is not becoming.' This was cruel on Linda's part, and her words also were untrue. Linda would be twenty-one at her next birthday, whereas Herr Steinmarc had not yet reached his fifty-second birthday.

Herr Steinmarc was a man who had a temper of his own, and who was a little touchy on the score of age. Linda knew that he was touchy on the score of age, and had exaggerated her statement with the view of causing pain. It was probably some appreciation of this fact which caused Herr Steinmarc to continue his solicitations with more of authority in his voice than he had hitherto used. 'I am not three times as old as you, Linda; but, whatever may be my age, your aunt, who has the charge of you, thinks that the marriage is a fitting one. You should remember that you cannot fly in her face without committing a great sin. I offer to you an honest household and a respectable position. As Madame Staubach thinks that you should accept them, you must know that you are wrong to answer me with scorn and ribaldry.'

'I have not answered you with ribaldry. It is not ribaldry to say that you are an old man.'

'You have answered me with scorn.'

'I do scorn you, Herr Steinmarc, when you come to me pretending to make love like a young man, with your Sunday clothes on, and your hair brushed smooth, and your new shoes. I do scorn you. And you may go and tell my aunt that I say so, if you like. And as for being an old man, you are an old man. Old men are very well in their way, I daresay; but they shouldn't go about making love to young women.'

Herr Steinmarc had not hoped to succeed on this his first personal venture; but he certainly had not expected to be received after the fashion which Linda had adopted towards him. He had, doubtless, looked very often into Linda's face, and had listened very often to the tone of her voice; but he had not understood what her face expressed, nor had he known what compass that voice would reach. Had he been a wise man,—a man wise as to his own future comfort,—he would have abandoned his present attempt after the lessons which he was now learning. But, as has before been said, he had a temper, and he was now angry with Linda. He was roused, and was disposed to make her know that, old as he was, and bald, and forced to wear awkward shoes, and to stump along heavily, still he could force her to become his wife and to minister to his wants. He understood it all. He knew what were his own deficiencies, and was as wide awake as was Linda herself to the natural desires of a young girl. Madame Staubach was, perhaps, equally awake, but she connected these desires directly with the devil. Because it was natural that a young woman should love a young man, therefore, according to the religious theory of Madame Staubach, it was well that a young woman should marry an old man, so that she might then be crushed and made malleable, and susceptible of that teaching which tells us that all suffering in this world is good for us. Now Peter Steinmarc was by no means alive to the truth of such lessons as these. Religion was all very well. It was an outward sign of a respectable life,—of a life in which men are trusted and receive comfortable wages,—and, beyond that, was an innocent occupation for enthusiastic women. But he had no idea that any human being was bound to undergo crushing in this world for his soul's sake. Had he not wished to marry Linda himself, it might be very well that Linda should marry a young man. But now that Linda so openly scorned him, had treated him with such plain-spoken contumely, he thought it would be well that Linda should be crushed. Yes; and he thought also that he might probably find a means of crushing her.

'I suppose, miss,' he said, after pausing for some moments, 'that the meaning of this is that you have got a young lover?'

'I have got no young lover,' said Linda; 'and if I had, why shouldn't I? What would that be to you?'

'It would be very much to me, if it be the young man I think. Yes, I understand; you blush now. Very well. I shall know now how to manage you;—or your aunt will know.'

'I have got no lover,' said Linda, in great anger; 'and you are a very wicked old man to say so.'

'Then you had better receive me as your future husband. If you will be good and obedient, I will forgive the great unkindness of what you have said to me.'

'I have not meant to be unkind, but I cannot have you for my husband. How am I to love you?'

'That will come.'

'It will never come.'

'Was it not unkind when you said that I was three times as old as you?'

'I did not mean to be unkind.' Since the allusion which had been made to some younger lover, from which Linda had gathered that Peter Steinmarc must know something of Ludovic's passion for herself, she had been in part quelled. She was not able now to stand up bravely before her suitor, and fight him as she had done at first with all the weapons which she had at her command. The man knew something which it was almost ruinous to her that he should know, something by which, if her aunt knew it, she would be quite ruined. How could it be that Herr Steinmarc should have learned anything of Ludovic's wild love? He had not been in the house,—he had been in the town-hall, sitting in his big official arm-chair,—when Ludovic had stood in the low-arched doorway and blown a kiss across the river from his hand. And yet he did know it; and knowing it, would of course tell her aunt! 'I did not mean to be unkind,' she said.

'You were very unkind.'

'I beg your pardon then, Herr Steinmarc.'

'Will you let me address you, then, as your lover?'

'Oh, no!'

'Because of that young man; is it?'

'Oh, no, no. I have said nothing to the young man— not a word. He is nothing to me. It is not that.'

'Linda, I see it all. I understand everything now. Unless you will promise to give him up, and do as your aunt bids you, I must tell your aunt everything.'

'There is nothing to tell.'

'Linda!'

'I have done nothing. I can't help any young man. He is only over there because of the brewery.' She had told all her secret now. 'He is nothing to me, Herr Steinmarc, and if you choose to tell aunt Charlotte, you must. I shall tell aunt Charlotte that if she will let me keep out of your way, I will promise to keep out of his. But if you come, then—then—then—I don't know what I may do.' After that she escaped, and went away back into the kitchen, while Peter Steinmarc stumped up again to his own room.

'Well, my friend, how has it gone?' said Madam Staubach, entering Peter's chamber, at the door of which she had knocked.

'I have found out the truth,' said Peter, solemnly.

'What truth?' Peter shook his head, not despondently so much as in dismay. The thing which he had to tell was so very bad! He felt it so keenly, not on his own account so much as on account of his friend! All that was expressed by the manner in which Peter shook his head. 'What truth have you found out, Peter? Tell me at once,' said Madame Staubach.

'She has got a—lover.'

'Who? Linda! I do not believe it.'

'She has owned it. And such a lover!' Whereupon Peter Steinmarc lifted up both his hands.

'What lover? Who is he? How does she know him, and when has she seen him? I cannot believe it. Linda has never been false to me.'

'Her lover is—Ludovic Valcarm.'

'Your cousin?'

'My cousin Ludovic—who is a good-for-nothing, a spendthrift, a fellow without a florin, a fellow that plays cards on Sundays.'

'And who fears neither God nor Satan,' said Madame Staubach. 'Peter Steinmarc, I do not believe it. The child can hardly have spoken to him.'

'You had better ask her, Madame Staubach.' Then with some exaggeration Peter told Linda's aunt all that he did know, and something more than all that Linda had confessed; and before their conversation was over they had both agreed that, let these tidings be true in much or in little, or true not at all, every exertion should be used to force Linda into the proposed marriage with as little delay as possible.

'I overheard him speaking to her out of the street window, when they thought I was out,' said the town-clerk in a whisper before he left Madame Staubach. 'I had to come back home for the key of the big chest, and they never knew that I had been in the house.' This had been one of the occasions on which Linda had been addressed, and had wanted breath to answer the bold young man who had spoken to her.

CHAPTER IV

ON the following morning, being Sunday morning, Linda positively refused to get up at the usual hour, and declared her intention of not going to church. She was, she said, so ill that she could not go to church. Late on the preceding evening Madame Staubach, after she had left Peter Steinmarc, had spoken to Linda of what she had heard, and it was not surprising that Linda should have a headache on the following morning. 'Linda,' Madame Staubach said, 'Peter has told me that Ludovic Valcarm has been—making love to you. Linda, is this true?' Linda had been unable to say that it was not true. Her aunt put the matter to her in a more cunning way than Steinmarc had done, and Linda felt herself unable to deny the charge. 'Then let me tell you, that of all the young women of whom I ever heard, you are the most deceitful,' continued Madame Staubach.

'Do not say that, aunt Charlotte; pray, do not say that.'

'But I do say it. Oh, that it should have come to this between you and me!'

'I have not deceived you. Indeed I have not. I don't want to see Ludovic again; never, if you do not wish it. I haven't said a word to him. Oh, aunt, pray believe me. I have never spoken a word to him;—in the way of what you mean.'

'Will you consent to marry Peter Steinmarc?' Linda hesitated a moment before she answered. 'Tell me, Miss; will you promise to take Peter Steinmarc as your husband?'

'I cannot promise that, aunt Charlotte.'

'Then I will never forgive you,—never. And God will never forgive you. I did not think it possible that my sister's child should have been so false to me.'

'I have not been false to you,' said Linda through her tears.

'And such a terrible young man, too; one who drinks, and gambles, and is a rebel; one of whom all the world speaks ill; a penniless spendthrift, to whom no decent girl would betroth herself. But, perhaps, you are to be his light-of-love!'*

'It is a shame,—a great shame,—for you to say—such things,' said Linda, sobbing bitterly. 'No, I won't wait, I must go. I would sooner be dead than hear you say such things to me. So I would. I can't help it, if it's wicked. You make me say it.' Then Linda escaped from the room, and went up to her bed; and on the next morning she was too ill either to eat her breakfast or to go to church.

Of course she saw nothing of Peter on that morning; but she heard the creaking of his shoes as he went forth after his morning meal, and I fear that her good wishes for his Sunday work did not go with him on that Sabbath morning. Three or four times her aunt was in her room, but to her aunt Linda would say no more than that she was sick and could not leave her bed. Madame Staubach did not renew the revilings which she had poured forth so freely on the preceding evening, partly influenced by Linda's headache, and partly, perhaps, by a statement which had been made to her by Tetchen as to the amount of love-making which had taken place. 'Lord bless you, ma'am, in any other house than this it would go for nothing. Over at Jacob Heisse's, among his girls, it wouldn't even have been counted at all,—such a few words as that. Just the compliments of the day, and no more.' Tetchen could not have heard it all, or she would hardly have talked of the compliments of the day. When Ludovic had told Linda that she was the fairest girl in all Nuremberg, and that he never could be happy, not for an hour, unless he might hope to call her his own, even Tetchen, whose notions about young men were not over strict, could not have taken such words as simply meaning the compliments of the day. But there was Linda sick in bed, and this was Sunday morning, and nothing further could be said or done on the instant. And, moreover, such love-making as had taken place did in truth seem to have been perpetrated altogether on the side of the young man. Therefore it was that Madame Staubach spoke with a gentle voice as she prescribed to Linda some pill or potion that might probably be of service, and then went forth to her church.

Madame Staubach's prayers on a Sunday morning were a long affair. She usually left the house a little after ten, and did not return till past two. Soon after she was gone, on the present occasion, Tetchen came up to Linda's room, and expressed her own desire to go to the

Frauenkirche,*—for Tetchen was a Roman Catholic.
'That is, if you mean to get up, miss, I'll go,' said Tetchen.
Linda, turning in her bed, thought that her head would
be better now that her aunt was gone, and promised
that she would get up. In half an hour she was alone
in the kitchen down-stairs, and Tetchen had started to
the Frauenkirche,—or to whatever other place was more
agreeable to her for the occupation of her Sunday
morning.

It was by no means an uncommon occurrence that
Linda should be left alone in the house on some part of
the Sunday, and she would naturally have seated herself
with a book at the parlour window as soon as she had
completed what little there might be to be done in the
kitchen. But on this occasion there came upon her a
feeling of desolateness as she thought of her present condition. Not only was she alone now, but she must be
alone for ever. She had no friend left. Her aunt was
estranged from her. Peter Steinmarc was her bitterest
enemy. And she did not dare even to think of Ludovic
Valcarm. She had sauntered now into the parlour, and,
as she was telling herself that she did not dare to think
of the young man, she looked across the river, and there
he was standing on the water's edge.

She retreated back in the room,—so far back that it
was impossible that he should see her. She felt quite sure
that he had not seen her as yet, for his back had been
turned to her during the single moment that she had
stood at the window. What should she do now? She
was quite certain that he could not see her, as she stood
far back in the room, within the gloom of the dark walls.
And then there was the river between him and her. So
she stood and watched, as one might watch a coming
enemy, or a lover who was too bold. There was a little
punt or raft moored against the bank just opposite to
the gateway of the warehouse, which often lay there, and
which, as Linda knew, was used in the affairs of the
brewery. Now, as she stood watching him, Ludovic
stepped into the punt without unfastening it from the
ring, and pushed the loose end of it across the river as

far as the shallow bottom would allow him. But still there was a considerable distance between him and the garden of the red house, a distance so great that Linda felt that the water made her safe. But there was a pole in the boat, and Linda saw the young man take up the pole and prepare for a spring, and in a moment he was standing in the narrow garden. As he landed, he flung the pole back into the punt, which remained stranded in the middle of the river. Was ever such a leap seen before? Then she thought how safe she would have been from Peter Steinmarc, had Peter Steinmarc been in the boat.

What would Ludovic Valcarm do next? He might remain there all day before she would go to him. He was now standing under the front of the centre gable, and was out of Linda's sight. There was a low window close to him where he stood, which opened from the passage that ran through the middle of the house. On the other side of this passage, opposite to the parlour which Madame Staubach occupied, was a large room not now used, and filled with lumber. Linda, as soon as she was aware that Ludovic was in the island, within a few feet of her, and that something must be done, re-treated from the parlour back into the kitchen, and, as she went, thoughtfully drew the bolt of the front door. But she had not thought of the low window into the passage, which in these summer days was always opened, nor, if she had thought of it, could she have taken any precaution in that direction. To have attempted to close the window would have been to throw herself into the young man's arms. But there was a bolt inside the kitchen door, and that she drew. Then she stood in the middle of the room listening. Had this been a thief who had come when she was left in charge of the house, is it thus she would have protected her own property and her aunt's? It was no thief. But why should she run from this man whom she knew,—whom she knew and would have trusted had she been left to her own judg-ment of him? She was no coward. Were she to face the man, she would fear no personal danger from him. He

would offer her no insult, and she thought that she could
protect herself, even were he to insult her. It was not
that that she feared,—but that her aunt should be able
to say that she had received her lover in secret on this
Sunday morning, when she had pretended that she was
too ill to go to church!

She was all ears, and could hear that he was within
the house. She had thought of the window the moment
that she had barred the kitchen door, and knew that
he would be within the house. She could hear him knock
at the parlour door, and then enter the parlour. But he
did not stay there a moment. Then she heard him at the
foot of the stair, and with a low voice he called to her by
her name. 'Linda, are you there?' But, of course, she
did not answer him. It might be that he would fancy that
she was not within the house and would retreat. He
would hardly intrude into their bedrooms; but it might
be that he would go as far as his cousin's apartments.
'Linda,' he said again,—'Linda, I know that you are in
the house.' That wicked Tetchen! It could not be but
that Tetchen had been a traitor. He went three or four
steps up the stairs, and then, bethinking himself of the
locality, came down again and knocked at once at
the kitchen door. 'Linda,' he said, when he found that the
door was barred,—'Linda, I know that you are here.'

'Go away,' said Linda. 'Why have you come here?
You know that you should not be here.'

'Open the door for one moment, that you may listen
to me. Open the door, and I will tell you all. I will go
instantly when I have spoken to you, Linda; I will indeed.'

Then she opened the door. Why should she be a
barred-up prisoner in her own house? What was there
that she need fear? She had done nothing that was
wrong, and would do nothing wrong. Of course, she
would tell her aunt. If the man would force his way into
the house, climbing in through an open window, how
could she help it? If her aunt chose to misbelieve her,
let it be so. There was need now that she should call
upon herself for strength. All heaven and earth together

should not make her marry Peter Steinmarc. Nor should earth and the evil one combined make her give herself to a young man after any fashion that should disgrace her mother's memory or her father's name. If her aunt doubted her, the sorrow would be great, but she must bear it. 'You have no right here,' she said as soon as she was confronted with the young man. 'You know that you should not be here. Go away.'

'Linda, I love you.'

'I don't want your love.'

'And now they tell me that my cousin Peter is to be your husband.'

'No, no. He will never be my husband.'

'You will promise that?'

'He will never be my husband.'

'Thanks, dearest; a thousand thanks for that. But your aunt is his friend. Is it not true?'

'Of course she is his friend.'

'And would give you to him?'

'I am not hers to give. I am not to be given away at all. I choose to stay as I am. You know that you are very wicked to be here; but I believe you want to get me into trouble.'

'Oh, Linda!'

'Then go. If you wish me to forgive you, go instantly.'

'Say that you love me, and I will be gone at once.'

'I will not say it.'

'And do you not love me,—a little? Oh, Linda, you are so dear to me!'

'Why do you not go? They tell me evil things of you, and now I believe them. If you were not very wicked you would not come upon me here, in this way, when I am alone, doing all that you possibly can to make me wretched.'

'I would give all the world to make you happy.'

'I have never believed what they said of you. I always thought that they were ill-natured and prejudiced, and that they spoke falsehoods. But now I shall believe them. Now I know that you are very wicked. You have no right to stand here. Why do you not go when I bid you?'

'But you forgive me?'

'Yes, if you go now,—at once.'

Then he seized her hand and kissed it. 'Dearest Linda, remember that I shall always love you; always be thinking of you; always hoping that you will some day love me a little. Now I am gone?

'But which way?' said Linda—'you cannot jump back to the boat. The pole is gone. At the door they will see you from the windows.'

'Nobody shall see me. God bless you, Linda.' Then he again took her hand, though he did not, on this occasion, succeed in raising it as far as his lips. After that he ran down the passage, and, having glanced each way from the window, in half a minute was again in the garden. Linda, of course, hurried into the parlour, that she might watch him. In another half minute he was down over the little wall, into the river, and in three strides had gained the punt. The water, in truth, on that side was not much over his knees; but Linda thought he must be very wet. Then she looked round, to see if there were any eyes watching him. As far as she could see, there were no eyes.

Linda, when she was alone, was by no means contented with herself; and yet there was a sort of joy at her heart which she could not explain to herself, and of which, being keenly alive to it, she felt in great dread. What could be more wicked, more full of sin, than receiving, on a Sunday morning, a clandestine visit from a young man, and such a young man as Ludovic Valcarm? Her aunt had often spoken to her, with fear and trembling, of the mode of life in which their neighbours opposite lived. The daughters of Jacob Heisse were allowed to dance, and talk, and flirt, and, according to Madame Staubach, were living in fearful peril. For how much would such a man as Jacob Heisse, who thought of nothing but working hard, in order that his four girls might always have fine dresses,—for how much would he be called upon to answer in the last day? Of what comfort would it be to him then that his girls, in this foolish vain world, had hovered about him, bringing him his pipe

and slippers, filling his glass stoup for him, and kissing
his forehead as they stood over his easy-chair in the
evening? Jacob Heisse and his daughters had ever been
used as an example of worldly living by Madame Staubach. But none of Jacob Heisse's girls would ever have
done such a thing as this. They flirted, indeed; but they
did it openly, under their father's nose. And Linda had
often heard the old man joke with his daughters about
their lovers. Could Linda joke with any one touching
this visit from Ludovic Valcarm?

And yet there was something in it that was a joy to
her,—a joy which she could not define. Since her aunt
had been so cruel to her, and since Peter had appeared
before her as her suitor, she had told herself that she
had no friend. Heretofore she had acknowledged Peter
as her friend, in spite of his creaking shoes and objection-
able hat. There was old custom in his favour, and he
had not been unkind to her as an inmate of the same
house with him. Her aunt she had loved dearly; but now
her aunt's cruelty was so great that she shuddered as she
thought of it. She had felt herself to be friendless. Then
this young man had come to her; and though she had
said to him all the hard things of which she could think
because of his coming, yet—yet—yet she liked him because he had come. Was any other young man in Nuremberg so handsome? Would any other young man have
taken that leap, or have gone through the river, that he
might speak one word to her, even though he were to
have nothing in return for the word so spoken? He had
asked her to love him, and she had refused;—of course
she had refused;—of course he had known that she would
refuse. She would sooner have died than have told him
that she loved him. But she thought she did love him—
a little. She did not so love him but what she would give
him up,—but what she would swear never to set eyes
upon him again, if, as part of such an agreement, she
might be set free from Peter Steinmarc's solicitations.
That was a matter of course, because, without reference
to Peter, she quite acknowledged that she was not free
to have a lover of her own choice, without her aunt's

consent. To give up Ludovic would be a duty,—a duty which she thought she could perform. But she would not perform it unless as part of a compact. No; let them look to it. If duty was expected from her, let duty be done to her. Then she sat thinking, and as she thought she kissed her own hand where Ludovic had kissed it.

The object of her thoughts was this;—what should she do now, when her aunt came home? Were she at once to tell her aunt all that had occurred, that comparison which she had made between herself and the Heisse girls, so much to her own disfavour, would not be a true comparison. In that case she would have received no clandestine young man. It could not be imputed to her as a fault,—at any rate not imputed by the justice of heaven, —that Ludovic Valcarm had jumped out of a boat and got in at the window. She could put herself right, at any rate, before any just tribunal, simply by telling the story truly and immediately. 'Aunt Charlotte, Ludovic Valcarm has been here. He jumped out of a boat, and got in at the window, and followed me into the kitchen, and kissed my hand, and swore he loved me, and then he scrambled back through the river. I couldn't help it;— and now you know all about it.' The telling of such a tale as that would, she thought, be the only way of making herself quite right before a just tribunal. But she felt, as she tried the telling of it to herself, that the task would be very difficult. And then her aunt would only half believe her, and would turn the facts, joined, as they would be, with her own unbelief, into additional grounds for urging on this marriage with Peter Steinmarc. How can one plead one's cause justly before a tribunal which is manifestly unjust,—which is determined to do injustice?

Moreover, was she not bound to secrecy? Had not secrecy been implied in that forgiveness which she had promised to Ludovic as the condition of his going? He had accepted the condition and gone. After that, would she not be treacherous to betray him? Why was it that at this moment it seemed to her that treachery to him,— to him who had treated her with such arrogant audacity,

—would be of all guilt the most guilty? It was true that she could not put herself right without telling of him; and not to put herself right in this extremity would be to fall into so deep a depth of wrong! But any injury to herself would now be better than treachery to him. Had he not risked much in order that he might speak to her that one word of love? But, for all that, she did not make up her mind for a time. She must be governed by things as they went.

Tetchen came home first, and to Tetchen, Linda was determined that she would say not a word. That Tetchen was in communication with young Valcarm she did not doubt, but she would not tell the servant what had been the result of her wickedness. When Tetchen came in, Linda was in the kitchen, but she went at once into the parlour, and there awaited her aunt. Tetchen had bustled in, in high good-humour, and had at once gone to work to prepare for the Sunday dinner. 'Mr. Peter is to dine with you to-day, Linda,' she had said; 'your aunt thinks there is nothing like making one family of it.' Linda had left the kitchen without speaking a word, but she had fully understood the importance of the domestic arrangement which Tetchen had announced. No stranger ever dined at her aunt's table; and certainly her aunt would have asked no guest to do so on a Sunday but one whom she intended to regard as a part of her own household. Peter Steinmarc was to be one of them, and therefore might be allowed to eat his dinner with them even on the Sabbath.

Between two and three her aunt came in, and Peter was with her. As was usual on Sundays, Madame Staubach was very weary, and, till the dinner was served, was unable to do much in the way of talking. Peter went up into his own room to put away his hat and umbrella, and then, if ever, would have been the moment for Linda to have told her story. But she did not tell it then. Her aunt was leaning back in her accustomed chair, with her eyes closed, as was often her wont, and Linda knew that her thoughts were far away, wandering in another world, of which she was ever thinking, living in a dream of bliss

with singing angels,—but not all happy, not all sure, because of the danger that must intervene. Linda could
not break in, at such a time as this, with her story of the
young man and his wild leap from the boat.

And certainly she would not tell her story before Peter
Steinmarc. It should go untold to her dying day before
she would whisper a word of it in his presence. When
they sat round the table, the aunt was very kind in her
manner to Linda. She had asked after her headache, as
though nothing doubting the fact of the ailment; and
when Linda had said that she had been able to rise almost
as soon as her aunt had left the house, Madame Staubach
expressed no displeasure. When the dinner was over,
Peter was allowed to light his pipe, and Madame Staubach either slept or appeared to sleep. Linda seated herself in the furthest corner of the room, and kept her eyes
fixed upon a book. Peter sat and smoked with his eyes
closed, and his great big shoes stuck out before him. In
this way they remained for an hour. Then Peter got up,
and expressed his intention of going out for a stroll in the
Nonnen Garten. Now the Nonnen Garten was close to
the house,—to be reached by a bridge across the river,
not fifty yards from Jacob Heisse's door. Would Linda
go with him? But Linda declined.

'You had better, my dear,' said Madame Staubach,
seeming to awake from her sleep. 'The air will do you
good.'

'Do, Linda,' said Peter; and then he intended to be
very gracious in what he added. 'I will not say a word
to tease you, but just take you out, and bring you back
again.'

'I am sure, it being the Sabbath, he would say nothing
of his hopes to-day,' said Madame Staubach.

'Not a word,' said Peter, lifting up one hand in token
of his positive assurance.

But, even so assured, Linda would not go with him,
and the town-clerk went off alone. Now, again, had
come the time in which Linda could tell the tale. It
must certainly be told now or never. Were she to tell it
now she could easily explain why she had been silent so

long; but were she not to tell it now, such explanation
would ever afterwards be impossible. 'Linda, dear, will
you read to me,' said her aunt. Then Linda took up the
great Bible. 'Turn to the eighth and ninth chapters of
Isaiah,* my child.' Linda did as she was bidden, and
read the two chapters indicated. After that, there was
silence for a few minutes, and then the aunt spoke.
'Linda, my child.'

'Yes, aunt Charlotte.'

'I do not think you would willingly be false to me.'
Then Linda turned away her face, and was silent. 'It is
not that the offence to me would be great, who am, as
we all are, a poor weak misguided creature; but that the
sin against the Lord is so great, seeing that He has placed
me here as your guide and protector.' Linda made no
promise in answer to this, but even then she did not tell
the tale. How could she have told it at such a moment?
But the tale must now go untold for ever!

CHAPTER V

A WEEK passed by, and Linda Tressel heard nothing of
Ludovic, and began at last to hope that that terrible
episode of the young man's visit to her might be allowed
to be as though it had never been. A week passed by,
during every day of which Linda had feared and had
half expected to hear some question from her aunt which
would nearly crush her to the ground. But no such
question had been asked, and, for aught that Linda knew,
no one but she and Ludovic were aware of the wonderful
jump that had been made out of the boat on to the
island. And during this week little, almost nothing, was
said to her in reference to the courtship of Peter Steinmarc. Peter himself spoke never a word; and Madame
Staubach had merely said, in reference to certain pipes
of tobacco which were smoked by the town-clerk in
Madame Staubach's parlour, and which would heretofore
have been smoked in the town-clerk's own room, that it
was well that Peter should learn to make himself at home

with them. Linda had said nothing in reply, but had sworn inwardly that she would never make herself at home with Peter Steinmarc.

In spite of the pipes of tobacco, Linda was beginning to hope that she might even yet escape from her double peril, and, perhaps, was beginning to have hope even beyond that, when she was suddenly shaken in her security by words which were spoken to her by Fanny Heisse. 'Linda,' said Fanny, running over to the gate of Madame Staubach's house, very early on one bright summer morning, 'Linda, it is to be to-morrow! And will you not come?'

'No, dear; we never go out here: we are so sad and solemn that we know nothing of gaiety.'

'You need not be solemn unless you like it.'

'I don't know but what I do like it, Fanny; I have become so used to it that I am as grave as an owl.'

'That comes of having an old lover, Linda.'

'I have not got an old lover,' said Linda, petulantly.

'You have got a young one, at any rate.'

'What do you mean, Fanny?'

'What do I mean? Just what I say. You know very well what I mean. Who was it jumped over the river that Sunday morning, my dear? I know all about it.' Then there came across Linda's face a look of extreme pain,—a look of anguish; and Fanny Heisse could see that her friend was greatly moved by what she had said. 'You don't suppose that I shall tell any one,' she added.

'I should not mind anything being told if all could be told,' said Linda.

'But he did come,—did he not?' Linda merely nodded her head. 'Yes; I knew that he came when your aunt was at church, and Tetchen was out, and Herr Steinmarc was out. Is it not a pity that he should be such a ne'er-do-well?'

'Do you think that I am a ne'er-do-well, Fanny?'

'No indeed; but, Linda, I will tell you what I have always thought about young men. They are very nice, and all that; and when old croaking hunkses have told me that I should have nothing to say to them, I have

always answered that I meant to have as much to say
to them as possible; but it is like eating good things;—
everybody likes eating good things, but one feels ashamed
of doing it in secret.'

This was a terrible blow to poor Linda. 'But I don't
like doing it,' she answered. 'It wasn't my fault. I did
not bid him come.'

'One never does bid them to come; I mean not till one
has taken up with a fellow as a lover outright. Then you
bid them, and sometimes they won't come for your
bidding.'

'I would have given anything in the world to have
prevented his doing what he did. I never mean to speak
to him again,—if I can help it.'

'Oh, Linda!'

'I suppose you think I expected him, because I stayed
at home alone?'

'Well,—I did think that possibly you expected something.'

'I would have gone to church with my aunt though my
head was splitting had I thought that Herr Valcarm
would have come here while she was away.'

'Mind I have not blamed you. It is a great shame to
give a girl an old lover like Peter Steinmarc, and ask her
to marry him. I wouldn't have married Peter Steinmarc
for all the uncles and all the aunts in creation; nor yet
for father,—though father would never have thought of
such a thing. I think a girl should choose a lover for herself, though how she is to do so if she is to be kept moping
at home always, I cannot tell. If I were treated as you
are I think I should ask somebody to jump over the river
to me.'

'I have asked nobody. But, Fanny, how did you know
it?'

'A little bird saw him.'

'But, Fanny, do tell me.'

'Max saw him get across the river with his own eyes.'
Max Bogen was the happy man who on the morrow was
to make Fanny Heisse his wife.

'Heavens and earth!'

'But, Linda, you need not be afraid of Max. Of all men in the world he is the very last to tell tales.'

'Fanny, if ever you whisper a word of this to any one, I will never speak to you again.'

'Of course, I shall not whisper it.'

'I cannot explain to you all about it,—how it would ruin me. I think I should kill myself outright if my aunt were to know it; and yet I did nothing wrong. I would not encourage a man to come to me in that way for all the world; but I could not help his coming. I got myself into the kitchen; but when I found that he was in the house I thought it would be better to open the door and speak to him.'

'Very much better. I would have slapped his face. A lover should know when to come and when to stay away.'

'I was ashamed to think that I did not dare to speak to him, and so I opened the door. I was very angry with him.'

'But still, perhaps, you like him,—just a little; is not that true, Linda?'

'I do not know; but this I know, I do not want ever to see him again.'

'Come, Linda; never is a long time.'

'Let it be ever so long, what I say is true.'

'The worst of Ludovic is that he is a ne'er-do-well. He spends more money than he earns, and he is one of those wild spirits who are always making up some plan of politics*—who live with one foot inside the State prison, as it were. I like a lover to be gay, and all that; but it is not well to have one's young man carried off and locked up by the burgomasters. But, Linda, do not be unhappy. Be sure that I shall not tell; and as for Max Bogen, his tongue is not his own. I should like to hear him say a word about such a thing when I tell him to be silent.'

Linda believed her friend, but still it was a great trouble to her that any one should know what Ludovic Valcarm had done on that Sunday morning. As she thought of it all, it seemed to her to be almost impossible that a secret should remain a secret that was known to three persons,—for she was sure that Tetchen knew it,—

to three persons besides those immediately concerned. She thought of her aunt's words to her, when Madame Staubach had cautioned her against deceit, 'I do not think that you would willingly be false to me, because the sin against the Lord would be so great.' Linda had understood well how much had been meant by this caution. Her aunt had groaned over her in spirit once, when she found it to be a fact that Ludovic Valcarm had been allowed to speak to her,—had been allowed to speak though it were but a dozen words. The dozen words had been spoken and had not been revealed, and Madame Staubach having heard of this sin, had groaned in the spirit heavily. How much deeper would be her groans if she should come to know that Ludovic had been received in her absence, had been received on a Sabbath morning, when her niece was feigning to be ill! Linda still fancied that her aunt might believe her if she were to tell her own story, but she was certain that her aunt would never believe her if the story were to be told by another. In that case there would be nothing for her, Linda, but perpetual war; and, as she thought, perpetual disgrace. As her aunt would in such circumstances range her forces on the side of propriety, so must she range hers on the side of impropriety. It would become necessary that she should surrender herself, as it were, to Satan; that she should make up her mind for an evil life; that she should cut altogether the cord which bound her to the rigid practices of her present mode of living. Her aunt had once asked her if she meant to be the light-of-love of this young man. Linda had well known what her aunt had meant, and had felt deep offence; but yet she now thought that she could foresee a state of things in which, though that degradation might yet be impossible, the infamy of such degradation would belong to her. She did not know how to protect herself from all this, unless she did so by telling her aunt of the young man's visit.

But were she to do so she must accompany her tale by the strongest assurance that no possible consideration would induce her to marry Peter Steinmarc. There must then be a compact, as has before been said, that the name neither of one man nor the other should ever again be mentioned as that of Linda's future husband. But would her aunt agree to such a compact? Would she not rather so use the story that would be told to her, as to draw from it additional reasons for pressing Peter's suit? The odious man still smoked his pipes of tobacco in Madame Staubach's parlour, gradually learning to make himself at home there. Linda, as she thought of this, became grave, settled, and almost ferocious in the working of her mind. Anything would be better than this,—even the degradation to be feared from hard tongues, and from the evil report of virtuous women. As she pictured to herself Peter Steinmarc with his big feet, and his straggling hairs, and his old hat, and his constant pipe, almost any lot in life seemed to her to be better than that. Any lot in death would certainly be better than that. No! If she told her story there must be a compact. And if her aunt would consent to no compact, then,—then she must give herself over to the Evil One. In that case there would be no possible friend for her, no ally available to her in her difficulties, but that one. In that case, even though Ludovic should have both feet within the State prison, he must be all in all to her, and she,—if possible,—all in all to him.

Then she was driven to ask herself some questions as to her feelings towards Ludovic Valcarm. Hitherto she had endeavoured to comfort herself with the reflection that she had in no degree committed herself. She had not even confessed to herself that she loved the man. She had never spoken,—she thought that she had never spoken a word, that could be taken by him as encouragement. But yet, as things were going with her now, she passed no waking hour without thinking of him; and in her sleeping hours he came to her in her dreams. Ah, how often he leaped over that river, beautifully, like an angel, and, running to her in her difficulties, dispersed all her troubles by the beauty of his presence. But then the scene would change, and he would become a fiend instead of a god, or a fallen angel; and at these moments it would become her fate to be carried off with him into uttermost darkness. But even in her saddest dreams she was never inclined to stand before the table in the church* and vow that she would be the loving wife of Peter Steinmarc. Whenever in her dreams such a vow was made, the promise was always given to that ne'er-do-well.

Of course she loved the man. She came to know it as a fact, to be quite sure that she loved him, without reaching any moment in which she first made the confession openly to herself. She knew that she loved him. Had she not loved him, would she have so easily forgiven him,— so easily have told him that he was forgiven? Had she not loved him, would not her aunt have heard the whole story from her on that Sunday evening, even though the two chapters of Isaiah had been left unread in order that she might tell it? Perhaps, after all, the compact of which she had been thinking might be more difficult to her than she had imagined. If the story of Ludovic's coming could be kept from her aunt's ears, it might even yet be possible to her to keep Steinmarc at a distance without any compact. One thing was certain to her. He should be kept at a distance, either with or without a compact.

Days went on, and Fanny Heisse was married, and all probability of telling the story was at an end. Madame Staubach had asked her niece why she did not go to her friend's wedding, but Linda had made no answer,—had shaken her head as though in anger. What business had her aunt to ask her why she did not make one of a gay assemblage, while everything was being done to banish all feeling of gaiety from her life? How could there be any pleasant thought in her mind while Peter Steinmarc still smoked his pipes in their front parlour? Her aunt understood this, and did not press the question of the wedding party. But, after so long an interval, she did find it necessary to press that other question of Peter's courtship. It was now nearly a month since the matter had first been opened to Linda, and Madame Staubach was resolved that the thing should be settled before the autumn was over. 'Linda,' she said one day, 'has Peter Steinmarc spoken to you lately?'

'Has he spoken to me, aunt Charlotte?'

'You know what I mean, Linda.'

'No, he has not—spoken to me. I do not mean that he should—speak to me.' Linda, as she made this answer, put on a hard stubborn look, such as her aunt did not know that she had ever before seen upon her countenance. But if Linda was resolved, so also was Madame Staubach.

'My dear,' said the aunt, 'I do not know what to think of such an answer. Herr Steinmarc has a right to speak if he pleases, and certainly so when that which he says is said with my full concurrence.'

'I can't allow you to think that I shall ever be his wife. That is all.'

After this there was silence for some minutes, and then Madame Staubach spoke again. 'My dear, have you thought at all about—marriage?'

'Not much, aunt Charlotte.'

'I daresay not, Linda; and yet it is a subject on which a young woman should think much before she either accepts or rejects a proposed husband.'

'It is enough to know that one doesn't like a man.'

'No, that is not enough. You should examine the causes of your dislike. And as far as mere dislike goes, you should get over it, if it be unjust. You ought to do that, whoever may be the person in question.'

'But it is not mere dislike.'

'What do you mean, Linda?'

'It is disgust.'

'Linda, that is very wicked. You should not allow yourself to feel what you call disgust at any of God's creatures. Have you ever thought who made Herr Steinmarc?'

'God made Judas Iscariot, aunt Charlotte.'

'Linda, that is profane,—very profane.' Then there was silence between them again; and Linda would have remained silent had her aunt permitted it. She had been called profane, but she disregarded that, having, as she thought, got the better of her aunt in the argument as to disgust felt for any of God's creatures. But Madame

Staubach had still much to say. 'I was asking you whether
you had thought at all about marriage, and you told me
that you had not.'

'I have thought that I could not possibly—under any
circumstances—marry Peter Steinmarc.'

'Linda, will you let me speak? Marriage is a very
solemn thing.'

'Very solemn indeed, aunt Charlotte.'

'In the first place, it is the manner in which the all-wise
Creator has thought fit to make the weaker vessel subject
to the stronger one.' Linda said nothing, but thought
that that old town-clerk was not a vessel strong enough
to hold her in subjection. 'It is this which a woman
should bring home to herself, Linda, when she first thinks
of marriage.'

'Of course I should think of it, if I were going to be
married.'

'Young women too often allow themselves to imagine
that wedlock should mean pleasure and diversion. Instead of that it is simply the entering into that state of life
in which a woman can best do her duty here below. All
life here must be painful, full of toil, and moistened with
many tears.' Linda was partly prepared to acknowledge
the truth of this teaching; but she thought that there was
a great difference in the bitterness of tears. Were she
to marry Ludovic Valcarm, her tears with him would
doubtless be very bitter, but no tears could be so bitter
as those which she would be called upon to shed as the
wife of Peter Steinmarc. 'Of course,' continued Madame
Staubach, 'a wife should love her husband.'

'But I could not love Peter Steinmarc.'

'Will you listen to me? How can you understand me
if you will not listen to me? A wife should love her husband. But young women, such as I see them to be,
because they have been so instructed, want to have something soft and delicate; a creature without a single serious
thought, who is chosen because his cheek is red and his
hair is soft; because he can dance, and speak vain,
meaningless words; because he makes love, as the foolish
parlance of the world goes. And we see what comes of

such lovemaking. Oh, Linda! God forbid that you
should fall into that snare! If you will think of it, what is
it but harlotry?'

'Aunt Charlotte, do not say such horrible things.'

'A woman when she becomes a man's wife should see,
above all things, that she is not tempted by the devil after
this fashion. Remember, Linda, how he goeth about,—
ever after our souls,—like a roaring lion.* And it is in this
way specially that he goeth about after the souls of young
women.'

'But why do you say those things to me?'

'It is to you only that I can say them. I would so speak
to all young women, if it were given me to speak to more
than to one. You talk of love.'

'No, aunt; never. I do not talk—of love.'

'Young women do, and think of it, not knowing what
love for their husband should mean. A woman should
revere her husband and obey him, and be subject to him
in everything.' Was it supposed, Linda thought, that she
should revere such a being as Peter Steinmarc? What
could be her aunt's idea of reverence? 'If she does that,
she will love him also.'

'Yes,—if she does,' said Linda.

'And will not this be much more likely, if the husband
be older than his wife?'

'A year or two,' said Linda, timidly.

'Not a year or two only, but so much so as to make him
graver and wiser, and fit to be in command over her.
Will not the woman so ruled be safer than she who trusts
herself with one who is perhaps as weak and inexperi-
enced as herself?' Madame Staubach paused, but Linda
would not answer the question. She did not wish for such
security as was here proposed to her. 'Is it not that of
which you have to think,—your safety here, so that, if
possible, you may be safe hereafter?' Linda answered
this to herself, within her own bosom. Not for security
here or hereafter, even were such to be found by such
means, would she consent to become the wife of the man
proposed to her. Madame Staubach, finding that no
spoken reply was given to her questions, at last proceeded

from generalities to the special case which she had under her consideration. 'Linda,' she said, 'I trust you will consent to become the wife of this excellent man.' Linda's face became very hard, but still she said nothing. 'The danger of which I have spoken is close upon you. You must feel it to be so. A youth, perhaps the most notorious in all Nuremberg for wickedness——'

'No, aunt; no.'

'I say yes; and this youth is spoken of openly as your lover.'

'No one has a right to say so.'

'It is said, and he has so addressed himself to your own ears. You have confessed it. Tell me that you will do as I would have you, and then I shall know that you are safe. Then I will trust you in everything, for I shall be sure that it will be well with you. Linda, shall it be so?'

'It shall not be so, aunt Charlotte.'

'Is it thus you answer me?'

'Nothing shall make me marry a man whom I hate.'

'Hate him! Oh, Linda.'

'Nothing shall make me marry a man whom I cannot love.'

'You fancy, then, that you love that reprobate?' Linda was silent. 'Is it so? Tell me. I have a right to demand an answer to that question.'

'I do love him,' said Linda. Using the moment for reflection allowed to her as best she could, she thought that she saw the best means of escape in this avowal. Surely her aunt would not press her to marry one man when she had declared that she loved another.

'Then, indeed, you are a castaway.'

'I am no castaway, aunt Charlotte,' said Linda, rising to her feet. 'Nor will I remain here, even with you, to be so called. I have done nothing to deserve it. If you will cease to press upon me this odious scheme, I will do nothing to disgrace either myself or you; but if I am perplexed by Herr Steinmarc and his suit, I will not answer for the consequences.' Then she turned her back upon her aunt and walked slowly out of the room.

On that very evening Peter came to Linda while she

was standing alone at the kitchen window. Tetchen was
out of the house, and Linda had escaped from the parlour
as soon as the hour arrived at which in those days Steinmarc was wont to seat himself in her aunt's presence
and slowly light his huge meerschaum pipe. But on this
occasion he followed her into the kitchen, and Linda was
aware that this was done before her aunt had had any
opportunity of explaining to him what had occurred on
that morning. 'Fraulein,' he said, 'as you are alone here,
I have ventured to come in and join you.'

'This is no proper place for you, Herr Steinmarc,' she
replied. Now, it was certainly the case that Peter rarely
passed a day without standing for some twenty minutes
before the kitchen stove talking to Tetchen. Here he
would always take off his boots when they were wet, and
here, on more than one occasion,—on more, probably,
than fifty,—had he sat and smoked his pipe, when there
was no other stove a-light in the house to comfort him
with its warmth. Linda, therefore, had no strong point
in her favour when she pointed out to her suitor that he
was wrong to intrude upon the kitchen.

'Wherever you are, must be good for me,' said Peter,
trying to smirk and to look pleased.

Linda was determined to silence him, even if she could
not silence her aunt. 'Herr Steinmarc,' she said, 'I have
explained to my aunt that this kind of thing from you
must cease. It must be made to cease. If you are a man
you will not persecute me by a proposal which I have
told you already is altogether out of the question. If
there were not another man in all Nuremberg, I would
not have you. You may perhaps make me hate you
worse than anybody in the world; but you cannot possibly do anything else. Go to my aunt and you will find
that I have told her the same.' Then she walked off to
her own bedroom, leaving the town-clerk in sole possession of the kitchen.

Peter Steinmarc, when he was left standing alone in
the kitchen, did not like his position. He was a man not
endowed with much persuasive gift of words, but he had
a certain strength of his own. He had a will, and some

firmness in pursuing the thing which he desired. He was industrious, patient, and honest with a sort of second-class honesty. He liked to earn what he took, though he had a strong bias towards believing that he had earned whatever in any way he might have taken, and after the same fashion he was true with a second-class truth. He was unwilling to deceive; but he was usually able to make himself believe that that which would have been deceit from another to him, was not deceit from him to another. He was friendly in his nature to a certain degree, understanding that good offices to him-wards could not be expected unless he also was prepared to do good offices to others; but on this matter he kept an accurate mental account-sheet, on which he strove hard to be able to write the balance always on the right side. He was not cruel by nature, but he had no tenderness of heart and no delicacy of perception. He could forgive an offence against his comfort, as when Tetchen would burn his soup; or even against his pocket, as when, after many struggles, he would be unable to enforce the payment of some municipal fee. But he was vain, and could not forgive an offence against his person. Linda had previously told him to his face that he was old, and had with premeditated malice and falsehood exaggerated his age. Now she threatened him with her hatred. If he persevered in asking her to be his wife, she would hate him! He, too, began to hate her; but his hatred was unconscious, a thing of which he was himself unaware, and he still purposed that she should be his wife. He would break her spirit, and bring her to his feet, and punish her with a life-long punishment for saying that he was sixty, when, as she well knew, he was only fifty-two. She should beg for his love,—she who had threatened him with her hatred! And if she held out against him, he would lead her such a life, by means of tales told to Madame Staubach, that she should gladly accept any change as a release. He never thought of the misery that might be forthcoming to himself in the possession of a young wife procured after such a fashion. A man requires some power of imagination to enable him to look forward to the circumstances of an untried existence, and Peter Stein-marc was not an imaginative man.

But he was a thoughtful man, cunning withal, and conscious that various resources might be necessary to him. There was a certain packer of casks, named Stobe, in the employment of the brewers who owned the ware-house opposite, and Stobe was often to be seen on the other side of the river in the Ruden Platz. With this man Steinmarc had made an acquaintance, not at first with any reference to Linda Tressel, but because he was desirous of having some private information as to the doings of his relative Ludovic Valcarm. From Stobe, however, he had received the first intimation of Ludovic's passion for Linda; and now on this very evening of which we are speaking, he obtained further information,— which shocked him, frightened him, pained him exceed-ingly, and yet gave him keen gratification. Stobe also had seen the leap out of the boat, and the rush through the river; and when, late on that evening, Peter Stein-marc, sore with the rebuff which he had received from Linda, pottered over to the Ruden Platz, thinking that it would be well that he should be very cunning, that he should have a spy with his eye always open, that he should learn everything that could be learned by one who might watch the red house, and watch Ludovic also, he learned, all of a sudden, by the speech of a moment, that Ludovic Valcarm had, on that Sunday morning, paid his wonderful visit to the island.

'So you mean that you saw him?' said Peter.

'With my own eyes,' said Stobe, who had his reasons, beyond Peter's moderate bribes, for wishing to do an evil turn to Ludovic. 'And I saw her at the parlour window, watching him, when he came back through the water.'

'How long was he with her?' asked Peter, groaning, but yet exultant.

'A matter of half an hour; not less anyways.'

'It was two Sundays since', said Peter, remembering well the morning on which Linda had declined to go to church because of her headache.

'I remember it well. It was the feast of St. Lawrence,'*

said Stobe, who was a Roman Catholic, and mindful of
the festivals of his Church.

Peter tarried for no further discourse with the brewer's
man, but hurried back again, round by the bridge, to the
red house. As he went he applied his mind firmly to the
task of resolving what he would do. He might probably
take the most severe revenge on Linda, the revenge which
should for the moment be the most severe, by summoning
her to the presence of her aunt, by there exposing her vile
iniquity, and by there declaring that it was out of the
question that a man so respectable as he should contami-
nate himself by marrying so vile a creature. But were he
to do this Linda would never be in his power, and the red
house would never be in his possession. Moreover, though
he continued to tell himself that Linda was vile, though
he was prepared to swear to her villany, he did not in
truth believe that she had done anything disgraceful.
That she had seen her lover he did not doubt; but that,
in Peter's own estimation, was a thing to be expected.
He must, no doubt, on this occasion pretend to view the
matter with the eyes of Madame Staubach. In punishing
Linda, he would so view it. But he thought that, upon
the whole bearing of the case, it would not be incumbent
upon his dignity to abandon for ever his bride and his
bride's property, because she had been indiscreet. He
would marry her still. But before he did so he would let
her know how thoroughly she was in his power, and how
much she would owe to him if he now took her to his
bosom. The point on which he could not at once quite
make up his mind was this: Should he tell Madame
Staubach first, or should he endeavour to use the power
over Linda, which his knowledge gave him, by threats
to her? Might he not say to her with much strength,
'Give way to me at once, or I will reveal to your aunt
this story of your vileness'? This no doubt would be the
best course, could he trust in its success. But, should it
not succeed, he would then have injured his position. He
was afraid that Linda would be too high-spirited, too
obstinate, and he resolved that his safest course would be
to tell everything at once to Madame Staubach.

As he passed between the back of Jacob Heisse's house and the river he saw the upholsterer's ruddy face looking out from an open window belonging to his workshop. 'Good evening, Peter,' said Jacob Heisse. 'I hope the ladies are well.'

'Pretty well, I thank you,' said Peter, as he was hurrying by.

'Tell Linda that we take it amiss that she did not come to our girl's wedding. The truth is, Peter, you keep her too much moped up there among you. You should remember, Peter, that too much work makes Jack a dull boy. Linda will give you all the slip some day, if she be kept so tight in hand.'

Peter muttered something as he passed on to the red house. Linda would give them the slip, would she? It was not improbable, he thought, that she should try to do so, but he would keep such a watch on her that it should be very difficult, and the widow should watch as closely as he would do. Give them the slip! Yes; that might be possible, and therefore he would lose no time.

When he entered the house he walked at once up to Madame Staubach's parlour, and entered it without any of that ceremony of knocking that was usual to him. It was not that he intended to put all ceremony aside, but that in his eager haste he forgot his usual precaution. When he entered the room Linda was there with her aunt, and he had again to turn the whole subject over in his thoughts. Should he tell his tale in Linda's presence or behind her back? It gradually became apparent to him that he could not possibly tell it before her face; but he did not arrive at this conclusion without delay, and the minutes which were so occupied were full of agony. He seated himself in his accustomed chair, and looked from the aunt to the niece and then from the niece to the aunt. Give him the slip, would she? Well, perhaps she would. But she should be very clever if she did.

'I thought you would have been in earlier, Peter,' said Madame Staubach.

'I was coming, but I saw the fraulein in the kitchen,

and I ventured to speak a word or two there. The reception which I received drove me away.'

'Linda, what is this?'

'I did not think, aunt, that the kitchen was the proper place for him.'

'Any room in this house is the proper place for him,' said Madame Staubach, in her enthusiasm. Linda was silent, and Peter replied to this expression of hospitality simply by a grateful nod. 'I will not have you give yourself airs, Linda,' continued Madame Staubach. 'The kitchen not a proper place! What harm could Peter do in the kitchen?'

'He tormented me, so I left him. When he torments me I shall always leave him.' Then Linda got up and stalked out of the room. Her aunt called her more than once, but she would not return. Her life was becoming so heavy to her, that it was impossible that she should continue to endure it. She went up now to her room, and looking out of the window fixed her eyes upon the low stone archway in which she had more than once seen Ludovic Valcarm. But he was not there now. She knew, indeed, that he was not in Nuremberg. Tetchen had told her that he had gone to Augsburg,—on pretence of business connected with the brewery, Tetchen had said, but in truth with reference to some diabolical political scheme as to which Tetchen expressed a strong opinion that all who dabbled in it were children of the very devil. But though Ludovic was not in Nuremberg, Linda stood looking at the archway for more than half an hour, considering the circumstances of her life, and planning, if it might be possible to plan, some future scheme of existence. To live under the upas-tree* of Peter Steinmarc's courtship would be impossible to her. But how should she avoid it? As she thought of this, her eyes were continually fixed on the low archway. Why did not he come out from it and give her some counsel as to the future? There she stood looking out of the window till she was called by her aunt's voice—'Linda, Linda, come down to me.' Her aunt's voice was very solemn, almost as though it came from the grave; but then solemnity was common to her aunt, and Linda, as she descended, had not on her mind any special fear.

When she reached the parlour Madame Staubach was alone there, standing in the middle of the room. For a moment or two after she entered, the widow stood there without speaking, and then Linda knew that there was cause for fear. 'Did you want me, aunt Charlotte?' she said.

'Linda, what were you doing on the morning of the Sabbath before the last, when I went to church alone, leaving you in bed?'

Linda was well aware now that her aunt knew it all, and was aware also that Steinmarc had been the informer. No idea of denying the truth of the story or of concealing anything, crossed her mind for a moment. She was quite prepared to tell everything now, feeling no doubt but that everything had been told. There was no longer a hope that she should recover her aunt's affectionate good-will. But in what words was she to tell her tale? That was now her immediate difficulty. Her aunt was standing before her, hard, stern, and cruel, expecting an answer to her question. How was that answer to be made on the spur of the moment?

'I did nothing, aunt Charlotte. A man came here while you were absent.'

'What man?'

'Ludovic Valcarm.' They were both standing, each looking the other full in the face. On Madame Staubach's countenance there was written a degree of indignation and angry shame which seemed to threaten utter repudiation of her niece. On Linda's was written a resolution to bear it all without flinching. She had no hope now with her aunt,—no other hope than that of being able to endure. For some moments neither of them spoke, and then Linda, finding it difficult to support her aunt's continued gaze, commenced her defence. 'The young man came when I was alone, and made his way into the house when the door was bolted. I had locked myself into the kitchen; but when I heard his voice I opened the door, thinking that it did not become me to be afraid of his presence.'

'Why did you not tell me,—at once?' Linda made no immediate reply to this question; but when Madame Staubach repeated it, she was obliged to answer.

'I told him that if he would go, I would forgive him. Then he went, and I thought that I was bound by my promise to be silent.'

Madame Staubach having heard this, turned round slowly, and walked to the window, leaving Linda in the middle of the room. There she stood for perhaps half a minute, and then came slowly back again. Linda had remained where she was, without stirring a limb; but her mind had been active, and she had determined that she would submit in silence to no rebukes. Any commands from her aunt, save one, she would endeavour to obey; but from all accusations as to impropriety of conduct she would defend herself with unabashed spirit. Her aunt came up close to her; and, putting out one hand, with the palm turned towards her, raising it as high as her shoulder, seemed to wave her away. 'Linda,' said Madame Staubach, 'you are a castaway.'*

'I am no castaway, aunt Charlotte,' said Linda, almost jumping from her feet, and screaming in her self-defence.

'You will not frighten me by your wicked violence. You have—lied to me;—have lied to me. Yes; and that after all that I said to you as to the heinousness of such wickedness. Linda, it is my belief that you knew that he was coming when you kept your bed on that Sabbath morning.'

'If you choose to have such thoughts of me in your heart, aunt Charlotte, I cannot help it. I knew nothing of his coming. I would have given all I had to prevent it. Yes,—though his coming could do me no real harm. My good name is more precious to me than anything short of my self-esteem. Nothing even that you can say shall rob me of that.'

Madame Staubach was almost shaken by the girl's firmness,—by that, and by her own true affection for the sinner. In her bosom, what remained of the softness of womanhood was struggling with the hardness of the religious martinet, and with the wilfulness of the domestic tyrant. She had promised to Steinmarc that she would be very stern. Steinmarc had pointed out to her that nothing but the hardest severity could be of avail. He, in telling his story, had taken it for granted that Linda had expected her lover, had remained at home on purpose that she might receive her lover, and had lived a life of deceit with her aunt for months past. When Madame Staubach had suggested that the young man's coming might have been accidental, he had treated the idea with ridicule. He, as the girl's injured suitor, was, he declared, obliged to treat such a suggestion as altogether incredible, although he was willing to pardon the injury done to him, if a course of intense severity and discipline were at once adopted, and if this were followed by repentance which to him should appear to be sincere. When he took this high ground, as a man having authority, and as one who knew the world, he had carried Madame Staubach with him, and she had not ventured to say a word in excuse for her niece. She had promised that the severity should be at any rate forthcoming, and, if possible, the discipline. As for the repentance, that, she said meekly, must be left in the hands of God. 'Ah!' said Peter, in his bitterness, 'I would make her repent in sackcloth and ashes!'* Then Madame Staubach had again promised that the sack-cloth and ashes should be there. She remembered all this as she thought of relenting,—as she perceived that to relent would be sweet to her, and she made herself rigid with fresh resolves. If the man's coming had been accidental, why had not the story been told to her? She could understand nothing of that forgiveness of which Linda had spoken; and had not Linda confessed that she loved this man? Would she not rather have hated him who had so intruded upon her, had there been real intrusion in the visit?

'You have done that,' she said, 'which would destroy the character of any girl in Nuremberg.'

'If you mean, aunt Charlotte, that the thing which has happened would destroy the character of any girl in Nuremberg, it may perhaps be true. If so, I am very unfortunate.'

'Have you not told me that you love him?'

'I do;—I do;—I do! One cannot help one's love. To love as I do is another misfortune. There is nothing but misery around me. You have heard the whole truth now, and you may as well spare me further rebuke.'

'Do you not know how such misery should be met?' Linda shook her head. 'Have you prayed to be forgiven this terrible sin?'

'What sin?' said Linda, again almost screaming in her energy.

'The terrible sin of receiving this man in the absence of your friends.'

'It was no sin. I am sinful, I know,—very; no one perhaps more so. But there was no sin there. Could I help his coming? Aunt Charlotte, if you do not believe me about this, it is better that we should never speak to each again. If so, we must live apart.'

'How can that be? We cannot rid ourselves of each other.'

'I will go anywhere,—into service, away from Nuremberg,—where you will. But I will not be told that I am a liar.'

And yet Madame Staubach was sure that Linda had lied. She thought that she was sure. And if so,—if it were the case that this young woman had planned an infamous scheme for receiving her lover on a Sunday morning;—the fact that it was on a Sunday morning, and that the hour of the Church service had been used, greatly enhanced the atrocity of the sin in the estimation of Madame Staubach;—if the young woman had intrigued in order that her lover might come to her, of course she would intrigue again. In spite of Linda's solemn protestation as to her self-esteem, the thing would be going on. This infamous young man, who, in Madame Staubach's eyes, was beginning to take the proportions of the Evil One himself, would be coming there beneath her very nose. It seemed to her that life would be impossible to her, unless Linda would consent to be married to the respectable suitor who was still willing to receive her; and that the only way in which to exact that consent would be to insist on the degradation to which Linda had subjected herself. Linda had talked of going into service. Let her go into that service which was now offered to her by those whom she was bound to obey. 'Of course Herr Steinmarc knows it all,' said Madame Staubach.

'I do not regard in the least what Herr Steinmarc knows,' replied Linda.

'But he is still willing to overlook the impropriety of your conduct, upon condition——'

'He overlook it! Let him dare to say such a word to me, and I would tell him that his opinion in this matter was of less moment to me than that of any other creature in all Nuremberg. What is it to him who comes to me? Were it but for him, I would bid the young man come every day.'

'Linda!'

'Do not talk to me about Peter Steinmarc, aunt Charlotte, or I shall go mad.'

'I must talk about him, and you must hear about him. It is now more than ever necessary that you should be his wife. All Nuremberg will hear of this.'

'Of course it will,—as Peter Steinmarc knows it.'

'And how will you cover yourself from your shame?'

'I will not cover myself at all. If you are ashamed of me, I will go away. If you will not say that you are not ashamed of me, I will go away. I have done nothing to disgrace me, and I will hear nothing about shame.' Having made this brave assertion, she burst into tears, and then escaped to her own bed.

When Madame Staubach was left alone, she sat down, closed her eyes, clasped her hands, and began to pray. As to what she should do in these terrible circumstances she had no light, unless such light might be given to her from above. A certain trust she had in Peter Steinmarc, because Peter was a man, and not a young man; but it was not a trust which made her confident. She thought that Peter was very good in being willing to take Linda at all after all that had happened, but she had begun to be aware that he himself was not able to make his own goodness apparent to Linda. She did not in her heart blame Peter for his want of eloquence, but rather imputed an increased degree of culpability to Linda, in that any eloquence was necessary for her conviction on such a matter. Eloquence in an affair of marriage, in reference to any preparation for marriage arrangements, was one of those devil's baits of which Madame Staubach was especially afraid. Ludovic Valcarm no doubt could be eloquent, could talk of love, and throw glances from his eyes, and sigh, and do worse things, perhaps, even than those. All tricks of Satan, these to ensnare the souls of young women! Peter could perform no such tricks, and therefore it was that his task was so difficult to him. She could not regard it as a deficiency that he was unable to do those very things which, when done in her presence, were abominable to her sight, and when spoken of were abominable to her ears, and when thought of were abominable to her imagination. But yet how was she to arrange this marriage, if Peter were able to say nothing for himself? So she sat herself down and clasped her hands and prayed earnestly that assistance might be given to her. If you pray that a mountain shall be moved, and will have faith, the mountain shall certainly be stirred. So she told herself; but she told herself this in an agony of spirit, because she still doubted,—she feared that she doubted,—that this thing would not be done for her by heaven's aid. Oh, if she could only make herself certain that heaven would aid her, then the thing would be done for her. She could not be certain, and therefore she felt herself to be a wretched sinner.

In the mean time, Linda was in bed up-stairs, thinking over her position, and making up her mind as to what should be her future conduct. As far as it might be possible, she would enter no room in which Peter Steinmarc was present. She would not go into the parlour when he was there, even though her aunt should call her. Should he follow her into the kitchen, she would instantly leave it. On no pretence would she speak to him. She had always the refuge of her own bedroom, and should he venture to follow her there, she thought that she would know how to defend herself. As to the rest, she must bear her aunt's thoughts, and if necessary her aunt's hard words also. It was very well to talk of going into service, but where was the house that would receive her? And then, as to Ludovic Valcarm! In regard to him, it was not easy for her to come to any resolution; but she still thought that she would be willing to make that compact, if her aunt, on the other side, would be willing to make it also.

CHAPTER VI

A LL September went by, and all October, and life in the red house in the island in Nuremberg was a very sad life indeed. During this time Linda Tressel never spoke to Ludovic Valcarm, nor of him; but she saw him once, standing among the beer-casks opposite to the warehouse. Had she not so seen him, she would have thought that he had vanished altogether out of the city, and that he was to be no more heard of or seen among them. He was such a man, and belonged to such a set, that his vanishing in this fashion would have been a thing to create no surprise. He might have joined his father, and they two might be together in any quarter of the globe,—on any spot,—the more distant, the more probable. It was one of Linda's troubles that she knew really nothing of the life of the man she loved. She had always heard things evil spoken of him, but such evil-speaking had come from those who were his enemies,— from his cousin, who had been angry because Ludovic had not remained with him on the stool in the town-hall; and from Madame Staubach, who thought ill of almost all young men, and who had been specially prejudiced against this young man by Peter Steinmarc. Linda did not know what she should believe. She had heard that the Brothers Sach were respectable tradesmen, and it was in Valcarm's favour that he was employed by them. She had thought that he had left them; but now, seeing him again among the barrels, she had reason to presume that his life could not be altogether unworthy of him. He was working for his bread, and what more could be required from a young man than that? Nevertheless, when she saw him, she sedulously kept herself from his sight, and went, almost at once, back to the kitchen, from whence there was no view on to the Ruden Platz.

During these weeks life was very sad in this house. Madame Staubach said but little to her niece of her past iniquity in the matter of Ludovic's visit, and not much of Peter's suit; but she so bore herself that every glance of her eye, every tone of her voice, every nod of her head, was a separate rebuke. She hardly ever left Linda alone, requiring her company when she went out to make her little purchases in the market, and always on those more momentous and prolonged occasions when she attended some public prayer-meeting. Linda resolved to obey in such matters, and she did obey. She went hither and thither by her aunt's side, and at home sat with her aunt, always with a needle in her hand,—never leaving the room, except when Peter Steinmarc entered it. This he did, perhaps, on every other evening; and when he did so, Linda always arose and went up to her own chamber, speaking no word to the man as she passed him. When her aunt had rebuked her for this, laying upon her a command that she should remain when Steinmarc appeared, she protested that in that matter obedience was impossible to her. In all other things she would do as she was bidden; nothing, she said, but force, should induce her to stay for five minutes in the same room with Peter Steinmarc. Peter, who was of course aware of all this, would look at her when he passed her, or met her on the stairs, or in the passages, as though she were something too vile for him to touch. Madame Staubach, as she saw this, would groan aloud, and then Peter would groan. Latterly, too, Tetchen had taken to groaning; so that life in that house had become very sad. But Linda paid back Peter's scorn with interest. Her lips would curl, and her nostrils would be dilated, and her eyes would flash fire on him as she passed him. He also prayed a little in these days that Linda might be given into his hands. If ever she should be so given, he should teach her what it was to scorn the offer of an honest man.

For a month or six weeks Linda Tressel bore all this with patience; but when October was half gone, her patience was almost at an end. Such a life, if prolonged much further, would make her mad. The absence of all smiles from the faces of those with whom she lived, was terrible to her. She was surrounded by a solemnity as of the grave, and came to doubt almost whether she were a living creature. If she were to be scorned always, to be treated ever as one unfit for the pleasant intercourse of life, it might be as well that she should deserve such treatment. It was possible that by deserving it she might avoid it! At first, during these solemn wearisome weeks, she would tell herself that because her aunt had condemned her, not therefore need she feel assured that she was condemned of her heavenly Father. She was not a castaway because her aunt had so called her. But gradually there came upon her a feeling, springing from her imagination rather than from her judgment, that she was a thing set apart as vile and bad. There grew upon her a conviction that she was one of the non-elect,* or rather, one of those who are elected to an eternity of misery. Her religious observances, as they came to her now, were odious to her; and that she supposed to be a certain sign that the devil had fought for her soul and had conquered. It could not be that she should be so terribly wretched if she were not also very wicked. She would tremble now at every sound; and though she still curled her lips, and poured scorn upon Peter from her eyes, as she moved away at his approach, she was almost so far beaten as to be desirous to succumb. She must either succumb to her aunt and to him, or else she must fly. How was she to live without a word of sympathy from any human being?

She had been careful to say little or nothing to Tetchen, having some indistinct idea that Tetchen was a double traitor. That Tetchen had on one occasion been in league with Ludovic, she was sure; but she thought that since that the woman had been in league with Peter also. The league with Ludovic had been very wicked, but that might be forgiven. A league with Peter was a sin to be forgiven never; and therefore Linda had resolutely declined of late to hold any converse with Tetchen other than that which the affairs of the house demanded. When Tetchen, who in this matter was most unjustly treated, would make little attempts to regain the confidence of her young mistress, her efforts were met with a repellant silence. And thus there was no one in the house to whom Linda could speak. This at last became so dreadful to her, the desolation of her position was so complete, that she had learned to regret her sternness to Tetchen. As far as she could now see, there was no alliance between Tetchen and Peter; and it might be the case, she thought, that her suspicions had been unjust to the old woman.

One evening, about the beginning of November, when it had already become dark at that hour in which Peter would present himself in Madame Staubach's parlour, he had entered the room, as was usual with him; and, as usual, Linda had at once left it. Peter, as he passed her, had looked at her with more than his usual anger, with an aggravated bitterness of condemnation in his eyes. She had been weeping in silence before he had appeared, and she had no power left to throw back her scorn at him. Still weeping, she went up into her room, and throwing herself on her bed, began, in her misery, to cry aloud for mercy. Some end must be brought to this, or the burden on her shoulders would be heavier than she could bear. She had gone to the window for a moment as she entered the chamber, and had thrown one glance in despair over towards the Ruden Platz. But the night was dark, and full of rain, and had he been there she could not have seen him. There was no one to befriend her. Then she threw herself on the bed and wept aloud.

She was still lying there when there came a very low tap at the door. She started up and listened. She had heard no footfall on the stairs, and it was, she thought, impossible that any one should have come up without her hearing the steps. Peter Steinmarc creaked whenever he went along the passages, and neither did her aunt or Tetchen tread with feet as light as that. She sat up, and

then the knock was repeated,—very low and very clear.
She still paused a moment, resolving that nothing should
frighten her,—nothing should startle her. No change
that could come to her would, she thought, be a change
for the worse. She hastened up from off the bed, and
stood upon the floor. Then she gave the answer that is
usual to such a summons. 'Come in,' she said. She spoke
low, but with clear voice, so that her word might certainly be heard, but not be heard afar. She stood about
ten feet from the door, and when she heard the lock
turned, her heart was beating violently.

The lock was turned, and the door was ajar, but it was
not opened. 'Linda,' said a soft voice—'Linda, will you
speak to me?' Heavens and earth! It was Ludovic,—
Ludovic in her aunt's house,—Ludovic at her chamber
door,—Ludovic there, within the very penetralia* of their
abode, while her aunt and Peter Steinmarc were sitting
in the chamber below! But she had resolved that in no
event would she be startled. In making that resolve, had
she not almost hoped that this would be the voice that
should greet her?

She could not now again say, 'Come in,' and the man
who had had the audacity to advance so far, was not bold
enough to advance farther, though invited. She stepped
quickly to the door, and, placing her hand upon the lock,
knew not whether to close it against the intruder or to
confront the man. 'There can be but a moment, Linda;
will you not speak to me?' said her lover.

What could her aunt do to her?—what Peter Steinmarc?—what could the world do, worse than had been
done already? They had told her that she was a castaway, and she had half believed it. In the moments of her
deepest misery she had believed it. If that were so, how
could she fall lower? Would it not be sweet to her to
hear one word of kindness in her troubles, to catch one
note that should not be laden with rebuke? She opened
the door, and stood before him in the gloom of the
passage.

'Linda,—dear, dearest Linda;'—and before she knew
that he was so near her, he had caught her hand.

'Hush! they are below;—they will hear you.'

'No; I could be up among the rafters before any one could be on the first landing; and no one should hear a motion.' Linda, in her surprise, looked up through the darkness, as though she could see the passage of which he spoke in the narrowing stair amidst the roof. What a terrible man was this, who had come to her bedroom door, and could thus talk of escaping amidst the rafters!

'Why are you here?' she whispered.

'Because I love you better than the light of heaven. Because I would go through fire and water to be near you. Linda,—dearest Linda, is it not true that you are in sorrow?'

'Indeed yes,' she said, shaking her head, while she still left her hand in his.

'And shall I not find an escape for you?'

'No, no; that is impossible.'

'I will try at least,' said he.

'You can do nothing for me,—nothing.'

'You love me, Linda? Say that you love me.' She remained silent, but her hand was still within his grasp. She could not lie to him, and say that she loved him not. 'Linda, you are all the world to me. The sweetest music that I could hear would be one word to say that I am dear to you.' She said not a word, but he knew now that she loved him. He knew it well. It is the instinct of the lover to know that his mistress has given him her heart heartily, when she does not deny the gift with more than sternness,—with cold cruelty. Yes; he knew her secret now; and pulling her close to him by her hand, by her arm, he wound his own arm round her waist tightly, and pressed his face close to hers. 'Linda, Linda,—my own, my own!—O God! how happy I am!' She suffered it all, but spoke not a word. His hot kisses were rained upon her lips, but she gave him never a kiss in return. He pressed her with all the muscles of his body, and she simply bore the pressure, uncomplaining, uncomplying, hardly thinking, half conscious, almost swooning, hysterical, with blood rushing wildly to her heart, lost in an agony of mingled fear and love. 'Oh, Linda!—oh, my own one!' But the kisses were still raining on her lips, and cheek, and brow. Had she heard her aunt's footsteps on the stairs, had she heard the creaking shoes of Peter Steinmarc himself, she could hardly have moved to save herself from their wrath. The pressure of her lover's arms was very sweet to her, but still, through it all, there was a consciousness that, in her very knowledge of that sweetness, the devil was claiming his own. Now, in very truth, was she a castaway. 'My love, my life!' said Ludovic, 'there are but a few moments for us. What can I do to comfort you?' She was still in his arms, pressed closely to his bosom, not trusting at all to the support of her own legs. She made one little struggle to free herself, but it was in vain. She opened her lips to speak, but there came no sound from them. Then there came again upon her that storm of kisses, and she was bound round by his arm, as though she were never again to be loosened. The waters that fell upon her were sweeter than the rains of heaven; but she knew,—there was still enough of life in her to remember,—that they were foul with the sulphur and the brimstone of the pit of hell.

'Linda,' he said, 'I am leaving Nuremberg; will you go with me?' Go with him! whither was she to go? How was she to go? And this going that he spoke of? Was it not thus usually with castaways? If it were true that she was in very fact already a castaway, why should she not go with him? And yet she was half sure that any such going on her part was a thing quite out of the question. As an actor will say of himself when he declines some proffered character, she could not see herself in that part. Though she could tell herself that she was a castaway, a very child of the devil, because she could thus stand and listen to her lover at her chamber door, yet could she not think of the sin that would really make her so without an abhorrence which made that sin frightful to her. She was not allured, hardly tempted, by the young man's offer as he made it. And yet, what else was there for her to do? And if it were true that she was a castaway, why should she struggle to be better than others who were of the same colour with herself? 'Linda, say, will you be my wife?'

His wife! Oh, yes, she would be his wife,—if it were possible. Even now, in the moment of her agony, there came to her a vague idea that she might do him some service if she were his wife, because she had property of her own. She was ready to acknowledge to herself that her duty to him was stronger than her duty to that woman below who had been so cruel to her. She would be his wife, if it were possible, even though he should drag her through the mud of poverty and through the gutters of tribulation. Could she walk down to her aunt's presence this moment his real wife, she would do so, and bear all that could be said to her. Could this be so, that storm which had been bitter with brimstone from the lowest pit, would at once become sweet with the air of heaven. But how could this be? She knew that it could not be. Marriage was a thing difficult to be done, hedged in with all manner of impediments, hardly to be reached at all by such a one as her, unless it might be such a marriage as that proposed to her with Peter Steinmarc. For girls with sweet, loving parents, for the Fanny Heisses of the world, marriage might be made easy. It was all very well for Ludovic Valcarm to ask her to be his wife; but in asking he must have known that she could not if she would; and yet the sound of the word was sweet to her. If it might be so, even yet she would not be a castaway.

But she did not answer his question. Struggling hard to speak, she muttered some prayer to him that he would leave her. 'Say that you love me,' demanded Ludovic. The demand was only whispered, but the words came hot into her ears.

'I do love you,' she replied.

'Then you will go with me.'

'No, no! It is impossible.'

'They will make you take that man for your husband.'

'They shall never do that;—never,—never.' In making this assertion, Linda found strength to extricate herself from her lover's arms and to stand alone.

'And how shall I come to you again?' said Ludovic.

'You must not come again. You should not have come

now. I would not have been here had I thought it possible you would have come.'

'But, Linda——' and then he went on to show to her how very unsatisfactory a courtship theirs would be, if, now that they were together, nothing could be arranged as to their future meeting. It soon became clear to Linda that Ludovic knew everything that was going on in the house, and had learned it all from Tetchen. Tetchen at this moment was quite aware of his presence up-stairs, and was prepared to cough aloud, standing at the kitchen door, if any sign were made that either Steinmarc or Madame Staubach were about to leave the parlour. Though it had seemed to Linda that her lover had come to her through the darkness, aided by the powers thereof, the assistance which had really brought him there was simply that of the old cook down-stairs. It certainly was on the cards that Tetchen might help him again after the same fashion, but Ludovic felt that such help would be but of little avail unless Linda, now that she had acknowledged her love, would do something to help also. With Ludovic Valcarm it was quite a proper course of things that he should jump out of a boat, or disappear into the roof among the rafters, or escape across the tiles and down the spouts in the darkness, as preliminary steps in a love affair. But in this special love affair such movements could only be preliminary; and therefore, as he was now standing face to face with Linda, and as there certainly had been difficulties in achieving this position, he was anxious to make some positive use of it. And then, as he explained to Linda in very few words, he was about to leave Nuremberg, and go to Munich. She did not quite understand whether he was always to remain in Munich; nor did she think of inquiring how he was to earn his bread there. But it was his scheme, that she should go with him and that there they should be married. If she would meet him at the railway station in time for the early train, they certainly could reach Munich without impediment. Linda would find no difficulty in leaving the house. Tetchen would take care that even the door should be open for her.

Linda listened to it all, and by degrees the impossibility of her assenting to such iniquity became less palpable. And though the wickedness of the scheme was still manifest to her, though she felt that, were she to assent to it, she would, in doing so, give herself up finally, body and soul, to the Evil One, yet was she not angry with Ludovic for proposing it. Nay, loving him well enough before, she loved him the better as he pressed her to go with him. But she would not go. She had nothing to say but, No, no, no. It was impossible. She was conscious after a certain fashion that her legs would refuse to carry her to the railway station on such an errand, that her physical strength would have failed her, and that were she to make ever so binding a promise, when the morning came she would not be there. He had again taken her hand, and was using all his eloquence, still speaking in low whispers, when there was heard a cough,—not loud, but very distinct,—Tetchen's cough as she stood at the kitchen door. Ludovic Valcarm, though the necessity for movement was so close upon him, would not leave Linda's hand till he had again pressed a kiss upon her mouth. Now, at last, in this perilous moment, there was some slightest movement on Linda's lips, which he flattered himself he might take as a response. Then, in a moment, he was gone and her door was shut, and he was escaping, after his own fashion, into the darkness,—she knew not whither and she knew not how, except that there was a bitter flavour of brimstone* about it all.

She seated herself at the foot of the bed lost in amazement. She must first think,—she was bound first to think, of his safety; and yet what in the way of punishment could they do to him comparable to the torments which they could inflict upon her? She listened, and she soon heard Peter Steinmarc creaking in the room below. Tetchen had coughed because Peter was as usual going to his room, but had Ludovic remained at her door no one would have been a bit the wiser. No doubt Ludovic, up among the rafters, was thinking the same thing; but there must be no renewal of their intercourse that night, and therefore Linda bolted her door. As she did so, she

swore to herself that she would not unbolt it again that
evening at Ludovic's request. No such encroaching
request was made to her. She sat for nearly an hour at
the foot of her bed, waiting, listening, fearing, thinking,
hoping,—hardly hoping, when another step was heard
on the stair and in the passage,—a step which she well
knew to be that of her aunt Charlotte. Then she arose,
and as her aunt drew near she pulled back the bolt and
opened the door. The little oil lamp which she held
threw a timid fitful light into the gloom, and Linda
looked up unconsciously into the darkness of the roof over
her head.

It had been her custom to return to her aunt's parlour
as soon as she heard Peter creaking in the room below,
and she had still meant to do so on this evening; but
hitherto she had been unable to move, or at any rate so to
compose herself as to have made it possible for her to go
into her aunt's presence. Had she not had the whole
world of her own love story to fill her mind and her
heart?

'Linda, I have been expecting you to come down to
me,' said her aunt, gravely.

'Yes, aunt Charlotte, and I was coming.'

'It is late now, Linda.'

'Then, if you please, I will go to bed,' said Linda, who
was by no means sorry to escape the necessity of returning to the parlour.

'I could not go to my rest,' said Madame Staubach,
'without doing my duty by seeing you and telling you
again, that it is very wicked of you to leave the room
whenever our friend enters it. Linda, do you ever think
of the punishment which pride will bring down upon
you?'

'It is not pride.'

'Yes, Linda. It is the worst pride in the world.'

'I will sit with him all the evening if he will promise me
never again to ask me to be his wife.'

'The time will perhaps come, Linda, when you will be
only too glad to take him, and he will tell you that you
are not fit to be the wife of an honest man.' Then, having

uttered this bitter curse,—for such it was,—Madame
Staubach went across to her own room.

Linda, as she knelt at her bedside, tried to pray that
she might be delivered from temptation, but she felt that
her prayers were not prayers indeed. Even when she was
on her knees, with her hands clasped together as though
towards her God, her very soul was full of the presence
of that arm which had been so fast wound round her
waist. And when she was in bed she gave herself up to
the sweetness of her love. With what delicious violence
had that storm of kisses fallen on her! Then she prayed
for him, and strove very hard that her prayer might be
sincere.

CHAPTER VII

ANOTHER month had passed by, and it was now nearly
mid-winter. Another month had passed by, and
neither had Madame Staubach nor Peter Steinmarc
heard ought of Ludovic's presence among the rafters;
but things were much altered in the red house, and
Linda's life was hot, fevered, suspicious, and full of a
dangerous excitement. Twice again she had seen Ludovic, once meeting him in the kitchen, and once she had
met him at a certain dark gate in the Nonnen Garten, to
which she had contrived to make her escape for half an
hour on a false plea. Things were much changed with
Linda Tressel when she could condescend to do this. And
she had received from her lover a dozen notes, always
by the hand of Tetchen, and had written to him more
than once a few short, incoherent, startling words, in which
she would protest that she loved him, and protest also at
the same time that her love must be all in vain. 'It is of
no use. Do not write, and pray do not come. If this goes
on it will kill me. You know that I shall never give
myself to anybody else.' This was in answer to a proposition made through Tetchen that he should come again
to her,—should come, and take her away with him. He
had come, and there had been that interview in the
kitchen, but he had not succeeded in inducing her to
leave her home.

There had been many projects discussed between them, as to which Tetchen had given much advice. It was Tetchen's opinion, that if Linda would declare to her aunt that she meant at once to marry Ludovic Valcarm, and make him master of the house in which they lived, Madame Staubach would have no alternative but to submit quietly; that she would herself go forth and instruct the clergyman to publish the banns, and that Linda might thus become Valcarm's acknowledged wife before the snow was off the ground. Ludovic seemed to have his doubts about this, still signifying his preference for a marriage at Munich. When Tetchen explained to him that Linda would lose her character by travelling with him to Munich before she was his wife, he merely laughed at such an old wife's tale. Had not he himself seen Fanny Heisse and Max Bogen in the train together between Augsburg and Nuremberg long before they were married, and who had thought of saying a word against Fanny's character? 'But everybody knew about that,' said Linda. 'Let everybody know about this,' said Ludovic.

But Linda would not go. She would not go, even though Ludovic told her that it was imperative that he himself should quit Nuremberg. Such matters were in training,*—he did not tell her what matters,—as would make his going quite imperative. Still she would take no step towards going with him. That advice of Tetchen's was much more in accordance with her desires. If she could act upon that, then she might have some happiness before her. She thought that she could make up her mind, and bring herself to declare her purpose to her aunt, if Ludovic would allow her to do so. But Ludovic declared that this could not be done, as preparatory to their being married at Nuremberg; and at last he was almost angry with her. Did she not trust him? Oh, yes, she would trust him with everything; with her happiness, her heart, her house,—with all that the world had left for her. But there was still that feeling left within her bosom, that if she did this thing which he proposed, she would be trusting him with her very soul.

Ludovic said a word to her about the house, and
Tetchen said many words. When Linda expressed an
opinion, that though the house might not belong to her
aunt legally, it was or ought to be her aunt's property in
point of honour, Tetchen only laughed at her. 'Don't let
her bother you about Peter then, if she chooses to live
here on favour,' said Tetchen. As Linda came to think
of it, it did appear hard to her that she should be tormented about Peter Steinmarc in her own house. She was not
Madame Staubach's child, nor her slave; nor, indeed,
was she of childish age. Gradually the idea grew upon
her that she might assert her right to free herself from the
tyranny to which she was made subject. But there was
always joined to this a consciousness, that though, according to the laws of the world, she might assert her right,
and claim her property, and acknowledge to everybody
her love to Ludovic Valcarm, she could do none of these
things in accordance with the laws of God. She had
become subject to her aunt by the circumstances of her
life, as though her aunt were in fact her parent, and the
fifth commandment was as binding on her as though she
were in truth the daughter of the guardian who had had
her in charge since her infancy. Once she said a word to
her aunt about the house, and was struck with horror by
the manner in which Madame Staubach had answered
her. She had simply said that, as the house was partly
hers, she had thought that she might suggest the expediency of getting another lodger in place of Peter Steinmarc.
But Madame Staubach had arisen from her chair and
had threatened to go at once out into the street,—'bare,
naked, and destitute,' as she expressed herself. 'If you
ever tell me again,' said Madame Staubach, 'that the
house is yours, I will never eat another meal beneath
your father's roof.' Linda, shocked at her own wickedness, had fallen at her aunt's knees, and promised that
she would never again be guilty of such wickedness. And
as she reflected on what she had done, she did believe
herself to have been very mean and very wicked. She
had known all her life that, though the house was hers
to live in, it was subject to the guidance of her aunt; and

so had she been subject till she had grown to be a woman. She could not quite understand that such subjection for the whole term of her life need be a duty to her; but when was the term of duty to be completed?

Between her own feelings on one side, and Tetchen's continued instigation on the other, she became aware that that which she truly needed was advice. These secret interviews and this clandestine correspondence were terrible to her very soul. She would not even yet be a castaway if it might be possible to save herself! There were two things fixed for her,—fixed, even though by their certainty she must become a castaway. She would never marry Peter Steinmarc, and she would never cease to love Ludovic Valcarm. But might it be possible that these assured facts should be reconciled to duty? If only there were somebody whom she might trust to tell her that!

Linda's father had had many friends in Nuremberg, and she could still remember those whom, as a child, she had seen from time to time in her father's house. The names of some were still familiar to her, and the memories of the faces even of one or two who had suffered her to play at their knees when she was little more than a baby, were present to her. Manners had so changed at the red house since those days, that few, if any, of these alliances had been preserved. The peculiar creed of Madame Staubach was not popular with the burghers of Nuremberg, and we all know how family friendships will die out when they are not kept alive by the warmth of familiar intercourse. There were still a few, and they among those most respected in the city, who would bow to Madame Staubach when they met her in the streets, and would smile and nod at Linda as they remembered the old days when they would be merry with a decorous mirth in the presence of her father. But there were none in the town,—no, not one,—who could interfere as a friend in the affairs of the widow Staubach's household, or who ever thought of asking Linda to sit at a friendly hearth. Close neighbourhood and school acquaintance had made Fanny Heisse her friend, but it was very rarely indeed that she had set her foot over the threshold of Jacob's door. Peter Steinmarc was their only friend, and his friendship had arisen from the mere fact of his residence beneath the same roof. It was necessary that their house should be divided with another, and in this way Peter had become their lodger. Linda certainly could not go to Peter for advice. She would have gone to Jacob Heisse, but that Jacob was a man slow of speech, somewhat timid in all matters beyond the making of furniture, and but little inclined to meddle with things out of his own reach. She fancied that the counsel which she required should be sought for from some one wiser and more learned than Jacob Heisse.

Among the names of those who had loved her father, which still rested in her memory, was that of Herr Molk, a man much spoken of in Nuremberg, one rich and of great repute, who was or had been burgomaster, and who occupied a house on the Egidien Platz,* known to Linda well, because of its picturesque beauty. Even Peter Steinmarc, who would often speak of the town magistrates as though they were greatly inferior to himself in municipal lore and general wisdom, would mention the name of Herr Molk with almost involuntary respect. Linda had seen him from time to time either in the Platz or on the market-place, and her father's old friend had always smiled on her and expressed some hope that she was well and happy. Ah, how vain had been that hope! What if she should now go to Herr Molk and ask him for advice? She would not speak to Tetchen, because Tetchen would at once tell it all to Ludovic; and in this matter, as Linda felt, she must not act as Ludovic would bid her. Yes; she would go to this noted pundit*of the city, and, if he would allow her so to do, would tell to him all her story.

And then she made another resolve. She would not do this without informing her aunt that it was about to be done. On this occasion, even though her aunt should tell her to remain in the house, she would go forth. But her aunt should not throw it in her teeth that she had acted on the sly. One day, one cold November morning, when the hour of their early dinner was approaching, she went up-stairs from the kitchen for her hat and cloak, and then, equipped for her walk, presented herself before her aunt.

'Linda, where are you going?' demanded Madame Staubach.

'I am going, aunt Charlotte, to Herr Molk, in the Egidien Platz.'

'To Herr Molk? And why? Has he bidden you come to him?' Then Linda told her story, with much difficulty. She was unhappy, she said, and wanted advice. She remembered this man,—that he was the friend of her father. 'I am sorry, Linda, that you should want other advice than that which I can give you.'

'Dear aunt, it is just that. You want me to marry this man here, and I cannot do it. This has made you miserable, and me miserable. Is it not true that we are not happy as we used to be?'

'I certainly am not happy. How can I be happy when I see you wandering astray? How can I be happy when you tell me that you love the man in Nuremberg whom I believe of all to be most wicked and ungodly? How can I be happy when you threaten to expel from the house, because it is your own, the only man whom I love, honour, and respect?'

'I never said so, aunt Charlotte;—I never thought of saying such a thing.'

'And what will you ask of this stranger should you find yourself in his presence?'

'I will tell him everything, and ask him what I should do.'

'And will you tell him truly?'

'Certainly, aunt Charlotte; I will tell him the truth in everything.'

'And if he bids you marry the man whom I have chosen as your husband?' Linda, when this suggestion was made to her, became silent. Truly it was impossible that any wise man in Nuremberg could tell her that such a sacrifice as that was necessary! Then Madame Staubach repeated the question. 'If he bids you marry Peter Steinmarc, will you do as he bids you?'

Surely she would not be so bidden by her father's friend! 'I will endeavour to do as he bids me,' said Linda.

'Then go to him, my child, and may God so give him grace that he may soften the hardness of your heart, and prevail with you to put down beneath your feet the temptations of Satan; and that he may quell the spirit of evil within you. God forbid that I should think that there is no wisdom in Nuremberg fitter than mine to guide you. If the man be a man of God, he will give you good counsel.'

Then Linda, wondering much at her aunt's ready acquiescence, went forth, and walked straightway to the house of Herr Molk in the Egidien Platz.

CHAPTER VIII

A WALK of ten minutes took Linda from the Schutt island to the Egidien Platz, and placed her before the door of Herr Molk's house. The Egidien Platz is, perhaps, the most fashionable quarter of Nuremberg, if Nuremberg may be said to have a fashion in such matters. It is near to the Rathhaus, and to St. Sebald's Church, and is not far distant from the old Burg or Castle in which the Emperors used to dwell when they visited the imperial city of Nuremberg. This large open Place has a church in its centre, and around it are houses almost all large, built with gables turned towards the street, quaint, picturesque, and eloquent of much burghers' wealth. There could be no such square in a city which was not or had not been very rich. And among all the houses in the Egidien Platz, there was no house to exceed in beauty of ornament, in quaintness of architecture, or in general wealth and comfort, that which was inhabited by Herr Molk.

Linda stood for a moment at the door, and then putting up her hand, pulled down the heavy iron bell-handle, which itself was a gem of art, representing some ancient and discreet burgher of the town, wrapped in his cloak, and almost hidden by his broad-brimmed hat. She heard the bell clank close inside the door, and then the portal was open, as though the very pulling of the bell had opened it. The lock at least was open, so that Linda could push the door with her hand and enter over the threshold. This she did, and she found herself within a long narrow court or yard, round which, one above another, there ran galleries, open to the court, and guarded with heavy balustrades of carved wood. From the narrowness of the enclosure, the house on each side seemed to be very high, and Linda, looking round with astonished eyes, could see that at every point the wood was carved. And the waterspouts were ornamented with grotesque figures, and the huge broad stairs which led to the open galleries on the left hand were of polished oak, made so slippery with the polishers' daily care that it was difficult to tread upon them without falling. All around the bottom of the court there were open granaries or warehouses; for there seemed to be nothing that could be called a room on the ground floor, beyond the porter's lodge; and these open warehouses seemed to be filled full with masses of stacked firewood. Linda knew well the value of such stores in Nuremberg, and lost none of her veneration for Herr Molk because of such nature were the signs of his domestic wealth.

As she timidly looked around her she saw an old woman within the gate of the porter's lodge, and inquired whether Herr Molk was at home and disengaged. The woman simply motioned her to the wicket gate by which the broad polished stairs were guarded. Linda, hesitating to advance into so grand a mansion alone, and yet knowing that she should do as she was bidden, entered the wicket and ascended carefully to the first gallery. Here was another bell ready to her hand, the handle of which consisted of a little child in iron-work. This also she pulled, and waited till some one should come. Presently there was a scuffling heard of quick feet in the gallery, and three children ran up to her. In the middle was the elder, a girl dressed in dark silk, and at her sides

were two boys habited in black velvet. They all had long
fair hair, and large blue eyes, and soft peach-like cheeks,
—such as those who love children always long to kiss.
Linda thought that she had never seen children so
gracious and so fair. She asked again whether Herr Molk
was at home, and at liberty to see a stranger. 'Quite a
stranger,' said poor Linda, with what emphasis she could
put upon her words. The little girl said that her grandfather was at home, and would see any visitor,—as a
matter of course. Would Linda follow her? Then the
child, still leading her little brothers, tripped up the
stairs to the second gallery, and opening a door which led
into one of the large front rooms, communicated to an
old gentleman who seemed to be taking exercise in the
apartment with his hands behind his back, that he was
wanted by a lady.

'Wanted, am I, my pretty one? Well, and here I am.'
Then the little girl, giving a long look up into Linda's
face, retreated, taking her brothers with her, and closing
the door. Thus Linda found herself in the room along
with the old gentleman, who still kept his hands behind
his back. It was a singular apartment, nearly square, but
very large, panelled with carved wood,* not only throughout the walls, but up to the ceiling also. And the floor
was polished even brighter than were the stairs. Herr
Molk must have been well accustomed to take his exercise there, or he would surely have slipped and fallen in
his course. There was but one small table in the room,
which stood unused near a wall, and there were perhaps
not more than half-a-dozen chairs,—all high-backed,
covered with old tapestry, and looking as though they
could hardly have been placed there for ordinary use.
On one of these, Linda sat at the old man's bidding; and
he placed himself on another, with his hands still behind
him, just seating himself on the edge of the chair.

'I am Linda Tressel,' said poor Linda. She saw at a
glance that she herself would not have known Herr Molk,
whom she had never before met without his hat, and she
perceived also that he had not recognised her.

'Linda Tressel! So you are. Dear, dear! I knew your

father well,—very well. But, lord, how long that is ago! He is dead ever so many years; how many years?'

'Sixteen years,' said Linda.

'Sixteen years dead! And he was a younger man than I,—much younger. Let me see,—not so much younger, but younger. Linda Tressel, your father's daughter is welcome to my house. A glass of wine will not hurt you this cold weather.' She declined the wine, but the old man would have his way. He went out, and was absent perhaps five minutes. Then he returned bearing a small tray in his own hands, with a long-necked bottle and glasses curiously engraved, and he insisted that Linda should clink her glass with his. 'And now, my dear, what is it that I can do for you?'

So far Linda's mission had prospered well; but now that the story was to be told, she found very much difficulty in telling it. She had to begin with the whole history of the red house, and of the terms upon which her aunt had come to reside in it. She had one point at least in her favour. Herr Molk was an excellent listener. He would nod his head, and pat one hand upon the other, and say, 'Yes, yes,' without the slightest sign of impatience. It seemed as though he had no other care before him than that of listening to Linda's story. When she experienced the encouragement which came from the nodding of his head and the patting of his hand, she went on boldly. She told how Peter Steinmarc had come to the house, and how her aunt was a woman peculiar from the strength of her religious convictions. 'Yes, my dear, yes; we know that,—we know that,' said Herr Molk. Linda did her best to say nothing evil of her aunt. Then she came to the story of Peter's courtship. 'He is quite an old man, you know,' said poor Linda, thoughtfully. Then she was interrupted by Herr Molk. 'A worthy man; I know him well,—well,—well. Peter Steinmarc is our clerk at the Rathhaus. A very worthy man is Peter Steinmarc. Your father, my dear, was clerk at the Rathhaus, and Peter followed him. He is not young,— not just young; but a very worthy man. Go on, my dear.' Linda had resolved to tell it all, and she did tell it all.

It was difficult to tell, but it all came out. Perhaps there could be no listener more encouraging to such a girl as Linda than the patient, gentle-mannered old man with whom she was closeted. 'She had a lover whom she loved dearly,' she said,—'a young man.'

'Oh, a lover,' said Herr Molk. But there seemed to be no anger in his voice. He received the information as though it were important, but not astonishing. Then Linda even told him how the lover had come across the river on the Sunday morning, and how it had happened that she had not told her aunt, and how angry her aunt had been. 'Yes, yes,' said Herr Molk; 'it is better that your elders should know such things,—always better. But go on, my dear.' Then she told also how the lover had come down, or had gone up, through the rafters, and the old man smiled. Perhaps he had hidden himself among rafters fifty years ago, and had some sweet remembrance of the feat. And now Linda wanted to know what was she to do, and how she ought to act. The house was her own, but she would not for worlds drive her aunt out of it. She loved her lover very dearly, and she could not love Peter Steinmarc at all,—not in that way.

'Has the young man means to support a wife?' asked Herr Molk. Linda hesitated, knowing that there was still a thing to be told, which she had not as yet dared to mention. She knew too that it must be told. Herr Molk, as she hesitated, asked a second question on this very point. 'And what is the young man's name, my dear? It all depends on his name and character, and whether he has means to support a wife.'

'His name——is——Ludovic Valcarm,' said Linda, whispering the words very low.

The old man jumped from his seat with an alacrity that Linda had certainly not expected. 'Ludovic—Valcarm!' he said; 'why, my dear, the man is in prison this moment. I signed the committal yesterday myself.'

'In prison!' said Linda, rising also from her chair.

'He is a terrible young man,' said Herr Molk—'a very terrible young man. He does all manner of things;—I can't explain what. My dear young woman, you must

not think of taking Ludovic Valcarm for your husband;
you must not, indeed. You had better make up your
mind to take Peter Steinmarc. Peter Steinmarc can
support a wife, and is very respectable. I have known
Peter all my life. Ludovic Valcarm! Oh dear! That
would be very bad,—very bad indeed!'

Linda's distress was excessive. It was not only that the
tidings which she heard of Ludovic were hard to bear,
but it seemed that Herr Molk was intent on ranging
himself altogether with her enemies respecting Peter
Steinmarc. In fact, the old man's advice to her respecting
Peter was more important in her mind that his denunciation of Ludovic. She did not quite credit what he said
of Ludovic. It was doubtless true that Ludovic was in
prison; probably for some political offence. But such
men, she thought, were not kept in prison long. It was
bad, this fact of her lover's imprisonment; but not so bad
as the advice which her counsellor gave her, and which
she knew she would be bound to repeat to her aunt.

'But, Herr Molk, sir, if I do not love Peter Steinmarc
—if I hate him——?'

'Oh, my dear, my dear! This is a terrible thing. There
is not such another ne'er-do-well in all Nuremberg as
Ludovic Valcarm. Support a wife! He cannot support
himself. And it will be well if he does not die in a jail.
Oh dear! oh dear! For your father's sake, fraulein—for
your father's sake, I would go any distance to save you
from this. Your father was a good man, and a credit to
the city. And Peter Steinmarc is a good man.'

'But I need not marry Peter Steinmarc, Herr Molk.'

'You cannot do better, my dear,—indeed you cannot.
See what your aunt says. And remember, my dear, that
you should submit yourself to your elders and your betters.
Peter is not so old. He is not old at all. I was one of the
city magistrates when Peter was a little boy. I remember
him well. And he began life in your father's office.
Nothing can be more respectable than he has been. And
then Ludovic Valcarm! oh dear! If you ask my advice,
I should counsel you to accept Peter Steinmarc.'

There was nothing more to be got from Herr Molk.

And with this terrible recommendation still sounding in her ears, Linda sadly made her way back from the Egidien Platz to the Schütt island.

CHAPTER IX

LINDA TRESSEL, as she returned home to the house in the Schütt island, became aware that it was necessary for her to tell to her aunt all that had passed between herself and Herr Molk. She had been half stunned with grief as she left the magistrate's house, and for a while had tried to think that she could keep back from Madame Staubach at any rate the purport of the advice that had been given to her. And as she came to the conclusion that this would be impossible to her,—that it must all come out, —various wild plans flitted across her brain. Could she not run away without returning to the red house at all? But whither was she to run, and with whom? The only one who would have helped her in this wild enterprise had been sent to prison by that ill-conditioned old man who had made her so miserable! At this moment, there was no longer any hope in her bosom that she should save herself from being a castaway; nay, there was hardly a wish. There was no disreputable life so terrible to her thoughts, no infamy so infamous in idea to her, as would be respectability in the form of matrimony with Peter Steinmarc. And now, as she walked along painfully, going far out of her way that she might have some little time for reflection, turning all this in her mind, she began almost to fear that if she went back to her aunt, her aunt would prevail, and that in very truth Peter Steinmarc would become her lord and master. Then there was another plan, as impracticable as that scheme of running away. What if she were to become sullen, and decline to speak at all? She was well aware that in such a contest her aunt's tongue would be very terrible to her; and as the idea crossed her mind, she told herself that were she so to act people would treat her as a mad woman. But even that, she thought, would be better than being forced to marry Peter Steinmarc. Before she had reached the island, she knew that the one scheme was as impossible as the other. She entered the house very quietly, and turning to the left went at once into the kitchen.

'Linda, your aunt is waiting dinner for you this hour,' said Tetchen.

'Why did you not take it to her by herself?' said Linda, crossly.

'How could I do that, when she would not have it? You had better go in now at once. But, Linda, does anything ail you?'

'Very much ails me,' said Linda.

Then Tetchen came close to her, and whispered, 'Have you heard anything about him?'

'What have you heard, Tetchen? Tell me at once.'

'He is in trouble.'

'He is in prison!' Linda said this with a little hysteric scream. Then she began to sob and cry, and turned her back to Tetchen and hid her face in her hands.

'I have heard that too,' said Tetchen. 'They say the burgomasters have caught him with letters on him from some terrible rebels up in Prussia,* and that he has been plotting to have the city burned down. But I don't believe all that, fraulein.'

'He is in prison. I know he is in prison,' said Linda. 'I wish I were there too;—so I do, or dead. I'd rather be dead.' Then Madame Staubach, having perhaps heard the lock of the front door when it was closed, came into the kitchen. 'Linda,' she said, 'I am waiting for you.

'I do not want any dinner,' said Linda, still standing with her face turned to the wall. Then Madame Staubach took hold of her arm, and led her across the passage into the parlour. Linda said not a word as she was being thus conducted, but was thinking whether it might not even yet serve her purpose to be silent and sullen. She was still sobbing, and striving to repress her sobs; but she allowed herself to be led without resistance, and in an instant the door was closed, and she was seated on the old sofa with her aunt beside her.

'Have you seen Herr Molk?' demanded Madame Staubach.

'Yes; I have seen him.'

'And what has he said to you?' Then Linda was silent. 'You told me that you would seek his counsel; and that you would act as he might advise you.'

'No; I did not say that.'

'Linda!'

'I did not promise. I made no promise.'

'Linda, surely you did promise. When I asked you whether you would do as he might bid you, you said that you would be ruled by him. Then, knowing that he is wise, and of repute in the city, I let you go. Linda, was it not so?' Linda could not remember what words had in truth been spoken between them. She did remember that in her anxiety to go forth, thinking it to be impossible that the burgomaster should ask her to marry a man old enough to be her father, she had in some way assented to her aunt's proposition. But yet she thought that she had made no definite promise that she would marry the man she hated. She did not believe that she would absolutely have promised that under any possible circumstances she would do so. She could not, however, answer her aunt's question; so she continued to sob, and endeavoured again to hide her face. 'Did you tell the man everything, my child?' demanded Madame Staubach.

'Yes, I did.'

'And what has he said to you?'

'I don't know.'

'You don't know! Linda, that cannot be true. It is not yet half an hour since, and you do not know what Herr Molk said to you? Did you tell him of my wish about our friend Peter?'

'Yes, I did.'

'And did you tell him of your foolish fancy for that wicked young man?'

'Yes, I did.'

'And what did he say?'

Linda was still silent. It was almost impossible for her to tell her aunt what the man had said to her. She could not bring herself to tell the story of what had passed in the panelled room. Had Madame Staubach been in any

way different from what she was,—had she been at all
less stubborn, less hard, less reliant on the efficacy of her
religious convictions to carry her over all obstacles,—she
would have understood something of the sufferings of the
poor girl with whom she was dealing. But with her the
only idea present to her mind was the absolute necessity
of saving Linda from the wrath to come by breaking her
spirit in regard to things of this world, and crushing her
into atoms here, that those atoms might be remoulded in
a form that would be capable of a future and a better
life. Instead therefore of shrinking from cruelty, Madame
Staubach was continually instigating herself to be cruel.
She knew that the image of the town-clerk was one
simply disgusting to Linda, and therefore she was determined to force that image upon her. She knew that the
girl's heart was set upon Ludovic Valcarm with all the
warmth of its young love, and therefore she conceived it
to be her duty to prove to the girl that Ludovic Valcarm
was one already given up to Satan and Satanic agencies.
Linda must be taught not only to acknowledge, but in
very fact to understand and perceive, that this world is a
vale of tears,* that its paths are sharp to the feet, and that
they who walk through it should walk in mourning and
tribulation. What though her young heart should be
broken by the lesson,—be broken after the fashion in
which human hearts are made to suffer? To Madame
Staubach's mind a broken heart and a contrite spirit
were pretty much the same thing. It was good that
hearts should be broken, that all the inner humanities
of the living being should be, as it were, crushed on a
wheel and ground into fragments, so that nothing should
be left capable of receiving pleasure from the delights of
this world. Such, according to her theory of life, was the
treatment to which young women should be subjected.
The system needed for men might probably be different.
It was necessary that they should go forth and work; and
Madame Staubach conceived it to be possible that the
work of the world could not be adequately done by men
who had been subjected to the crushing process which
was requisite for women. Therefore it was that she

admitted Peter Steinmarc to her confidence as a worthy friend, though Peter was by no means a man enfranchised from the thralls of the earth. Of young women there was but one with whom she could herself deal; but in regard to that one Madame Staubach was resolved that no softness of heart should deter her from her duty. 'Linda,' she said, after pausing for a while, 'I desire to know from you what Herr Molk has said to you!' Then there was a short period of silence. 'Linda, did he sanction your love for Ludovic Valcarm?'

'No,' said Linda, sullenly.

'I should think not, indeed! And, Linda, did he bid you be rebellious in that other matter?'

Linda paused again before she answered; but it was but for a moment, and then she replied, in the same voice, 'No.'

'Did he tell you that you had better take Peter Steinmarc for your husband?' Linda could not bring herself to answer this, but sat beating the floor with her foot, and with her face turned away and her eyes fixed upon the wall. She was no longer sobbing now, but was hardening herself against her aunt. She was resolving that she would be a castaway,—that she would have nothing more to do with godliness, or even with decency. She had found godliness and decency too heavy to be borne. In all her life, had not that moment in which Ludovic had held her tight bound by his arm round her waist been the happiest? Had it not been to her, her one single morsel of real bliss? She was thinking now whether she would fly round upon her aunt and astonish her tyrant by a declaration of principles that should be altogether new. Then came the question again in the same hard voice, 'Did he not tell you that you had better take Peter Steinmarc for your husband?'

'I won't take Peter Steinmarc for my husband,' said Linda; and she did in part effect that flying round of which she had been thinking. 'I won't take Peter Steinmarc for my husband, let the man say what he may. How can I marry him if I hate him? He is a—beast.'

Then Madame Staubach groaned. Linda had often

heard her groan, but had never known her to groan as she groaned now. It was very deep and very low, and prolonged with a cadence that caused Linda to tremble in every limb. And Linda understood it thoroughly. It was as though her aunt had been told by an angel that Satan was coming to her house in person that day. And Linda did that which the reader also should do. She gave to her aunt full credit for pure sincerity in her feelings. Madame Staubach did believe that Satan was coming for her niece, if not actually come; he was close at hand, if not arrived. The crushing, if done at all, must be done instantly, so that Satan should find the spirit so broken and torn to paltry fragments as not to be worth his acceptance. She stretched forth her hand and took hold of her niece. 'Linda,' she said, 'do you ever think of the bourne to which the wicked ones go;—they who are wicked as you now are wicked?'

'I cannot help it,' said Linda.

'And did he not bid you take this man for your husband?'

'I will not do his bidding, then! It would kill me. Do you not know that I love Ludovic better than all the world? He is in prison, but shall I cease to love him for that reason? He came to me once up-stairs at night when you were sitting here with that—beast, and I swore to him then that I would never love another man,—that I should never marry anybody else!'

'Came to you once up-stairs at night! To your own chamber?'

'Yes, he did. You may know all about it, if you please. You may know everything. I don't want anything to be secret. He came to me, and when he had his arms round me I told him that I was his own,—his own,—his own. How can I be the wife of another man after that?'

Madame Staubach was so truly horrified by what she had first heard, was so astonished, that she omitted even to groan. Valcarm had been with this wretched girl up in her own chamber! She hardly even now believed that which it seemed to her that she was called upon to believe, having never as yet for a moment doubted the real purity of her niece even when she was most vehemently denouncing her as a reprobate, a castaway, and a child of Satan. The reader will know to what extent Linda had been imprudent, to what extent she had sinned. But Madame Staubach did not know. She had nothing to guide her but the words of this poor girl who had been so driven to desperation by the misery which enveloped her, that she almost wished to be taken for worse than she was in order that she might escape the terrible doom from which she saw no other means of escape. Nobody, it is true, could have forced her to marry Peter Steinmarc. There was no law, no custom in Nuremberg, which would have assisted her aunt, or Peter, or even the much-esteemed and venerable Herr Molk himself, in compelling her to submit to such nuptials. She was free to exercise her own choice, if only she had had strength to assert her freedom. But youth, which rebels so often against the authority and wisdom of age, is also subject to much tyranny from age. Linda did not know the strength of her own position, had not learned to recognise the fact of her own individuality. She feared the power of her aunt over her, and through her aunt the power of the man whom she hated; and she feared the now provoked authority of Herr Molk, who had been with her weak as a child is weak, counselling her to submit herself to a suitor unfitted for her, because another man who loved her was also unfit. And, moreover, Linda, though she was now willing in her desperation to cast aside all religious scruples of her own, still feared those with which her aunt was armed. Unless she did something, or at least said something, to separate herself entirely from her aunt, this terrible domestic tyrant would overcome her by the fear of denunciation, which would terrify her soul even though she had dared to declare to herself that in her stress of misery she would throw overboard all consideration of her soul's welfare. Though she intended no longer to live in accordance with her religious belief, she feared what religion could say to her,—dreaded to the very marrow of her bones the threats of God's anger and of Satan's power with which her aunt would harass her. If only she could rid herself of it all!

Therefore, though she perceived that the story which she had told of herself had filled her aunt's mind with a horrible and a false suspicion, she said nothing to correct the error. Therefore she said nothing further, though her aunt sat looking at her with open mouth, and eyes full of terror, and hands clasped, and pale cheeks.

'In this house,—in this very house!' said Madame Staubach, not knowing what it might best become her to say in such a strait as this.

'The house is as much mine as yours,' said Linda, sullenly. And she too, in saying this, had not known what she meant to say, or what she ought to have said. Her aunt had alluded to the house, and there seemed to her, in her distress, to be something in that on which she could hang a word.

For a while her aunt sat in silence looking at Linda, and then she fell upon her knees, with her hands clasped to heaven. What was the matter of her prayers we may not here venture to surmise; but, such as they were, they were sincere. Then she arose and went slowly as far as the door, but she returned before she had reached the threshold. 'Wretched child!' she said.

'Yes, you have made me wretched,' said Linda.

'Listen to me, Linda, if so much grace is left to you. After what you have told me, I cannot but suppose that all hope of happiness or comfort in this world is over both for you and me.'

'For myself, I wish I were dead,' said Linda.

'Have you no thought of what will come after death? Oh, my child, repentance is still possible to you, and with repentance there will come at length grace and salvation. Mary Magdalene was blessed,—was specially blessed among women.'

'Pshaw!' said Linda, indignantly. What had she to do with Mary Magdalene? The reality of her position then came upon her, and not the facts of that position which she had for a moment almost endeavoured to simulate.

'Do you not hate yourself for what you have done?'

'No, no, no. But I hate Peter Steinmarc, and I hate Herr Molk, and if you are so cruel to me I shall hate you.

I have done nothing wrong. I could not help it if he came up-stairs. He came because he loved me, and because you would not let him come in a proper way. Nobody else loves me, but he would do anything for me. And now they have thrown him into prison!'

The case was so singular in all its bearings, that Madame Staubach could make nothing of it. Linda seemed to have confessed her iniquity, and yet, after her confession, spoke of herself as though she were the injured person,—of herself and her lover as though they were both ill used. According to Madame Staubach's own ideas, Linda ought now to have been in the dust, dissolved in tears, wiping the floor with her hair, utterly subdued in spirit, hating herself as the vilest of God's creatures. But there was not even an outward sign of contrition. And then, in the midst of all this real tragedy, Tetchen brought in the dinner. The two women sat down together, but neither of them spoke a word. Linda did eat something,—a morsel or two; but Madame Staubach would not touch the food on the table. Then Tetchen was summoned to take away the all but unused plates. Tetchen, when she saw how it had been, said nothing, but looked from the face of one to the face of the other. 'She has heard all about that scamp Ludovic,' said Tetchen to herself, as she carried the dishes back into the kitchen.

It had been late when the dinner had been brought to them, and the dusk of the evening came upon them as soon as Tetchen's clatter with the crockery was done. Madame Staubach sat in her accustomed chair, with her eyes closed, and her hands clasped on her lap before her. A stranger might have thought that she was asleep, but Linda knew that her aunt was not sleeping. She also sat silent till she thought that the time was drawing near at which Steinmarc might probably enter the parlour. Then she arose to go, but could not leave her aunt without a word. 'Aunt Charlotte,' she said, 'I am ill,—very ill; my head is throbbing, and I will go to bed.' Madame Staubach merely shook her head, and shook her hands, and remained silent, with her eyes still closed. She had not even yet resolved upon the words with which it would be expedient that she should address her niece. Then Linda left the room, and went to her own apartment.

Madame Staubach, when she was alone, sobbed and cried, and knelt and prayed, and walked the length and breadth of the room in an agony of despair and doubt. She also was in want of a counsellor to whom she could go in her present misery. And there was no such counsellor. It seemed to her to be impossible that she should confide everything to Peter Steinmarc. And yet it was no more than honest that Peter should be told before he was allowed to continue his courtship. Even now, though she had seen Linda's misery, Madame Staubach thought that the marriage which she had been so anxious to arrange would be the safest way out of all their troubles,—if only Peter might be brought to consent to it after hearing all the truth. And she fancied that those traits in Peter's character, appearance, and demeanour which were so revolting to Linda would be additional means of bringing Linda back from the slough of despond,—if only such a marriage might still be possible. But the crushing must be more severe than had hitherto been intended, the weights imposed must be heavier, and the human atoms smaller and more like the dust.

While she was meditating on this there came the usual knock at the door, and Steinmarc entered the room. She greeted him, as was her wont, with but a word or two, and he sat down and lighted his pipe. An observant man might have known, even from the sound of her breathing, that something had stirred Madame Staubach more than usual. But Peter was not an observant man, and, having something on his own mind, paid but little attention to the widow. At last, having finished his first pipe and filled it again, he spoke. 'Madame Staubach,' he said, 'I have been thinking about Linda Tressel.'

'And so have I, Peter,' said Madame Staubach.

'Yes,—of course; that is natural. She is your niece, and you and she have interests in common.'

'What interests, Peter? Ah me! I wish we had.'

'Of course it is all right that you should, and I say nothing about that. But, Madame Staubach, I do not like to be made a fool of;—I particularly object to be made a fool of. If Linda is to become my wife, there is not any time to be lost.' Then Peter recommended the smoking of his new-lighted pipe with great vigour.

Madame Staubach at this moment became a martyr to great scruples. Was it her duty, or was it not her duty, to tell Peter at this moment all that she had heard to-day? She rather thought that it was her duty to do so, and yet she was restrained by some feeling of feminine honour from disgracing her niece,—by some feeling of feminine honour for which she afterwards did penance with many inward flagellations of the spirit.

'You must not be too hard upon her, Peter,' said Madame Staubach with a trembling voice.

'It is all very well saying that, and I do not think that I am the man to be hard upon any one. But the fact is that this young woman has got a lover, which is a thing of which I do not approve. I do not approve of it at all, Madame Staubach. Some persons who stand very high indeed in the city,—indeed I may say that none in Nuremberg stand higher,—have asked me to-day whether I am engaged to marry Linda Tressel. What answer am I to make when I am so asked, Madame Staubach? One of our leading burgomasters*was good enough to say that he hoped it was so for the young woman's sake.' Madame Staubach, little as she knew of the world of Nuremberg, was well aware who was the burgomaster. 'That is all very well, my friend; but if it be so that Linda will not renounce her lover,—who, by the by, is at this moment locked up in prison, so that he cannot do any harm just now,—why then, in that case, Madame Staubach, I must renounce her.' Having uttered these terrible words, Peter Steinmarc smoked away again with all his fury.

A fortnight ago, had Peter Steinmarc ventured to speak to her in this strain, Madame Staubach would have answered him with some feminine pride, and would have told him that her niece was not a suppliant for his hand.

This she did not dare to do now. She was all at fault as to facts, and did not know what the personages of Nuremberg might be saying in respect to Linda. Were she to quarrel altogether with Steinmarc, she thought that there would be left to her no means of bringing upon Linda that salutary crushing which alone might be efficacious for her salvation. She was therefore compelled to temporise. Let Peter be silent for a week, and at the end of that week let him speak again. If things could not then be arranged to his satisfaction, Linda should be regarded as altogether a castaway.

'Very well, Madame Staubach. Then I will ask her for the last time this day week.' In coarsest sackcloth, and with bitterest ashes, did Madame Staubach on that night do spiritual penance for her own sins and for those of Linda Tressel.

This week had nearly passed to the duration of which Peter Steinmarc had assented, and at the end of which it was to be settled whether Linda would renounce Ludovic Valcarm, or Peter himself would renounce Linda. With a manly propriety he omitted any spoken allusion to the subject during those smoking visits which he still paid on alternate days to the parlour of Madame Staubach. But, though he said nothing, his looks and features and the motions of his limbs were eloquent of his importance and his dignity during this period of waiting. He would salute Madame Staubach when he entered the chamber with a majesty of demeanour which he had not before affected, and would say a few words on subjects of public interest—such as the weather, the price of butter, and the adulteration of the city beer—in false notes, in tones which did not belong to him, and which in truth disgusted Madame Staubach, who was sincere in all things. But Madame Staubach, though she was disgusted, did not change her mind or abandon her purpose. Linda was to be made to marry Peter Steinmarc, not because he was a pleasant man, but because such a discipline would be for the good of her soul. Madame Staubach therefore listened, and said little or nothing; and when Peter on a certain Thursday evening remarked as he was leaving the parlour that the week would be over on the following morning, and that he would do himself the honour of asking for the fraulein's decision on his return from the town-hall at five P.M. on the morrow, apologising at the same time for the fact that he would then be driven to intrude on an irregular day, Madame Staubach merely answered by an assenting motion of her head, and by the utterance of her usual benison, 'God in His mercy be with you, Peter Steinmarc.' 'And with you too, Madame Staubach.' Then Peter marched forth with great dignity, holding his pipe as high as his shoulder.

Linda Tressel had kept her bed during nearly the whole week, and had in truth been very ill. Hitherto it had been her aunt's scheme of life to intermit in some slight degree the acerbity of her usual demeanour in periods of illness. At such times she would be very constant with the reading of good books by the bedside and with much ghostly advice to the sufferer, but she would not take it amiss if the patient succumbed to sleep while she was thus employed, believing sleep to be pardonable at such times of bodily weakness, and perhaps salutary; and she would be softer in her general manner, and would sometimes descend to the saying of tender little words, and would administer things agreeable to the palate which might at the same time be profitable to the health. So thus there had been moments in which Linda had felt that it would be comfortable to be always ill. But now, during the whole of this week, Madame Staubach had been very doubtful as to her conduct. At first it had seemed to her that all tenderness must be misplaced in circumstances so terrible, till there had been an actual resolution of repentance, till the spirit had been made to pass seven times through the fire,* till the heart had lost all its human cords and fibres. But gradually, and that before the second day had elapsed, there came upon her a conviction that she had in some way mistaken the meaning of Linda's words, and that matters were not as she had supposed. She did not now in the least doubt Linda's truth. She was convinced that Linda had intentionally told no falsehood, and that she would tell none. But there were questions which she would not ask, which she could not ask at any rate except by slow degrees. Something, however, she learned from Tetchen, something from Linda herself, and thus there came upon her a conviction that there might be no frightful story to tell to Peter,—that in all probability there was no such story to be told. What she believed at this time was in fact about the truth.

But if it were as she believed, then was it the more incumbent on her to see that this marriage did not slip through her fingers. She became very busy, and in her eagerness she went to Herr Molk. Herr Molk had learned something further about Ludovic, and promised that he would himself come down and see 'the child.' He would see 'the child,' ill as she was, in bed, and perhaps say a word or two that might assist. Madame Staubach found that the burgomaster was quite prepared to advocate the Steinmarc marriage, being instigated thereto apparently by his civic horror at Valcarm's crimes. He would shake his head, and swing his whole body, and blow out the breath from behind his cheeks, knitting his eyebrows and assuming a look of terror when it was suggested to him that the daughter of his old friend, the undoubted owner of a house in Nuremberg, was anxious to give herself and her property to Ludovic Valcarm. 'No, no, Madame Staubach, that mustn't be; —that must not be, my dear Madame. A rebel! a traitor! I don't know what the young man hasn't done. It would be confiscated;—confiscated! Dear, dear, only to think of Josef Tressel's daughter! Let her marry Peter Steinmarc, a good man,—a very good man! Followed her father, you know, and does his work very well. The city is not what it used to be, Madame Staubach, but still Peter does his work very well.' Then Herr Molk promised to come down to the red house, and he did come down.

But Madame Staubach could not trust everything to Herr Molk. It was necessary that she should do much before he came, and much probably after he went. As her conception of the true state of things became strong,

LINDA TRESSEL

and as she was convinced also that Linda was really far
from well, her manner became kinder, and she assumed
that sickbed tenderness which admitted of sleep during
the reading of a sermon. But it was essential that she
should not forget her work for an hour. Gradually Linda
was taught to understand that on such a day Steinmarc
was to demand an answer. When Linda attempted to
explain that the answer had been already given, and could
not be altered, her aunt interrupted her, declaring that
nothing need be said at the present moment. So that the
question remained an open question, and Linda understood that it was so regarded. Then Madame Staubach
spoke of Ludovic Valcarm, putting up her hands with
dismay, and declaring what horrid things Herr Molk had
told of him. It was at that moment that Linda was told
that she was to be visited in a day or two by the burgomaster. Linda endeavoured to explain that though it
might be necessary to give up Ludovic,—not saying that
she would give him up,—still it was not on that account
necessary also that she should marry Peter Steinmarc.
Madame Staubach shook her head, and implied that the
necessity did exist. Things had been said, and things
had been done, and Herr Molk was decidedly of opinion
that the marriage should be solemnised without delay.
Linda, of course, did not submit to this in silence; but
gradually she became more and more silent as her aunt
continued in a low tone to drone forth her wishes and her
convictions, and at last Linda would almost sleep while
the salutary position of Peter Steinmarc's wife was being
explained to her.

The reader must understand that she was in truth ill,
prostrated by misery, doubt, and agitation, and weak
from the effects of her illness. In this condition Herr Molk
paid his visit to her. He spoke, in the first place, of the
civil honour which she had inherited from her respected
father, and of all that she owed to Nuremberg on this
account. Then he spoke also of that other inheritance,
the red house, explaining to her that it was her duty as
a citizen to see that this should not be placed by her in
evil hands. After that he took up the subject of Peter

Steinmarc's merits; and according to Herr Molk, as he now drew the picture, Peter was little short of a municipal demigod. Prudent he was, and confidential. A man deep in the city's trust, and with money laid out at interest. Strong and healthy he was,—indeed lusty for his age, if Herr Molk spoke the truth. Poor Linda gave a little kick beneath the clothes when this was said, but she spoke no word of reply. And then Peter was a man not given to scolding, of equal temper, who knew his place, and would not interfere with things that did not belong to him. Herr Molk produced a catalogue of nuptial virtues, and endowed Peter with them all. When this was completed, he came to the last head of his discourse,—the last head and the most important. Ludovic Valcarm was still in prison, and there was no knowing what might be done to him. To be imprisoned for life in some horrible place among the rats seemed to be the least of it. Linda, when she heard this, gave one slight scream, but she said nothing. Because Herr Molk was a burgomaster, she need not on that account believe every word that fell from his mouth. But the cruellest blow of all was at the end. When Ludovic was taken, there had been—a young woman with him.

'What young woman?' said Linda, turning sharply upon the burgomaster.

'Not such a young woman as any young man ought to be seen with,' said Herr Molk.

'What matters her name?' said Madame Staubach, who, during the whole discourse, had been sitting silent by the bedside.

'I don't believe a word of it,' said Linda.

'I saw the young woman in his company, my dear. She had a felt hat and a blue frock. But, my child, you know nothing of the lives of such young men as this. It would not astonish me if he knew a dozen young women! You don't suppose that such a one as he ever means to be true?'

'I am sure he meant to be true to me,' said Linda.

'T-sh, t-sh, t-sh! my dear child; you don't know the world, and how should you? If you want to marry a husband who will remain at home and live discreetly, and be true to you, you must take such a man as Peter Steinmarc.

'Of course she must,' said Madame Staubach.

'Such a one as Ludovic Valcarm would only waste your property and drag you into the gutters.'

'No more—no more,' said Madame Staubach.

'She will think better of it, Madame Staubach. She will not be so foolish nor so wicked as that,' said the burgomaster.

'May the Lord in His mercy give her light to see the right way,' said Madame Staubach.

Then Herr Molk took his departure with Madame Staubach at his heels, and Linda was left to her own considerations. Her first assertion to herself was that she did not believe a word of it. She knew what sort of a man she could love as her husband without having Herr Molk to come and teach her. She could not love Peter Steinmarc, let him be ever so much respected in Nuremberg. As to what Herr Molk said that she owed to the city, that was nothing to her. The city did not care for her, nor she for the city. If they wished to take the house from her, let them do it. She was quite sure that Ludovic Valcarm had not loved her because she was the owner of a paltry old house. As to Ludovic being in prison, the deeper was his dungeon, the more true it behoved her to be to him. If he were among the rats, she would willingly be there also. But when she tried to settle in her thoughts the matter of the young woman with the felt hat and the blue frock, then her mind became more doubtful.

She knew well enough that Herr Molk was wrong in the picture which he drew of Peter; but she was not so sure that he was wrong in that other picture about Ludovic. There was something very grand, that had gratified her spirit amazingly, in the manner in which her lover had disappeared among the rafters; but at the same time she acknowledged to herself that there was much in it that was dangerous. A young man who can disappear among the rafters so quickly must have had much experience. She knew that Ludovic was wild,—

very wild, and that wild young men do not make good
husbands. To have had his arm once round her waist
was to her almost a joy for ever. But she had nearly come
to believe that if she were to have his arm often round
her waist, she must become a castaway. And then, to be
a castaway, sharing her treasure with another! Who was
this blue-frocked woman, with a felt hat, who seemed to
have been willing to do so much more for Ludovic than
she had done,—who had gone with him into danger, and
was sharing with him his perils?

But though she made a great fight against the wisdom
of Herr Molk when she was first left to herself, the words
of the burgomaster had their effect. Her enemies were
becoming too strong for her. Her heart was weak within
her. She had eaten little or nothing for the last few days,
and the blood was running thinly through her veins.
It was more difficult to reply to tenderness from her aunt
than to harshness. And there came upon her a feeling
that after all it signified but little. There was but a
choice between one misery and another. The only really
good thing would be to die and to have done with it all,
—to die before she had utterly thrown away all hope, all
chance of happiness in that future world in which she
thoroughly believed. She was ill now, and if it might be
that her illness would bring her to death;—but would
bring her slowly, so that she might yet repent, and all
would be right.

Madame Staubach said nothing more to her about
Peter till the morning of that day on which Peter was to
come for his answer. A little before noon Madame
Staubach brought to her niece some weak broth, as she
had done once before, on that morning. But Linda, who
was sick and faint at heart, would not take it.

'Try, my dear,' said Madame Staubach.

'I cannot try,' said Linda.

'I wish particularly to speak to you,—now,—at once;
and this will give you strength to listen to me.' But
Linda declined to be made strong for such a purpose, and
declared that she could listen very well as she was. Then
Madame Staubach began her great argument. Linda

had heard what the burgomaster had said. Linda knew well what she, her aunt and guardian, thought about it. Linda could not but know that visits from a young man at her chamber door, such as that to which she herself had confessed, were things so horrible that they hardly admitted of being spoken of even between an aunt and her niece; and Madame Staubach's cheeks were hot and red as she spoke of this.

'If he had come to your door, aunt Charlotte, you could not have helped it.'

'But he embraced you?'

'Yes, he did.'

'Oh, my child, will you not let me save you from the evil days? Linda, you are all in all to me;—the only one that I love. Linda, Linda, your soul is precious to me, almost as my own. Oh, Linda, shall I pray for you in vain?' She sank upon her knees as she spoke, and prayed with all her might that God would turn the heart of this child, so that even yet she might be rescued from the burning. With arms extended, and loud voice, and dishevelled hair, and streaming tears, shrieking to Heaven in her agony, every now and again kissing the hand of the poor sinner, she besought the Lord her God that He would give to her the thing for which she asked;—and that thing prayed for with such agony of earnestness, was a consent from Linda to marry Peter Steinmarc! It was very strange, but the woman was as sincere in her prayer as is faith itself. She would have cut herself with knives, and have swallowed ashes whole, could she have believed that by doing so she could have been nearer her object. And she had no end of her own in view. That Peter, as master of the house, would be a thorn in her own side, she had learned to believe; but thorns in the sides of women were, she thought, good for them; and it was necessary to Linda that she should be stuck full of thorns, so that her base human desires might, as it were, fall from her bones and perish out of the way. Once, twice, thrice, Linda besought her aunt to arise; but the half frantic woman had said to herself that she would remain on her knees, on the hard boards, till this thing was granted to her. Had it not been said by lips that could not lie, that faith would move a mountain? and would not faith, real faith, do for her this smaller thing? Then there came questions to her mind, whether the faith was there. Did she really believe that this thing would be done for her? If she believed it, then it would be done. Thinking of all this, with the girl's hands between her own, she renewed her prayers. Once and again she threw herself upon the floor, striking it with her forehead. 'Oh, my child! my child, my child! If God would do this for me! my child, my child! Only for my sin and weakness this thing would be done for me.'

For three hours Linda lay there, hearing this, mingling her screams with those of her aunt, half fainting, half dead, now and again dozing for a moment even amidst the screams, and then struggling up in bed, that she might embrace her aunt, and implore her to abandon her purpose. But the woman would only give herself with the greater vehemence to the work. 'Now, if the Lord would see fit, now,—now; if the Lord would see fit!'

Linda had swooned, her aunt being all unconscious of it, had dozed afterwards, and had then risen and struggled up, and was seated in her bed. 'Aunt Charlotte,' she said, 'what is it—that—you want of me?'

'That you should obey the Lord, and take this man for your husband.'

Linda stayed a while to think, not pausing that she might answer her aunt's sophistry, which she hardly noticed, but that she might consider, if it were possible, what it was that she was about to do;—that there might be left a moment to her before she had surrendered herself for ever to her doom. And then she spoke. 'Aunt Charlotte,' she said, 'if you will get up I will do as you would have me.'

Madame Staubach could not arise at once, as it was incumbent on her to return thanks for the mercy that had been vouchsafed to her; but her thanks were quickly rendered, and then she was on the bed, with Linda in her arms. She had succeeded, and her child was saved. Perhaps there was something of triumph that the earnestness of her prayer should have been efficacious. It was a great thing that she had done, and the Scriptures had proved themselves to be true to her. She lay for a while fondling her niece and kissing her, as she had not done for years. 'Linda, dear Linda!' She almost promised to the girl earthly happiness, in spite of her creed as to the necessity for crushing. For the moment she petted her niece as one weak woman may pet another. She went down to the kitchen and made coffee for her,—though she herself was weak from want of food,—and toasted bread, and brought the food up with a china cup and a china plate, to show her gratitude to the niece who had been her convert. And yet, as she did so, she told herself that such gratitude was mean, vile, and mistaken. It had been the Lord's doing, and not Linda's.

Linda took the coffee and the toast, and tried to make herself passive in her aunt's hands. She returned Madame Staubach's kisses and the pressure of her hand, and made some semblance of joy, that peace should have been re-established between them two. But her heart was dead within her, and the reflection that this illness might even yet be an illness unto death was the only one in which she could find the slightest comfort. She had promised Ludovic that she would never become the wife of any one but him; and now, at the first trial of her faith, she had promised to marry Peter Steinmarc. She was for-sworn, and it would hardly be that the Lord would be satisfied with her, because she had perjured herself! When her aunt left her, which Madame Staubach did as the dusk came on, she endeavoured to promise herself that she would never get well. Was not the very thought that she would have to take Peter for her husband enough to keep her on her sickbed till she should be beyond all such perils as that?

Madame Staubach, before she left the room, asked Linda whether she would not be able to dress herself and come down, so that she might say one word to her affianced husband. It should be but one word, and then she should be allowed to return. Linda would have declined to do this,—was refusing utterly to do it,—

when she found that if she did not go down Peter would be brought up to her bedroom, to receive her troth there, by her bedside. The former evil, she thought, would be less than the latter. Steinmarc as a lover at her bedside would be intolerable to her; and then if she descended, she might ascend again instantly. That was part of the bargain. But if Peter were to come up to her room, there was no knowing how long he might stay there. She promised therefore that she would dress and come down as soon as she knew that the man was in the parlour. We may say for her, that when left alone she was as firmly resolved as ever that she would never become the man's wife. If this illness did not kill her, she would escape from the wedding in some other way. She would never put her hand into that of Peter Steinmarc, and let the priest call him and her man and wife. She had lied to her aunt —so she told herself,—but her aunt had forced the lie from her.

When Peter entered Madame Staubach's parlour he was again dressed in his Sunday best, as he had been when he made his first overture to Linda. 'Good evening, Madame Staubach,' he said.

'Good evening, Peter Steinmarc.'

'I hope you have good news for me, Madame Staubach, from the maiden up-stairs.'

Madame Staubach took a moment or two for thought before she replied. 'Peter Steinmarc, the Lord has been good to us, and has softened her heart, and has brought the child round to our way of thinking. She has consented, Peter, that you should be her husband.'

Peter was not so grateful perhaps as he should have been at this good news,—or rather perhaps at the manner in which the result seemed to have been achieved. Of course he knew nothing of those terribly earnest petitions which Madame Staubach had preferred to the throne of heaven on behalf of his marriage, but he did not like being told at all of any interposition from above in such a matter. He would have preferred to be assured, even though he himself might not quite have believed the assurance, that Linda had yielded to a sense of his own

merits. 'I am glad she has thought better of it, Madame
Staubach,' he said; 'she is only just in time.'

Madame Staubach was very nearly angry, but she
reminded herself that people cannot be crushed by rose-
leaves. Peter Steinmarc was to be taken, because he was
Peter Steinmarc, not because he was somebody very
different, better mannered, and more agreeable.

'I don't know how that may be, Peter.'

'Ah, but it is so;—only just in time, I can assure you.
But "a miss is as good as a mile;" so we will let that pass.'

'She is now ready to come down and accept your troth,
and give you hers. You will remember that she is ill and
weak; and, indeed, I am unwell myself. She can stay
but a moment, and then, I am sure, you will leave us for
to-night. The day has not been without its trouble and
its toil to both of us.'

'Surely,' said Peter; 'a word or two shall satisfy me
to-night. But, Madame Staubach, I shall look to you to
see that the period before our wedding is not protracted,
—you will remember that.' To this Madame Staubach
made no answer, but slowly mounted to Linda's chamber.

Linda was already nearly dressed. She was not
minded to keep her suitor waiting. Tetchen was with
her, aiding her; but to Tetchen she had refused to say a
single word respecting either Peter or Ludovic. Something Tetchen had heard from Madame Staubach, but
from Linda she heard nothing. Linda intended to go
down to the parlour, and therefore she must dress herself.
As she was weak almost to fainting, she had allowed
Tetchen to help her. Her aunt led her down, and there
was nothing said between them as they went. At the
door her aunt kissed her, and muttered some word of
love. Then they entered the room together.

Peter was found standing in the middle of the chamber,
with his left hand beneath his waistcoat, and his right
hand free for the performance of some graceful salutation.
'Linda,' said he, as soon as he saw the two ladies standing
a few feet away from him, 'I am glad to see you down-
stairs again,—very glad. I hope you find yourself better.'
Linda muttered, or tried to mutter, some words of thanks;

but nothing was audible. She stood hanging upon her aunt, with eyes turned down, and her limbs trembling beneath her. 'Linda,' continued Peter, 'your aunt tells me that you have accepted my offer. I am very glad of it. I will be a good husband to you, and I hope you will be an obedient wife.'

'Linda,' said Madame Staubach, 'put your hand in his.' Linda put forth her little hand a few inches, and Peter took it within his own, looking the while into Madame Staubach's face, as though he were to repeat some form of words after her. 'You are now betrothed in the sight of God, as man and wife,' said Madame Staubach; 'and may the married life of both of you be passed to His glory.—Amen.'

'Amen,' said Steinmarc, like the parish clerk. Linda pressed her lips close together, so that there should be no possibility of a chance sound passing from them.

'Now, I think we will go back again, Peter, as the poor child can hardly stand.' Peter raised no objection, and then Linda was conducted back again to her bed. There was one comfort to her in the remembrance of the scene. She had escaped the dreaded contamination of a kiss.

CHAPTER X

PETER STEINMARC, now that he was an engaged man, affianced to a young bride, was urgent from day to day with Madame Staubach that the date of his wedding should be fixed. He soon found that all Nuremberg knew that he was to be married. Perhaps Herr Molk had not been so silent and discreet as would have been becoming in a man so highly placed, and perhaps Peter himself had let slip a word to some confidential friend who had betrayed him. Be this as it might, all Nuremberg knew of Peter's good fortune, and he soon found that he should have no peace till the thing was completed. 'She is quite well enough, I am sure,' said Peter to Madame Staubach, 'and if there is anything amiss she can finish getting well afterwards.' Madame Staubach was sufficiently eager herself that Linda should be married without delay; but, nevertheless, she was angry at being so pressed, and used rather sharp language in explaining to Peter that he would not be allowed to dictate on such a subject. 'Ah! well; if it isn't this year it won't be next,' said Peter, on one occasion when he had determined to show his power. Madame Staubach did not believe the threat, but she did begin to fear that, perhaps, after all, there might be fresh obstacles. It was now near the end of November, and though Linda still kept her room, her aunt could not see that she was suffering from any real illness. When, however, a word was said to press the poor girl, Linda would declare that she was weak and sick—unable to walk; in short, that at present she would not leave her room. Madame Staubach was beginning to be angered at this; but, for all that, Linda had not left her room.

It was now two weeks since she had suffered herself to be betrothed, and Peter had twice been up to her chamber, creaking with his shoes along the passages. Twice she had passed a terrible half-hour, while he had sat, for the most part silent, in an old wicker chair by her bedside. Her aunt had, of course, been present, and had spoken most of the words that had been uttered during these visits; and these words had nearly altogether referred to Linda's ailments. Linda was still not quite well, she had said, but would soon be better, and then all would be properly settled. Such was the purport of the words which Madame Staubach would speak on those occasions.

'Before Christmas?' Peter had once asked.

'No,' Linda had replied, very sharply.

'It must be as the Lord shall will it,' said Madame Staubach. That had been so true that neither Linda nor Peter had found it necessary to express dissent. On both these occasions Linda's energy had been chiefly used to guard herself from any sign of a caress. Peter had thought of it, but Linda lay far away upon the bed, and the lover did not see how it was to be managed. He was not sure, moreover, whether Madame Staubach would not have been shocked at any proposal in reference to an antenuptial embrace. On these considerations he abstained.

It was now near the end of November, and Linda knew that she was well. Her aunt had proposed some day in January for the marriage, and Linda, though she had never assented, could not on the moment find any plea for refusing altogether to have a day fixed. All she could do was to endeavour to stave off the evil. Madame Staubach seemed to think that it was indispensable that a day in January should be named; therefore, at last, the thirtieth of that month was after some fashion fixed for the wedding. Linda never actually assented, but after many discourses it seemed to be decided that it should be so. Peter was so told, and with some grumbling expressed himself as satisfied; but when would Linda come down to him? He was sure that Linda was well enough to come down if she would. At last a day was fixed for that also. It was arranged that the three should go to church together on the first Sunday in December. It would be safer so than in any other way. He could not make love to her in church.

On the Saturday evening Linda was down-stairs with her aunt. Peter, as she knew well, was at the Rothe Ross on that evening, and would not be home till past ten. Tetchen was out, and Linda had gone down to take her supper with her aunt. The meal had been eaten almost in silence, for Linda was very sad, and Madame Staubach herself was beginning to feel that the task before her was almost too much for her strength. Had it not been that she was carried on by the conviction that things stern and hard and cruel would in the long-run be comforting to the soul, she would have given way. But she was a woman not prone to give way when she thought that the soul's welfare was concerned. She had seen the shrinking, retreating horror with which Linda had almost involuntarily contrived to keep her distance from her future husband. She had listened to the girl's voice, and knew that there had been not one light-hearted tone from it since that consent had been wrung from the sufferer by the vehemence of her own bedside prayers. She was aware that Linda from day to day was becoming thinner and thinner, paler and still paler. But she knew, or thought that she knew, that it was God's will; and so she went on. It was not a happy time even for Madame Staubach, but it was a time in which to Linda it seemed that hell had come to her beforehand with all its terrors.

There was, however, one thing certain to her yet. She would never put her hand into that of Peter Steinmarc in God's house after such a fashion that any priest should be able to say that they two were man and wife in the sight of God.

On this Saturday evening Tetchen was out, as was the habit with her on alternate Saturday evenings. On such occasions Linda would usually do what household work was necessary in the kitchen, preparatory to the coming Sabbath. But on this evening Madame Staubach herself was employed in the kitchen, as Linda was not considered to be well enough to perform the task. Linda was sitting alone, between the fire and the window, with no work in her hand, with no book before her, thinking of her fate, when there came upon the panes of the window sundry small, sharp, quickly-repeated rappings, as though gravel had been thrown upon them. She knew at once that the noise was not accidental, and jumped up on her feet. If it was some mode of escape, let it be what it might, she would accept it. She jumped up, and with short hurried steps placed herself close to the window. The quick, sharp, little blows upon the glass were heard again, and then there was a voice. 'Linda, Linda.' Heavens and earth! it was his voice. There was no mistaking it. Had she heard but a single syllable in the faintest whisper, she would have known it. It was Ludovic Valcarm, and he had come for her, even out of his prison. He should find that he had not come in vain. Then the word was repeated—'Linda, are you there?' 'I am here,' she said, speaking very faintly, and trembling at the sound of her own voice. Then the iron pin was withdrawn from the wooden shutter on the outside, as it could not have been withdrawn had not some traitor within the house prepared the way for it, and the heavy Venetian blinds were folded back, and Linda could see the outlines of the man's head and shoulders, in the dark, close to the panes of the window. It was raining at the time, and the night was very dark, but still she could see the outline. She stood and watched him; for, though she was willing to be with him, she felt that she could do nothing. In a moment the frame of the window was raised, and his head was within the room, within her aunt's parlour, where her aunt might now have been for all that he could have known; —were it not that Tetchen was watching at the corner, and knew to the scraping of a carrot how long it would be before Madame Staubach had made the soup for to-morrow's dinner.

'Linda,' he said, 'how is it with you?'

'Oh, Ludovic!'

'Linda, will you go with me now?'

'What! now, this instant?'

'To-night. Listen, dearest, for she will be back. Go to her in ten minutes from now, and tell her that you are weary and would be in bed. She will see you to your room perhaps, and there may be delay. But when you can, come down silently, with your thickest cloak and your strongest hat, and any little thing you can carry easily. Come without a candle, and creep to the passage window. I will be there. If she will let you go up-stairs alone, you may be there in half-an-hour. It is our only chance.' Then the window was closed, and after that the shutter, and then the pin was pushed back, and Linda was again alone in her aunt's chamber.

To be there in half-an-hour! To commence such a job as this at once! To go to her aunt with a premeditated lie that would require perfect acting, and to have to do this in ten minutes, in five minutes, while the minutes were flying from her like sparks of fire! It was impossible. If it had been enjoined upon her for the morrow, so that there should have been time for thought, she might have done it. But this call upon her for instant action almost paralysed her. And yet what other hope was there? She had told herself that she would do anything, however wicked, however dreadful, that would save her from the proposed marriage. She had sworn to herself that she would do something; for that Steinmarc's wife she would never be. And here had come to her a possibility of escape,—of escape too which had in it so much of sweetness! She must lie to her aunt. Was not every hour of life a separate lie? And as for acting a lie, what was the difference between that and telling it, except in the capability of the liar. Her aunt had forced her to lie. No truth was any longer possible to her. Would it not be better to lie for Ludovic Valcarm than to lie for Peter Steinmarc? She looked at the upright clock which stood in the corner of the room, and, seeing that the ten minutes was already passed, she crossed at once over into the kitchen. Her aunt was standing there, and Tetchen with her bonnet on, was standing by. Tetchen, as soon as she saw Linda, explained that she must be off again at once. She had only returned to fetch some article for a little niece of hers which Madame Staubach had given her.

'Aunt Charlotte,' said Linda, 'I am very weary. You will not be angry, will you, if I go to bed?'

'It is not yet nine o'clock, my dear.'

'But I am tired, and I fear that I shall lack strength for to-morrow.' Oh, Linda, Linda! But, indeed, had you foreseen the future, you might have truly said that you would want strength on the morrow.

'Then go, my dear;' and Madame Staubach kissed her niece and blessed her, and after that, with careful hand, threw some salt into the pot that was simmering on the stove. Peter Steinmarc was to dine with them on the morrow, and he was a man who cared that his soup should be well seasoned. Linda, terribly smitten by the consciousness of her own duplicity, went forth, and crept up-stairs to her room. She had now, as she calculated, a quarter of an hour, and she would wish, if possible, to be punctual. She looked out for a moment from the window, and could only see that it was very dark, and could hear that it was raining hard. She took her thickest cloak and her strongest hat. She would do in all things as he bade her; and then she tried to think what else she would take.

She was going forth,—whither she knew not. Then came upon her a thought that on the morrow,—for many morrows afterwards, perhaps for all morrows to come, —there would be no comfortable wardrobe to which she could go for such decent changes of raiment as she required. She looked at her frock, and having one darker and thicker than that she wore, she changed it instantly. And then it was not only her garments that she was leaving behind her. For ever afterwards, —for ever and ever and ever,—she must be a castaway. The die had been thrown now, and everything was over. She was leaving behind her all decency, all feminine respect, all the clean ways of her pure young life, all modest thoughts, all honest, serviceable daily tasks, all godliness, all hope of heaven! The silent, quick-running tears streamed down her face as she moved rapidly about the room. The thing must be done, must be done,—must be done, even though earth and heaven were to fail her for ever afterwards. Earth and heaven would fail her for ever afterwards, but still the thing must be done. All should be endured, if by that all she could escape from the man she loathed.

She collected a few things, what little store of money she had,—four or five gulden, perhaps,—and a pair of light shoes and clean stockings, and a fresh handkerchief or two, and a little collar, and then she started. He had told her to bring what she could carry easily. She must not disobey him, but she would fain have brought more had she dared. At the last moment she returned, and took a small hair-brush and a comb. Then she looked round the room with a hurried glance, put out her candle, and crept silently down the stairs. On the first landing she paused, for it was possible that Peter might be returning. She listened, and then remembered that she would have heard Peter's feet even on the walk outside. Very quickly, but still more gently than ever, she went down the last stairs. From the foot of the stairs into the passage there was a moment in which she must be within sight of the kitchen door. She flew by, and felt that she must have been seen. But she was not seen. In an instant she was at the open window, and in another instant she was standing beside her lover on the gravel path. What he said to her she did not hear; what he did she did not know. She had completed her task now; she had done her part, and had committed herself entirely into his hands. She would ask no question. She would trust him entirely. She only knew that at the moment his arm was round her, and that she was being lifted off the bank into the river.

'Dearest girl! can you see? No; nothing, of course, as yet. Step down. There is a boat here. There are two boats. Lean upon me, and we can walk over. There. Do not mind treading softly. They cannot hear because of the rain. We shall be out of it in a minute. I am sorry you should be wet, but yet it is better for us.'

She hardly understood him, but yet she did as he told her, and in a few minutes she was standing on the other bank of the river, in the Ruden Platz. Here Linda perceived that there was a man awaiting them, to whom Ludovic gave certain orders about the boats. Then Ludovic took her by the hand and ran with her across the Platz, till they stood beneath the archway of the brewery warehouse where she had so often watched him as he went in and out. 'Here we are safe,' he said, stooping down and kissing her, and brushing away the drops of rain from the edges of her hair. Oh, what safety! To be there, in the middle of the night, with him, and not know whither she was to go, where she was to lie, whether she would ever again know that feeling of security which had been given to her throughout her whole life by her aunt's presence and the walls of her own house. Safe! Was ever peril equal to hers? 'Linda, say that you love me. Say that you are my own.'

'I do love you,' she said; 'otherwise how should I be here?'

'And you had promised to marry that man!'

'I should never have married him. I should have died.'

'Dearest Linda! But come; you must not stand here.' Then he took her up, up the warehouse stairs into a gloomy chamber, from which there was a window looking on to the Ruden Platz, and there, with many caresses, he explained to her his plans. The caresses she endeavoured to avoid, and, when she could not avoid them, to moderate. 'Would he remember,' she asked, 'just for the present, all that she had gone through, and spare her for a while, because she was so weak?' She made her little appeal with swimming eyes and low voice, looking into his face, holding his great hand the while between her own. He swore that she was his queen, and should have her way in everything. But would she not give him one kiss? He reminded her that she had never kissed him. She did as he asked her, just touching his lips with hers, and then she stood by him, leaning on him, while he explained to her something of his plans. He kept close to the window, as it was necessary that he should keep his eyes upon the red house.

His plan was this. There was a train which passed by the Nuremberg station on its way to Augsburg*at three o'clock in the morning. By this train he proposed that they should travel to that city. He had, he said, the means of providing accommodation for her there, and no one would know whither they had gone. He did not anticipate that any one in the house opposite would learn that Linda had escaped till the next morning; but should any suspicion have been aroused, and should the fact be ascertained, there would certainly be lights moving in the house, and light would be seen from the window of Linda's own chamber. Therefore he proposed, during the long hours that they must yet wait, to stand in his present spot and watch, so that he might know at the first moment whether there was any commotion among the inmates of the red house. 'There goes old Peter to bed,' said he; 'he won't be the first to find out, I'll bet a florin.' And afterwards he signified the fact that Madame Staubach had gone to her chamber. This was the moment of danger, as it might be very possible that Madame Staubach would go into Linda's room. In that case, as he said, he had a little carriage outside the walls which would take them to the first town on the route to Augsburg. Had a light been seen but for a moment in Linda's room they were to start; and would certainly reach the spot where the carriage stood before any followers could be on their heels. But Madame Staubach went to her own room without noticing that of her niece, and then the red house was all dark and all still. They would have made the best of their way to Augsburg before their flight would be discovered.

During the minutes in which they were watching the lights Linda stood close to her lover, leaning on his shoulder, and supported by his arm. But this was over by ten, and then there remained nearly five hours, during which they must stay in their present hiding-place. Up to this time Linda's strength had supported her under the excitement of her escape, but now she was like to faint, and it was necessary at any rate that she should be allowed to lie down. He got sacks for her from some part of the building, and with these constructed for her a bed on the floor, near to the spot which he must occupy himself in still keeping his eye upon the red house. He laid her down and covered her feet with sacking, and put sacks under her head for a pillow. He was very gentle with her, and she thanked him over and over again, and endeavoured to think that her escape had been fortunate, and that her position was happy. Had she not succeeded in flying from Peter Steinmarc? And after such a flight would not all idea of a marriage with him be out of the question? For some little time she was cheered by talking to him. She asked him about his imprisonment. 'Ah!' said he; 'if I cannot be one too many for such an old fogey as Herr Molk, I'll let out my brains to an ass, and take to grazing on thistles.'* His offence had been political, and had been committed in conjunction with others. And he and they were sure of success ultimately,—were sure of success very speedily Linda could understand nothing of the subject. But she could hope that her lover might prosper in his undertaking, and she could admire and love him for encountering the dangers of such an enterprise. And then, half sportively, half in earnest, she taxed him with that matter which was next her heart. Who had been the young woman with the blue frock and the felt hat who had been with him when he was brought before the magistrates?

'Young woman;——with blue frock! who told you of the young woman, Linda?' He came and knelt beside her as he asked the question, leaving his watch for the moment; and she could see by the dim light of the lamp outside that there was a smile upon his face,—almost joyous, full of mirth.

'Who told me? The magistrate you were taken to; Herr Molk told me himself,' said Linda, almost happily. That smile upon his face had in some way vanquished her feeling of jealousy.

'Then he is a greater scoundrel than I took him to be, or else a more utter fool. The girl in the blue frock, Linda, was one of our young men, who was to get out of the city in that disguise. And I believe Herr Molk knew it when he tried to set you against me, by telling you the story.'

Whether Herr Molk had known this, or whether he had simply been fool enough to be taken in by the blue frock and the felt hat, it is not for us to inquire here. But Ludovic was greatly amused at the story, and Linda was charmed at the explanation she had received. It was only an extra feather in her lover's cap that he should have been connected with a blue frock and felt hat under such circumstances as those now explained to her. Then he went back to the window, and she turned on her side and attempted to sleep.

To be in all respects a castaway,—a woman to whom other women would not speak! She knew that such was her position now. She had done a deed which would separate her for ever from those who were respectable, and decent, and good. Peter Steinmarc would utterly despise her. It was very well that something should have occurred which would make it impossible that he should any longer wish to marry her; but it would be very bitter to her to be rejected even by him because she was unfit to be an honest man's wife. And then she asked herself questions about her young lover, who was so handsome, so bold, so tender to her; who was in all outward respects

just what a lover should be. Would he wish to marry her
after she had thus consented to fly with him, alone, at
night: or would he wish that she should be his light-of-
love, as her aunt had been once cruel enough to call her?
There would be no cruelty, at any rate no injustice, in so
calling her now. And should there be any hesitation on
his part, would she ask him to make her his wife? It was
very terrible to her to think that it might come to pass
that she should have on her knees to implore this man to
marry her. He had called her his queen, but he had
never said that she should be his wife. And would any
pastor marry them, coming to him, as they must come,
as two runaways? She knew that certain preliminaries
were necessary,—certain bidding of banns, and processes
before the magistrates. Her own banns and those of her
betrothed, Peter Steinmarc, had been asked once in the
church of St. Lawrence,* as she had heard with infinite
disgust. She did not see that it was possible that Ludovic
should marry her, even if he were willing to do so. But
it was too late to think of all this now; and she could only
moisten the rough sacking with her tears.

'You had better get up now, dearest,' said Ludovic,
again bending over her.

'Has the time come?'

'Yes; the time has come, and we must be moving. The
rain is over, which is a comfort. It is as dark as pitch,
too. Cling close to me. I should know my way if I were
blindfold.'

She did cling close to him, and he conducted her
through narrow streets and passages out to the city gate,*
which led to the railway station. Nuremberg has still
gates like a fortified town, and there are, I believe,
porters at the gates with huge keys. Nuremberg delights
to perpetuate the memories of things that are gone. But
ingress and egress are free to everybody, by night as well
as by day, as it must be when railway trains arrive and
start at three in the morning; and the burgomaster and
warders, and sentinels and porters, though they still
carry the keys, know that the glory of their house has
gone.

Railway tickets for two were given to Linda without a question,—for to her was intrusted the duty of procuring them,—and they were soon hurrying away towards Augsburg through the dark night. At any rate they had been successful in escaping. 'After to-morrow we will be as happy as the day is long,' said Ludovic, as he pressed his companion close to his side. Linda told herself, but did not tell him, that she never could be happy again.

CHAPTER XI

THEY were whirled away through the dark cold night with the noise of the rattling train ever in their ears. Though there had been a railway running close by Nuremberg now for many years,* Linda was not herself so well accustomed to travelling as will probably be most of those who will read this tale of her sufferings. Now and again in the day-time, and generally in fair weather, she had gone as far as Fürth, and on one occasion even as far as Würzburg* with her aunt when there had been a great gathering of German Anabaptists at that town; but she had never before travelled at night, and she had certainly never before travelled in such circumstances as those which now enveloped her. When she entered the carriage, she was glad to see that there were other persons present. There was a woman, though the woman was so closely muffled and so fast asleep that Linda, throughout the whole morning, did not know whether her fellow-traveller was young or old. Nevertheless, the presence of the woman was in some sort a comfort to her, and there were two men in the carriage, and a little boy. She hardly understood why, but she felt that it was better for her to have fellow-travellers. Neither of them, however, spoke above a word or two either to her or to her lover. At first she sat at a little distance from Ludovic,— or rather induced him to allow that there should be some space between them; but gradually she suffered him to come closer to her, and she dozed with her head upon his shoulder. Very little was said between them. He whispered to her from time to time sundry little words of love, calling her his queen, his own one, his life, and the joy of his eyes. But he told her little or nothing of his future plans, as she would have wished that he should do. She asked him, however, no questions;—none at least till their journey was nearly over. The more that his conduct warranted her want of trust, the more unwilling did she become to express any diffidence or suspicion.

After a while she became very cold;—so cold that that now became for the moment her greatest cause of suffering. It was mid-winter, and though the cloak she had brought was the warmest garment that she possessed, it was very insufficient for such work as the present night had brought upon her. Besides her cloak, she had nothing wherewith to wrap herself. Her feet became like ice, and then the chill crept up her body; and though she clung very close to her lover, she could not keep herself from shivering as though in an ague fit. She had no hesitation now in striving to obtain some warmth by his close proximity. It seemed to her as though the cold would kill her before she could reach Augsburg. The train would not be due there till nine in the morning, and it was still dark night as she thought that it would be impossible for her to sustain such an agony of pain much longer. It was still dark night, and the violent rain was pattering against the glass, and the damp came in through the crevices, and the wind blew bitterly upon her; and then as she turned a little to ask her lover to find some comfort for her, some mitigation of her pain, she perceived that he was asleep. Then the tears began to run down her cheeks, and she told herself that it would be well if she could die.

After all, what did she know of this man who was now sleeping by her side,—this man to whom she had intrusted everything, more than her happiness, her very soul? How many words had she ever spoken to him? What assurance had she even of his heart? Why was he asleep, while her sufferings were so very cruel to her? She had encountered the evils of this elopement to escape what had appeared to her the greater evils of a detested marriage. Steinmarc was very much to be hated. But might it not be that even that would have been better than this? Poor girl! the illusion even of her love was being frozen cold within her during the agony of that morning. All the while the train went thundering on through the night, now rushing into a tunnel, now crossing a river, and at every change in the sounds of the carriages she almost hoped that something might be amiss. Oh, the cold! She had gathered her feet up and was trying to sit on them. For a moment or two she had hoped that her movement would waken Ludovic, so that she might have had the comfort of a word; but he had only tumbled with his head hither and thither, and had finally settled himself in a position in which he leaned heavily upon her. She thought that he was heartless to sleep while she was suffering; but she forgot that he had watched at the window while she had slumbered upon the sacks in the warehouse. At length, however, she could bear his weight no longer, and she was forced to rouse him. 'You are so heavy,' she said; 'I cannot bear it;' when at last she succeeded in inducing him to sit upright.

'Dear me! oh, ah, yes. How cold it is! I think I have been asleep.'

'The cold is killing me,' she said.

'My poor darling! What shall I do? Let me see. Where do you feel it most.'

'All over. Do you not feel how I shiver? Oh, Ludovic, could we get out at the next station?'

'Impossible, Linda. What should we do there?'

'And what shall we do at Augsburg? Oh dear, I wish I had not come. I am so cold. It is killing me.' Then she burst out into floods of sobbing, so that the old man opposite to her was aroused. The old man had brandy in his basket and made her drink a little. Then after a while she was quieted, and was taken by station after station without demanding of Ludovic that he should bring this weary journey to an end.

Gradually the day dawned, and the two could look at

each other in the grey light of the morning. But Linda thought of her own appearance rather than that of her lover. She had been taught that it was required of a woman that she should be neat, and she felt now that she was dirty, foul inside and out,—a thing to be scorned. As their companions also bestirred themselves in the daylight, she was afraid to meet their eyes, and strove to conceal her face. The sacks in the warehouse had, in lieu of a better bed, been acceptable; but she was aware now, as she could see the skirts of her own dress and her shoes, and as she glanced her eyes gradually round upon her shoulders, that the stains of the place were upon her, and she knew herself to be unclean. That sense of killing cold had passed off from her, having grown to a numbness which did not amount to present pain, though it would hardly leave her without some return of the agony; but the misery of her disreputable appearance was almost as bad to her as the cold had been. It was not only that she was untidy and dishevelled, but it was that her condition should have been such without the company of any elder female friend whose presence would have said, 'This young woman is respectable, even though her dress be soiled with dust and meal.' As it was, the friend by her side was one who by his very appearance would condemn her. No one would suppose her to be his wife. And then the worst of it was that he also would judge her as others judged her. He also would say to himself that no one would suppose such a woman to be his wife. And if once he should learn so to think of her, how could she expect that he would ever persuade himself to become her husband? How she wished that she had remained beneath her aunt's roof! It now occurred to her, as though for the first time, that no one could have forced her to go to church on that thirtieth of January and become Peter Steinmarc's wife. Why had she not remained at home and simply told her aunt that the thing was impossible?

At last they were within an hour of Augsburg, and even yet she knew nothing as to his future plans. It was very odd that he should not have told her what they were to do at Augsburg. He said that she should be his queen, that she should be as happy as the day was long, that everything would be right as soon as they reached Augsburg; but now they were all but at Augsburg, and she did not as yet know what first step they were to take when they reached the town. She had much wished that he would speak without being questioned, but at last she thought that she was bound to question him. 'Ludovic, where are we going to at Augsburg?'

'To the Black Bear first. That will be best at first.'

'Is it an inn?'

'Yes, dear; not a great big house like the Rothe Ross at Nuremberg, but very quiet and retired, in a back street.'

'Do they expect us?'

'Well, no; not exactly. But that won't matter.'

'And how long shall we stay there?'

'Ah! that must depend on tidings from Berlin and Munich. It may be that we shall be compelled to get away from Bavaria altogether.' Then he paused for a moment, while she was thinking what other question she could ask. 'By the by,' he said, 'my father is in Augsburg.'

She had heard of his father as a man altogether worthless, one ever in difficulties, who would never work, who had never seemed to wish to be respectable. When the great sins of Ludovic's father had been magnified to her by Madame Staubach and by Peter, with certain wise hints that swans never came out of the eggs of geese, Linda would declare with some pride of spirit that the son was not like the father; that the son had never been known to be idle. She had not attempted to defend the father, of whom it seemed to be acknowledged by the common consent of all Nuremberg that he was utterly worthless, and a disgrace to the city which had produced him. But Linda now felt very thankful for the assurance of even his presence. Had it been Ludovic's mother, how much better would it have been! But that she should be received even by his father,—by such a father,—was much to her in her desolate condition.

'Will he be at the station?' Linda asked.

'Oh, no.'

'Does he expect us?'

'Well, no. You see, Linda, I only got out of prison yesterday morning.'

'Does your father live in Augsburg?'

'He hardly lives anywhere. He goes and comes at present as he is wanted by the cause.* It is quite on the cards that we should find that the police have nabbed him. But I hope not. I think not. When I have seen you made comfortable, and when we have had something to eat and drink, I shall know where to seek him. While I am doing so, you had better lie down.'

She was afraid to ask him whether his father knew, or would suspect, aught as to his bringing a companion, or whether the old man would welcome such a companion for his son. Indeed, she hardly knew how to frame any question that had application to herself. She merely assented to his proposition that she should go to bed at the Black Bear, and then waited for the end of their journey. Early in the morning their fellow-passengers had left them, and they were now alone. But Ludovic distressed her no more by the vehemence of his caresses. He also was tired and fagged and cold and jaded. It is not improbable that he had been meditating whether he, in his present walk of life, had done well to encumber himself with the burden of a young woman.

At last they were at the platform at Augsburg. 'Don't move quite yet,' he said. 'One has to be a little careful.' When she attempted to raise herself she found herself to be so numb that all quickness of motion was out of the question. Ludovic, paying no attention to her, sat back in the carriage, with his cap before his face, looking with eager eyes over the cap on to the platform.

'May we not go now?' said Linda, when she saw that the other passengers had alighted.

'Don't be in a hurry, my girl. By God, there are those ruffians, the gendarmerie. It's all up. By Jove! yes, it's all up. That is hard, after all I did at Nuremberg.'

'Ludovic!'

'Look here, Linda. Get out at once and take these

letters. Make your way to the Black Bear, and wait for me.'

'And.you?'

'Never mind me, but do as you're told. In a moment it will be too late. If we are noticed to be together it will be too late.'

'But how am I to get to the Black Bear?'

'Heaven and earth! haven't you a tongue? But here they are, and it's all up.' And so it was. A railway porter opéned the door, and behind the railway porter were two policemen. Linda, in her dismay, had not even taken the papers which had been offered to her, and Valcarm, as soon as he was sure that the police were upon him, had stuffed them down the receptacle made in the door for the fall of the window.

But the fate of Valcarm and of his papers is at the present moment not of so much moment to us as is that of Linda Tressel. Valcarm was carried off, with or without the papers, and she, after some hurried words, which were unintelligible to her in her dismay, found herself upon the platform amidst the porters. A message had come from Nuremberg by the wires to Augsburg, requiring the arrest of Ludovic Valcarm, but the wires had said nothing of any companion that might be with him. Therefore Linda was left standing amidst the porters on the platform. She asked one of the men about the Black Bear. He shook his head, and told her that it was a house of a very bad sort,—of a very bad sort indeed.

CHAPTER XII

A DOZEN times during the night Linda had remembered that her old friend Fanny Heisse, now the wife of Max Bogen, lived at Augsburg, and as she remembered it, she had asked herself what she would do were she to meet Fanny in the streets. Would Fanny condescend to speak to her, or would Fanny's husband allow his wife to hold any communion with such a castaway? How might she dare to hope that her old friend would do other than shun her, or, at the very least, scorn her, and pass her as a thing unseen? And yet, through all the days of their life, there had been in Linda's world a supposition that Linda was the good young woman, and that Fanny Heisse was, if not a castaway, one who had made the frivolities of the world so dear to her that she could be accounted as little better than a castaway. Linda's conclusion, as she thought of all this, had been, that it would be better that she should keep out of the way of the wife of an honest man who knew her. All fellowship hereafter with the wives and daughters of honest men must be denied to her. She had felt this very strongly when she had first seen herself in the dawn of the morning.

But now there had fallen upon her a trouble of another kind, which almost crushed her,—in which she was not as yet able to see that, by God's mercy, salvation from utter ruin might yet be extended to her. What should she do now,—now, at this moment? The Black Bear, to which her lover had directed her, was so spoken of that she did not dare to ask to be directed thither. When a compassionate railway porter pressed her to say whither she would go, she could only totter to a seat against the wall, and there lay herself down and sob. She had no friends, she said; no home; no protector except him who had just been carried away to prison. The porter asked her whether the man were her husband, and then again she was nearly choked with sobs. Even the manner of the porter was changed to her when he perceived that she was not the wife of him who had been her companion. He handed her over to an old woman who looked after the station, and the old woman at last learned from Linda the fact that the wife of Max Bogen the lawyer had once been her friend. About two hours after that she was seated with Max Bogen himself, in a small close carriage, and was being taken home to the lawyer's house. Max Bogen asked her hardly a question. He only said that Fanny would be so glad to have her;—Fanny, he said, was so soft, so good, and so clever, and so wise, and always knew exactly what ought to be done. Linda heard it all, marvelling in her dumb half-consciousness.

This was the Fanny Heisse of whom her aunt had so often told her that one so given to the vanities of the world could never come to any good!

Max Bogen handed Linda over to his wife, and then disappeared. 'Oh, Linda, what is it? Why are you here? Dear Linda.' And then her old friend kissed her, and within half an hour the whole story had been told.

'Do you mean that she eloped with him from her aunt's house in the middle of the night?' asked Max, as soon as he was alone with his wife. 'Of course she did,' said Fanny; 'and so would I, had I been treated as she has been. It has all been the fault of that wicked old saint, her aunt.' Then they put their heads together as to the steps that must be taken. Fanny proposed that a letter should be at once sent to Madame Staubach, explaining plainly that Linda had run away from her marriage with Steinmarc, and stating that for the present she was safe and comfortable with her old friend. It could hardly be said that Linda assented to this, because she accepted all that was done for her as a child might accept it. But she knelt upon the floor with her head upon her friend's lap, kissing Fanny's hands, and striving to murmur thanks. Oh, if they would leave her there for three days, so that she might recover something of her strength! 'They shall leave you for three weeks, Linda,' said the other. 'Madame Staubach is not the Emperor,' that she is to have her own way in everything. And as for Peter——'

'Pray, don't talk of him;—pray, do not,' said Linda, shuddering.

But all this comfort was at an end about seven o'clock on that evening. The second train in the day from Nuremberg was due at Augsburg at six, and Max Bogen, though he said nothing on the subject to Linda, had thought it probable that some messenger from the former town might arrive in quest of Linda by that train. At seven there came another little carriage up to the door, and before her name could be announced, Madame Staubach was standing in Fanny Bogen's parlour. 'Oh, my child!' she said. 'Oh, my child, may God in His mercy forgive my child!' Linda cowered in a corner of the sofa and did not speak.

'She hasn't done anything in the least wrong,' said Fanny; 'nothing on earth. You were going to make her marry a man she hated, and so she came away. If father had done the same to me, I wouldn't have stayed an hour.' Linda still cowered on the sofa, and was still speechless.

Madame Staubach, when she heard this defence of her niece, was hardly pushed to know in what way it was her duty to answer it. It would be very expedient, of course, that some story should be told for Linda which might save her from the ill report of all the world,—that some excuse should be made which might now, instantly, remove from Linda's name the blight which would make her otherwise to be a thing scorned, defamed, useless, and hideous; but the truth was the truth, and even to save her child from infamy Madame Staubach would not listen to a lie without refuting it. The punishment of Linda's infamy had been deserved, and it was right that it should be endured. Hereafter, as facts came to disclose themselves, it would be for Peter Steinmarc to say whether he would take such a woman for his wife; but whether he took her or whether he rejected her, it could not be well that Linda should be screened by a lie from any part of the punishment which she had deserved. Let her go seven times seven through the fire,* if by such suffering there might yet be a chance for her poor desolate half-withered soul.

'Done nothing wrong, Fanny Heisse!' said Madame Staubach, who, in spite of her great fatigue, was still standing in the middle of the room. 'Do you say so, who have become the wife of an honest God-fearing man?'

But Fanny was determined that she would not be put down in her own house by Madame Staubach. 'It doesn't matter whose wife I am,' she said, 'and I am sure Max will say the same as I do. She hasn't done anything wrong. She made up her mind to come away because she wouldn't marry Peter Steinmarc. She came here in company with her own young man, as I used

to come with Max. And as soon as she got here she
sent word up to us, and here she is. If there's anything very wicked in that, I'm not religious enough to
understand it. But I tell you what I can understand,
Madame Staubach,—there is nothing on earth so horribly
wicked as trying to make a girl marry a man whom she
loathes, and hates, and detests, and abominates. There,
Madame Staubach; that's what I've got to say; and now
I hope you'll stop and have supper with Max and Linda
and me.'

Linda felt herself to be blushing in the darkness of her
corner as she heard this excuse for her conduct. No;
she had not made the journey to Augsburg with Ludovic
in such fashion as Fanny had, perhaps more than once,
travelled the same route with her present husband.
Fanny had not come by night, without her father's
knowledge, had not escaped out of a window; nor had
Fanny come with any such purpose as had been hers.
There was no salve to her conscience in all this, though
she felt very grateful to her friend, who was fighting her
battle for her.

'It is not right that I should argue the matter with
you,' said Madame Staubach, with some touch of true
dignity. 'Alas, I know that which I know. Perhaps you
will allow me to say a word in privacy to this unfortunate
child.'

But Max Bogen had not paid his wife a false compliment for cleverness. She perceived at once that the
longer this interview between the aunt and her niece
could be delayed,—the longer that it could be delayed,
now that they were in each other's company,—the
lighter would be the storm on Linda's head when it did
come. 'After supper, Madame Staubach; Linda wants
her supper; don't you, my pet?' Linda answered nothing.
She could not even look up, so as to meet the glance of
her aunt's eyes. But Fanny Bogen succeeded in arranging
things after her own fashion. She would not leave the
room, though in sooth her presence at the preparation
of the supper might have been useful. It came to be
understood that Madame Staubach was to sleep at the

lawyer's house, and great changes were made in order
that the aunt and niece might not be put in the same
room. Early in the morning they were to return together
to Nuremberg, and then Linda's short hour of comfort
would be over.

She had hardly as yet spoken a word to her aunt when
Fanny left them in the carriage together. 'There were
three or four others there,' said Fanny to her husband,
'and she won't have much said to her before she gets
home.'

'But when she is at home!' Fanny only shrugged her
shoulders. 'The truth is, you know,' said Max, 'that it
was not at all the proper sort of thing to do!'

'And who does the proper sort of thing?'

'You do, my dear.'

'And wouldn't you have run away with me if father
had wanted me to marry some nasty old fellow who cares
for nothing but his pipe and his beer? If you hadn't,
I'd never have spoken to you again.'

'All the same,' said Max, 'it won't do her any good.'

The journey home to Nuremberg was made almost in
silence, and things had been so managed by Fanny's craft
that when the two women entered the red house hardly
a word between them had been spoken as to the affairs
of the previous day. Tetchen, as she saw them enter,
cast a guilty glance on her young mistress, but said not a
word. Linda herself, with a veil over her face which she
had borrowed from her friend Fanny, hurried up-stairs
towards her own room. 'Go into my chamber, Linda,'
said Madame Staubach, who followed her. Linda did as
she was bid, went in, and stood by the side of her aunt's
bed. 'Kneel down with me, Linda, and let us pray that
the great gift of repentance may be given to us,' said
Madame Staubach. Then Linda knelt down, and hid
her face upon the counterpane.

All her sins were recapitulated to her during that
prayer. The whole heinousness of the thing which she
had done was given in its full details, and the details
were repeated more than once. It was acknowledged
in that prayer that though God's grace might effect

absolute pardon in the world to come, such a deed as that
which had been done by this young woman was beyond
the pale of pardon in this world. And the Giver of all
mercy was specially asked so to make things clear to that
poor sinful creature, that she might not be deluded into
any idea that the thing which she had done could be
justified. She was told in that prayer that she was im-
pure, vile, unclean, and infamous. And yet she probably
did not suffer from the prayer half so much as she would
have suffered had the same things been said to her face
to face across the table. And she recognised the truth of
the prayer, and she was thankful that no allusion was
made in it to Peter Steinmarc, and she endeavoured to
acknowledge that her conduct was that which her aunt
represented it to be in her strong language. When the
prayer was over Madame Staubach stood before Linda
for a while, and put her two hands on the girl's arms, and
lightly kissed her brow. 'Linda,' she said, 'with the Lord
nothing is impossible; with the Lord it is never too late;
with the Lord the punishment need never be unto
death!' Linda, though she could utter no articulate
word, acknowledged to herself that her aunt had been
good to her, and almost forgot the evil things that her
aunt had worked for her.

CHAPTER XIII

LINDA TRESSEL, before she had gone to bed on that
night which she had passed at Augsburg, had written
a short note which was to be delivered, if such delivery
should be possible, to Ludovic Valcarm. The condition
of her lover had, of course, been an added trouble to
those which were more especially her own. During the
last three or four hours which she had passed with him in
the train her tenderness for him had been numbed by her
own sufferings, and she had allowed herself for a while
to think that he was not sufficiently alive to the great
sacrifice she was making on his behalf. But when he was
removed from her, and had been taken, as she well

knew, to the prison of the city, something of the softness of her love returned to her, and she tried to persuade herself that she owed to him that duty which a wife would owe. When she spoke to Fanny on the subject, she declared that even if it were possible to her she would not go back to Ludovic. 'I see it differently now,' she said; 'and I see how bad it is.' But, still,—though she declared that she was very firm in that resolve,—she did not like to be carried back to her old home without doing something, making some attempt, which might be at least a token to herself that she had not been heartless in regard to her lover. She wrote therefore with much difficulty the following few words, which Fanny promised that her husband should endeavour to convey to the hands of Ludovic Valcarm:

'DEAR LUDOVIC,—My aunt has come here for me, and takes me back to Nuremberg to-morrow. When you left me at the station I was too ill to go to the place you told me; so they sent to this house, and my dear, dear friend Fanny Heisse got her husband to come for me, and I am in their house now. Then my aunt came, and she will take me home to-morrow. I am so unhappy that you should be in trouble! I hope that my coming with you did not help to bring it about. As for me, I know it is best that I should go back, though I think that it will kill me. I was very wicked to come. I feel that now, and I know that even you will have ceased to respect me. Dear Ludovic, I hope that God will forgive us both. It will be better that we should never meet again, though the thought that it must be so is almost more than I can bear. I have always felt that I was different from other girls, and that there never could be any happiness for me in this world. God bless you, Ludovic. Think of me some-times,—but never, never, try to come for me again.

L. T.'

It had cost her an hour of hard toil to write this little letter, and when it was written she felt that it was cold, un-grateful, unloving,—very unlike the words which he would feel that he had a right to expect from her. Nevertheless,

such as it was, she gave it to her friend Fanny, with many
injunctions that it might, if possible, be placed in the
hands of Ludovic. And thus, as she told herself repeatedly
on her way home, the romance of her life was over.* After
all, the journey to Augsburg would have been serviceable
to her,—would be serviceable although her character
should be infamous for ever in the town that knew her,—
if by that journey she would be saved from all further
mention of the name of Peter Steinmarc. No disgrace
would be so bad as the prospect of that marriage. Therefore, as she journeyed homeward, sitting opposite to her
aunt, she endeavoured to console herself by reflecting
that his suit to her would surely be at an end. Would it
ever reach his dull heart that she had consented to destroy
her own character, to undergo ill-repute and the scorn
of all honest people, in order that she might not be forced
into the horror of a marriage with him? Could he be
made to understand that in her flight from Nuremberg
her great motive had been to fly from him?

On the second morning after her return even this
consolation was taken from her, and she learned from
her aunt that she had not given up all hope in the direction of the town-clerk. On the first day after her return
not a word was said to Linda about Peter, nor would she
have had any notice of his presence in the house had she
not heard his shoes creaking up and down the stairs.
Nor was the name of Ludovic Valcarm so much as
mentioned in her presence. Between Tetchen and her
there was not a word passed, unless such as were spoken
in the presence of Madame Staubach. Linda found that
she was hardly allowed to be for a moment out of her
aunt's presence, and at this time she was unable not to
be submissive. It seemed to her that her aunt was so
good to her in not positively upbraiding her from morning to night, that it was impossible for her not to be
altogether obedient in all things! She did not therefore
even struggle to escape the long readings, and the longer
prayers, and the austere severity of her aunt's presence.
Except in prayer,—in prayers delivered out loud by the
aunt in the niece's presence,—no direct mention was

made of the great iniquity of which Linda had been guilty. Linda was called no heartrending name to her face; but she was required to join, and did join over and over again, in petitions to the throne of mercy 'that the poor castaway might be received back again into the pale of those who were accepted.' And at this time she would have been content to continue to live like this, to join in such prayers day after day, to have her own infamy continually brought forward as needing some special mercy, if by such means she might be allowed to live in tranquillity without sight or mention of Peter Steinmarc. But such tranquillity was not to be hers.

On the afternoon of the second day her aunt went out, leaving Linda alone in the house with Tetchen. Linda at once went to her chamber, and endeavoured to make herself busy among those possessions of her own which she had so lately thought that she was leaving for ever. She took out her all, the articles of her wardrobe, all her little treasures, opened the sweet folds of her modest raiment and refolded them, weeping all the while as she thought of the wreck she had made of herself. But no; it was not she who had made the wreck. She had been ruined by the cruelty of that man whose step at this moment she heard beneath her. She clenched her fist, and pressed her little foot against the floor, as she thought of the injury which this man had done her. There was not enough of charity in her religion to induce her even to think that she would ever cease to hate him with all the vigour of her heart. Then Tetchen came to her, and told her that her aunt had returned and desired to see her. Linda instantly went down to the parlour. Up to this moment she was as a child in her aunt's hands.

'Sit down, Linda,' said Madame Staubach, who had taken off her bonnet, and was already herself stiffly seated in her accustomed chair. 'Sit down, my dear, while I speak to you.' Linda sat down at some distance from her aunt, and awaited dumbly the speech that was to be made to her. 'Linda,' continued Madame Staubach, 'I have been this afternoon to the house of your friend Herr Molk.' Linda said nothing out loud, but she

declared to herself that Herr Molk was no friend of hers.
Friend indeed! Herr Molk had shown himself to be one
of her bitterest enemies. 'I thought it best to see him
after what—has been done, especially as he had been
with you when you were ill, before you went.' Still
Linda said nothing. What was there that she could
possibly say? Madame Staubach paused, not expecting
her niece to speak,.but collecting her own thoughts and
arranging her words. 'And Peter Steinmarc was there
also,' said Madame Staubach. Upon hearing this Linda's
heart sank within her. Had all her sufferings, then, been
for nothing? Had she passed that terrible night, that
terrible day, with no result that might be useful to her?
But even yet might there not be hope? Was it not
possible that her aunt was about to communicate to her
the fact that Peter Steinmarc declined to be bound by
his engagement to her? She sighed deeply and almost
sobbed, as she clasped her hands together. Her aunt
observed it all, and then went on with her speech. 'You
will, I hope, have understood, Linda, that I have not
wished to upbraid you.'

'You have been very good, aunt Charlotte.'

'But you must know that that which you have done is,
—is,—is a thing altogether destructive of a young
woman's name and character.' Madame Staubach's
voice, as she said this, was tremulous with the excess of
her eagerness. If this were Peter Steinmarc's decision,
Linda would bear it all without a complaint. She bowed
her head in token that she accepted the disgrace of which
her aunt had spoken. 'Of course, Linda,' continued
Madame Staubach, 'recovery from so lamentable a
position is very difficult,—is almost impossible. I do not
mean to say a word of what has been done. We believe,
—that is, I believe, and Herr Molk, and Peter also
believes it——'

'I don't care what Peter Steinmarc believes,' exclaimed
Linda, unable to hold her peace any longer.

'Linda, Linda, would you be a thing to be shuddered
at, a woman without a name, a byword for shame for
ever?' Madame Staubach had been interrupted in her

statement as to the belief entertained in respect to
Linda's journey by herself and her two colleagues, and
did not recur to that special point in her narrative. When
Linda made no answer to her last appeal, she broadly
stated the conclusion to which she and her friends had
come in consultation together in the panelled chamber of
Herr Molk's house. 'I may as well make the story short,'
she said. 'Herr Molk has explained to Peter that things
are not as bad as they have seemed to be.' Every muscle
and every fibre in Linda's body was convulsed when she
heard this, and she shuddered and shivered so that she
could hardly keep her seat upon her chair. 'And Peter
has declared that he will be satisfied if you will at once
agree that the marriage shall take place on the thirtieth
of the month. If you will do this, and will make him a
promise that you will go nowhere without his sanction
before that day, he will forget what has been done.'
Linda answered not a word, but burst into tears, and fell
at her aunt's feet.

Madame Staubach was a woman who could bring herself to pardon any sin that had been committed,—that
was done, and, as it were, accomplished,—hoping in all
charity that it would be followed by repentance. Therefore she had forgiven, after a fashion, even the last
tremendous trespass of which her niece had been guilty,
and had contented herself with forcing Linda to listen
to her prayers that repentance might be forthcoming.
But she could forgive no fault, no conduct that seemed
to herself to be in the slightest degree wrong, while it was
in the course of action. She had abstained from all hard
words against Linda, from all rebuke, since she had found
that the young man was gone, and that her niece was
willing to return to her home. But she would be prepared
to exercise all the power which Linda's position had
given her, to be as severe as the austerity of her nature
would permit, if this girl should persist in her obstinacy.
She regarded it as Linda's positive duty to submit to
Peter Steinmarc as her husband. They had been betrothed with Linda's own consent. The banns had been
already once called. She herself had asked for God's

protection over them as man and wife. And then how much was there not due to Peter, who had consented, not without much difficult persuasion from Herr Molk, to take this soiled flower to his bosom, in spite of the darkness of the stain. 'There will be no provoking difficulties made about the house?' Peter had said in a corner to the burgomaster. Then the burgomaster had undertaken that in the circumstances as they now existed, there should be no provoking difficulties. Herr Molk understood that Linda must give up something on receiving that position of an honest man's wife, which she was now hardly entitled to expect. Thus the bargain had been made, and Madame Staubach was of opinion that it was her first duty to see that it should not be again endangered by any obstinacy on behalf of Linda. Obstinate, indeed! How could she be obstinate after that which she had done? She had now fallen at her aunt's feet, was weeping, sobbing, praying for mercy. But Madame Staubach could have no mercy on the girl in this position. Such mercy would in itself be a sin. The sin done she could forgive; the sin a-doing must be crushed, and put down, and burnt out, and extinguished, let the agony coming from such process be as severe as might be. There could be no softness for Linda while Linda was obstinate. 'I cannot suppose,' she said, 'that you mean to hesitate after what has taken place.'

'Oh, aunt Charlotte! dear aunt Charlotte!'

'What is the meaning of this?'

'I don't love him. I can't love him. I will do anything else that you please. He may have the house if he wants it. I will promise;—promise never to go away again or to see anybody.' But she might as well have addressed such prayers to a figure of stone. On such a matter as this Madame Staubach could not be other than relentless. Even while Linda was kneeling at her feet convulsed with sobs, she told the poor girl, with all the severity of language which she could use, of the vileness of the iniquity of that night's proceedings. Linda had been false to her friend, false to her vows, false to her God, immodest, unclean, had sinned against all the laws by

which women bind themselves together for good conduct,
—had in fact become a castaway in very deed. There
was nothing that a female could do more vile, more
loathsome than that which Linda had done. Madame
Staubach believed that the time had come in which it
would be wicked to spare, and she did not spare. Linda
grovelled at her feet, and could only pray that God
might take her to Himself at once. 'He will never take
you; never, never, never,' said Madame Staubach;
'Satan will have you for his own, and all my prayers will
be of no avail.'

There were two days such as this, and Linda was still
alive and still bore it. On the third day, which was the
fifth after her return from Augsburg, Herr Molk came to
her, and at his own request was alone with her. He did
not vituperate her as her aunt had done, nor did he
express any special personal horror at her sin; but he
insisted very plainly on the position which she had made
for herself. 'You see, my dear, the only thing for you is
to be married out of hand at once, and then nobody will
say anything about it. And what is the difference if he
is a little old? girls forget to think about that after a
month or two; and then, you see, it will put an end to all
your troubles;—to all your troubles.' Such were the
arguments of Herr Molk; and it must be acknowledged
that such arguments were not lacking in strength, nor
were they altogether without truth. The little story of
Linda's journey to Augsburg had been told throughout
the city, and there were not wanting many who said that
Peter Steinmarc must be a very good-natured man
indeed, if, after all that had passed, he would still accept
Linda Tressel as his wife. 'You should remember all that
of course, my dear,' said Herr Molk.

How was it possible that Linda should stand alone
against such influence as had been brought to bear
against her? She was quite alone, for she would not
admit of any intimacy with Tetchen. She would hardly
speak to the old woman. She was quite aware that
Tetchen had arranged with Ludovic the manner of her
elopement; and though she felt no anger with him, still

she was angry with the servant whose duplicity had
helped to bring about the present misery. Had she not
fled with her lover she might then,—so she thought now,
—have held her ground against her aunt and against
Peter. As things had gone with her since, such obstinacy
had become impossible to her. On the morning of the
seventh day she bowed her head, and though she did not
speak, she gave her aunt to understand that she had
yielded. 'We will begin to purchase what may be necessary to-morrow,' said Madame Staubach.

But even now she had not made up her mind that she
would in truth marry the man. She had simply found it
again impossible to say that she would not do so. There
was still a chance of escape. She might die, for instance!
Or she might run away again. If she did that, surely the
man would persecute her no further. Or at the last
moment she might stolidly decline to move; she might
refuse to stand on her legs before the altar. She might be
as a dead thing even though she were alive,—as a thing
dead and speechless. Oh! if she could only be without
ears to hear those terrible words which her aunt would
say to her! And then there came another scheme into
her mind. She would make one great personal appeal
to Steinmarc's feelings as a man. If she implored him
not to make her his wife, kneeling before him, submitting
herself to him, preferring to him with all her earnestness
this one great prayer, surely he would not persevere!

Hitherto, since her return from Augsburg, Peter had
done very little to press his own suit. She had again had
her hand placed in his since she had yielded, and had
accepted as a present from him a great glass brooch
which to her eyes was the ugliest thing in the guise of a
trinket which the world of vanity had ever seen. She had
not been a moment in his company without her aunt's
presence, and there had not been the slightest allusion
made by him to her elopement. Peter had considered
that such allusion had better come after marriage when
his power would, as he thought, be consolidated. He
was surprised when he was told, early in the morning
after that second hand-pledging, by Linda herself that

she wanted to see him. Linda came to his door and made her request in person. Of course he was delighted to welcome his future bride to his own apartment, and begged her with as soft a smile as he could assume to seat herself in his own arm-chair. She took a humbler seat, however, and motioned to him to take that to which he was accustomed. He looked at her as he did so, and perceived that the very nature of her face was changed. She had lost the plumpness of her cheeks, she had lost the fresh colour of her youth, she had lost much of her prettiness. But her eyes were brighter than ever they had been, and there was something in their expression which almost made Peter uneasy. Though she had lost so much of her prettiness, he was not on that account moved to doubt the value of his matrimonial prize; but there did come across his mind an idea that those eyes might perhaps bring with them some discomfort into his house-hold. 'I am very glad to see you, Linda,' he said. 'It is very good of you to come to me here. Is there anything I can do for you?'

'There is one thing, Peter Steinmarc, that you can do for me.'

'What is that, my dear?'

'Let me alone.' As she spoke she clenched her small fist and brought it down with some energy on the table that was close to her. She looked into his face as she did so, and his eyes quailed before her glance. Then she repeated her demand. 'Let me alone.'

'I do not know what you mean, Linda. Of course you are going to be my wife now.'

'I do not wish to be your wife. You know that; and if you are a man you will not force me.' She had intended to be gentle with him, to entreat him, to win him by humility and softness, and to take his hand, and even kiss it if he would be good to her. But there was so much of tragedy in her heart, and such an earnestness of purpose in her mind, that she could not be gentle. As she spoke it seemed to him that she was threatening him.

'It is all settled, Linda. It cannot be changed now.'

'It can be changed. It must be changed. Tell her that

I am not good enough. You need not fear her. And if you will say so, I will never be angry with you for the word. I will bless you for it.'

'But, Linda, you did nothing so very much amiss;—did you?' Then there came across her mind an idea that she would lie to him, and degrade herself with a double disgrace. But she hesitated, and was not actress enough to carry on the part. He winked at her as he continued to speak. 'I know,' he said. 'It was just a foolish business, but no worse than that.'

Oh heavens, how she hated him! She could have stabbed him to the heart that moment, had the weapon been there, and had she possessed the physical energy necessary for such an enterprise. He was a thing to her so foul that all her feminine nature recoiled from the closeness of his presence, and her flesh crept as she felt that the same atmosphere encompassed them. And this man was to be her husband! She must speak to him, speak out, speak very plainly. Could it be possible that a man should wish to take a woman to his bosom who had told him to his face that he was loathed? 'Peter,' she said, 'I am sure that you don't think that I love you.'

'I don't see why you shouldn't, Linda.'

'I do not;—not the least; I can promise you that. And I never shall;—never. Think what it would be to have a wife who doesn't love you a bit. Would not that be bad?'

'Oh, but you will.'

'Never! Don't you know that I love somebody else very dearly?' On hearing this there came something of darkness upon Peter's brow,—something which indicated that he had been touched. Linda understood it all. 'But I will never speak to him again, never see him, if you will let me alone.'

'See him, Linda! He is in prison, and will be sent to the quarries to work. He will never be a free man again. Ha! ha! I need not fear him, my dear.'

'But you shall fear me. Yes; I will lead you such a life! Peter Steinmarc, I will make you rue the day you first saw me. You shall wish that you were at the quarries

yourself. I will disgrace you, and make your name
infamous. I will waste everything that you have. There
is nothing so bad I will not do to punish you. Yes; you
may look at me, but I will. Do you think that you are to
trample me under foot, and that I will not have my
revenge? You said it was a foolish business that I did.
I will make it worse than foolish.' He stood with his
hands in the pockets of his broad flaps, looking at her,
not knowing how to answer her. He was no coward,—
not such a coward as to be intimidated at the moment by
the girl's violence. And being now thoroughly angry,
her words had not worked upon him as she had intended
that they should work. His desire was to conquer her and
get the best of her; but his thoughts worked slowly, and
he did not know how to answer her. 'Well, what do you
say to me? If you will let me escape, I will always be
your friend.'

'I will not let you escape,' he said.

'And you expect that I shall be your wife?'

'I do expect it.'

'I shall die first; yes;—die first. To be your wife! Oh,
there is not a beggar in the streets of Nuremberg whom
I would not sooner take for my husband.' She paused,
but again he was at a loss for words. 'Come, Peter, think
of it. Do not drive a poor weak girl to desperation. I
have been very unhappy,—very; you do not know how
unhappy I have been. Do not make it worse for me.'
Then the chord which had been strung so tightly was
broken asunder. Her strength failed her, and she burst
into tears.

'I will make you pay dearly for all this one of these
days, fraulein,' said Peter, as, with his hands still in his
pockets, he left the room. She watched him as he
creaked down-stairs, and went into her aunt's apartments. For a moment she felt disposed to go and confront him there before her aunt. Together, the two of
them, could not force her to marry him. But her courage
failed her. Though she could face Peter Steinmarc without flinching, she feared the words which her aunt could
say to her. She had not scrupled to threaten Steinmarc

with her own disgrace, but she could not endure to be
told by her aunt that she was degraded.

CHAPTER XIV

PETER STEINMARC, when he went into Madame Staubach's parlour, found that lady on her knees in prayer.
He had entered the room without notice, having been
urged to this unwonted impetuosity by the severity of the
provocation which he had received. Madame Staubach
raised her head; but when she saw him she did not rise.
He stood there for some seconds looking at her, expecting
her to get up and greet him; but when he found that such
was not her purpose, he turned angrily on his heel, and
went out of the house, up to his office in the town-hall.
His services were not of much service to the city on that
day,—neither on that day nor on the two following days.
He was using all his mental faculties in endeavouring to
decide what it might be best for him to do in the present
emergency. The red house was a chattel*of great value
in Nuremberg,—a thing very desirable,—the possession
of which Peter himself did desire with all his heart. But
then, even in regard to the house, it was not to be arranged
that Peter was to become the sole and immediate possessor of it on his marriage. Madame Staubach was to live
there, and during her life the prize would be but a half-
and-half possession. Madame Staubach was younger
than himself; and though he had once thought of marrying her, he was not sure that he was now desirous of
living in the same house with her for the remainder of his
life. He had wished to marry Linda Tressel, because she
was young, and was acknowledged to be a pretty girl;
and he still wished to marry her, if not now for these
reasons, still for others which were quite as potent. He
wanted to be her master, to get the better of her, to
punish her for her disdain of him, and to bring her to his
feet. But he was not a man so carried away by anger or
by a spirit of revenge as to be altogether indifferent to his
own future happiness. There had already been some

among his fellow-citizens, or perhaps citizenesses, kind enough to compliment him on his good-nature. He had been asked whether Linda Tressel had told him all about her little trip to Augsburg, and whether he intended to ask his cousin Ludovic Valcarm to come to his wedding. And now Linda herself had said things to him which made him doubt whether she was fit to be the wife of a man so respectable and so respected as himself. And were she to do those things which she threatened, where would he be then? All the town would laugh at him, and he would be reduced to live for the remainder of his days in the sole company of Madame Staubach as the result of his enterprise. He was sufficiently desirous of being revenged on Linda, but he was a cautious man, and began to think that he might buy even that pleasure too dear. He had been egged on to the marriage by Herr Molk and one or two others of the city pundits,—by the very men whose opposition he had feared when the idea of marrying Linda was first suggested to him. They had told him that Linda was all right, that the elopement had been in point of fact nothing. 'Young girls will be young before they are settled,' Herr Molk had said. Then the extreme desirability of the red house had been mentioned, and so Peter had been persuaded. But now, as the day drew near, and as Linda's words sounded in his ears, he hardly knew what to think of it. On the evening of the third day of his contemplation, he went again to his friend Herr Molk.

'Nonsense, Peter,' said the magistrate; 'you must go on now, and there is no reason why you should not. Is a man of your standing to be turned aside by a few idle words from a young girl?'

'But she told me——— You can't understand what she told me. She's been away with this young fellow once, and she said as much as that she'd go again.'

'Pshaw! you haven't had to do with women as I have, or you would understand them better. Of course a young girl likes to have her little romance. But when a girl has been well brought up,—and there is no better bringing up than what Linda Tressel has had,—marriage steadies them directly. Think of the position you'll have in the city when the house belongs to yourself.'

Peter, when he left the magistrate, was still tossed about by an infinity of doubts. If he should once take the girl as his wife, he could never unmarry himself again. He could not do so at least without trouble, disgrace, and ruinous expense. As for revenge, he thought that he might still have a certain amount of that pleasure in repudiating his promised spouse for her bad conduct, and in declaring to her aunt that he could not bring himself to make a wife of a woman who had first disgraced herself, and then absolutely taken glory in her disgrace. As he went along from Herr Molk's house towards the island, taking a somewhat long path by the Rothe Ross where he refreshed himself, and down the Carls Strasse, and by the Church of St. Lawrence,* round which he walked twice, looking up to the tower for inspiration,—he told himself that circumstances had been most cruel to him. He complained bitterly of his misfortune. If he refused to marry Linda he must leave the red house altogether, and would, of course, be ridiculed for his attempt at matrimony; and if he did marry her —— Then, as far as he could see, there would be the very mischief. He pitied himself with an exceedingly strong compassion, because of the unmerited hardness of his position. It was very dark when he got to the narrow passage leading to the house along the river, and when there, in the narrowest and darkest part of the passage, whom should he meet coming from Madame Staubach's house,—coming from Linda's house, for the passage led from the red house only,—but Ludovic Valcarm his cousin?

'What, uncle Peter?' said Ludovic, assuming a name which he had sometimes used in old days when he had wished to be impertinent to his relative. Peter Steinmarc was too much taken aback to have any speech ready on the occasion. 'You don't say a word to congratulate me on having escaped from the hands of the Philistines.'*

'What are you doing here?' said Peter.

'I've been to see my young woman,' said Ludovic,

who, as Peter imagined, was somewhat elated by strong drink.

'She is not your young woman,' said Peter.

'She is not yours at any rate,' said the other.

'She is mine if I like to take her,' said Peter.

'We shall see about that. But here I am again, at any rate. The mischief take them for interfering old fools! When they had got me they had nothing to say against me.'

'Pass on, and let me go by,' said Peter.

'One word first, uncle Peter. Among you, you are treating that girl as cruelly as ever a girl was treated. You had better be warned by me, and leave off. If she were forced into a marriage with you, you would only disgrace yourself. I don't suppose you want to see her dead at your feet. Go on now, and think of what I have said to you.' So Ludovic had been with her again! No; he, Peter Steinmarc, would not wed with one who was so abandoned. He would reject her;—would reject her that very night. But he would do so in a manner that should leave her very little cause for joy or triumph.

We must now go back for a while to Linda and her aunt. No detailed account of that meeting between Linda and Steinmarc, in Steinmarc's room, ever reached Madame Staubach's ears. That there had been an interview, and that Linda had asked Steinmarc to absolve her from her troth, the aunt did learn from the niece; and most angry she was when she learned it. She again pointed out to the sinner the terrible sin of which she was guilty in not submitting herself entirely, in not eradicating and casting out from her bosom all her human feelings, in not crushing herself, as it were, upon a wheel, in token of her repentance for what she had done. Sackcloth and ashes, in their material shape, were odious to the imagination of Madame Staubach, because they had a savour of Papacy, and implied that the poor sinner who bore them could do something towards his own salvation by his own works;* but that moral sackcloth, and those ashes of the heart and mind, which she was ever prescribing to Linda, seemed to her to have none of this taint. And yet, in what is the difference? The school of religion to which Madame Staubach belonged was very like that early school of the Church of Rome in which material ashes were first used for the personal annoyance of the sinner. But the Church of Rome in Madame Staubach's day had, by the force of the human nature of its adherents, made its way back to the natural sympathies of mankind; whereas in Madame Staubach's school the austerity of self-punishment was still believed to be all in all. During the days of Steinmarc's meditation, Linda was prayed for and was preached to with an unflagging diligence which, at the end of that time, had almost brought the girl to madness. For Linda the worst circumstance of all was this, that she had never as yet brought herself to disbelieve her aunt's religious menaces. She had been so educated that what fixed belief she had on the subject at all was in accordance with her aunt's creed rather than against it. When she was alone, she would tell herself that it was her lot to undergo that eternal condemnation with which her aunt threatened her; though in telling herself so she would declare to herself also that whatever that punishment could be, her Creator, let Him be ever so relentless, could inflict nothing on her worse than that state of agony with which His creatures had tormented her in this world.

She was in this state when Tetchen crept up to her room, on that evening on which Peter had been with Herr Molk. 'Fraulein,' said Tetchen, 'you are very unkind to me.'

'Never mind,' said Linda, not looking up into the woman's face.

'I have done everything in my power for you, as though you had been my own.'

'I am not your own. I don't want you to do anything for me.'

'I love you dearly, and I love him,—Ludovic. Have I not done everything in my power to save you from the man you hate?'

'You made me go off with him in the night, like a— like a——! Oh, Tetchen, was that treating me as though

I had been your own? Would you have done that for your own child?'

'Why not,—if you are to be his wife?'

'Tetchen, you have made me hate you, and you have made me hate myself. If I had not done that, I should not be such a coward. Go away. I do not want to speak to you.'

Then the old woman came close up to Linda, and stood for a moment leaning over her. Linda took no notice of her, but continued by a certain tremulous shaking of her knee to show how strongly she was moved. 'My darling,' said Tetchen, 'why should you send away from you those who love you?'

'Nobody loves me,' said Linda.

'I love you,—and Ludovic loves you.'

'That is of no use,—of none at all. I do not wish to hear his name again. It was not his fault, but he has disgraced me. It was my own fault,—and yours.'

'Linda, he is in the house now.'

'Who,—Ludovic?'

'Yes; Ludovic Valcarm.'

'In the house? How did he escape?'

'They could do nothing to him. They let him go. They were obliged to let him go.'

Then Linda got up from her seat, and stood for a minute with her eyes fixed upon the old woman's face, thinking what step she had better take. In the confusion of her mind, and in the state to which she had been reduced, there was no idea left with her that it might yet be possible that she would become the wife of Ludovic Valcarm, and live as such the life of a respectable woman. She had taught herself to acknowledge that her elopement with him had made that quite impossible;—that by what they had done they had both put themselves beyond the pale of such gentle mercy. Such evil had come to her from her secret interviews with this man who had become her lover almost without her own acquiescence, that she dreaded him even though she loved him. The remembrance of the night she had passed with him, partly in the warehouse and partly in the railway train, had nothing in it of the sweetness of love, to make her thoughts of it acceptable to her. This girl was so pure at heart, was by her own feelings so prone to virtue, that she looked back upon what she had done with abhorrence. Whether she had sinned or not, she hated what she had done as though it had been sinful; and now, when she was told that Ludovic Valcarm was again in the house, she recoiled from the idea of meeting him. On the former occasions of his coming to her, a choice had hardly been allowed to her whether she would see him or not. He had been with her before she had had time to fly from him. Now she had a moment for thought,—a moment in which she could ask herself whether it would be good for her to place herself again in his hands. She said that it would not be good, and she walked steadily down to her aunt's parlour. 'Aunt Charlotte,' she said, 'Ludovic Valcarm is in the house.'

'In this house,—again!' exclaimed Madame Staubach. Linda, having made her statement, said not a word further. Though she had felt herself compelled to turn informant against her lover, and by implication against Tetchen, her lover's accomplice, nevertheless she despised herself for what she was doing. She did not expect to soften her aunt by her conduct, or in any way to mitigate the rigour of her own sufferings. Her clandestine meetings with Ludovic had brought with them so much of pain and shame, that she had resolved almost by instinct to avoid another. But having taken this step to avoid it, she had nothing further to say or to do. 'Where is the young man?' demanded Madame Staubach.

'Tetchen says that he is here, in the house,' said Linda. Then Madame Staubach left the parlour, and crossed into the kitchen. There, standing close to the stove and warming himself, she found this terrible youth who had worked her so much trouble. It seemed to Madame Staubach that for months past she had been hearing of his having been constantly in and about the house, entering where he would and when he would, and in all those months she had never seen him. When last she had beheld him he had been to her simply a foolish idle youth with whom his elder cousin had been forced to quarrel. Since that, he had become to her a source of infinite terror. He had been described to her as one guilty of crimes which, much as she hated them, produced, even in her breast, a kind of respect for the criminal. He was a rebel of whom the magistrates were afraid. When in prison he had had means of escaping. When arrested at Nuremberg he would be the next day at Augsburg; when arrested at Augsburg he would be the next day at Nuremberg. He could get in and out of the roofs of houses, and could carry away with him a young maiden. These are deeds which always excite a certain degree of admiration in the female heart, and Madame Staubach, though she was a Baptist, was still a female. When, therefore, she found herself in the presence of Ludovic, she could not treat him with the indignant scorn with which she would have received him had he intruded upon her premises before her fears of him had been excited. 'Why are you here, Ludovic Valcarm?' she said advancing hardly a step beyond the doorway. Ludovic looked up at her with his hand resting on the table. He was not drunk, but he had been drinking; his clothes were soiled; he was unwashed and dirty, and the appearance of the man was that of a vagabond. 'Speak to me, and tell me why you are here,' said Madame Staubach.

'I have come to look for my wife,' said Ludovic.

'You have no wife;—at any rate you have none here.'

'Linda Tressel is my true and lawful wife, and I have come to take her away with me. She went with me once, and now she will go again. Where is she? You're not going to keep her locked up. It's against the law to make a young woman a prisoner.'

'My niece does not wish to see you;—does not intend to see you. Go away.'

But he refused to go, and threatened her, alleging that Linda Tressel was of an age which allowed her to dispose as she pleased of her person and her property. Of course this was of no avail with Madame Staubach, who was determined that, whatever might happen, the young man

should not force himself into Linda's presence. When
Ludovic attempted to leave the kitchen, Madame Staubach stood in the doorway and called for Tetchen. The
servant, who had perched herself on the landing, since
Linda had entered the parlour, was down in a moment,
and with various winks and little signs endeavoured to
induce Valcarm to leave the house. 'You had better go,
or I shall call at once for my neighbour Jacob Heisse,'
said Madame Staubach. Then she did call, as lustily as
she was able, though in vain. Upon this Ludovic, not
knowing how to proceed, unable or unwilling to force
his way further into the house in opposition to Madame
Staubach, took his departure, and as he went met Peter
Steinmarc in the passage at the back of Heisse's house.
Madame Staubach was still in the kitchen asking questions of Tetchen which Tetchen did not answer with
perfect truth, when Peter appeared among them.
'Madame Staubach,' he said, 'that vagabond Ludovic
Valcarm has just been here, in this house.'

'He went away but a minute since,' said Madame
Staubach.

'Just so. That is exactly what I mean. This is a thing
not to be borne,—not to be endured, and shows that
your niece Linda is altogether beyond the reach of any
good impressions.'

'Peter Steinmarc!'

'Yes, that is all very well; of course I expect that you
will take her part; although, with your high ideas of
religion and all that sort of thing, it is almost unaccount-
able that you should do so. As far as I am concerned
there must be an end of it. I am not going to make myself
ridiculous to all Nuremberg by marrying a young woman
who has no sense whatever of self-respect. I have over-
looked a great deal too much already,—a great deal too
much.'

'But Linda has not seen the young man. It was she
herself who told me that he was here.'

'Ah, very well. I don't know anything about that. I
saw him coming away from here, and it may be as well
to tell you that I have made up my mind. Linda Tressel

is not the sort of young woman that I took her to be, and I shall have nothing more to say to her.'

'You are an old goose,' said Tetchen.

'Hold your tongue,' said Madame Staubach angrily to her servant. Though she was very indignant with Peter Steinmarc, still it would go much against the grain with her that the match should be broken off. She had resolved so firmly that this marriage was proper for all purposes, that she had almost come to look at it as though it were a thing ordained of God. Then, too, she remembered, even in this moment, that Peter Steinmarc had received great provocation. Her immediate object was to persuade him that nothing had been done to give him further provocation. No fault had been committed by Linda which had not already been made known to him and been condoned by him. But how was she to explain all this to him in privacy, while Tetchen was in the kitchen, and Linda was in the parlour opposite? 'Peter, on my word as an honest truthful woman, Linda has been guilty of no further fault.'

'She has been guilty of more than enough,' said Peter.

'That may be said of all us guilty, frail, sinful human beings,' rejoined Madame Staubach.

'I doubt whether there are any of us so bad as she is,' said Peter.

'I wonder, madame, you can condescend to argue with him,' said Tetchen; 'as if all the world did not know that the fraulein is ten times too good for the like of him!'

'Hold your tongue,' said Madame Staubach.

'And where is Miss Linda at the present moment?' demanded Peter. Madame Staubach hesitated for an instant before she answered, and then replied that Linda was in the parlour. It might seem, she thought, that there was some cause for secrecy if she made any concealment at the present moment. Then Peter made his way out of the kitchen and across the passage, and without any invitation entered the parlour. Madame Staubach followed him, and Tetchen followed also. It was unfortunate for Madame Staubach's plans that the meeting between Peter and Linda should take place in this way, but she could not help it. But she was already making up her mind to this,—that if Peter Steinmarc ill-treated her niece, she would bring all Nuremberg about his ears.

'Linda Tressel,' he said;—and as he spoke, the impetuosity of indignation to which he had worked himself had not as yet subsided, and therefore he was full of courage;—'Linda Tressel, I find that that vagabond Ludovic Valcarm has again been here.'

'He is no vagabond,' said Linda, turning upon him with full as much indignation as his own.

'All the city knows him, and all the city knows you too. You are no better than you should be, and I wash my hands of you.'

'Let it be so,' said Linda; 'and for such a blessing I will pardon you the unmanly cruelty of your words.'

'But I will not pardon him,' said Madame Staubach. 'It is false; and if he dares to repeat such words, he shall rue them as long as he lives. Linda, this is to go for nothing,—for nothing. Perhaps it is not unnatural that he should have some suspicion.' Poor Madame Staubach, agitated by divided feelings, hardly knew on which side to use her eloquence.

'I should think not indeed,' said Peter, in triumph. 'Unnatural! Ha! ha!'

'I will put his eyes out of him if he laughs like that,' said Tetchen, looking as though she were ready to put her threat into execution upon the instant.

'Peter Steinmarc, you are mistaken in this,' said Madame Staubach. 'You had better let me see you in private.'

'Mistaken, am I? Oh! am I mistaken in thinking that she was alone during the whole night with Ludovic? A man does not like such mistakes as that. I tell you that I have done with her,—done with her,—done with her! She is a bad piece. She does not ring sound.* Madame Staubach, I respect you, and am sorry for you; but you know the truth as well as I do.'

'Man,' she said to him, 'you are ungrateful, cruel, and unjust.'

'Aunt Charlotte,' said Linda, 'he has done me the only

favour that I could accept at his hands. It is true that I have done that which, had he been a man, would have prevented him from seeking to make me his wife. All that is true. I own it.'

'There; you hear her, Madame Staubach.'

'And you shall hear me by-and-by,' said Madame Staubach.

'But it is no thought of that that has made him give me up,' continued Linda. 'He knows that he never could have got my hand. I told him that I would die first, and he has believed me. It is very well that he should give me up; but no one else, no other man alive, would have been base enough to have spoken to any woman as he has spoken to me.'

'It is all very well for you to say so,' said Peter.

'Aunt Charlotte, I hope I may never be asked to hear another word from his lips, or to speak another word to his ears.' Then Linda escaped from the room, thinking as she went that God in His mercy had saved her at last.

CHAPTER XV

ALL January had passed by. That thirtieth of January had come and gone which was to have made Linda Tressel a bride, and Linda was still Linda Tressel. But her troubles were not therefore over, and Peter Steinmarc was once again her suitor. It may be remembered how he had reviled her in her aunt's presence, how he had reminded her of her indiscretion, and how he had then rejected her; but, nevertheless, in the first week of February he was again her suitor.

Madame Staubach had passed a very troubled and uneasy month. Though she was minded to take her niece's part when Linda was so ungenerously attacked by the man whom she had warmed in the bosom of her family, still she was most unwilling that Linda should triumph. Her feminine instincts prompted her to take Linda's part on the spur of the moment, as similar instincts had prompted Tetchen to do the same thing;

but hardly the less on that account did she feel that it
was still her duty to persevere with that process of crushing by which all human vanity was to be pressed out of
Linda's heart. Peter Steinmarc had misbehaved himself
grossly, had appeared at that last interview in a guise
which could not have made him fascinating to any
young woman; but on that account the merit of submitting to him would be so much the greater. There
could hardly be any moral sackcloth and ashes too coarse
and too bitter for the correction of a sinful mind in this
world, but for the special correction of a mind sinful as
Linda's had been, marriage with such a man as Peter
Steinmarc would be sackcloth and ashes of the most
salutary kind. The objection which Linda would feel for
the man would be the exact antidote to the poison with
which she had been infected by the influence of the Evil
One. Madame Staubach acknowledged, when she was
asked the question, that a woman should love her husband; but she would always go on to describe this
required love as a feeling which should spring from a
dutiful submission. She was of opinion that a virtuous
child would love his parent, that a virtuous servant
would love her mistress, that a virtuous woman would
love her husband, even in spite of austere severity on the
part of him or her who might be in authority. When,
therefore, Linda would refer to what had taken place in
the parlour, and would ask whether it were possible that
she should love a man who had ill-used her so grossly,
Madame Staubach would reply as though love and
forgiveness were one and the same thing. It was Linda's
duty to pardon the ill-usage and to kiss the rod that had
smitten her. 'I hate him so deeply that my blood curdles
at the sight of him,' Linda had replied. Then Madame
Staubach had prayed that her niece's heart might be
softened, and had called upon Linda to join her in these
prayers. Poor Linda had felt herself compelled to go
down upon her knees and submit herself to such prayer
as well as she was able. Could she have enfranchised her
mind altogether from the trammels of belief in her aunt's
peculiar religion, she might have escaped from the

waters which seemed from day to day to be closing over her head; but this was not within her power. She asked herself no questions as to the truth of these convictions. The doctrine had been taught to her from her youth upwards, and she had not realised the fact that she possessed any power of rejecting it. She would tell herself, and that frequently, that to her religion held out no comfort, that she was not of the elect, that manifestly she was a castaway, and that therefore there could be no reason why she should endure unnecessary torments in this life. With such impressions on her mind she had suffered herself to be taken from her aunt's house, and carried off by her lover to Augsburg. With such impressions strong upon her, she would not hesitate to declare her hatred for the man, whom, in truth, she hated with all her heart, but whom, nevertheless, she thought it was wicked to hate. She daily told herself that she was one given up by herself to Satan. But yet, when summoned to her aunt's prayers, when asked to kneel and implore her Lord and Saviour to soften her own heart,—so to soften it that she might become a submissive wife to Peter Steinmarc,—she would comply, because she still believed that such were the sacrifices which a true religion demanded. But there was no comfort to her in her religion. Alas! alas! let her turn herself which way she might, there was no comfort to be found on any side.

At the end of the first week in February no renewed promise of assent had been extracted from Linda; but Peter, who was made of stuff less stern, had been gradually brought round to see that he had been wrong. Madame Staubach had, in the first instance, obtained the co-operation of Herr Molk and others of the leading city magistrates. The question of Linda's marriage had become quite a city matter. She had been indiscreet; that was acknowledged. As to the amount of her indiscretion, different people had different opinions. In the opinion of Herr Molk, that was a thing that did not signify. Linda Tressel was the daughter of a city officer who had been much respected. Her father's successor in that office was just the man who ought to be her husband.

Of course he was a little old and rusty; but then Linda had been indiscreet. Linda had not only been indiscreet, but her indiscretion had been, so to say, very public. She had run away from the city in the middle of the night with a young man,—with a young man known to be a scamp and a rebel. It must be acknowledged that indiscretion could hardly go beyond this. But then was there not the red house to make things even, and was it not acknowledged on all sides that Peter Steinmarc was very rusty?—The magistrates had made up their minds that the bargain was a just one, and as it had been made, they thought that it should be carried out. When Peter complained of further indiscretion on the part of Linda, and pointed out that he was manifestly absolved from his contract by her continued misconduct, Herr Molk went to work with most demure diligence, collected all the evidence, examined all the parties, and explained to Peter that Linda had not misbehaved herself since the contract had last been ratified. 'Peter, my friend,' said the burgomaster, 'you have no right to go back to any-thing,—to anything that happened before the twenty-third.' The twenty-third was the day on which Peter had expressed his pardon for the great indiscretion of the elopement. 'Since that time there has been no breach of trust on her part. I have examined all the parties, Peter.' It was in vain that Steinmarc tried to show that he was entitled to be absolved because Linda had said that she hated him. Herr Molk did not lose above an hour or two in explaining to him that little amenities of that kind were to be held as compensated in full by the possession of the red house. And then, had it not been acknow-ledged that he was very rusty,—a man naturally to be hated by a young woman who had shown that she had a preference for a young lover? 'Oh, bah!' said Herr Molk, almost angry at this folly; 'do not let me hear anything more about that, Peter.' Steinmarc had been convinced, had assented, and was now ready to accept the hand of his bride.

Nothing more had been heard of Ludovic since the day on which he had come to the house and had disappeared. Herr Molk, when he was interrogated on the subject, would shake his head, but in truth Herr Molk knew nothing. It was the fact that Valcarm, after being confined in prison at Augsburg for three days, had been discharged by the city magistrates; and it was the case, also, though the fact was not generally known, that the city magistrates of Augsburg had declared the city magistrates of Nuremberg to be——geese. Ludovic Valcarm was not now in prison, but he had left Nuremberg, and no one knew whither he was gone. The brewers, Sach, by whom he had been employed, professed that they knew nothing respecting him; but then, as Herr Molk declared, the two brothers Sach were men who ought themselves to be in prison. They, too, were rebels, according to Herr Molk.

But in truth, as regarded Linda, no trouble need have been taken in inquiring after Ludovic. She made no inquiry respecting him. She would not even listen to Tetchen when Tetchen would suggest this or that mode of ascertaining where he might be. She had allowed herself to be reconciled to Tetchen, because Tetchen had taken her part against Peter Steinmarc; but she would submit to no intrigue at the old woman's instance. 'I do not want to see him ever again, Tetchen.'

'But, fraulein, you loved him.'

'Yes, and I do. But of what use is such love? I could do him no good. If he were there, opposite,—where he used to be,—I would not cross the river to him.'

'I hope, my dear, that it mayn't be so with you always, that's all,' Tetchen had said. But Linda had no vestige of such hope at her heart. The journey to Augsburg had been to her the cause of too much agony, had filled her with too real a sense of maidenly shame, to enable her to look forward with hope to any adventure in which Ludovic should have to take a part. To escape from Peter Steinmarc, whether by death, or illness, or flight, or sullen refusal,—but to escape from him let the cost to herself be what it might,—that was all that she now desired. But she thought that escape was not possible to her. She was coming at last to believe that she would have to stand up in the church and give her hand. If it were so, all Nuremberg should ring with the tragedy of their nuptials.

Since Peter had returned, and expressed to Madame Staubach his willingness to go on with the marriage, he had, after a fashion, been again taken into that lady's favour. He had behaved very badly, but a fault repented was a fault to be forgiven. 'I am sorry that there was a rumpus, Madame Staubach,' he had said, 'but you see that there is so much to put a man's back up when a girl runs away with a man in the middle of the night, you know.'

'Peter,' the widow had replied, interrupting him, 'that need not be discussed again. The wickedness of the human heart is so deep that it cannot be fathomed; but we have the word of the Lord to show to us that no sinner is too vile to be forgiven. What you said in your anger was cruel and unmanly, but it has been pardoned.' Then Peter sat down and lighted his pipe. He did not like the tone of his friend's remarks, but he knew well that there was nothing to be gained by discussing such matters with Madame Staubach. It was better for him to take his old seat quietly, and at once to light his pipe. Linda, on that occasion, and on many others subsequently, came and sat in the room, and there would be almost absolute silence. There might be a question asked about the household, and Linda would answer it; or Peter might remark that such a one among the small city dealers had been fined before the magistrates for some petty breach of the city's laws. But of conversation there was none, and Peter never on these evenings addressed himself specially to Linda. It was quite understood that she was to undergo persuasion, not from Peter, but from her aunt.

About the middle of February her aunt made her last attack on poor Linda. For days before something had been said daily; some word had been spoken in which Madame Staubach alluded to the match as an affair which would certainly be brought about sooner or later. And there were prayers daily for the softening of Linda's heart. And it was understood that every one in the house was supposed to be living under some special cloud of God's anger till Linda's consent should have been given. Madame Staubach had declared during the ecstasy of her devotion, that not only she herself, but even Tetchen also, would become the prey of Satan if Linda did not relent. Linda had almost acknowledged to herself that she was in the act of bringing eternal destruction on all those around her by her obstinacy. Oh, if she could only herself be dead, let the eternal consequences as they regarded herself alone be what they might!

'Linda,' said her aunt, 'is it not time at length that you should give us an answer?'

'An answer, aunt Charlotte?' As if she had not given a sufficiency of answers.

'Do you not see how others suffer because of your obstinacy?'

'It is not my doing.'

'It is your doing. Do not allow any such thought as that to get into your mind, and assist the Devil in closing the door of your heart. They who are your friends are bound to you, and cannot separate themselves from you.'

'Who are my friends?'

'I am sorry you should ask that question, Linda.'

'I have no friends.'

'Linda, that is ungrateful to God, and thankless. I say nothing of myself.'

'You are my friend, but no one else.'

'Herr Molk is your friend, and has shown himself to be so. Jacob Heisse is your friend.' He, too, using such wisdom as he possessed, had recommended Linda to take the husband provided for her. 'Peter Steinmarc is your friend.'

'No, he is not,' said Linda.

'That is very wicked,—heinously wicked.' Whereupon Madame Staubach went towards the door for the purpose of bolting it, and Linda knew that this was preparatory to a prayer. Linda felt that it was impossible that she should fall on her knees and attempt to pray at this moment. What was the use of it? Sooner or later she must yield. She had no weapon with which to carry on the battle, whereas her aunt was always armed.

'Aunt Charlotte,' she said, suddenly, 'I will do what you want,—only not now; not quite yet. Let there be time for me to make myself ready for it.'

The dreaded visitation of that special prayer was at any rate arrested, and Madame Staubach graciously accepted Linda's assent as sufficient quittance at any rate for the evil words that had been spoken on that occasion. She was too wise to demand a more gracious acquiescence, and did not say a word then even in opposition to the earnest request which had been made for delay. She kissed her niece, and rejoiced as the woman rejoiced who had swept diligently and had found her lost piece. If Linda would at last take the right path, all former deviations from it should be as nothing. And Madame Staubach half-trusted, almost thought, that it could not be but that her own prayers should prevail at last. Linda indeed had twice before assented, and had twice retracted her word. But there had been causes. The young man had come and had prevailed, who surely would not come again, and who surely, if coming, would not prevail. And then Peter himself had misbehaved. It must now be Madame Staubach's care that there should arise no further stumbling-block. There were but two modes of taking this care at her disposal. She could watch Linda all the day, and she could reiterate her prayers with renewed diligence. On neither points would she be found lacking.

'And when shall be the happy day?' said Peter. On the occasion of his visit to the parlour subsequent to the scene which has just been described, Madame Staubach left the room for a while so that the two lovers might be together. Peter had been warned that it would be so, and had prepared, no doubt, his little speech.

'There will be no happy day,' said Linda.

'Don't say that, my dear.'

'I do say it. There will be no happy day for you or for me.'

'But we must fix a day, you know,' said Peter.

'I will arrange it with my aunt.' Then Linda got up and left the room. Peter Steinmarc attempted no further conversation with her, nor did Madame Staubach again endeavour to create any intercourse between them. It must come after marriage. It was clearly to her God's will that these two people should be married, and she could not but be right to leave the result to His wisdom. A day was named. With a simple nod of her head Linda agreed that she would become Peter's wife on the fifteenth of March; and she received visits from Herr Molk and from Jacob Heisse to congratulate her on her coming happiness.

CHAPTER XVI

THROUGHOUT February Linda never flinched. She hardly spoke at all except on matters of household business, but to them she was sedulously attentive. She herself insisted on understanding what legal arrangement was made about the house, and would not consent to sign the necessary document preparatory to her marriage till there was inserted in it a clause giving to her aunt a certain life-interest in the property in the event either of her marriage or of her death. Peter did his best to oppose this, as did also Madame Staubach herself; but Linda prevailed, and the clause was there. 'She would have to live with you whether or no,' said Herr Molk to the town-clerk. 'You couldn't turn the woman out into the street.' But Peter had wished to be master of his own house, and would not give up the point till much eloquence and authority had been used. He had come to wish with all his heart that he had never seen Linda Tressel or the red house; but he had gone so far that he could not retract. Linda never flinched, never uttered a word of complaint; sat silent while Peter was smoking, and awaited her doom. Once her aunt spoke to her about her feelings as a bride. 'You do love him, do you not, Linda?' said Madame Staubach. 'I do not love him,' Linda had replied. Then Madame Staubach dared to ask no further question, but prayed that the necessary affection might be given.

There were various things to be bought, and money

for the purpose was in a moderate degree forthcoming. Madame Staubach possessed a small hoard, which was now to be spent, and something she raised on her own little property. A portion of this was intrusted wholly to Linda, and she exercised care and discretion in its disposition. Linen for the house she purchased, and things needed for the rooms and the kitchen. But she would expend nothing in clothes for herself. When pressed on the subject by her aunt, she declared that her marriage would be one that required no finery. Her own condition and that of her proposed husband, she said, made it quite unnecessary. When she was told that Steinmarc would be offended by such exaggerated simplicity, she turned upon her aunt with such a look of scorn that Madame Staubach did not dare to say another word. Indeed at this time Madame Staubach had become almost afraid of her niece, and would sit watching the silent stern industry of the younger woman with something of awe. Could it be that there ever came over her heart a shock of regret for the thing she was doing? Was it possible that she should already be feeling remorse? If it was so with her, she turned herself to prayer, and believed that the Lord told her that she was right.

But there were others who watched, and spoke among themselves, and felt that the silent solemnity of Linda's mode of life was a cause for trembling. Max Bogen's wife had come to her father's house, and had seen Linda, and had talked to Tetchen, and had said at home that Linda was——mad. Her father had become frightened, and had refused to take any part in the matter. He acknowledged that he had given his advice in favour of the marriage, but he had done this merely as a matter of course,—to oblige his neighbour, Madame Staubach. He would have nothing more to do with it. When Fanny told him that she feared that Linda would lose her senses, he went into his workshop and busied himself with a great chair. But Tetchen was not so reticent. Tetchen said much to Madame Staubach;—so much that the unfortunate widow was nearly always on her knees, asking for help, asking in very truth for new gifts of

obstinate persistency; and Tetchen also said much to
Fanny Bogen.

'But what can we do, Tetchen?' asked Fanny.

'If I had my will,' said Tetchen, 'I would so handle
him that he would be glad enough to be off his bargain.
But you'll see they'll never live together as man and wife,
—never for a day.'

They who said that Linda was mad at this time were
probably half-right; but if so, her madness had shown
itself in none of those forms which are held to justify
interference by authority. There was no one in Nuremberg who could lock a woman up because she was silent;
or could declare her to be unfit for marriage because she
refused to buy wedding clothes. The marriage must go
on. Linda herself felt that it must be accomplished. Her
silence and her sternness were not now consciously used
by her as means of opposing or delaying the coming
ceremony, but simply betrayed the state of mind to which
she was reduced. She counted the days and she counted
the hours as a criminal counts them who sits in his cell
and waits for the executioner. She knew, she thought
she knew, that she would stand in the church and have
her hand put into that of Peter Steinmarc; but what
might happen after that she did not know.

She would stand at the altar and have her hand put
into that of Peter Steinmarc, and she would be called his
wife in sight of God and man. She spent hours in solitude
attempting to realise the position with all its horrors.
She never devoted a minute to the task of reconciling
herself to it. She did not make one slightest endeavour
towards teaching herself that after all it might be possible
for her to live with the man as his companion in peace
and quietness. She hated him with all the vigour of her
heart, and she would hate him to the end. On that subject
no advice, no prayer, no grace from heaven, could be of
service to her. Satan, with all the horrors of hell, as they
had been described to her, was preferable to the com-
panionship of Peter Steinmarc. And yet she went on
without flinching.

She went on without flinching till the night of the

tenth of March. Up to that time, from the day on which she had last consented to her martyrdom, no idea of escape had occurred to her. As she left her aunt on that evening, Madame Staubach spoke to her. 'You should at any rate pray for him,' said Madame Staubach. 'I hope that you pray that this marriage may be for his welfare.' How could she pray for him? And how could she utter such a prayer as that? But she tried; and as she tried, she reflected that the curse to him would be as great as it was to her. Not only was she to be sacrificed, but the miserable man was bringing himself also to utter wretchedness. Unless she could die, there would be no escape for him, as also there would be none for her. That she should speak to him, touch him, hold intercourse with him, was, she now told herself, out of the question. She might be his servant, if he would allow her to be so at a distance, but nothing more. Or it might be possible that she should be his murderess! A woman who has been taught by her religion that she is and must be a child of the Evil One, may become guilty of what most terrible crime you please without much increase of damage* to her own cause,—without much damage according to her own views of life and death. Linda, as she thought of it in her own chamber, with her eyes wide open, looking into the dark night from out of her window, declared to herself that in certain circumstances she would certainly attempt to kill him. She shuddered and shook till she almost fell from her chair. Come what might, she would not endure the pressure of his caress.

Then she got up and resolved that she would even yet make one other struggle to escape. It would not be true of her to say that at this moment she was mad, but the mixed excitement and terror of her position as she was waiting her doom, joined to her fears, her doubts, and, worse than all, her certainties as to her condition in the sight of God, had almost unstrung her mind. She had almost come to believe that the world was at its end, and that the punishment of which she had heard so much was already upon her. 'If this is to be a doom for ever,' she said to herself, 'the God I have striven to love is very

cruel.' But then there came an exercise of reason which
told her that it could not be a doom for ever. It was clear
to her that there was much as yet within her own power
which could certainly not be so in that abode of the
unblessed to which she was to be summoned. There was
the window before her, with the silent river running
below; and she knew that she could throw herself from
it if she chose to put forth the power which she still
possessed. She felt that 'she herself might her quietus
make with a bare bodkin.' Why should she

> 'Fardels bear,
> To grunt and sweat under a weary life,
> But that the dread of something after life,
> The undiscovered country from whose bourne
> No traveller returns, puzzles the will,
> And makes us rather bear those ills we have
> Than fly to others that we know not of.'*

Linda knew nothing of Hamlet, but the thought was
there, exact; and the knowledge that some sort of choice
was still open to her, if it were only the choice of sending
herself at once to a world different from this, a world in
which Peter Steinmarc would not be the avenger of
her life's wickedness, made her aware that even yet
something might be done.

On the following morning she was in the kitchen, as
was usual with her now, at an early hour, and made the
coffee for her aunt's breakfast, and for Peter's. Tetchen
was there also, and to Tetchen she spoke a word or two
in good humour. Tetchen said afterwards that she knew
that something was to happen, because Linda's manner
to her had been completely changed that morning. She
sat down with her aunt at eight, and ate a morsel of
bread, and endeavoured to swallow her coffee. She was
thinking at the time that it might be the case that she
would never see her aunt again. All the suffering that
she had endured at Madame Staubach's hands had never
quenched her love. Miserable as she had been made by
the manner in which this woman had executed the trust
which circumstances had placed in her hands, Linda
had hardly blamed her aunt even within her own bosom.

When with a frenzy of agony Madame Staubach would repeat prayer after prayer, extending her hands towards heaven, and seeking to obtain that which she desired by the painful intensity of her own faith, it had never occurred to Linda that in such proceedings she was ill-treated by her aunt. Her aunt, she thought, had ever shown to her all that love which a mother has for her child, and Linda in her misery was never ungrateful. As soon as the meal was finished she put on her hat and cloak, which she had brought down from her room, and then kissed her aunt.

'God bless you, my child,' said Madame Staubach, 'and enable you to be an affectionate and dutiful wife to your husband.' Then Linda went forth from the room and from the house, and as she went she cast her eyes around, thinking that it might be possible that she should never see them again.

Linda told no lie as she left her aunt, but she felt that she was acting a lie. It had been arranged between them, before she had entertained this thought of escaping from Nuremberg, that she should on this morning go out by herself and make certain purchases. In spite of the things that had been done, of Valcarm's visit to the upper storeys of the house, of the flight to Augsburg, of Linda's long protracted obstinacy and persistently expressed hatred for the man who was to be her husband, Madame Staubach still trusted her niece. She trusted Linda perhaps the more at this time from a feeling that she had exacted so much from the girl. When, therefore, Linda kissed her and went out, she had no suspicion on her mind; nor was any aroused till the usual dinner-hour was passed, and Linda was still absent. When Tetchen at one o'clock said something of her wonder that the fraulein had not returned, Madame Staubach had suggested that she might be with her friend Herr Molk. Tetchen knew what was the warmth of that friendship, and thought that such a visit was not probable. At three o'clock the postman brought a letter which Linda herself had dropped into the box of the post-office that morning, soon after leaving the house. She had known when, in ordinary course, it would be delivered. Should it lead by any misfortune to her discovery before she could escape, that she could not help. Even that, accompanied by her capture, would be as good a mode as any other of telling her aunt the truth. The letter was as follows:—

'*Thursday Night.*

'DEAREST AUNT,—I think you hardly know what are my sufferings. I truly believe that I have deserved them, but nevertheless they are insupportable. I cannot marry Peter Steinmarc. I have tried it, and cannot. The day is very near now; but were it to come nearer, I should go mad, or I should kill myself. I think that you do not know what the feeling is that has made me the most wretched of women since this marriage was first proposed to me. I shall go away to-morrow, and shall try to get to my uncle's house in Cologne. It is a long way off, and perhaps I shall never get there: but if I am to die on the road, oh, how much better will that be! I do not want to live. I have made you unhappy, and everybody unhappy, but I do not think that anybody has been so unhappy as I am. I shall give you a kiss as I go out, and you will think that it was the kiss of Judas;*but I am not a Judas in my heart. Dear aunt Charlotte, I would have borne it if I could,—Your affectionate, but undutiful niece.

'LINDA TRESSEL.'

Undutiful! So she called herself; but had she not, in truth, paid duty to her aunt beyond that which one human being can in any case owe to another? Are we to believe that the very soul of the offspring is to be at the disposition of the parent? Poor Linda! Madame Staubach, when the letter was handed to her by Tetchen, sat aghast for a while, motionless, with her hands before her. 'She is off again, I suppose,' said Tetchen.

'Yes; she has gone.'

'It serves you right. I say it now, and I will say it. Why was she so driven?' Madame Staubach said never a word. Could she have had Linda back at the instant, just now, at this very moment, she would have yielded.

It was beginning to become apparent to her that God did not intend that her prayers should be successful. Doubtless the fault was with herself. She had lacked faith. Then as she sat there she began to reflect that it might be that she herself was not of the elect. What if, after all, she had been wrong throughout! 'Is anything to be done?' said Tetchen, who was still standing by her side.

'What ought I to do, Tetchen?'

'Wring Peter Steinmarc's neck,' said Tetchen. 'That would be the best thing.' Even this did not bring forth an angry retort from Madame Staubach. About an hour after that Peter came in. He had already heard that the bird had flown. Some messenger from Jacob Heisse's house had brought him the tidings to the town-hall.

'What is this?' said he. 'What is this? She has gone again.'

'Yes,' said Tetchen, 'she has gone again. What did you expect?'

'And Ludovic Valcarm is with her?'

'Ludovic Valcarm is not with her!' said Madame Staubach, with an expression of wrath which made him start a foot back from where he stood.

'Ah!' he exclaimed, when he had recovered himself, and reflected that he had no cause for fear, 'she is no better than she should be.'

'She is ten times too good for you. That is all that is the matter with her,' said Tetchen.

'I have done with her,—have done with her altogether,' said Peter, rubbing his hands together.

'I should think you have,' said Tetchen.

'Tell him to leave me,' said Madame Staubach, waving Peter away with her hand. Then Tetchen took the town-clerk by his arm, and led him somewhat roughly out of the room. So he shall disappear from our sight. No reader will now require to be told that he did not become the husband of Linda Tressel.

Madame Staubach did nothing and said nothing further on the matter that night. Tetchen indeed went up to the railway station, and found that Linda had

taken a ticket through to Mannheim, and had asked
questions there, openly, in reference to the boats from
thence down the Rhine. She had with her money
sufficient to take her to Cologne,* and her aunt endeavoured to comfort herself with thinking that no
further evil would come of this journey than the cost,
and the rumours it would furnish. As to Peter Steinmarc,
that was now all over. If Linda would return, no further
attempt should be made. Tetchen said nothing on the
subject, but she herself was by no means sure that Linda
had no partner in her escape. To Tetchen's mind it was
so natural that there should be a partner.

Early on the following morning Madame Staubach
was closeted with Herr Molk in the panelled chamber of
the house in the Egidien Platz, seeking advice. 'Gone
again, is she?' said Herr Molk, holding up his hand.
'And that fellow is with her of course?'

'No, no, no!' exclaimed Madame Staubach.

'Are you sure of that! At any rate she must marry him
now, for nobody else will take her. Peter won't bite
again at that bait.' Then Madame Staubach was compelled to explain that all ideas of matrimony in respect
to her niece must be laid aside, and she was driven also
to confess that she had persevered too long in regard to
Peter Steinmarc. 'He certainly is a little rusty for such a
young woman as Linda,' said Herr Molk, confessing also
his part of the fault. At last he counselled Madame
Staubach that she could do nothing but follow her niece
to Cologne, as she had before followed her to Augsburg.
Such a journey would be very terrible to her. She had
not been in Cologne for years, and did not wish to see
again those who were there. But she felt that she had no
alternative, and she went.

CHAPTER XVII

FOR very many years no connection had been maintained between the two women who lived together in
Nuremberg, and their nearest relative, who was a half-
brother of Madame Staubach's, a lawyer, living in

Cologne. This uncle of Linda's was a Roman Catholic, and had on this account been shunned by Madame Staubach. Some slight intercourse there had been on matters of business, and thus it had come to pass that Linda knew the address of her uncle. But this was all that she knew, and knowing this only, she had started for Cologne. The reader will hardly require to be told that she had not gone in company with him who a few weeks since had been her lover. The reader, perhaps, will have understood Linda's character so thoroughly as to be convinced that, though she had submitted to be dragged out of her window by her lover, and carried away to Augsburg in the night, still it was not probable that she should again be guilty of such indiscretion as that. The lesson had not been in vain. If there be any reader who does not know Linda's character better than it was known to Herr Molk, or even to Tetchen, this story has been told in vain. All alone she started, and all alone she made the entire journey. Long as it was, there was no rest for her on the way. She went by a cheap and slow train, and on she went through the long day and the long night, and on through the long day again. She did not suffer with the cold as she had suffered on that journey to Augsburg, but the weariness of the hours was very great, and the continuation of the motion oppressed her sorely. Then joined to this suffering was the feeling that she was going to a strange world in which no one would receive her kindly. She had money to take her to Cologne, but she would have none to bring her back again. It seemed to her as she went that there could be no prospect to her returning to a home which she had disgraced so thoroughly.

At Mannheim she found that she was obliged to wait over four hours before the boat started. She quitted the railway a little after midnight, and she was told that she was to be on board before five in the morning. The night was piercing cold, though never so cold as had been that other night; and she was dismayed at the thought of wandering about in that desolate town. Some one, however, had compassion on her, and she was taken to a small inn, in which she rested on a bed without removing her clothes. When she rose in the morning, she walked down to the boat without a word of complaint, but she found that her limbs were hardly able to carry her. An idea came across her mind that if the people saw that she was ill they would not take her upon the boat. She crawled on, and took her place among the poorer passengers before the funnels. For a considerable time no one noticed her, as she sat shivering in the cold morning air on a damp bench. At last a market-woman going down to Mayence asked her a question. Was she ill? Before they had reached Mayence she had told her whole story to the market-woman. 'May God temper the wind for thee, my shorn lamb!'* said the market-woman to Linda, as she left her; 'for it seems that thou hast been shorn very close.' By this time, with the assistance of the woman, she had found a place below in which she could lie down, and there she remained till she learned that the boat had reached Cologne. Some one in authority on board the vessel had been told that she was ill; and as they had reached Cologne also at night, she was allowed to remain on board till the next morning. With the early dawn she was astir, and the full daylight of the March morning was hardly perfect in the heavens when she found herself standing before the door of a house in the city, to which she had been brought as being the residence of her uncle.

She was now, in truth, so weak and ill that she could hardly stand. Her clothes had not been off her back since she left Nuremberg, nor had she come prepared with any change of raiment. A woman more wretched, more disconsolate, on whose shoulders the troubles of this world lay heavier, never stood at an honest man's door to beg admittance. If only she might have died as she crawled through the streets!

But there she was, and she must make some petition that the door might be opened for her. She had come all the way from Nuremberg to this spot, thinking it possible that in this spot alone she might receive succour; and now she stood there, fearing to raise the knocker on the door. She was a lamb indeed, whose fleece had been shorn very close; and the shearing had been done all in the sacred name of religion! It had been thought necessary that the vile desires of her human heart should be crushed within her bosom, and the crushing had brought her to this. She looked up in her desolation at the front of the house. It was a white, large house, as belonging to a moderately prosperous citizen, with two windows on each side of the door, and five above, and then others again above them. But there seemed to be no motion within it, nor was there any one stirring along the street. Would it not be better, she thought, that she should sit for a while and wait upon the door-step? Who has not known that frame of mind in which any post-ponement of the thing dreaded is acceptable?

But Linda's power of postponement was very short. She had hardly sunk on to the step, when the door was opened, and the necessity for explaining herself came upon her. Slowly and with pain she dragged herself on to her feet, and told the suspicious servant, who stood filling the aperture of the doorway, that her name was Linda Tressel, and that she had come from Nuremberg. She had come from the house of Madame Staubach at Nuremberg. Would the servant be kind enough to tell Herr Grüner that Linda Tressel, from Madame Stau-bach's house in Nuremberg, was at his door? She claimed no kindred then, feeling that the woman might take such claim as a disgrace to her master. When she was asked to call again later, she looked piteously into the woman's face, and said that she feared she was too ill to walk away.

Before the morning was over she was in bed, and her uncle's wife was at her bedside, and there had been fair-haired cousins in her room, creeping in to gaze at her with their soft blue eyes, touching her with their young soft hands, and calling her Cousin Linda with their soft voices. It seemed to her that she could have died happily, so happily, then, if only they might have been allowed to stand round her bed, and still to whisper and still to touch her. But they had been told that they might only

just see their new cousin and then depart,— because the
new cousin was ill. The servant at the front door had
doubted her, as it is the duty of servants to doubt in such
cases; but her uncle had not doubted, and her uncle's
wife, when she heard the story, wept over her, and told
her that she should be at rest.

Linda told her story from the first to the last. She told
everything,—her hatred for the one man, her love for the
other; her journey to Augsburg. 'Ah, dear, dear, dear,'
said aunt Grüner when this was told to her. 'I know how
wicked I have been,' said Linda, sorrowing. 'I do not
say that you have been wicked, my dear, but you have
been unfortunate,' said aunt Grüner. And then Linda
went on to tell her, as the day so much dreaded by her
drew nearer and nearer, as she came to be aware that,
let her make what effort she would, she could not bring
herself to be the man's wife,—that the horror of it was
too powerful for her,—she resolved at the last moment
that she would seek the only other relative in the world
of whom she knew even the name. Her aunt Grüner
thoroughly commended her for this, saying, however,
that it would have been much better that she should have
made the journey at some period earlier in her troubles.
'Aunt Charlotte does not seem to be a very nice sort of
woman to live with,' said aunt Grüner. Then Linda,
with what strength she could, took Madame Staubach's
part. 'She always thought that she was doing right,' said
Linda, solemnly. 'Ah, that comes of her religion,' said
aunt Grüner. 'We think differently, my dear. Thank
God, we have got somebody to tell us what we ought to
do and what we ought not to do.'* Linda was not strong
enough to argue the question, or to remind her aunt that
this somebody, too, might possibly be wrong.

Linda Tressel was now happier than she had remembered herself to have been since she was a child, though
ill, so that the doctor who came to visit her could only
shake his head and speak in whispers to aunt Grüner.
Linda herself, perceiving how it was with the doctor,—
knowing that there were whispers though she did not
hear them, and shakings of the head though she did not

see them,—told her aunt with a smile that she was contented to die. Her utmost hope, the extent of her wishes,
had been to escape from the extremity of misery to which
she had been doomed. She had thought often, she said,
as she had been making that journey, that her strength
would not serve her to reach the house of her relative.
'God,' she said, 'had been very good to her, and she was
now contented to go.'

Madame Staubach arrived at Cologne four days after
her niece, and was also welcomed at her brother's house.
But the welcome accorded to her was not that which had
been given to Linda. 'She has been driven very nearly
to death's door among you,' said the one aunt to the
other. To Linda Madame Staubach was willing to own
that she had been wrong, but she could make no such
acknowledgment to the wife of her half-brother,—to a
benighted Papist.* 'I have endeavoured to do my duty by
my niece,' said Madame Staubach, 'asking the Lord
daily to show me the way.' 'Pshaw!' said the other
woman. 'Your always asking the way, and never knowing it, will end in her death. She will have been murdered by your prayers.' This was very terrible, but for
Linda's sake it was borne.

There was nothing of reproach either from Linda to
her aunt or from Madame Staubach to her niece, nor
was the name of Peter Steinmarc mentioned between
them for many days. It was, indeed, mentioned but
once again by poor Linda Tressel. For some weeks, for
nearly a month, they all remained in the house of Herr
Grüner, and then Linda was removed to apartments in
Cologne, in which all her earthly troubles were brought
to a close. She never saw Nuremberg again, or Tetchen,
who had been faithful at least to her, nor did she ever
even ask the fate of Ludovic Valcarm. His name
Madame Staubach never dared to mention; and Linda
was silent, thinking always that it was a name of offence.
But when she had been told that she must die,—that her
days were indeed numbered, and that no return to
Nuremberg was possible for her,—she did speak a word
of Peter Steinmarc. 'Tell him, aunt Charlotte, from me,'

she said, 'that I prayed for him when I was dying, and that I forgave him. You know, aunt Charlotte, it was impossible that I should marry him. A woman must not marry a man whom she does not love.' Madame Staubach did not venture to say a word in her own justification. She did not dare even to recur to the old tenets of her fierce religion, while Linda still lived. She was cowed, and contented herself with the offices of a nurse by the sickbed of the dying girl. She had been told by her sister-in-law that she had murdered her niece. Who can say what were the accusations brought against her by the fury of her own conscience?

Every day the fair-haired cousins came to Linda's bedside, and whispered to her with their soft voices, and looked at her with their soft eyes, and touched her with their soft hands. Linda would kiss their plump arms and lean her head against them, and would find a very paradise of happiness in this late revelation of human love. As she lay a-dying she must have known that the world had been very hard to her, and that her aunt's teaching had indeed crushed her,—body as well as spirit. But she made no complaint; and at last, when the full summer had come, she died at Cologne in Madame Staubach's arms.

During those four months at Cologne the zeal of Madame Staubach's religion had been quenched, and she had been unable to use her fanaticism, even towards herself. But when she was alone in the world the fury of her creed returned. 'With faith you shall move a mountain,' she would say, 'but without faith you cannot live.' * She could never trust her own faith, for the mountain would not be moved.

A small tombstone in the Protestant burying-ground at Cologne tells that Linda Tressel, of Nuremberg, died in that city on the 20th of July 1863, and that she was buried in that spot.

THE END

one and virtual prayed for him when I was dying, and
that I forgave him. You know, aunt Charlotte, it was
impossible that I should marry him. A woman must not
marry a man whom she does not love.' Madame
Staubach did not understand in any way a word in her own justification. She did not discuss even in her own mind the old sores
of her love 'régime', with Linda still alive. She sat
cowed, and embittered in itself with the offence of a mind
by the wicked of the dying girl. She had been told by
the sister-in-law that she had purchased her niece? Who
can say what were the accusations brought against her
by the fury of her own conscience?

Every day the bewildered cousin came to Linda's
bedside, and whispered to her with their soft voices and
looked at her with their soft eyes, and touched her with
their soft hands. Linda would kiss their plump arms
and draw her hands about them, and would feel a very
paradise of happiness in this late revelry of happiness
love. 'As she lay a-dying, she must have known that the
world had been very hard to her, and that there was no
reaching had indeed crushed her—body as well as spirit.
But she made no complaint; and at last, when the full
summer had come, she died at Cologne in Madame
Staubach's arms.

During those four months at Cologne the zeal of
Madame Staubach's religion had been quenched, and
she had been unable to use her fanaticism, even towards
herself. But when she was alone in the world the fury of
her creed returned. 'With faith you shall have a region
gain,' she would say, 'but without faith you cannot live.'
She could never trust her own faith, for the mountain
would not be removed.

* * * *

A small tombstone in the Protestant burying-ground
at Cologne tells that Linda Tressel, of Nuremberg, died
in that city on the 10th of July 1863; and that she was
buried in that spot.

THE END.

EXPLANATORY NOTES

Nina Balatka

Ger.: German; Cz.: Czech.

2 THE PERSONS OF THE STORY: Trollope tried to use authentic Czech and Jewish names for his characters, with some success. Josef Balatka is correctly named. Nina's proper surname is Balatkova; Trollope probably suspected that English readers would find two forms of a family name confusing. Luxa simplifies the correct form, Luxova. Souchey should be Souchek; here a printer may have misread Trollope's handwriting. Karil (usually Karel) is correct, but Zamenoy is unlikely. The Zamenoys have named their son Zižka after a Bohemian hero, John Žižka (*c*.1376–1424), commemorated in Prague by the Žižkaberg (Žižka's mountain), where he won a great victory over imperial forces (14 July 1420). Czech nationalists revered Žižka as a defender of Czech liberties against the Empire, but Žižka was also a Hussite leader; it is unlikely that the Catholic Zamenoys should have so named their son. I am grateful to Ms Martina Ladova for assistance with some of the Czech names.

A 1787 edict of Joseph II ordered all Czech Jews to adopt German names. Jacobi and Loth are correct. Rapinski (Rapinsky in text, p. 111) may be so named because Trollope remembered that the 'Old-New' Synagogue stood on Rabínská Ulice (Rabbi Street). Trendellsohn is not an authentic name, but *trendel* is the German term for *dredl* (Yiddish), the top which Jewish children spin at Hanukkah.

3 *of Prague*: at the time of the story, Prague was the capital of Bohemia, then a province of the Austrian Empire; the Austrian Emperor was also King of Bohemia, which is roughly the western third of what is now (with Moravia and Slovakia) Czechoslovakia. Bohemians are Slavs, speaking Czech, a Slavic language, and describing themselves as Czechs. The independent Kingdom of Bohemia disappeared in 1526, when Ferdinand of Habsburg was elected King, and

merged Bohemia with Austria, Hungary, and other Habsburg possessions.

Jews' quarter ... still is now: the Prague ghetto or Judenstadt, renamed Josefstadt (Cz. Josefov) in honour of Joseph II, is on the east bank of the Moldau (Cz. Vltava) River, north of the Charles Bridge. Prague's Jewish community claimed to be the oldest in Europe, allegedly founded by refugees from the fall of Jerusalem (AD 70). With its synagogue and burial ground (each also claiming to be the oldest in Europe), it was a recommended sight for tourists visiting Prague. 'Enforced' Jewish residence in the ghetto was legally abolished in 1848, as was the ghetto as a separate jurisdiction in 1852; however, in 1870 over half Prague's Jews still lived in the ghetto. Most of the old ghetto buildings were demolished for sanitary reasons in the mid-1890s. (See *Encyclopaedia Judaica*, article 'Prague'.)

4 *vial of her wrath*: 'And I heard a great voice out of the temple saying to the seven angels, Go your ways, and pour out the vials of the wrath of God upon the earth' (Revelation 16: 1).

into the wilderness: a Biblical phrase implying exile from the community.

Kleinseite: Prague's 'Little Side' (Cz. Malá Strana), on the west side of the Moldau. Trollope uses German names for Prague's streets and districts, following Murray's *Handbook for Travellers in Southern Germany*, the guide he used on his visit to Prague and Nuremberg. The *Handbook* was frequently updated and reprinted in the 1850s and 1860s; for Murray, 'Southern Germany' included Austria, Hungary, and most of modern Czechoslovakia and Yugoslavia.

5 *alas! ... Austrian barracks*: Bohemian nationalism was kept in check by a large military garrison drawn from other parts of the Empire. The 'Old Traveller' notes Prague's numerous 'soldiers, wherewith all Austrian cities are filled even to encumbrance'. See the nearly contemporary *Travels in Bohemia with a Walk through the Highlands of Saxony* by an Old Traveller (London: T. Cautley Newby, 1857), i. 320.

main street of the Kleinseite: the Brückengasse or Bridge Street (Cz. Mostska ulice), connecting St Nicholas's Church and the Charles Bridge.

Hradschin . . . ex-emperor of the House of Hapsburg: the Hradschin (Cz. Hradčany), on a hill overlooking Kleinseite, is, like the Kremlin, a kind of royal city, containing palaces and Prague's cathedral. It began as a castle (Cz. hrad) of the kings of Bohemia. Ferdinand I (1793–1875), Emperor of Austria (1835–48), was feeble-minded and at times insane; in 1848 he abdicated in favour of his nephew, Francis Joseph (Emperor 1848–1916), and thereafter lived in the Hradschin.

7 *Windberg-gasse*: on the southern outskirts of the New Town, in a then newly built area.

fatuously: thus in *Blackwood's* and all early printings; perhaps a misprint for 'forcefully', 'furiously'?

9 *old Jewish synagogue*: the Altneuschul or 'Old-New' schule (Cz. Staronová skola or Synagóga), a small Gothic structure (c.1265). It has survived the ghetto demolition of the 1890s and use by the Nazis as an anti-Semitic museum. Like the Trendellsohn house, it has a 'high-pitched sharp roof'.

10 *away in Palestine*: the Zionist movement, advocating a Jewish return to their ancient homeland, properly began in the 1890s under the leadership of Theodore Herzl (1860–1904), but as early as the 1850s Sir Moses Montefiore and the Rothschilds were assisting Jews to settle in Palestine; Daniel Deronda is heading there at the end of the novel (1876) which bears his name.

looking babies: staring at the small image of oneself in another person's eye. In a letter (7 February 1833), Tennyson reminds James Spedding 'of the many intellectual, spirituous, and spiritual evenings we have spent together . . . while we sat . . . looking smoky babies in each other's eyes (for you know, James, you were ever fond of a pipe)' (*The Letters of Alfred Lord Tennyson*, ed. Cecil Y. Lang and Edgar F. Shannon, Jr. (1981), i. 87).

15 *on the bridge*: the Charles Bridge (Ger. Karlsbrücke; Cz. Karlúv most) across the Moldau, connecting the Kleinseite with the rest of Prague. The bridge was begun (1357) by Charles IV of Bohemia, and completed by his successor, Wenceslaus (Václav) IV (1378–1419).

16 *St. John Nepomucene*: the Charles Bridge buttresses hold

twenty-eight statues or groups of statues, most of them baroque. The bronze statue (1683) of St John Nepomuk stands in the centre of the bridge, on its northern parapet; the nearby spot where the saint was thrown into the river is marked by a marble slab (not a 'plate') bearing a cross and five stars; the stars are said to have hovered over the spot where his body lay under water until it was retrieved. St John was drowned (1383) by order of Wenceslaus IV for refusing to reveal what the Queen had told him in confession. The Old Traveller (*Travels in Bohemia*, i. 266) notes that passers-by often kissed the stars and crossed themselves; men usually lifted their hats.

17 *woman taken in adultery . . . Samaritan woman at the well*: Christ declined to assist in stoning to death, as Mosaic law decreed, a woman taken in adultery; the crowd assembled to stone her melted away after Christ told them, 'He that is without sin among you, let him first cast a stone at her' (John 8: 3–11). Though Jews scorned Samaritans, Christ asked the Samaritan woman for water, rebuked her gently for living adulterously, and explained that he was the Messiah, come for Samaritans as well as Jews (John 4: 5–42).

St. Nicholas . . . her own Church: Nina's parish church (built 1673–1752) was dedicated to St Nicholas; it stands in the centre of 'Little Side Square' (Ger. Kleinseitner Ring; Cz. Malostranské náměstí) at the west end of the Brückengasse.

beyond Purgatory: Catholic doctrine describes purgatory as a posthumous state of torment, where sins are eventually purged through suffering, making admission to Heaven possible. Unrepentant sinners are sent 'beyond Purgatory' to hell's 'everlasting torments'.

20 *a couple of kreutzers*: four pfennigs made one kreutzer, then worth an English farthing, one-quarter of an English penny.

a florin: the florin was worth sixty kreutzers, or about two English shillings.

22 *Diana's dart*: apparently an arrow-shaped hair ornament, worn in Bohemia by unmarried women. The goddess Diana, usually portrayed as a huntress, with bow and arrows, was the patroness of virginity.

27 *as the law now stood in Austria*: Emperor Francis Joseph's Constitutional Edict (1849) made Jews equal to Christians under law, and so removed civil barriers to intermarriage.

armed men . . . seldom countrymen of her own: another reminder that Prague was occupied by Austrian troops drawn from various parts of the Empire.

29 *Bohemian . . . head of the police*: under Austrian rule, Bohemian mayors and other local authorities had little power; the police were headed by an Austrian German, appointed by the central government.

into a convent . . . the very mischief: Mme Zamenoy's idea, to imprison Nina in a convent and so prevent her marriage, recalls the plots of Gothic novels by Anne Radcliffe and 'Monk' Lewis, where such imprisonments are common. Lotta may be remembering the furore aroused by the Mortara case, in which a Catholic nurse in Rome secretly baptized a Jewish child (1858), then kidnapped him to be raised in a convent as a Catholic. When the papal government declined to order the child returned, protest meetings were held in various European cities, and the French and British governments formally protested.

34 *no twopenny notes*: Ziska gives Balatka about 15 florins, or 25 English shillings.

35 *glozing*: softening, palliating.

39 *Ross Markt*: the 'horse market', according to the Old Traveller an outmoded name by 1852 (*Travels in Bohemia*, i. 256). The 'Zamenoy . . . house of business' is in Wenceslaus, or St Wenceslaus Square (Ger. Wenzelplatz; Cz. Václavské náměstí), the heart of Prague's New Town. Despite the name, it is not a square but a broad open rectangle, about sixty yards wide and nearly half a mile long.

70 *those mighty commercial names*: Anton is probably thinking of the House of Rothschild, a Jewish banking family established in Frankfurt, Paris, and London. Their name had become a byword for wealth and financial acumen.

84 *short white surplices*: a surplice is a cotton or linen tunic, coming roughly to the hips, worn by Catholic priests for certain religious ceremonies; it is also used in the Church of

England and other denominations. Ashkenazic Jews (which includes Bohemian Jews) wore the similar *kittel* or *kitel* (Yiddish: gown) on religious festivals, and often on the Sabbath.

black with the dirt of ages: Murray's *Handbook* (1858) calls the synagogue 'remarkable for its antiquity ... and for its filth ... the smoky and gloomy walls have exactly the hue of the background of a picture by Rembrandt' (pp. 456–7). The Old Traveller calls it 'very dirty' (*Travels in Bohemia*, ii. 9), and George Eliot speaks of 'blackened, groined arches' (*The Lifted Veil*, (1985), 9).

cage ... or iron grille: in the Altneuschul, the *almemar* or *bimah* (raised reading platform) is surrounded by a 'cage' of fifteenth-century ironwork.

85 *altar ... High Priest*: the 'altar' is the ark holding the Torah scrolls, in the centre of the eastern wall, 'the place where the altar stands in a ch.' (Murray, *Handbook* (1858), 457). The 'High Priest' is a cantor or rabbi. Trollope clearly witnessed a service at the Altneuschul, possibly an ordinary Sabbath service (the next morning is 'the morning of the Christian Sunday', p. 91). However, he specifies a festival. He may have been present on Yom Kippur, the Day of Atonement, celebrated on the tenth day of the Jewish month Tishri (in 1865, 30 September). Less likely festivals are Sukkoth, the Feast of Tabernacles, celebrated over an extended period (15–22 Tishri; 5–12 October 1865), or Simchath Torah, Rejoicing in the Law (23 Tishri; 13 October). Trollope's 1865 European tour lasted from 17 September until 29 October. *Nina Balatka* begins around 'the beginning of September' (p. 9); by Chapter 15 it is 'something beyond the middle of October' (p. 175). Nina and Anton meet on Sunday (pp. 91, 105), the day after Ziska's visit to the synagogue; she sells her necklace the following Tuesday (pp. 106, 110); then 'ten or twelve' days pass before Rebecca Loth visits her (pp. 116–17) in mid-October. This makes Yom Kippur the most likely festival for Trollope to have observed. Though Rebecca's costume (p. 83) hardly suggests atonement, she would wear her best for a festival, even Yom Kippur.

95 *buttresses of St. Nicholas*: see note to p. 17.

105 *needle upon the Sunday*: to do any kind of work on Sunday was considered a violation of the commandment to 'keep ... holy ... the sabbath day ... in it thou shalt not do any work' (Exodus 20: 8–10).

110 *Grosser Ring ... Theinkirche ... Huss*: the Grosser Ring (Cz. Velké náměstí, Staroměstské náměstí) is the centre of the Old Town (Altstadt). On the east side of the square is the Gothic Týn Church (1370–1460; from Cz. Týn, stockade, since the church was once part of a stockaded enclosure); Trollope copies Murray's 'Theinkirche'. Jan Hus, or John Huss (*c*.1369–1415), influenced by the ideas of the English reformer John Wyclif, advocated clerical reform and an end to the sale of indulgences. He also emphasized Czech as opposed to German interests. He was condemned and burned as a heretic at the Council of Constance; his followers then rebelled, and controlled large areas of Bohemia until 1436. After the Reformation, most Hussites considered themselves Protestants.

133 *through the fire again*: 'The words of the Lord are pure words: as silver tried in a furnace ... purified seven times' (Psalms 12: 6).

150 *gulden*: another term for florin.

152 *son of Galen*: Galen (AD 129?–99) was a famous Graeco-Roman physician, author of medical treatises which served as textbooks for centuries.

159 *ghostly comfort*: spiritual comfort.

160 *extreme unction*: the 'last anointing', a Catholic sacrament administered to the dying. The priest anoints the eyes, ears, nostrils, lips, hands, and feet of the dying person, each a possible instrument of sin. As here, the priest first hears the dying person's confession and then offers absolution.

viaticum: (Latin: provision for a journey), the Eucharist given to the dying, usually before rather than after Extreme Unction.

162 *that side of the water*: the east, or Old Town–New Town side of the Moldau.

169 *privity*: knowledge of a secret.

176 *barracks and old palaces*: the palaces of many noble families stood in the Kleinseite, under the Hradschin, among them the Wallenstein, Nostiz, Lobkowitz, and Czernin Palaces.

vespers: an evening service of psalms, prayers, and hymns.

a lay friar: probably a brother (one not ordained a priest) in a religious order, though Trollope may mean a layman who is a tertiary (third-class member) of a religious order, and who could, under certain circumstances, wear a religious habit and preside at such an informal ceremony.

177 *that saint who was so powerful over the waters*: St John Nepomuk.

182 *St. Mark ... St. Bartholomew with ... his own skin*: Trollope is recalling sacred art seen in various museums and churches, and the insignia which identify the saints portrayed. St Mark usually appears with a lion; St Christopher, 'stout' in the sense of sturdy, is often depicted carrying the Christ child on his shoulders. St Peter thrice denied knowing Christ after his arrest (Matthew 26: 69-75; Mark 14: 66-72; Luke 22: 55-62; John 18: 25-7). St Lawrence is conventionally shown with the gridiron on which he was burned alive, and St Bartholomew, who was flayed alive, with the knife and evidence of his martyrdom. St Christopher's statue (1857) stands on Charles Bridge near that of St John Nepomuk.

189 *medicines of Mercury ... flasks of the gods*: the Roman god Mercury was a patron of physicians and healing. The gods drank nectar, which sustained eternal life.

Linda Tressel

198 THE PERSONS OF THE STORY: German names were more familiar to English readers than Czech names, and most of these are authentic, though Steinmark is more likely than Steinmarc. Valcarm, however, is improbable. Ludovic is a version of Ludwig (Louis). In naming Herr Molk, Trollope perhaps thought of Field Marshall Helmuth von Moltke (1800-91), the successful Prussian commander in the Austro-Prussian or Seven Weeks' War, which ended in July 1866, a little under a year before Trollope began *Linda Tressel*.

199 *picturesque ... Schütt island ... middle of the town*: the Pegnitz

River runs east–west, dividing Nuremberg (Ger. Nürnberg) in half. The Old Traveller (*Travels in Bohemia*, i. 172–3) and Murray's *Handbook for Travellers in Southern Germany* comment on the carefully preserved medieval appearance of Nuremberg.

200 *patient Bavaria*: at the time of the story (1862–3) Bavaria was an independent kingdom.

201 *St. Sebald and St. Lawrence*: Both were Catholic churches until the Reformation. Neither was ever a cathedral, since Nuremberg was never the seat of a bishop. The churches give names to the north or 'St Sehald's' and the south or 'St Lawrence' side of the Pegnitz.

a German Anabaptist ... a Calvinist: the Anabaptists were sixteenth-century Protestant reformers more extreme than Martin Luther. They denied Christ's human nature, and the validity of infant baptism (Anabaptist means 'rebaptizer'). Anabaptists did not exist as an organized sect in nineteenth-century Germany; Trollope uses the term to suggest Mme Staubach's extreme form of Lutheranism. Calvinists followed the teachings of the Protestant reformer John Calvin (1509–64): each individual is born depraved as a consequence of Adam's sin; however, God has predestined certain individuals for salvation (the Elect), giving them the gift of faith and an inner conviction that they will be saved. This salvation depends entirely on faith, not on good works or behaviour. Trollope uses 'Anabaptist' and 'Calvinist' imprecisely, to suggest a rigid puritanical attitude that considers any physical pleasure or self-indulgence to be sinful.

bairns: small children (Scots dialect).

202 *few hundred florins*: in Bavaria, as in the Austrian Empire, the florin (sixty kreutzers) was worth a little less than two English shillings.

204 *gulden*: as in *Nina Balatka*, another term for florin.

If your eye offend ... pluck it out: 'And if thine eye offend thee, pluck it out, and cast it from thee' (Matthew, 18: 9; see also Matthew 5: 29).

206 *Gasper Staubach*: Gasper (Caspar) was a popular name in Cologne (Ger. Köln), where relics of the Magi or Three

Kings (Caspar, Melchior, and Balthazar) are enshrined in the cathedral.

216 *an Apollo*: Apollo was supposedly the handsomest of the Greek male gods.

224 *political society . . . from Munich*: presumably a society advocating the unification of the German states under an emperor. The Bavarian government was opposed to German unification at this time, since it would end Bavarian independence. Munich was the capital of Bavaria. Such societies were particularly active after the unification of Italy in 1859–60.

225 *Sach Brothers*: Murray's *Handbook* calls the tourist's attention to the house of Hans Sachs (1494–1576), the Nuremberg poet–shoemaker. Coincidentally, Richard Wagner was completing *Die Meistersinger von Nürnberg*, with Sachs as hero (first performed 21 June 1868), while Trollope was writing *Linda Tressel*; both stories feature a middle-class young woman with an unattractive elderly suitor and a handsome younger suitor.

227 *the Rothe Ross*: Murray describes the Rothe Ross (Red Horse) as 'good', noting (1871) 'obliging landlord'. It stood on Irrerstrasse, in the north-east quarter of St Sebald's Side.

228 *fraulein*: young lady.

frock-coat: a man's full-skirted coat, extending to the knee.

civic collars: gold or silver chains worn by magistrates as insignia of office.

234 *light-of-love*: sharer in a brief love affair, with overtones of harlot, prostitute.

236 *the Frauenkirche*: the fourteenth-century Church of Our Lady, given back to the Catholics in 1810. It stands in the Haupt Markt (Chief or Central Marketplace) on St Sebald's Side.

245 *eighth and ninth chapters of Isaiah*: Isaiah 8–9 warns that Assyria will destroy Israel unless the people mend their ways and fear the Lord. Christians read chapter 9 as a prophecy of Christ's birth ('For unto us a child is born, unto us a son is given . . . and his name shall be called Wonderful, Counseller, The mighty God, The everlasting Father, The Prince of Peace', Isaiah 9: 6). However, the chapter ends ominously: 'For

wickedness burneth as the fire: it shall devour the briers and thorns ... Through the wrath of the LORD of hosts is the land darkened ... his anger is not turned away, but his hand is stretched out still' (9: 18–21).

248 *some plan of politics*: see note to 224.

251 *the table in the church*: the altar. English Evangelicals considered 'altar' a Catholic term, and insisted on 'table'. Trollope assumes that Mme Staubach and her co-religionists would have the same prejudice.

254 *the devil ... like a roaring lion*: 'Be sober, be vigilant; because your adversary the devil, as a roaring lion, walketh about, seeking whom he may devour' (1 Peter 5: 8).

258 *the feast of St. Lawrence*: 10 August.

261 *the upas-tree*: a Javanese tree, from whose bark poison can be made; it was said to be fatal to sleep under or near its branches.

263 *a castaway*: a reprobate, here a fallen woman. Mr Kennedy (*Phineas Finn*, *Phineas Redux*), who shares Mme Staubach's moral theology, suspects his estranged wife of adultery and suspects she might be 'a castaway' (*Phineas Redux*, i. 91).

264 *sackcloth and ashes*: the appropriate garb for mourners and repentant sinners in the Bible. 'And I set my face unto the Lord God, to seek by prayer and supplications, with fasting, and sackcloth, and ashes' (Daniel 9: 3; see also Esther 4: 1; Matthew 11: 21; Luke 10: 13).

270 *the non-elect*: those predestined to damnation.

272 *penetralia*: the innermost and most private rooms in a house.

277 *brimstone*: the odour of brimstone traditionally indicated the Devil's presence.

280 *Such matters ... in training*: presumably the political conspiracy is coming to a head.

283 *Egidien Platz*: a square in Nuremberg's Old Town, on St Sebald's Side, containing the eighteenth-century Egidienkirche (Church of St Giles; Lutheran) and a number of picturesque old houses.

pundit: one considered knowledgeable or wise; an expert.

287 *a singular apartment ... carved wood*: the courtyard with its
carved galleries and staircase, and this panelled room,
suggest that Trollope visited, and bestowed upon Herr Molk,
the Peller'sche Haus (1605), on the north side of the Egidienplatz: 'Within is a picturesque courtyard and staircase, and
upstairs a room with finely-panelled wood covering the walls
and ceiling' (Murray, *Handbook* (1858), 100).

292 *rebels up in Prussia*: those working for German unification
looked to Prussia, then an independent kingdom, for leadership; Otto von Bismarck (1815–98), Prime Minister of Prussia from 1862, worked for German unification with the King
of Prussia as German Emperor, a goal he achieved in 1871.

294 *vale of tears*: the earth, the place of ordinary human life.

301 *leading burgomasters*: a burgomaster is usually a mayor, but can
also mean any respected citizen who has served on the city's
governing council.

303 *seven times through the fire*: Psalms 12: 6. See note to page 133.

322 *Augsburg*: a Bavarian city, 105 miles south of Nuremberg by
rail. At the time of the story, an express train made the
journey in four and a half hours.

323 *brains to an ass ... grazing on thistles*: he will exchange brains
with an ass, and eat as asses do.

325 *banns ... church of St. Lawrence*: banns are the official
announcement of an impending marriage in the parish
church of the betrothed couple, so that anyone knowing a
reason why the marriage should not take place may reveal
that reason. Banns are usually 'called' on three successive
Sundays. St Lawrence's Church, in the Lorenzerplatz would
have been the parish church for Peter and Linda.

city gate: the Frauenthor, a tower-gate in the old city wall,
opposite the main railway station.

326 *a railway ... close by Nuremberg ... for many years*: the first
railway in Germany (1835) ran from Nuremberg to Fürth;
Fürth is about five miles north-west of Nuremberg.

Würzburg: sixty-three miles north-west of Nuremberg by rail.

331 *the cause*: the political cause.

334 *the Emperor*: here a conventional term for someone powerful.

335 *seven times seven through the fire*: see notes to pp. 133, 303.

340 *the romance of her life was over*: in *An Autobiography* Trollope
describes Lady Glencora's love for the worthless Burgo
Fitzgerald, her forced marriage to Plantagenet Palliser, her
narrow escape from running off with Fitzgerald (*Can You
Forgive Her?*). 'Lady Glencora overcomes that trouble,' Trollope comments, 'and is brought, partly by her own sense of
right and wrong, and partly by the genuine nobility of her
husband's conduct, to attach herself to him after a certain
fashion. The romance of her life is gone, but there remains a
rich reality of which she is fully able to taste the flavour' (*An
Autobiography* (London: Oxford University Press, 1950), 183).

350 *chattel*: strictly speaking, an item of personal property; the red
house is 'real' property.

352 *Rothe Ross . . . St. Lawrence*: Peter goes home by a roundabout
route, walking west from Egidienplatz (his direct way lay
south) to the Rothe Ross, then south along the Karlstrasse
and across the river, south-east to St Lawrence's Church, and
finally north to Schütt Island.

the Philistines: in the Bible, the enemies of Israel. Students in
nineteenth-century Germany used the term contemptuously
for those who were not students, professors, or mere peas-
ants—that is, for those who were middle class. Trollope
probably remembered the term from Matthew Arnold's
frequent use of it to label those concerned with wealth and
respectability rather than things of the mind and spirit.
Arnold found the term in Heinrich Heine's *Reisebilder* (1826),
and introduced and defined it in his Oxford lecture on Heine
(12 June 1863), published in *Cornhill Magazine* (August 1863)
where Trollope's *The Small House at Allington* was then
appearing. Arnold attacks Philistines in *Essays in Criticism,
First Series* (1865); in his fourth lecture on Celtic literature
(26 May 1866), published in *Cornhill* together with an episode
of Trollope's *The Claverings* (July 1866); and later in *Culture
and Anarchy*. Contemporary newspapers and journals often
commented on the propriety of calling the English middle
class Philistine.

353 *Papacy . . . salvation by his own works*: Papacy is Catholicism.
Mme Staubach's Calvinist doctrine taught that one's works
and action in this world were irrelevant to one's salvation.

360 *a bad piece . . . ring sound*: a counterfeit coin, recognizable by its leaden sound when dropped on a counter or table.

372 *without much increase of damage*: Linda's Calvinist sense that she is not among the Elect, and so is predestined to hell, suggests that a murder would have no effect on her salvation.

373 *she herself might . . . we know not of*: Hamlet, III. 75–82.

375 *kiss of Judas*: Judas betrayed Christ to 'the chief priests and elders'; he identified Christ for those sent to arrest him by kissing him (Matthew 26: 47–50; Mark 14: 42–6; Luke 22: 47–8).

377 *Mannheim . . . down the Rhine . . . Cologne*: Linda's rail journey would have been roundabout, probably via Würzburg with several changes, since there was no direct Nuremberg–Mannheim connection; she travelled two full days and the intervening night by 'a cheap and slow train' (p. 378). From Mannheim via Mayence (Mainz) to Cologne by steamer took about fourteen hours (Murray, *Handbook for Northern Germany* (1860), p. xxxiv). By 1860 it was possible, quicker, and much easier to travel by rail from Nuremberg to Cologne, but the journey by rail cost twice as much as the steamer fare.

379 *May God temper the wind . . . my shorn lamb!*: the market-woman quotes from *A Sentimental Journey* (1768) by Laurence Sterne, ii, 'Maria' ('*God tempers the wind*, said Maria, to the shorn lamb,'), though Sterne apparently drew on a well-known French proverb. See *A Sentimental Journey*, ed. Gardner D. Stout, Jr. (1967), 272.

381 *we have got somebody to tell us . . . what we ought not to do*: aunt Grüner makes a crude distinction between Catholicism, with its authoritative priesthood, and the Protestant reliance on private judgement of right and wrong.

382 *Papist*: Catholic.

383 *With faith you shall move . . . cannot live*: Mme Staubach's version of 1 Corinthians 13: 2: 'And though I have the gift of prophecy, and understand all mysteries, and all knowledge; and though I have all faith, so that I could remove mountains, and have not charity, I am nothing.'

THE WORLD'S CLASSICS

A Select List

SERGEI AKSAKOV: A Russian Gentleman
Translated by J. D. Duff
Edited by Edward Crankshaw

HANS ANDERSEN: Fairy Tales
Translated by L. W. Kingsland
Introduction by Naomi Lewis
Illustrated by Vilhelm Pedersen and Lorenz Frølich

ARTHUR J. ARBERRY (Transl.): The Koran

LUDOVICO ARIOSTO: Orlando Furioso
Translated by Guido Waldman

ARISTOTLE: The Nicomachean Ethics
Translated by David Ross

JANE AUSTEN: Emma
Edited by James Kinsley and David Lodge

Northanger Abbey, Lady Susan, The Watsons,
and Sanditon
Edited by John Davie

Persuasion
Edited by John Davie

ROBERT BAGE: Hermsprong
Edited by Peter Faulkner

WILLIAM BECKFORD: Vathek
Edited by Roger Lonsdale

KEITH BOSLEY (Transl.): The Kalevala

CHARLOTTE BRONTË: Jane Eyre
Edited by Margaret Smith

JOHN BUNYAN: The Pilgrim's Progress
Edited by N. H. Keeble

FRANCES HODGSON BURNETT: The Secret Garden
Edited by Dennis Butts

The Two Drovers and Other Stories
Edited by Graham Tulloch
Introduction by Lord David Cecil

SIR PHILIP SIDNEY:
The Countess of Pembroke's Arcadia (The Old Arcadia)
Edited by Katherine Duncan-Jones

TOBIAS SMOLLETT: The Expedition of Humphry Clinker
Edited by Lewis M. Knapp
Revised by Paul-Gabriel Boucé

ROBERT LOUIS STEVENSON: Treasure Island
Edited by Emma Letley

ANTHONY TROLLOPE: The American Senator
Edited by John Halperin

A complete list of Oxford Paperbacks, including The World's Classics, OPUS, Past Masters, Oxford Authors, Oxford Shakespeare, and Oxford Paperback Reference, is available in the UK from the Arts and Reference Publicity Department (RS), Oxford University Press, Walton Street, Oxford OX2 6DP.

In the USA, complete lists are available from the Paperbacks Marketing Manager, Oxford University Press, 200 Madison Avenue, New York, NY 10016.

Oxford Paperbacks are available from all good bookshops. In case of difficulty, customers in the UK can order direct from Oxford University Press Bookshop, Freepost, 116 High Street, Oxford, OX1 4BR, enclosing full payment. Please add 10 per cent of published price for postage and packing.